A View To A Kiss

CAROLINE LINDEN

AVON

An Imprint of HarperCollinsPublishers

This is a work of fiction. Names, characters, places, and incidents are drawn from the author's imagination or are used fictitiously and are not to be construed as real. Any resemblance to actual events, locales, organizations, or persons, living or dead, is entirely coincidental.

AVON BOOKS
An Imprint of HarperCollins*Publishers*
10 East 53rd Street
New York, New York 10022-5299

Copyright © 2009 by P. F. Belsley
ISBN 978-0-06-170635-6
www.avonromance.com

First Avon Books paperback printing: February 2009

Avon Trademark Reg. U.S. Pat. Off. and in Other Countries, Marca Registrada, Hecho en U.S.A.
HarperCollins® is a registered trademark of HarperCollins Publishers.

Printed in the U.S.A.

10 9 8 7 6 5 4 3 2 1

For Stephanie Kip Rostan,
who has been hearing about this story
for four years now and has
never once wavered in her enthusiasm for it
(or in her belief that I would ever finish writing it);
And for Eric,
who indulges my passion for
James Bond and Jason Bourne

A View To A Kiss

Prologue

She called herself Madame de la Tource and claimed to be related to French aristocracy. She was handsome, in a bold way, and she liked to entertain, although most respectable people would never dream of attending her salon. Like most Frenchwomen, she had expensive taste and an imperious attitude, and she treated her servants with disdain.

Which meant that when the household next door acquired a striking new footman, none of Madame's maids thought twice about making eyes at him. Working for Madame didn't offer many benefits, and if a bit of fun with the neighboring servants were the only one a girl could discover, so be it.

Tom, the second footman of the Greaves household, was tall and handsome, with sharp hazel eyes and the finest calves in London. He was dark and charming and gave an air of being meant for so much more than a footman. Before long there was nearly open strife belowstairs for his attentions, and within a fortnight Tom could have had any of Madame's maids for a wink and a crook of his finger.

And the evening of Madame's spring soiree, he

winked at Polly, Madame's ladies' maid, slipping through the open kitchen door behind her.

"Good eve to you, Miss Polly," he whispered as she hastily arranged a tray of tarts for the guests. Polly gasped, almost upsetting her tray, but recovered quickly.

"And to you." She turned around and set down the tray on a table. Tom's shoulders looked even broader up close, and Polly felt a thrill of excitement that she might explore them, personally, tonight. "No work tonight at Greaves's?"

He shrugged, lounging against the door but staying in the shadows. "Not much. The master's away, so I've a night out. Got a bit of a to-do here, aye?"

Any fool could see that, with people coming and going and various guests playing on the pianoforte at intervals. Madame's guests weren't the most dignified sort. Polly wiped her hands on the edge of her apron. She was supposed to be serving those guests, having been pressed into extra duties tonight like all the servants. But Tom was here, with a wicked twinkle in his eye . . .

"Not much." Tom's mouth curved knowingly. "Not too much for me to take a minute, that is," she amended coyly. "If you had a minute to spend with me . . . "

"Tonight, Poll," he said, "I've got more than a minute to spend with you."

Polly abandoned her tray of tarts without a backward glance.

She spirited him up the back stairs into the only room she knew would remain undisturbed during the evening, the mistress's dressing room.

All was proceeding very much according to Polly's fondest wishes when Tom lifted his head in an air of listening. "Hush," he whispered, catching her hands. "Hush."

She paused, listening intently. From the next room came the sound of voices, a man and a woman. Madame had come back upstairs, with a companion. "Bugger all," she gasped. "I'll be sack—" Tom cut her off with a hand over her mouth, and she remained silent, hardly daring to breathe. It was one thing to sneak away from her duties, and another to be caught by the mistress doing it.

"You 'ave been ignoring me," Madame was whining in her thick French accent. "You 'ave hardly been to see me this fortnight, and I *miss* you . . . "

"Yes, yes," said a man over her complaints. His voice was distinctive, sharp and hasty. "Don't fret. Look what I've brought you."

There was a moment of silence, then a rapturous gasp. "Oh, Gerald, you darling man—"

"Yes, look," he interrupted her. He didn't sound like a man eager to bask in her gratitude. "Look." Another moment's silence. "I can't give you more."

"Oh, Gerry." Her tone had turned wheedling. "You say that every time. It is not so much, is it? And I do depend on you so, Gerry . . . "

"Yes." He sounded nervous now. "But be wary what you do with it. It's an awful risk I took . . . "

She laughed, a confident trill of amusement. "*Oui,* but for me, Gerry, you would risk anything, *non*?"

"I shouldn't," he said. Almost pleaded. "I can't do it again, please don't ask me . . . "

In the dressing room, Polly's brow wrinkled. In response, Tom slipped his finger under the shoulder of her neckline and gave a tiny tug. She jumped and grabbed his hand, setting off a small tussle, during which neither clearly heard what was said next in the other room.

"We should go back downstairs now. Your guests will miss you, pet." Gerry still sounded nervous, but there was an undercurrent of relief in his words. Madame laughed again, and a moment later the door opened and closed. Polly exhaled loudly.

"Thought we'd be treated to a real show for a moment there," said her companion, his fingers still running along the edge of her undone bodice.

"Hush!" she scolded him. "Madame would flay me alive."

"Can't have that, can we?" He squeezed her bottom in one hand. Polly gulped back a sigh and tried not to melt; he had such lovely hands. "I suppose you'll be tossing me out, then."

She pulled a face even as she slid from his lap and began tugging her dress back into place. "Not because I want to."

"Who's the bloke? Not the master, I gather."

"Not the master, just the money. Sir Gerald somebody." Polly squinted in thought as she put her dress to rights. "Walton? No, Wollaston. Some fancy gent in the government. The Treasury, that's it. Madame's quite pleased to have such an important one, for all he's a fool. He's the one what pays for all her jewels and whatnot. Thinks he's God, and wants to be treated like it."

"All gents feel that way." Tom leaned back and put his hands behind his head as he watched her with hot, dark eyes. Polly frowned in pique despite that look. He hadn't removed more than his gloves and queue wig. She'd not had so much as a glimpse of his finer assets.

"I've got to get back," she told him. He just continued to look at her bosom. "Do you hear me? I've got to get back to my post."

"All right." He sat up with a sigh and plopped his powdered wig back on his head. He pulled on one glove, then looked around. "Where's my glove?"

"I don't know," she said. The clock on Madame's mantel in the other room chimed the hour and she jumped. How long had she been up here with him—a quarter hour? Half?

"I can't find it," he said, searching around. Polly hadn't yet tidied the room from Madame's whirlwind dressing, and female clothing littered every surface.

"Haven't you got another?" Now that it was clear she wouldn't have any fun, Polly began to feel anxious about being discovered missing. Cook would complain to Madame if she were missed, and the other girls would be sure to tattle on her if they knew she had Tom up here. No matter how clever his hands, she didn't want to lose her employment over Tom. She tossed aside some gowns as he looked behind the chaise.

"No, I haven't."

Polly sighed in distraction. "I don't see it. And I've got to get back."

"Go on, then, if you aren't of a mind to help." He got down on his knees and looked under the chaise where Polly had been sure she would be tumbled good and proper. She eyed his finely shaped arse for a moment, but the danger of getting the sack weighed too heavily.

"Well, don't be too long about it. If the mistress finds you here, I'll be turned out without a reference, I will."

"I heard you. Go on, then."

Polly didn't like his tone, but now was not the time to argue. She hurried to the door. "Don't take on, Tommy. I'll make it up to you, I vow." She winked at him. "Not before tomorrow, though." One corner of Tom's mouth curled lasciviously, and she slipped away, feeling like a queen among maids.

The left-behind footman from next door rummaged under the chaise until her footsteps died away completely. Then he got to his feet and crossed to the door she had exited, listening for a moment before rushing to the other door, the one to Madame de la Tource's bedchamber. With only a swift glance inside to assure himself that the room was empty, he slipped through the door, closing it softly behind him.

It was an expensive room, done up in the costliest of materials if not the finest of taste. A room meant to impress, no doubt, although Tom spared it barely a moment's inspection. Without hesitation he went to Madame's dressing table and slid open each drawer in succession, sifting quickly and quietly through the contents. He examined some items for a few moments, but returned everything to its place. Next he went to the writing desk by the window and repeated his search, but still took nothing. Wheeling about, he scanned the room, his gaze catching on the clock ticking on the mantel.

He moved to the chest opposite the bed and pulled open each drawer, his hands skimming through the unmentionables they contained, disturbing each item just enough to ascertain its ordinary nature. When he had rifled the entire chest, he slid the last drawer quietly home, his brow drawn into a slight frown. He swung around, scanning the room again. Not in the dressing table, not in the desk, not in the bureau. He didn't have time to search the entire room, and so had to choose. Where, then?

And then he saw the jewel case, left on the table. It was too obvious . . . and yet . . . He crossed the room with three strides and flipped open the lid. Inside lay a stunning emerald and diamond necklace with matching ear bobs, on a bed of pale green silk. Very nice indeed for a Treasury clerk, he thought, lifting the jewels out and setting them on the table. He whisked aside the silk, and there lay his object, a paper folded small and covered with lines of narrow script. He unfolded it and read a few lines, a satisfied smile lifting his mouth.

It took only a moment to restore the silk and jewels to the same attitude they'd had before he disturbed them. He left the jewel case on the table, exactly as he had found it; the entire room was exactly as he had found it, he assured himself before he slipped back into the dressing room, with only the paper from the jewel case missing. To look at it, no one would ever suspect he had been in the room.

Now, though, haste was more important than stealth. He stripped off his long footman's frockcoat, then the more elegant evening coat concealed beneath it, the tails pinned up at the shoulders. Keeping one eye on the door, he pulled off his powdered queue wig and swiftly unbuttoned the old-fashioned waistcoat and tossed it aside, revealing another, far more fashionable short waistcoat. He pulled the buckles, which were only pinned on, from his shoes, and retied his footman's stock into a simple but fashionable cravat before redonning the evening coat, tails unpinned. From one pocket he pulled a small piece of oilcloth, which held a bit of pomade darkened with boot blacking. He rubbed the pomade between his fingers, then ran his hands through his hair, twisting the hair at his brow into a wild mass of waves and smoothing down the back.

Tom paused just a moment to study his work in Madame's looking glass. Now he was no longer a footman, but a modern young gentlemen of the ton. He flicked one of his new curls to the side, smirking at his reflection; in less than a few minutes he'd achieved nearly the same appearance most gentleman took hours to perfect.

Then he turned away, bundling up the discarded footman's livery, including the supposedly missing gloves. Nothing must remain to indicate that he'd been here. He opened the window, taking a cautious glance out into the darkness below. It was deserted. He dropped the footman's clothing to the ground and had closed the window again almost before it landed.

Checking once more to make certain the folded paper from the jewel box was safe in his waistcoat pocket, he crossed the room and cracked open the door. A maid was hurrying down the hall away from him. He watched her disappear around the corner before he slipped into the hallway himself. Tugging on a pair of evening gloves, he strolled leisurely toward the stairs and down to join the party.

The parlor was a truly impressive crush, and guests spilled out into the hall and down into the dining room. He wound his way through the crowd, nodding politely to anyone who looked his way.

"Ponsonby!" A drunken fellow stumbled into him, seizing his arm. "By Jove, good man, I thought you'd made for Devonshire!"

"Devonshire? No, no, you mean Somerset, of course," Tom replied without blinking an eye.

The other man blinked, his eyes small and puzzled in his flushed round face. "Somerset? No, Devonshire."

"No, Somerset," Tom repeated in frosty indignation. "I went to Somerset. Nothing of value in Devonshire, I'm sure. What made you think that?"

"Er . . . " The man looked befuddled. "Don't fairly know."

"Then let's not speak of it again," said Tom, unhooking the man's fingers from his sleeve. "I'm looking for Carstairs. Have you seen him?"

"Carstairs?" His companion blinked again. "No, can't say I have. I say, are you sure it wasn't Devonshire?"

"Quite," Tom assured him. "I must be off. Carstairs, you see."

"Yes, yes," murmured the man in confusion, wandering off. "Thought for sure it was Devonshire . . . "

Tom continued on his way, lifting a glass of wine from a passing servant's tray. He took a healthy sip as he strolled through the parlor before depositing his half-full glass on a table under a flower arrangement and stepping into the hall. There, he walked up to one of the waiting footmen. "Fetch my things," he said with careless arrogance.

"Yes, sir, immediately." The footman bowed and hurried away, returning a moment later with a high-crowned hat, walking stick, and evening cloak. Tom tossed the cloak around his shoulders.

"Have a good time up there?" breathed the footman as he handed over the hat.

"Not too bad," Tom murmured in reply, his lips barely moving. He set the hat on his head at a jaunty angle and took the stick. "Back of the house, under the dressing room window."

The footman bowed. "Yes, sir," he said again in a

normal voice. "Good evening, sir." Tom ignored him and strode out the door, down the steps, and into the London night.

He walked for some time, through the quiet, well-swept avenues lit with gas into darker, dirtier streets that echoed with the invitations of whores and the racket of pubs, almost to Covent Garden, where he turned into a public house. He paused inside the door, letting his eyes adjust to the smoky, tallow-and-ale-scented air before taking a seat on a bench at the end of one table. A serving girl with a tightly laced bodice was upon him in a moment. He sent her for some ale, then leaned back and let his gaze wander about the room.

Within a few minutes another man, paunchy and colorless, slid onto the bench beside him. "Fine night, eh?" said the new fellow.

"The finest," Tom replied in languid tones.

His companion gave a sharp, satisfied nod. "Good work, Sinclair."

Tom the footman, who was neither named Tom nor a footman, tilted his head to look at the other man. "Did you think I wouldn't get it?"

"Never know," muttered Mr. Phipps. "Any trouble?"

"None."

Phipps just grunted as the girl brought the ale, leaning forward to display her overflowing bosom. Sinclair gave her a slow smile and a golden coin. She sashayed away, casting him an inviting look over one shoulder.

"Mighty free with his lordship's coin," Phipps said over his tankard.

Sinclair lifted one shoulder. "What are his lordship's coins for, if not to spend?"

Phipps took a long drink, then wiped the back of his hand over his mouth. Under the table he opened his hand between them. With no apparent attention, Sinclair dropped the paper from Madame's jewel case into it. "Take this," Phipps said, pushing a tightly folded note no larger than a shilling back into Sinclair's hand.

"What is it?" Sinclair palmed the note without looking at it, then lifted his ale again.

"An opportunity." Phipps slipped the paper Sinclair had given him into his own pocket. "You'll be wanting to read that soon."

"Indeed." Sinclair seemed utterly uninterested. "Why?"

"Word is you've got ambition."

Sinclair was watching the barmaid, who was smiling and winking at him as she wiped down a nearby table. "Every man has ambition—even you, I daresay."

Phipps's lips twisted. "Not like yours."

One corner of Sinclair's mouth quirked, but he said nothing.

"You should take it as a commendation," Phipps went on. "Not everyone gets a chance like that."

Sinclair just looked at him from under lowered eyelids. "Indeed."

Phipps gulped down the rest of his ale before shoving to his feet. With only a brief nod, he slapped a cap on his head and started to turn toward the door.

"One question," said Sinclair behind him, although without much curiosity. "Why Wollaston?"

Phipps braced his hands on the table and leaned over him, lowering his voice to a harsh whisper. "*Why* is not your concern. You do what you're told, Sinclair."

"But I notice no one's taking much notice of what the Frenchwoman does with the information he gives her." Sinclair's eyes glittered before sliding away, back to the buxom barmaid. "And it's not your neck in the noose, is it, Mr. Phipps? It's mine, if I get caught."

"You knew that at the beginning."

"Aye," agreed Sinclair in the same emotionless voice. "I did."

Phipps hesitated, then swung around and stomped out the door.

Sinclair stayed where he was and drank his ale. After a while the serving wench came back, running her fingers along the collar of his evening jacket and whispering an invitation in his ear. He gave her a half-hearted smile and his last coin, then gathered his hat and walking stick and left.

Outside, he stopped beneath the first gas lamp he came to, fishing the small note from his pocket. He held it up to the light, squinting at the cramped hand-writing, reading it three times before understanding everything it said.

For a moment he stood motionless, his face drawn in thought. A hackney clattered by, and he stuffed the note back into his pocket. Then he strolled off into the darkness, swinging his walking stick and lightly, quietly, whistling a tune.

Chapter 1

Doncaster House was a true mansion, an imposing edifice in the grandest style set in Mayfair. Tall windows glowed with candlelight and the front doors were thrown wide open to admit the throngs of elegantly attired guests climbing the steps. The air was filled with the soft strains of music from inside the house, mixed with the jingle of harnesses and the clatter of carriage wheels outside. The guests must number in the hundreds, all of them wealthy, fashionable, and important.

One man surveyed the scene from under lowered brows as he mounted the steps, rapping his cane sharply on each tread. He had never been to Doncaster House before, and his eyes roamed over the expanse of stone and glass and wrought iron as if he were counting the windowpanes and pediments. Halfway up the steps he paused, fishing a handkerchief from his pocket to blot his face.

A pair of young men—dandies from the looks of them—burst through the doors, talking and laughing in the careless, too-loud manner of men who have drunk too much. They clattered down the steps, jostling him out of the way without so much as a backward glance. He teetered on the steps for a moment before a footman hurrying in their wake came to his aid, offering his arm and a murmured solicitation. The guest nodded, leaning heavily on the footman until he got his balance back.

"Blasted scoundrels," he muttered, now breathing heavily. "In my day young men knew better than to go about too foxed to walk straight."

"Yes, sir," murmured the footman, discreetly slipping one hand under the gentleman's elbow as he helped him up another step.

"And mind, I'm not sorry to be in my dotage, if that is England's future," the old man went on. "Save for your old age now, lad, and pray they don't bring the country to complete ruin!"

"Yes, sir." The footman eased him up another step.

"If my boys had behaved that way, I'd have taken a cane to them, I would have . . . " His voice trailed off and he sighed. "Eh, but they're both dead now. Gone with my dear wife in 'ninety-six to the consumption."

"Terribly sorry, sir," said the footman, urging him up the last step.

"What, what? Not your fault." He patted the footman's arm. "There's a good lad. Write to your mother, would you?"

"Er—yes, sir." The footman bowed as the old man went into the house, leaning on his cane and favoring his left leg.

Inside the house, the elderly gentleman shuffled through the bustle, handing off his cloak and hat to another footman and making his way toward the ballroom to greet his host. It was a grand ball, but he'd arrived rather late, and the receiving line had dwindled to almost naught.

"Lord Henry Wroth," a servant announced him.

The Earl of Doncaster bowed, tall and urbane, his dark hair threaded with silver. "Good evening, sir."

"And to you." Lord Wroth executed a shaky bow over the countess's hand. "Madam."

"Welcome to our home," said Lady Doncaster with a gracious smile. She was younger than her husband, with a face more handsome than beautiful. "How kind of you to come."

Wroth chuckled, a hoarse, rusty sound. "And my great pleasure it is, too. But I hope you've not served a surfeit of punch. It tends to go to the young men's heads, it does."

"Indeed not," she replied smoothly. "I quite agree with you, sir."

He nodded his shaggy gray head. "Well done, madam, well done."

He bowed again and hobbled away, but slowly enough to overhear the exchange behind him in low tones.

"Wroth?" murmured the earl. "I thought that title died out."

"Apparently they found an heir," said his wife. "A distant cousin, I believe."

"Ah." This satisfied the question for Doncaster. He greeted his next guest with the same cordial manner as he'd shown the unknown Lord Wroth. Lady Doncaster followed suit, the curious old man dismissed from her mind as well.

The man called Lord Wroth listened with satisfaction, and went on his way. They would hardly be so calm if they suspected they had just welcomed a common spy named Harry Sinclair into their ballroom, in the completely fabricated guise of a recently discovered Lord Wroth. Then again, if he did his job properly, they'd never suspect anything like that at all.

The ballroom was a sight to behold. Long swaths of pale green silk hung from the walls, glowing in the light of dozens of fine wax candles augmenting the gas lamps. Harry had been to balls before, but never seen anything quite like this. There were flowers everywhere, all white; everything in the room was either green or white, he noted, scanning the room over his spectacles. It must have cost a bloody fortune just to decorate for an evening's entertainment.

His gaze flitted over the three sets of French windows standing open onto a wide terrace, just visible beyond the glow of the ballroom. Beyond that, he knew, lay a large garden. Guests were strolling in and out of the doors, for it was a warm evening and the mass of tapers made it warmer. It would be entirely possible for anyone to slip around to the back of the house, go through the garden, and in the terrace doors. There was no attempt to secure the house at all. Eyebrows lowered, he trudged on.

When he had gone halfway around the room, he plopped down into a chair too near the musicians for anyone to be sitting and conversing nearby. He pulled out his handkerchief again and mopped his face. Within moments a footman stopped beside him. "May I fetch you a drink, sir?"

"Aye," said Harry. "None of that pissy champagne. Some good port."

The footman bowed his head. "Yes, sir." He hurried away and returned in a moment with a glass. As he offered the tray, he tilted it too much and sent a wave of plum-colored port sloshing onto Lord Wroth's yellowed cuff.

"Oh, you blasted lummox," Harry grumbled. The servant stepped nearer, leaning solicitously forward until his powdered wig almost brushed Harry's cheek.

"Beg pardon, sir, I do apologize." The footman whisked out a cloth and dabbed at the spilled wine. "Nice to see you this evening," he murmured. "A bit late, of course."

Harry scowled. "Be more careful, sirrah," he said peevishly. "That's a waste of fine wine, and my linen also." Then he added in a much quieter tone, dabbing at his upper lip with the handkerchief, "It takes an eternity to get this bloody suit on, you know. Care to switch jobs? I'll give you the shoes this instant."

The footman's lips twitched as he rubbed a little harder at the stain. "Not at present, no. You look better gray and humped, actually." He glanced around and lowered his voice even more. "All quiet here tonight."

"That's good to hear." Harry leaned back a little, scanning the room again over the other man's bent head. Doncaster was still greeting guests, his dark head visible above the crowd. After a moment Harry located Lord Crane, a thin stooped figure who stood across the room opposite the musicians. He was talking to Lord Castlereagh, the Foreign Secretary, accenting his remarks with emphatic slashes of one hand. Whatever they were talking about, Castlereagh seemed to be getting the sharp edge of Crane's temper.

Harry glanced down at the man still scrubbing at his cuff. Alec Brandon would make a fine servant if he ever decided to give up spying. He considered telling Brandon so, after the snide remark about his tardiness. He'd done well to make it here at this hour, given the constraints of old Wroth's clothing. The coat was too tight in the sleeves and too loose in the shoulders, having been let out in back to accommodate the thick padding that gave Wroth a humped back. The shoes were too small and pinched his feet, forcing him to shuffle along with a genuinely grim expression, as any elderly man with gout might. It was a good disguise, and he was rather brilliant in it if he did say so himself, but it was horribly uncomfortable.

"Spill a little more next time, would you?" he muttered as Brandon continued working. "Go to, man, just fetch another glass," he said loudly, pulling free. "I'm not a damned teapot to be polished all night long."

Brandon's eyes flashed but he merely bowed. "Yes, sir."

Harry leaned back again and half closed his eyes as he surveyed the room again. There were over three hundred of the most prominent people in London here tonight, and the doors stood open wide enough for a dozen radicals to storm in with powder kegs under their arms and blow the whole lot to bits. That would certainly win him no favors, if it were to happen under his nose. Harry stifled his impatience, reminding himself he was only strictly responsible for the safety of two men present.

Lord Doncaster was moving into the room, his countess on his arm. Lord Crane was still haranguing Castlereagh. All looked calm and normal, at least so far as Harry was responsible for noticing. He reached for his cane, prepared to circle the room to keep them both in his sight.

And then he saw her.

"Your wine, sir. I do beg your pardon once more—" Brandon's voice died abruptly. Harry tore his eyes off the woman and snatched the glass from his fellow agent's hand, but the damage had been done.

"Have you lost your mind?" Brandon hissed between his teeth. "She's not for you."

"Of course not." Harry raised his eyebrows insolently and tossed back a gulp of wine. He could still see her from the corner of his eye, dancing with a scarlet-coated officer.

"Remember it," Brandon was saying in his ear. "Doncaster's daughter is the prize of the season. You wouldn't be good enough to wipe her shoes even if you were as you appear, Lord Wroth."

Doncaster's daughter. That would be Lady Mariah Dunmore, only child of the wealthy and influential earl. Of all the females to catch his eye . . . She was so far above his reach, it was somewhat surprising lightning hadn't smote him from on high just for looking at her. Harry said nothing.

"Just keep your eyes and mind where they belong." Brandon pressed his lips together; he'd been standing next to Harry too long and they both knew it. "May I fetch you anything else, my lord?"

Harry made a vaguely dismissive gesture. He'd gotten the message. "No, no, leave me in peace." He raised his glass again and turned his back on Brandon, shuffling away. Brandon spoke cold hard sense. A woman—any woman, let alone that woman—was not for him, not now. He was supposed to be guarding Lord Doncaster's life, not having lustful thoughts about his daughter. Over the rim of the glass he looked out into the crowd, in any direction but hers.

Lord, but she was a beauty, he thought, giving in to temptation within a few minutes. He sipped his wine again, in case Brandon or anyone else was watching. From the corner of his eyes he watched her leave the dancers, escorted by her partner. The officer bowed over her hand, but Harry could see her face and knew the fellow didn't have a chance. She was smiling politely, but her eyes conveyed something else entirely. Harry was quite good at reading expressions. Her feelings were as clear to him as if she had whispered it in his ear: *Stop talking and go away . . .*

Harry drank some more of his wine to hide a smirk. Poor fool, that captain. The officer lingered a moment while Lady Mariah turned away and spoke to someone else, then awkwardly took his leave. He might have felt sorry for the man, except that the captain had danced with her, held her in his arms, and basked in her smile, even if it had been forced and insincere. And Harry, who would be doing none of those things, couldn't pity that.

Of course, he knew he was leaping to conclusions, which was just what he was not supposed to do. He moved through the crowd, studying the guests from all angles without appearing to do so, always keeping one eye on his two principal marks. Brandon was correct that he would be entirely beneath Lady Mariah's notice no matter what he wore or called himself. Even if not, she was just a beautiful young woman, nothing more, nothing less, no doubt as fickle and vain as any of the species. He knew how women were; he had put the knowledge to use many times, and there was no reason to think this beautiful, wealthy, well-born lady would be any different.

And yet . . . He caught sight of her again, speaking to her mother the countess. Glossy dark braids were pinned high on her head, with little white flowers here and there. She was upset, her cheeks rosy but her mouth hard. There wasn't much of frail delicacy about her that he could see. There was a passion and vitality in her every movement that commanded his attention. Oh yes, there was something different about her, at least to him.

He drifted around the room twice over the next hour, like a comet in orbit, always keeping his gaze scrupulously away from *her*. A few people he had become loosely acquainted with stopped to greet him, and Harry chatted with them as long as he must; Lord Wroth couldn't move about society without knowing anyone, after all. But when they moved away, he breathed a sigh of relief. It was much easier to do his job if he didn't have to attend to any conversation, and the conversation at these affairs was invariably pointless and dull.

Satisfied everything was secure inside the ballroom, Harry strolled toward a draped doorway he knew led to a balcony overlooking the garden. Alec Brandon had supplied him with painstakingly exact drawings of the house and grounds, and he wanted to see it himself. As he had already noted, there were more than enough places someone could sneak in and cause mischief, and it was his job to prevent anything like that. He waited until Brandon caught his eye from across the room, then gave the slightest of nods. Dabbing his face with the handkerchief again, he slipped out into the darkness of the night.

There was something wrong with her.

There simply had to be. It was humiliating, but there

didn't seem to be another explanation. Instead of enjoying the ball, her first in London, Mariah Dunmore was wildly impatient for it to be over. That had rarely happened to her before, and she didn't know what to make of it.

She was hardly unused to gatherings like this. For the last five years her father, the Earl of Doncaster, had been an emissary of the Crown to various European capitals, and his wife and daughter had gone with him. Mariah had attended royal levees in Vienna, had tea with the czarina of Russia, and danced with a Spanish prince. With few exceptions, she had loved every minute of it. Even the dull people she met were interesting on some level, as they were so different from her, and she'd been almost sorry when her parents decided to return home.

But returning home meant she must have a Season, since she'd been too young to come out before they embarked on their travels. She was now getting well past the age most girls married, and her parents made it clear they considered this ball her presentation to the ton. The very best of English society had been invited, the most powerful, the most influential, the most fashionable. It was, without a doubt, one of the most coveted invitations in town . . . and Mariah was bored almost to tears.

Her mother had assured her the gentlemen in London would be eager to meet her, and Mariah had to admit that she was curious to meet them. A mild flirtation with an Italian count could not lead to anything; a flirtation with an English earl might. Unfortunately, the Englishmen were terribly disappointing. Every man she'd met tonight had fallen over himself to flatter and charm her. She had expected that, for her mother had warned her against it. Unfortunately, she had also expected that at least *some* of them would intrigue her, and so far not a one had even come close.

"Well, dear, are you having a good time?" her mother smiled fondly, catching her in a rare moment of quiet.

Mariah sighed. "I suppose."

Her mother's smile faded in surprise. "What is the matter? Have you a headache?"

"No, Mama." Mariah shook her head, tapping her fan on her wrist in frustration. "But all the gentlemen are so . . . so . . . *dull*!" She whispered the last, almost embarrassed. She could see other young ladies smiling and chatting with the same gentlemen she found unbearably boring, and wondered again what she was missing about them.

The countess laughed and laid her hand on Mariah's arm. "We've spoiled you, I fear. One cannot always have the excitement of foreign capitals and political intrigue."

"I know, Mama. But plenty of gentlemen here are interested in political intrigue. Most especially they are interested in the Aldhampton borough, and whom Papa might have in mind for it."

Her mother gave her a sideways, thoughtful look. "You cannot expect the gentlemen to see you independently of your family, Mariah. You might find it objectionable, but there are practical concerns to finding a wife, just as there are practical concerns to finding a husband."

"Well, I'm not ready to be found, then, not that way and not by them." She looked into her mother's sympathetic face and smiled contritely. "I'm sorry, Mama. I just wasn't prepared to be appraised so bluntly. I can almost hear them totting up my value as if I were a horse or a sheep at market."

Her mother smiled gently. "I know. It is hard. I, too, had a prominent father. But remember, you don't have to marry until you are ready."

"Thank you, Mama." Mariah sighed.

"There. Perhaps you need a breath of fresh air. I'll explain to the next young man on your dance card."

Mariah consulted her card. "Sir Charles Fitzroy." Even the man's name sounded dull. Why had she let him sign her dance card in the first place? And how horrible was she, for wanting to avoid him just because of his name?

Her mother squeezed her hand and released her. "I shall see you in a few minutes."

"Yes, Mama."

The countess left in a whisper of silk, and Mariah slipped through the guests and onto a small balcony off the ballroom. The breeze was cool but refreshing, as was the quiet. She pulled the drape, not wanting anyone to find her, and took a deep breath, glad to have a moment's peace at last.

Perhaps the problem really was with her, not with the gentlemen. Mama said she didn't have to choose quickly, but Mariah was old enough that people would think there was something wrong with her if she took too long. It was a little disconcerting; somehow, she'd thought the answer to the question about when and whom to wed would be obvious. She would meet someone, he would be as drawn to her as she was to him, they would fall in love, he would ask for her hand, and she would accept. Now that she had met dozens of the most eligible men in London, she realized how much her assumptions depended on chance. What if the man for her hadn't been able to attend tonight? What if she never managed to meet him? What if there *were* no such man? What if she had to choose between being a spinster and marrying one of the prosy fellows who'd swooned over her tonight?

"Blast it all," she said out loud, cross at herself for discovering she was a silly romantic—something she hadn't considered herself before—and at the gentlemen of London for being so inconsiderately dull. "A pox on men."

"Come now," spoke a voice from the darkness. "On all of us?"

Chapter 2

Mariah leaped back into the stone wall behind her. "Who is there?" she squeaked, hands flying to her throat.

"A poxy man, it seems."

She strained her eyes in the direction of the voice. It was very dark out here, away from the blaze of the chandeliers in the ballroom, but she could just barely make out a shadow. A very large shadow; why, he must be a giant, or a—

The shadow moved, and there was a quiet thud. He'd been sitting on the balcony railing and then jumped down. "Quite a sweeping condemnation, don't you think?" he asked.

"What are you doing out here?" she demanded, recovering her tongue.

"Enjoying the night air." He sounded rather amused. She scowled, annoyed at him for overhearing what she would never have said in front of anyone. "What are *you* doing out here?"

Her lips parted in astonishment. "How dare you! Why, I—I—"

"Are annoyed with all men, yes; I overheard."

"You should have announced your presence!"

"You gave me no opportunity, bursting out all in a passion. Perhaps *you* ought to have announced *your* presence. Heaven only knows what you might have interrupted out here."

Mariah gaped in his direction. She was an earl's daughter, and not used to being spoken to with such impertinence. And yet, she had an absurd urge to laugh. Now that she'd gotten over the surprise, she realized it must have been just as shocking for him as for her. She *had* burst onto the balcony in a fine fury. "Then we are even, sir," she said primly, not sure if she wanted him to apologize and leave, or stay and make her laugh in truth.

He laughed, a low dark rumble. "Not quite, but it will serve for now."

Her eyes opened wide. "What do you mean by that?"

"It means I accept your apology."

"Apology?" She was speechless again. "I, apologize?"

"And I accept."

"That wasn't—I didn't—"

He laughed again. There was something dangerous in the sound, as if he were deliberately luring her into impropriety. "And I apologize in turn for interrupting your tirade against the male sex. Fair enough?"

Mariah hesitated. "I suppose," she said at last.

"Excellent."

Silence descended. Mariah strained her eyes to see him better, but it was too dark to make out his features. There was no moon, and the drape blocked all light from the ballroom. The only thing she knew for certain was that he was tall; his voice came from above. It was a very nice voice, rich and even but with an enigmatic edge. She was sure she hadn't met him tonight, for she would have remembered that voice. She wished he would say something else, then realized she was standing in the dark with a strange man. A strange man who was, nevertheless, the most intriguing man she'd met all night. "Shall we introduce ourselves, now that the insults and forgiveness have been dispensed with?" she suggested, feeling a prickle of interest.

"Of course not," he said. "Situations like these were made for anonymity." She opened her mouth to reply, then closed it, nonplussed. "What made you call down a plague on mankind?"

The frustration bubbled up inside her chest again at once, and recklessly she gave in to the urge to vent it. He didn't know who she was, after all. Perhaps it would make her feel better to tell someone.

"Because they are boring." Goodness, it did feel good to say that aloud. "Or stupid, or greedy, or vain. I've not met one wholly decent gentleman tonight."

"Hmm, that is a risk one takes at parties like these," he said in a thoughtful tone. "Still, there are a great many men who could not attend tonight; perhaps one among them would satisfy your requirements."

Mariah sighed. "Of course there are more gentlemen in London society than those here tonight. But my mother—" She caught herself. "My mother assured me the gentlemen here are the finest in English society."

"Ah, there's the rub: if the finest are insufferable, how much worse must be the rest?"

Mariah nodded. That was exactly what she feared, even though she'd not put it into words.

"Perhaps it is your fault. Perhaps you have such an effect that sane, sensible men turn into stammering idiots in your presence," her companion went on.

She almost snorted. Without being vain—well, not

too vain—Mariah knew her own advantages. She was pretty, even in her own eyes. She was reasonably accomplished in the usual repertoire of maidenly skills, playing the pianoforte, dancing, embroidery. She rode well, spoke French and a modest bit of German, and wrote a very lovely hand.

But she wasn't slow-witted, and she knew very well the gentlemen in the ballroom hadn't been drawn to her embroidery talents. What drew them to her was nothing to do with *her* at all, and that was what she hated most of all.

"Then they are even bigger fools than I take them for." Mariah folded her arms and raised her chin. "What sort of man would be reduced to a babbling fool by any young lady, particularly a young lady they've never met before?"

"More than you might expect," he murmured.

"Then they have injured only themselves. They look at me as some *thing*, a prize to win. I am more than just my father's daughter, and yet I could clearly see each one of them thinking, as he looked at me, 'What an advantageous match she would be,'" she finished in a mocking lowered voice. It was a great deal of confidence she'd bestowed on a complete stranger. Her mother would be appalled if she knew. But Mariah didn't care, even though she had probably said enough to give away her identity.

"What a terrible cross it must be, to be the daughter of wealth and privilege. Terribly sought after, and never certain of the reason why." The man in the shadows nodded sagely—or so she imagined. She didn't know whether to be glad or upset that he understood. But perhaps it was something all young ladies of high birth suffered. Perhaps this man had a sister who was one. She glanced sideways toward him under her lashes. Perhaps he had even married such a lady.

"There is only one thing to do, in cases such as these," he continued.

"Really?" she asked, surprised and a bit hopeful. "What is it?"

"Take off your shoes."

Her mouth fell open. "How will that help?"

"First, you'll feel better; a cool breeze on the feet is terribly refreshing. Second, I've already gone and taken mine off, which is unpardonably rude, and if I can persuade you to do the same, I shan't feel so guilty."

She looked down even though she couldn't see his feet any better than his face. "Why did you take off your shoes?"

He heaved a sigh. "They pinched. Dreadfully. And I feel much better without them—why do you think I hid out on the balcony? Here—" And before she could protest, he put his hands at her waist and swung her into the air.

Mariah let out a small squeak as she landed on the balustrade. "Oh, no! I'll fall!"

"You won't. It's quite wide." She could hear the amusement in his voice as she snatched her hands from his shoulders. She hadn't even been aware she'd grabbed onto him. But as she sat up, she felt the truth of his statement: the carved stone balustrade was very wide, and she was in no danger of falling.

"Now the shoes, miss." Before she could react, he had taken her ankle in his hands—good heavens!—and flipped off her slipper.

"Oh, stop!" she gasped. "You mustn't!"

"Too late. I've already done it." He released her foot, his fingers sliding over her stocking. With the same deliberate care, he took her other foot, removed her other slipper, and let it fall to the floor of the balcony. Mariah didn't say anything. It felt shockingly personal, but it was only her shoes, after all. And then he released her foot and that was it. There was a rustle and a quiet thump as he climbed back onto the balustrade, and his voice came from her left. "Don't tell me you don't feel better already."

She wiggled her toes. She could still feel the stroke of his fingers on her ankle. "Perhaps."

He gave a low sigh of pleasure. "*I* feel immensely better."

Mariah squirmed a bit, settling more comfortably on the balustrade. "It does feel lovely," she admitted. A breeze ruffled her skirts, and she pulled them up just a little, letting the cool air swirl around her ankles. She tipped back her head, surprised to find that she did feel better, either from the fresh air or from expressing her frustration. "I don't think it will make the gentlemen more interesting, though."

It was quiet for a minute. Then he spoke. "Do you see the bright star there, near the horizon, to our left?"

Mariah looked. "Yes."

"That is Venus. The goddess of love and beauty. And yet, we can only see her because the moon is hidden." She caught the dim shape of his arm, sweeping across the heavens. "All these stars, many larger and brighter than our sun, are hidden when the moon comes out. And yet, the moon gives no light of its own; it's all reflected from the sun. Odd, isn't it, how that reflected light can drown out natural brilliance?"

Mariah smiled wryly, touched by his analogy. "So I'm destined never to be seen, in the reflected glow of my father's glory."

"And yet more men are intrigued by the mysteries of the stars and Venus than by the common moon. No doubt many are gazing at her this very night." She shot a sharp glance in his direction, but he didn't say anything else.

"Thank you," she said. "It was very kind of you to say that. I *had* been feeling very outshone tonight, or at least drowned in someone else's brilliance. Most people would have thought I reveled in the attention."

"No, I . . . " He paused. She heard the soft thud as he landed on his feet again. "Someone is calling you," he said, all trace of levity gone from his voice.

"Oh? Oh—really?" Mariah tried to listen over the sudden pounding of her blood. He had put his hands on her waist. Other gentlemen tonight had put their hands on her waist as they danced, but not like this. Not when they were alone in the dark.

"Yes. Here, let me help you down." She put her hands gingerly on his shoulders again, and he lifted her off the balustrade. This time he let her go at once, melting back into the darkness. Mariah felt around with her foot for her slippers and stepped back into them as she heard her mother calling her name, her voice growing nearer and more concerned.

"It's my mother," she whispered. The realization jolted her back to sense. "Just a moment." She brushed the back of her skirt and hurried to the drape, slipping through and holding it closed behind her. "Yes, Mama?"

Her mother turned, her frown clearing. "Heavens, Mariah, where did you go? Your partner for the supper dance is waiting."

"I'm sorry, I needed some air. I felt a slight headache coming on."

Mama cupped her chin, examining her face. "You do look flushed. Are you recovered?"

"Nearly, Mama," she said with a determined smile. "I shall be in directly."

Her mother's eyebrow arched. "Now, Mariah."

"A moment, Mama," said Mariah just as firmly. "Please."

Her mother's other eyebrow went up. "Is there someone on the balcony with you?"

Mariah wet her lips. "Why would you think that?" Should she lie to her mother—something she rarely did—or tell the truth, and find herself in trouble? "Of course not."

Her mother trusted her. "All right. Compose yourself, but you must return soon. Your father will not put up with the young man forever."

"I will, Mama. Thank you."

The countess smiled and was gone. With a sigh of relief, Mariah ducked back behind the drape and turned toward the end of the balcony. It seemed even blacker now after a few moments back in the light. She felt utterly blind. "It's the supper dance," she said, feeling suddenly awkward. Would they walk back into the ballroom together, after he declared the night made for anonymity and she told him how silly she found most of her parents' guests? But she didn't want *not* to see him again. "You must put on your shoes again." There was no reply. She edged toward where her mysterious companion had been. She didn't even know how to hail him. "Sir?"

"Good-bye," came his quiet voice, but now from below, far below. Her eyes widened, and she hurried to the balustrade and peered over into the darkness.

"How did you get down there?" she exclaimed.

"I thought it would be best if your mother didn't discover you alone on the balcony with a stranger."

"But—" What could she say to that? "You never told me your name," she said, suddenly wishing she had not agreed to anonymity. And he knew *her* name; he had known Mama was calling her.

"No, I never did," he said absently. She could hear rustlings in the garden below, but it was even darker down there than on the balcony. "Damn," she thought he muttered. "Where is it?"

Where is *what*? she wondered, and then it dawned on her. She felt around the floor of the balcony and found a gentleman's shoe, rather old-fashioned, with a raised heel and square toe. No wonder it pinched. She set it on the balustrade and leaned over, smiling broadly now. "Do you mean this shoe?"

"Yes!" He sounded relieved. "Would you be so kind as to toss it down?"

"I don't believe I shall. Not until you tell me your name."

There was a long silence. "Not even if I ask very politely?"

"No."

"If I were to beg?"

"No."

Another long silence, very long. "My friends call me Harry."

Mariah waited, but he said nothing more. "And your family?"

"Oh, they call me Harry as well," he said at once. "Except my mother, when she's angry with me."

"Your family's name," she said, exasperated enough to laugh.

He laughed, too, his tone easy again. "Come now, one shoe, one name. Toss it down, please."

"I shall discover it anyway," she declared. "My mother will have the guest list."

"No doubt. I wish you luck."

Mariah's eyes narrowed. "Do you think I cannot do it?"

This time his laugh was too confident, with that underlying darkness in it again. "I *know* you cannot."

Her mouth fell open in surprise. "Of all the cheek!" Without thinking, she hurled the shoe, rewarded with a faint, "Ow!" But her moment of satisfaction was brief.

"Thank you, Lady Mariah," he said, his voice growing fainter.

"Oh, wait!" She hurried along, trying to follow the direction his voice was going, and was brought up short by the end of the balcony. "How did you get down there?" It must have been fifteen feet to the ground at that point. She reached out blindly and felt leaves and vines: the ivy that crawled up much of the house's exterior. He had climbed down the side of the house. She was impressed against her will. She would have to come back and take a better look in the daylight to see how he'd done it. But now the scoundrel was walking out on her! "Where are you?" she demanded.

"Good-bye . . ." He was heading toward the terrace. Mariah tried to think how long it would take to go back through the house and around to the garden. Too long to catch him. She strained her eyes into the blackness below.

"Harry?" There was no reply. All she heard was the

murmur of noise from inside the house and the swish of the breeze through the tree branches. "Harry!"

But he was gone.

Harry held his breath as he waited in the pitch-black shadow of a tree until she turned and went back into the house, the flash of light from the ballroom illuminating her figure for a second as she threw open the drape. For a moment he had feared she would try to follow him over the balustrade and down the ivy, and he told himself that he'd waited to make sure she didn't; he had almost certainly damaged the vines' grip on the wall in his mad scramble down.

But finally she did leave, and he let out his breath. He must have lost his mind. Not only had he spoken in his real voice, he'd gone and told her his real name. He'd be sacked at once if Phipps found out. Lord Wroth had been painstakingly constructed and brought to life, and he almost threw it all away for the pleasure of talking to a pretty female.

No—not a pretty female, a beautiful one. Tall and slender, dark-haired and spirited. Harry wondered what color her eyes were: blue, or perhaps gray? He could imagine the way they flashed as she fought down her temper in annoyance at him. His mouth curved as he remembered the shock in her voice when he teased her. And the frustration in her tone as she confessed to feeling like an object. And the trill of her laughter. And the faint scent of her perfume. And the feel of her slim waist beneath his hands, and the touch of her hands on his shoulders—

He stopped himself. That way lay madness. The spark of interest he had felt in her would be extin-

guished the moment she laid eyes on him—especially
dressed as he was now.

Harry squeezed his foot back into the too-small
shoe. What a careless piece of work that had been,
leaving it on the balcony when he pitched his things
off and all but jumped after them. If she had refused
to give it back, he would have been stuck, unable to
return to the house, and then he would have been in
real trouble. As it was, he had spent far too much time
outside, and not seen a thing he meant to see. The
longer it took him to search the grounds, the longer it
would be before he could steal another glimpse of her
in the ballroom.

Straightening his coat and picking up his walking
stick, he set off through the darkened gardens.

Chapter 3

Mariah flung back the drape and hurried through the ballroom toward the terrace. The doors were open wide to allow the guests to move freely from the crowded ballroom into the gardens. The scoundrel had climbed straight down a wall—to get away from her!—and if he thought to sneak back into the ballroom without explaining himself, he was sadly mistaken.

The guests had begun moving toward the supper room, where a feast for hundreds was spread. Mariah threaded her way through them as quickly as she could, barely returning the greetings people called to her. *See, Harry,* she told him in her mind, *everyone here wants to greet me and be introduced to me. Why don't you?*

"Mariah!" A tall, plump girl with bouncing chest-nut ringlets caught her arm. "Where are you going in such a rush?"

"Joan, have you been on the terrace?" Mariah demanded.

Her cousin Joan smiled coyly. "Well. I'm sure I'd never admit it, if I had been."

"Bother that. Did you see a . . . " Oh blast, how was she to describe him? "A tall gentleman with a sly laugh?"

Joan blinked. "Only ten or twelve. Why?"

Mariah seized her arm and towed her through the doors out onto the terrace. "Point them out," she whispered. "Especially any who have not been here all along."

Joan stared at her. "Why? I refuse to incriminate anyone until you tell me what happened. Did he make an improper advance? Did—"

"Just do it." Mariah pushed her cousin forward, following close behind.

Joan huffed, but put on a bright smile and began nodding at the guests returning to the house from the terrace and garden. Mariah kept one eye on the other doors, too, although they were farther from where Harry had left her. He would have to make a very wide circle to get in that way without her seeing him.

"This one?" whispered Joan through her fixed smile. Mariah stared at the approaching tall gentleman with golden good looks. She doubted he was the one; he did not fit her mental picture of Harry at all; much too elegant and proper-looking. Harry was sly, bold, charming . . . and took off his shoes at a ball. The gentleman paused in front of Joan, probably because she was staring at him and grinning like a fool.

"Good evening, Miss Bennet." He bowed. "Lady Mariah."

It was not Harry. His voice was nowhere near the same, too cool and too languid. Mariah immediately turned away, scanning the terrace for any other candidates as he spoke to Joan.

"How kind of you, sir," Joan was saying. "But we are already engaged for supper, thank you." Thank heavens Joan was such a good friend.

Mariah murmured something to the gentleman as he bowed again and excused himself with a lingering puzzled glance. No doubt he thought them quite strange for staring at him, then brushing him aside. She would worry about that later, after cornering the impertinent Harry.

If she found him, that is. There were only a few people crossing the terrace now. A pair of gentlemen talking in low voices went back into the ballroom, but Joan whispered that she had seen them both talking outside for some time. A woman strolled out of the garden, smiling secretively, and a few moments later a man followed, too obviously intent on her to fool anyone. Soon it was only she and Joan.

"Now," exclaimed Joan when it became clear they were alone. "Tell me everything!"

"There's nothing much to tell," said Mariah, a little let down. "I met a gentleman, and he only told me his given name."

"Which is?" Joan prompted, her brown eyes shining.

"Harry." Mariah put up her chin as she said it. Harry was a rather common sort of name, now that she thought about it.

"You mean Henry. Or Harold. Perhaps Harris?" Joan frowned. "I met a Mr. Harris Cortney the other day, but he was quite short."

Mariah shook her head. "No, no, this Harry was tall, taller than I am."

"What does he look like?"

"I don't know," she muttered.

Joan gasped. "You don't know! Why not? Did you have your eyes closed? Were you—Oh! Mariah Dunmore!" she squealed. "Were you alone with him in the dark?"

"Yes!" Mariah glanced around. "Quiet, you ninny."

Joan laughed. "And you, such a good girl," she whispered in glee. "Alone with a strange man in the dark, and you didn't even learn his name!"

"I did not mean to be alone with him." Mariah gave up searching. The terrace was deserted, the garden seemed empty. Anyone still outside wanted to remain outside. She sank onto a nearby bench, half annoyed and half disappointed. Joan immediately sat next to her, alive with excitement.

"So how did it happen?"

"I went out on the balcony for some fresh air—I went alone, and thought I would be alone," she added at Joan's wicked smile. "He was out there already, and very impertinent."

"Mmm, a saucy fellow," said Joan with delight. "Are you in love with him?"

"No!" Mariah looked at her incredulously. "How could I be? I don't even know his proper name or what he looks like."

"But he's tall," Joan said. "And has a nice voice."

Mariah smiled. "Yes."

"Why do you suppose he was out there? Hiding from someone? Waiting for someone? Planning to steal the silver? Oh, perhaps he's a very scandalous person and was trying to avoid a duel!"

"I don't think my mother invited anyone scandalous."

Joan made a face. "I was afraid of that."

Mariah got to her feet. Joan could tease and laugh all she wanted, but Mariah knew—somehow—that Harry had not been on the balcony to avoid a duel or to steal the silver. "But then—you'll never believe it, Joan—he climbed down the side of the house!"

Her cousin's mouth opened in surprise. "What do you mean, climbed down the side of the house? How?"

"The ivy." He wouldn't try to climb back up the wall and sneak into the house, would he? She hadn't thought of it, but if he could go down the ivy, why couldn't he go up? Mariah took a few steps toward the path leading toward the balcony. Perhaps if she ran around now, she could catch him trying it.

"The ivy!" Joan was saying. "Oh, Mariah, just like Romeo!"

"Yes, only it was to get *away* from me," she grumbled.

"Show me." Joan hurried over. "Let's go see how far he must have climbed. This is so romantic. A mystery suitor! I knew you would have a flock of gentlemen at your feet, but I never dreamed you'd find someone so exciting, and at your very first ball, too! While I have lived here all my life and had two full Seasons, and never met anyone nearly so interesting."

"You are too particular," said Mariah.

Joan shrugged cheerfully. "You're right. I *am* too particular. But let's go see the ivy, quickly, before my mother comes looking for me."

Mariah glanced quickly back at the ballroom doors. Her mother would soon come looking for her, too. "All right. But hurry!" They picked up their skirts and ran across the terrace, down the steps, and along the gravel path. Mariah scanned the walls, squinting against the deep shadows that cloaked the house.

"There." She pointed at the balcony. From below, it didn't look so very far, actually; perhaps he hadn't been quite as daring as she'd thought. The English ivy that crawled up vast swaths of stone was particularly thick near the balcony, and when she leaned out and tugged a thick stalk, it felt as sturdy as a tree.

"All that way down." Joan sounded very impressed. "Just to get away from you. What on earth did you say to him?"

"Nothing!" Mariah protested. "I—I might have been a bit abrupt at the beginning . . . "

Joan sighed. "Well, it's still a lovely story. You didn't by any chance share one perfect kiss, did you?"

Mariah choked on her laughter. "Joan, you're really intolerable."

"I know." She linked her arm through Mariah's. "We'd better go back before my intolerable curiosity lands us in the suds. Perhaps we can discover him inside."

Mariah turned to go with her, but cast one last thoughtful glance back at the ivy, innocently rustling in the breeze. Joan might laugh it off as a smashing good tale, but her determination to track down the wretched, infuriating, intriguing man hadn't faltered. No, indeed, not in the least.

Harry took great care to keep his distance from her the rest of the evening. After making his rounds of the garden and examining the doors in the high wall that ran around it, he turned back toward the house. There were only guests out in the grounds, and he was powerless to do anything about them unless they drew a weapon. The gates were secure, so he went back to the ball.

Inside the ballroom he scanned the room and located Lady Heath, a plump old lady who would sit and talk with anyone about her dogs. He headed in her direction, needing some subterfuge.

"Good evening, Lady Heath. A pleasure to see you again." He bowed as the elderly lady looked vacantly at him.

"Oh, yes, good evening . . . er . . . " She trailed off with an expectant look.

Harry answered it. "Wroth, madam, Henry Wroth at your service. We met at the Roxbury affair a fortnight past."

Her smile was relieved. "Oh yes. Now I remember. You've an interest in greyhounds."

Harry nodded, settling into the chair next to her. "Indeed I have, most particularly after our conversation. You contended they were superior to pointers. I've always preferred pointers myself."

A gleam of near-mania appeared in Lady Heath's eyes. "Far superior, sir, far superior. You must start with some young bitches of good blood . . . " One mention of greyhounds was enough to set her off for hours. Harry knew he would be free to monitor the entire room while paying minimal attention.

He watched Lord Doncaster navigate the room with aplomb, conversing with the Prime Minister and other prominent persons. Brandon had been keeping his eyes on Doncaster for nearly a month now, but as the Season began in earnest, it would also be his responsibility to know the man and his habits.

The earl appeared to be all Harry had been told he was, a natural diplomat who managed to be agreeable to most everyone. His wife was obviously an asset, sophisticated and elegant, and a brilliant hostess, cordial to Tories and Whigs alike. Doncaster was rumored to be the new King's choice for Prime Minister, should Liverpool step down, and many in London openly hoped that would happen soon. Harry wished Lord

Wroth had been given an interest in politics; what he wouldn't give to be a party to that conversation, to know if Doncaster would be more open to reform and progress than Liverpool . . .

That was what had drawn Harry to this assignment, in fact: his interest in politics. Stafford had offered him the post and held out the promise of a patron, should Harry wish to stand for the House of Commons. How Stafford had guessed that his ambitions and hopes lay in that direction, Harry didn't know, but the lure was too strong to resist. And ever since accepting, he had been surrounded by members of Parliament, with policy and intrigue discussed almost within his earshot. But it was more maddening than anything else. He had been explicitly told that Wroth was not to be a political creature. He couldn't call attention to himself by spouting opinions and suggestions, and rarely had a reason to linger even close enough to eavesdrop. With a silent sigh he turned his gaze elsewhere.

Lord Crane, his other responsibility tonight, was at once harder and easier to watch. Harder, because of his prickly, impatient nature: Crane was a brilliant legal mind whose body had begun to fail, and it made him irritable and somewhat unpredictable. Easier, because he'd already been watching Crane for a few weeks and had a good sense of his habits. Through lecturing the Foreign Secretary, Crane was now expounding on something to Lord Sidmouth, hammering one fist into his palm as he spoke. Harry watched them for a while, his erstwhile employer and his real one, and wondered what they spoke of so passionately. No doubt it was the question of Queen Caroline, who was threatening to return to England

and claim her crown now that her husband was King George IV. It was a particular passion of Lord Crane's, who thought the King a fool for trying to divorce his wife. Harry took some small amusement at Sidmouth being harangued, reassured that Crane's infirmity would keep him where he was.

He saw Mariah Dunmore again. He couldn't help noticing that she spent a great deal of time in close conversation with a tall buxom brunette. Harry wondered who she was and what the two of them talked about with such intensity. He wondered if they talked of his odd introduction to Lady Mariah. He wondered if she were offended or intrigued by his secretive manner. He wondered if she had dismissed it—and him—from her mind the instant he left. But it was not his job to know, so he forced himself to look away.

He cast his eyes around the room again, murmuring some vague but encouraging reply to Lady Heath, who had paused for breath. He spied Doncaster across the dance floor, just behind his daughter. Again Harry's eyes snagged on her, watching the way the candlelight gleamed on her dark hair and the way her breasts swelled against her bodice as she curtsied to her partner. She raised her face to the fellow and smiled. She was flirting with him. A challenge shone in those clear gray eyes, as if she were daring the man to be impertinent to her. Or perhaps she merely found him as interesting as she had hoped a London gentleman would be. No doubt there were several who could catch her interest if they chose to try, gentlemen of suitable rank and fortune who could speak to her openly and dance with her in front of all society. If anyone recognized her taste for a little adventure and her desire to be viewed as a woman . . . Harry reined in his thoughts and turned his eyes away yet again.

Doncaster was dancing with his wife, but Crane was no longer speaking to Sidmouth. In fact, he was nowhere to be seen. Instantly, Harry sprang to alertness, his muscles tensing even though he didn't move. Where the devil was Crane?

It took him several seconds to locate the viscount. His jerking limp was distinctive, but he was moving behind a large group of people and was screened from Harry's vision for a while. Only when he had Crane's stooped figure firmly in sight did he relax, but only for a moment. Crane was heading for the door.

"Beg pardon, Lady Heath," he said, cutting into her exposition on the importance of proper weaning. "I must excuse myself." He tugged at his waistcoat and groped for his cane.

"Of course, of course! But don't neglect the bloodlines, Lord Wroth, or you shall be very sorry. Your litters shall be no better than any mongrel litter." She nodded decisively.

Harry made a hasty bow. "Thank you, madam, I shall." He hobbled through the crowd as quickly as he could in his cramped shoes, keeping one eye fixed on Lord Crane. The old man was leaving at a good pace. Harry wondered what had set him off. Normally, Crane didn't do anything quickly.

Still, he wasn't terribly sorry. Once he saw Crane safely through his own front door, he would be free to go home, shed the trappings of Lord Wroth, and go to bed. Doncaster would still be under Brandon's watchful eye. His own work tonight was almost done.

A footman was already bringing Crane his hat and cloak in the hall. Harry motioned to another servant to fetch his things, but Crane was turning toward the door, obligingly held open by another footman. Knowing all too well what a clean target Crane's thin, crippled figure would make on the broad front steps, Harry snapped sharply after the servant to hurry. When the man finally appeared with his hat, he had to remind himself not to snatch it away and race after Crane. He paused in the doorway and searched the street until he located the viscount again.

Crane was not waiting for his driver to draw near. He was walking to his carriage, some ways down the street. Harry hurried down the steps, gritting his teeth with each step. Damn shoes, he thought, but pushed onward. Crane was only a few yards ahead of him now, almost to his carriage. Crane's driver was opening the door, setting the step in place, and Harry's heart started to slow to a more regular rhythm.

Then a man emerged from a crowd of servants nearby, and the back of Harry's neck prickled. The coachmen and footmen of the guests were wont to wait about outside the house, enjoying a mug of ale and dancing to the music that drifted through the open doors and windows, forming a crowd that could all too easily conceal an assailant, an assassin, a common thief with a knife. Harry couldn't see clearly enough which class this fellow belonged to, but it didn't matter anyway. He quickened his step, glancing around for any possible accomplices lurking nearby, and closed his hand around the hilt of the dagger under his coat.

The man lurched toward Crane, groping for his shoulder and almost sending the old man off his feet. Crane's voice rose in indignation as he struggled under the man's hold. Harry gripped his walking cane and measured the remaining distance. Even now he was not supposed to reveal himself to Crane, so this had to be done quickly. He wedged the end of his cane between the man's boots and twisted, affecting a stumbling sidestep at the same moment. With a yelp the man tripped and sprawled on his back, then let out a feeble groan but didn't move.

"Oh dear," said Harry in Wroth's voice. He stooped over the felled man to hide his face, his hand still on his dagger. "So sorry, sir. The cobbles are slippery tonight."

Crane's driver had come running and was hovering beside his employer. "Are you injured, my lord?"

The viscount waved him away with a scowl. "No, no. Just a touch of assault while you were busy with the step. Fortunately I am not so easy to wound." He pulled up his cloak where it had slipped off his shoulder and limped away with only a brief nod in Harry's direction. The coachman gave him a sympathetic look before following his master.

Harry listened to Crane walk away. He nudged the man on the ground with his toe, then took hold of his coat and pulled him up. A strong smell of gin hit him in the face as the fellow moaned again, and Harry released him, letting him flop back onto the street. Just a common drunk. "Drink is a wicked thing," he told his victim, then slowly rose and turned. Lord Crane was getting settled into his carriage, none the worse for his encounter with a cup-shot lamplighter. Harry exhaled, pried his fingers from the dagger, then ducked his head and hurried on to his own carriage.

It was farther than he remembered, and by the time he reached the familiar horses, his shins burned. He glanced over his shoulder and saw that Crane's carriage had already started off. He rapped once on the driver's box with his cane to get Ian's attention, then flung open the door.

"Here here, now, my lord! Can't injure yourself, sir." Ian jumped down and seized his arm. Harry scowled as Ian's fingers bit into his flesh. "Feeling spry tonight, eh?" muttered the Scot as he practically heaved Harry into the carriage.

"Crane's already gone," he bit back, slamming the door in Ian's face. The carriage rocked as Ian leaped back onto his seat, then lurched as he set the horses off without pause. Harry knelt on the front seat and slid open the little door.

"He's headed home," Ian said as they passed the last of the clustered carriages near Doncaster House.

"He left in quite a rush." Harry couldn't see around Ian, and he could barely hear him. "I almost missed it."

Ian grunted. "Getting slow in your old age, aye?"

Harry ignored the dig. Ian was driving along at a rapid pace, and this carriage was not particularly luxurious or well-sprung. His knees bounced on the hard seat with every jerk and sway of the wheels. He had to brace himself on the door as they went around one corner on two wheels, from the feel of it. "Have we passed him yet?" he yelled at Ian, who merely laughed, the blighter.

Before long Ian slowed, then turned another corner and stopped altogether. Harry slid to the window and peered out. They were stopped in a narrow alley three doors down from Crane's town house. Harry's eyes swept up and down the well-lit street as the driver opened the door for the viscount and lowered the step. There was no one else about, no other carriages on the street. All seemed safe enough . . .

Lord Crane emerged, leaning heavily on the driver's arm. A footman came out of the house and hurried down the steps, only to jump back as Crane waved him away. Slowly, he climbed the steps into his house, trailed by the obedient footman. The door closed behind them both. The driver returned to his box and flicked the whip, setting the horses into motion.

"Home again, safe and sound." Ian broke the silence. "Where to, m'lord?"

"Home," Harry said, falling back into the seat and plucking the spectacles off his face to rub his nose. "We're done here."

The carriage rocked as Ian started the team, more sedately this time, and Harry rested his head and sighed. When they turned into the mews behind the house in Fenton Lane, he put the spectacles back on. This time Ian didn't bother to help him down, and Harry clenched his jaw as he had to put his full weight back on his sore feet. He jerked his head at Ian, who nodded and drove off to tend the horses.

Harry crossed the narrow way to the back door of the house and let himself in. There was little pretense of nobility in this house; it was plainly and practically furnished, just enough to be lived in. It was small and somewhat dingy and no one could call its location fashionable. Mr. Phipps certainly had spared the expense when he arranged this for their headquarters.

At the top of the stairs Harry turned toward his room, catching up the lamp left burning for him on the hall table. Ian slept in the stables most nights, and Angelique was on duty at Lord Bethwell's. He was nearly alone in the house tonight.

Grimacing, Harry shed the padded coat and laid it aside, then tossed the spectacles on top of it. He raised his arms above his head and stretched, feeling the muscles in his back pull tight in protest. Damn, it felt good to stand upright again after stooping for so many hours.

Next went the shoes, the despicable narrow shoes meant for a man half his size. He peeled off the waistcoat and cravat, stripping off the pieces of Wroth. First the outer layers of musty wool, then the layers of old linen, until he was bare to the waist and finally felt almost like himself again.

For a moment he just stood there with his arms folded, flexing his toes in relief. Those shoes were a torment from hell. But he'd been given them as part of his disguise and told not to ask questions. That was a common refrain in this job: don't ask, just do. He had accepted that so far, but from time to time as he sat on the edge of his seat, hardly breathing as he watched Crane labor up his front steps, he couldn't help wondering just where the true threat was coming from. Surely they hadn't been given this assignment merely to prevent Crane and the others from being harassed by drunks and pickpockets.

He sighed and shook it off. It was enough that Phipps and Stafford believed Crane, Doncaster, and Bethwell were in danger. It was his lot to keep them safe, not to worry about who might harm them. Tonight he had been successful, and he ought to be content with that.

In stockinged feet he crossed the room to the wash basin. He splashed his face, sucking in his breath at the coldness of the water, then dunked his head and scrubbed his hair to get rid of the sticky powder that turned it gray.

When he raised his dripping head, he braced his arms on the washstand and stared at himself in the mirror. Now he even looked like himself, although a drowned version. Dark hair spiked along his crown and clung to his forehead in sodden snakes. Water dripped off a square jaw. He leaned closer, scrutinizing his reflection in the dim lamplight. A straight, sharp nose. Piercing hazel eyes. Scullery maids and tavern wenches liked his face well enough . . .

"She wouldn't want you anyway," he muttered. He turned away from the mirror and buried his wet face in a towel, trying not to think anymore of the wealthy, pampered, gloriously beautiful and utterly forbidden Lady Mariah.

Chapter 4

Mariah went to her mother's suite as soon as she was dressed the next morning. Her curiosity about the mysterious Harry had, if anything, grown stronger overnight. Although she'd kept her eyes and ears open the rest of the night, she hadn't come across anyone who could be the same man. It was more than a little puzzling. How could he simply disappear? She even made it a point to meet as many gentlemen as possible after supper, to no avail. She'd never heard his voice again. His challenge, not to mention his sly laugh, rang in her ears as she rapped at the door and pushed it open when her mother called out.

"Good morning, Mariah." Mama was still in bed, sipping tea. "You're awake early for a young lady who danced until the dawn."

Mariah smiled. "I wasn't up so very late."

Her mother's gaze turned shrewd. "And you were not so taken by the dancing."

"No," Mariah admitted without pretense. "At least not by the dancing partners."

Cassandra Dunmore put down her teacup. "Mariah, you do know you shall see those same gentlemen at many other events. I hope you're not being too quick to condemn."

"Condemn? Oh, no, Mama," she protested. "I did not know what to expect. Now I do."

"And now you will expect to be bored," murmured her mother with a wry look. "Perhaps your father and I were wrong to keep you from London for so long. This is your home, after all, not St. Petersburg or Vienna. I hope the excitement of those cities hasn't spoiled England for you."

"Not at all! I am glad to be home. And I would never have forgiven you and Papa if you had left me here alone for the last five years." Her mother laughed, and Mariah grinned. Then she tried to shift the subject to what she wanted to discuss. It had to be done delicately. "There were *some* interesting people present last night, and I expect they shall improve even more upon further acquaintance." Mariah paused, then added as casually as she could, "Might I see the guest list?"

"Of course, darling. May I ask why?"

Mariah hesitated. At twenty-two years, soon to be three and twenty, she was past the age when most girls married. Her father had worried about this upon their return to England, but her mother firmly put his doubts aside; a girl with Mariah's family and beauty, to say nothing of her charm and intelligence, could have a husband as soon as she decided to get one. The earl gave way, agreeing with his wife on all accounts about their adored only child, and Mariah had felt none of the pressure to find a husband that her friends and peers had felt.

Still, she knew just how pleased her mother would be if she showed any interest in a gentleman. Papa would probably have him fetched at once to make his intentions and expectations known. Which was of course impossible with Harry until she discovered who he was, and even then she preferred not to arouse her parents' suspicions. She might not like him so very much after all. "I met a gentleman last night, and he refused to tell me his proper name," she settled on saying. "It was most vexing."

"Indeed," her mother replied in surprise. "Exceedingly vexing, I should say. What did he tell you?"

"He said he was called Harry." Mariah faced her mother with as unconcerned an expression as she could manage. "He laughed when I said I would discover his name on my own, and said he knew I could not."

Cassandra set aside her tea. "He laughed?"

Mariah gave a small sniff of disgust. "No doubt he thought I lacked the intelligence."

Her mother flung back her covers and got out of bed, a martial gleam in her eye. "Did he? We shall see about that." She pulled on her dressing gown as she crossed the room to her writing desk. Mariah watched, quietly gloating, while her mother pulled several pages from a drawer. "Now, come here, Mariah," she said, taking a seat on the chaise. "Let us discover the scoundrel."

"Yes, Mama." Mariah hurried over.

A half hour later, however, all her plans to fling the discovery triumphantly in his face lay in ruins. They had gone over the list two, three, four times, examining every name that could possibly imply *Harry*, and found nothing.

"Mariah, I think he must have lied to you." Cassandra put down the list. "We didn't invite anyone named Harry."

"But he was here, Mama!" She scowled at the list in frustration. "Who is this?" She tapped one name. Her mother looked.

"Mr. Harold Graves. Tall and bald. Not a terribly charming fellow."

Mariah didn't want that to be her Harry, and besides, she had found him perfectly charming. She looked down the page. "And this one?"

"Sir Henry Gates? I'm certain he never left the card room. Appalling weakness in a man of his position."

"What position?"

"He advises the Lord Chancellor, dear. Best of friends with him."

"Ah." Mariah flipped the pages, grasping at straws. "This one, then."

Cassandra sighed wearily. "Lord Wroth is elderly, Mariah. He walks with a cane and has a hump."

Mariah flung the useless list across the room. "Then who the devil is he?"

"Mariah, please!"

She flopped back with something dangerously close to a pout at her mother's reprimand. How on earth was she ever to meet the man again if she didn't know his name or his face?

"Tell me more about him," said her mother. "What does he look like?"

Mariah frowned uneasily. This was dangerous. "He was tall, but rather unexceptional looking. I hardly remember, in fact." True enough, she supposed. "It was only his mocking manner and his challenge that I would not be able to discover his name! What a thoroughly infuriating man!"

Cassandra patted her hand. "They all are, dear, at one point or another. But it matters not. I daresay you'll run into him again. It's only a matter of time before you discover him."

Mariah propped her chin on one hand. "I suppose." So Harry had won this point; she hadn't been able to learn his name on her own. "Wretched man," she muttered.

He wasn't worth this much aggravation. If he didn't have the backbone to introduce himself, he wasn't much of a man at all. Let *him* find *her* again; she certainly wouldn't spend another minute thinking of him.

At ten minutes before eight in the morning, Harry arrived at his other employment, the far less thrilling—and less dangerous—side of his job. Slipping in through the servants' door, he winked at the scullery maid sweeping the floor but didn't dare linger.

He hurried up three flights of back stairs, pushing his spectacles up on his nose. Unlike Wroth's useless lenses, he actually needed these; while his vision was perfect at a distance, things closer than arm's length, particularly small type, were a bit fuzzy. Today he would be spending the next several hours as Lord Crane's private secretary, reading and writing extremely small writing, and so wore his own spectacles.

He walked down the corridor and tapped lightly at a door. Jasper, Crane's valet, opened it. "Good morning, Mr. Towne."

"Good morning, Jasper." Harry stepped into the room as the valet left, then waited to be acknowledged by the slight figure sitting at a mahogany table, bent over a book with a magnifying lens in his hand. Who would have thought such a weak old man would be one of the most important men in England?

Ever since the so-called "Massacre at Manchester" the previous year, radicals had been fomenting revolt and rebellion against the government, even including the mass assassination of the Cabinet heads to wipe the government's slate clean. Lord Crane, like Lord Doncaster and the Marquis of Bethwell, had been identified as a likely target of their rage because his counsel was still invaluable to Lord Eldon, the Lord Chancellor. Crane had suffered a mild attack of palsy earlier in the year, leaving his hands unsteady. Stafford seized upon the opportunity to get one of his agents into Crane's household, though the viscount was notorious for disdaining secretaries and conducting most of his correspondence himself. Thus Harry—under the name Henry Towne—was sent to apply for the position, charged with ensuring Crane's safety without letting him suspect he was doing so.

It certainly gave Harry an intimate view of the viscount. Thin and rawboned, with a face like a hawk, Crane was as renowned for his legal brilliance as for his fierce will and even fiercer temper. He was as likely to sit and patiently lecture Harry on some obscure legal point as he was to upbraid him for not copying out a letter fast enough. Harry had quickly learned three things in his employ: don't be late, don't be meek, and don't make a mistake.

Now he stood at attention just inside the door, waiting. His muscles ached for a stretch, just a little easing of his posture, but he didn't move. He knew this routine by now, and fidgeting was not permitted. The only thing he could do was stretch his toes, which were still sore from last night. If only he could take off his shoes again and feel the cool night air on his feet . . .

That thought revived his spirits a great deal. This morning his indiscreet conversation with Lady Mariah had taken on a new character in his mind. No, she wouldn't want him if she knew who he was—but she didn't know, and he certainly couldn't tell her. It was quite likely he would cross her path again, since he'd be following her father from now on. It was almost his duty to think of her, if only to brace himself for their next encounter. He swallowed a smirk, for working so hard to justify his own desires, and allowed himself a few pleasurable moments anticipating his next glimpse of Mariah Dunmore.

The silence in the room wore on. Crane had made no sign he was aware of Harry's presence, but Harry knew better than to think this was the case. He kept his eyes on the far wall and concentrated on his breathing, willing away the remnants of weariness and sleep and illicit interest in young ladies. He knew there was a long day ahead of him.

"You are late." Crane pronounced each word as if it were a revelation.

Harry hadn't been late since his third day, when he came in as the clock struck eight and Crane informed him it would cost him a day's wages. "No, sir."

"You are," the viscount said firmly.

"No, sir," repeated Harry in the same calm voice. The first week, he had been all deference, until he realized Crane actually wanted someone to disagree with him.

Crane pursed his lips as the clock began to chime the hour, then turned back to his work. "See that it doesn't happen again," he muttered.

"Yes, sir." Harry moved to the small writing desk near the window.

"Take a letter." His employer didn't wait for him to seat himself or uncap his ink. "To John Rusk at Brimstow. Mind the peach trees particularly this season, as I hear there is a blight . . . "

Hurriedly taking his seat, Harry began making notes as fast as he could. Rusk was the head gardener at Crane's country estate, Brimstow, and Harry had learned early that Rusk was Lord Crane's most valued correspondent. Day after day Harry transcribed long letters to the gardener, letters filled with precisely detailed instructions for the care of the viscount's extensive gardens. It shouldn't have mattered much, but after a month of taking notes on the proper way to rake a rose bed and which tulips to plant under which tree at Brimstow, he would have been happy never to see another tulip bulb or even a leaf ever again. It was rather cruel of Crane to keep him out so late at night, then try to bore him to sleep the next day, Harry thought with a dash of black humor as he filled page after page with notes on peach trees.

After Crane finished dictating the letter, he waved Harry off to copy it out. "Go to, Towne. That letter must go off today."

Letters to Brimstow were always Crane's highest priority. Harry took out several sheets of paper as a servant slipped into the room and brought him the post. There were four invitations—it seemed London hostesses weren't put off by Crane's abrupt manners— a letter from Brimstow, and a note from Lord Billington seeking Crane's advice on some legal question. Harry detailed the post, hoping against hope that Billington's letter—which couldn't possibly be about fruit trees— would receive some notice, but the viscount merely grunted and took the gardener's letter, ignoring the rest.

"Good morning, Uncle!" Lord Crane's nephew, Tobias, had come in with the post. A big, handsome fellow, Tobias had taken up residence in the house when the palsy struck Crane, but what good he did his uncle was beyond Harry. Tobias enjoyed society and exercise and gambling, all things Crane despised. Harry was privately certain one of them would drive the other mad before the end of the Season, with his own money going on Tobias driving Crane mad first. Crane *liked* being grim and dour, while Tobias was anything but, and the two clashed regularly.

Harry lowered his head over his work. Crane hunched in his deep leather chair, pointedly turning his shoulder to the younger man. Tobias was undaunted.

"Well!" He rubbed his hands together. "It's a fine day out. Would you care to take a ride in my new curricle?"

Harry supposed one should credit Tobias for persistence, but no one could call his efforts successful. "No," growled Crane from behind the pages of Rusk's letter.

"Now, Uncle, it's the latest style. It cost me a pretty penny to get one so quickly, in time for the Season, but I had no choice."

"No choice," snapped Crane. "Walk!"

Tobias laughed, although a shade uncomfortably. "Well, a gentleman can hardly walk everywhere, Uncle."

"If he tried he could," was Crane's waspish reply.

Tobias cleared his throat, still grinning awkwardly. "Yes. Perhaps."

There was a moment of silence as Crane turned over his page, still reading. Harry finished one page of instruction and moved on to the next. Crane's peach trees were more cosseted than any human he knew.

"Will you attend the Steele soiree tonight, Uncle?" Tobias tried again.

"Of course not." Crane leaned forward and pulled his large horticultural reference toward him. He picked up his magnifying lens and examined something on the page.

"Oh . . . but Uncle—"

"No," said Crane again. "Go away, young man."

Tobias flushed. He noticed the stack of invitations then, sitting on the corner of Harry's desk, and held one up. "Why, Uncle, it seems you are still quite popular. Look, an invitation from Lady Jaffey!"

Crane turned a page in his almanac and made no reply.

Tobias didn't seem to notice, or care. "Lady Jaffey is one of the leading hostesses in London," he went on with growing enthusiasm. "Her parties are renowned for their elegance. You cannot refuse her invitation."

"Lady Jaffey is a shrill and vain woman," retorted his uncle. "I most certainly can refuse her."

Tobias's brow creased in frustration. He aspired to the society Crane disdained. He was Crane's only heir, and Harry suspected he had come to town this Season not only out of any affection or concern for his uncle, but to enjoy the prospect of his inheritance as well. "*I* should like to attend," Tobias muttered.

Crane finally looked up. "Then go! Go, go, go, and leave me in peace."

His nephew beamed. "Of course. Thank you, Uncle." He bowed and left, having secured at least one of his objects.

Lord Crane made a disgusted noise when the door had closed. "Empty-headed fribble. The sooner he gets himself an empty-headed wife, the happier he'll be and the more peace I'll have." He sighed, raising one hand to his brow. "Are you done with that letter yet, Towne?"

"Nearly, sir. Another moment only." Harry sped through the last of it, then brought it across the room. Crane read it over with a scowl, ready to make him recopy the entirety if there were a single mistake, but Harry had learned that lesson in his first days, too. Finding no fault, Crane signed the letter, his blue-veined hand trembling noticeably, and finally turned to his other correspondence.

"Shall you accept?" Harry asked as Crane rolled his eyes over each invitation.

"No," the viscount muttered again and again. Each time Harry made a mental note, totting up how often Crane would go out and require Lord Wroth's protective surveillance. Not often in the next fortnight, he realized, paging through Crane's diary.

"You are to dine tonight with Admiral Northby, sir," Harry said. "At his home." He did not look forward to it. When Crane spent the evening at a private affair, Harry couldn't follow as Mr. Towne or as Lord Wroth.

Four times already, he, and sometimes Ian, had spent
hours patrolling the shadows outside a home while
Crane or Lord Bethwell dined within, and twice they
had been soaked to the skin. Stafford at least managed
to get him invited to most balls or larger gatherings
their marks attended, and save him a night in the
rain.

"Am I? Lord, no," said Crane with a sigh. He leaned
back in his chair and closed his eyes, and for a moment
looked like the frail old man he was. "I shall stay at
home tonight. There were too many people at the ball
last night, hardly anyone who could speak sense, and
the streets were full of vagabonds. Send Northby my
regrets."

Harry obediently made a note of it in the diary,
breathing a silent sigh of relief. That left merely Doncaster. He already knew Bethwell was still ill and
would be abed under Angelique's watchful eye. And
surely after the affair at his own house last night, Doncaster would want a quiet evening at home . . . with his
family . . .

A terrible, tantalizing thought stole across Harry's
mind. It was out of the question, even if it were fea-
sible. Brandon would most likely send word that Doncaster was going out this evening, and he would find
himself sipping port and shuffling Lord Wroth's too-
tight shoes around another ballroom or parlor. But if
he didn't . . .

He didn't. By the time Harry returned to Fenton
Lane, Brandon had sent word that Doncaster was planning to go to his club, one of the few places they were
not responsible for following him. Whether Stafford
had other agents inside the gentlemen's clubs or just
considered their marks safe enough surrounded by

other nobility, Harry didn't know. But it meant he was completely free for the night.

He used the time to catch up on his reports, which were to be written nightly and then turned in to Stafford as soon as convenient. He hadn't done the one from last night, and then there was the one for today. Nothing much to report, though, he thought as his pen skimmed across the paper. There was rarely anything more significant than the drunk bothering Crane last night.

In short order the reports were done. Angelique's maid, Lisette, carried away Wroth's clothing for a brushing, for which Harry gave her a grateful smile. Ian had taken his night off at the local pub, glad to get away from the horses for a while. Angelique and Brandon were still in their respective posts. Harry found himself alone and unoccupied for the first time in weeks. He sat down in the rarely used sitting room and opened a book.

Time slowed to a crawl. The book lay unread in his hand. His eyes were fixed instead out the window, on the evening star hanging low and bright in the sky like a jewel against the dark velvet of the night. Venus was uncommonly bright tonight again . . .

Finally, he laid the book aside. He was utterly mad, damned if he did and damned if he didn't. Which meant there was no reason to fight the urge, no matter how mad. He reflected a moment on the possible consequences of his contemplated actions, then got up, put on his coat, and let himself out the door.

Chapter 5

After a whole day of not thinking about Harry, Mariah found she couldn't stop thinking of him once night fell.

Was he out somewhere, at some other ball, standing in the dark on another balcony with another young lady? Or was he in a ballroom, holding that other lady in his arms and teasing her in that droll tone? What did his smile look like? Even though she didn't want to know—vexing man—it was killing her that she didn't. If she could meet him again, just once, just to put her nose in the air and sniff at him . . . Or perhaps sneak up on him and startle him . . . Or simply gloat, victoriously, that she had found him out after all . . .

She sighed and tossed her book aside. She hadn't managed to read more than a page. Papa had gone out to his club, and even though it still felt early, Mariah thought she might as well go to bed. She and her mother had spent the evening at home, dining with Aunt Marion and Joan. Her cousin seemed to have forgotten all about Harry, which put Mariah even more out of sorts. She found she still had some feelings about him she would have liked to voice, and

Joan was the only person who could possibly have sympathized.

"Good night, Mama," she said with a sigh, getting to her feet. "I shall see you in the morning." Mariah stopped to kiss her mother's cheek as she passed.

"Good night, dear." Her mother put a hand on her arm. "Are you well, child?"

"Yes, perfectly. Just a bit tired."

Mama smiled fondly. "I understand. Sleep well."

Mariah trudged up the stairs, wretched curiosity still simmering in her mind. She wasn't sure she would even be able to fall asleep, with the restless buzzing of all her questions. She sat idly tracing circles on the dressing table with one finger while Sally, her maid, brushed out and braided her hair, then caught a glimpse of herself in the mirror. She looked petulant and cross, like a child denied a sweet. It brought a reluctant smile to her face. "Ninny," she whispered to herself. She couldn't believe she was acting this way over a gentleman.

"Pardon, my lady?"

Sally's voice recalled her to sense. "Nothing. Just woolgathering." She stood up and let Sally unfasten her dress. "Have you got a sweetheart, Sally?"

The maid's eyes barely flickered as she helped Mariah undress. "No, m'lady."

"Mmm." Mariah pulled on her nightgown thoughtfully. "You're better off, you know. Men are such vexing creatures."

"Yes, ma'am. My mum always did say so."

Mariah looked at her in surprise, then burst out laughing. Sally smiled a little, too. "Your mum was right. Well, you may go."

Sally curtsied and slipped out of the room. Mariah flung her long braid over her shoulder and crossed to the window. It was a warm night with a gentle breeze, very like last night. She leaned out to feel the breeze, wiggling her toes against the carpet, but it wasn't the same as having them caressed by the night air. So that was one thing Harry had done for her: shown her how lovely it was to go barefoot at night. She pulled the drapes open a little more to allow that breeze in and crossed the room to her bed, putting out the lamps as she went.

Perhaps there was some other way she could discover who he was. She considered it while plumping up the pillows behind her head. Mama had said she was likely to meet him again at another social gathering, and Mama was probably right. She would just have to keep her eyes open—and her ears alert. It wasn't very satisfying, but what else could she do? Wait for him to seek her out again, after he had said quite confidently that she could not find him? And been right, too, blast him.

"Lady Mariah."

Mariah opened her eyes and frowned, listening hard. She'd been so absorbed in her thoughts she wasn't sure she had actually heard anything. Had Sally come back? No, the door hadn't opened; it must have been her imagination.

"Lady Mariah."

She sat up in bed, this time sure she had heard someone call her name. "Yes?" she said tentatively. "Who is there?"

"Just I," came the quiet reply, just now resolving into a familiar voice. "Harry."

She bolted out of bed, her heart slamming, and looked around. "Where are you?" she cried, grabbing her extinguished candle.

"The window." She looked closer, and sure enough, saw the faint outline of a head and shoulders.

"What on earth are you doing there?" she exclaimed, taking a step toward him.

"Seeing if I am welcome to come in," he said in the same barely amused, utterly assured tone she remembered too well.

Mariah stopped dead, wide-eyed in disbelief. He had climbed up the side of the house to call on her? Here? *Now*? "Come in?" she repeated stupidly. "This is my bedroom." Only a scoundrel would try to climb into a young lady's bedroom, and only a young lady with no morals would invite him in. Why was he even asking?

"Yes, I know. It took devilishly long to figure that out. Shall I stay, or go?"

"Stay!" The word was out of her mouth before she even realized what she was saying. "Come in," she said more calmly. "Please."

Mariah backed up as he hoisted himself silently over the windowsill. She strained her eyes to make him out in the dark room, her curiosity burning like a bonfire: Who was he, why was he sneaking around like this, and what did he intend by it? She gripped her candlestick, just in case. Out of the corner of her eye she could see the bell, which would bring Sally on the run. Or she could scream, which would bring any number of servants, or even her mother.

"Go back to your bed," he said, unfolding his frame in front of the window.

Mariah felt a moment of alarm. "Why?"

He put his hands on his hips. "Because I can't stay if you don't. I shall stay here, and you shall stay there, or I really must go." She still hesitated, and he half turned to the window again. "All right, then. Good night."

"No, no! Don't go." She retreated to her bed as she spoke. "But why must I stay over here?"

"We hardly know each other, miss," he said with affected affront. "Keep your distance, if you please."

Mariah choked back a snort of laughter. "You're afraid of me?"

"A wise man never underestimates a woman."

She leaned forward and stared hard. He was still nothing more than an indistinct shape, standing as he was in front of the only source of light, however dim, in the room. "And I suppose you want to be able to jump out the window if someone should come, like you did last night."

His laugh was low. "I didn't jump. I climbed."

"And how did you manage that?" she asked, astonished all over again that he had done it. "You might have broken your neck."

"I might have done." He didn't sound bothered by the prospect at all.

"Why did you do it?"

"Your mother was calling you. Would she have been pleased to discover you lurking in the dark with a man?"

"I wasn't lurking—"

"Would she?"

"Well—no—"

"So I left."

Mariah pressed her lips shut. "Left the ball entirely?"

"I never said that." He folded his arms and leaned back on the windowsill, his shadow firming into a more definite silhouette. His hair was wavy, she saw with interest—or perhaps just tousled from his climb. Oh, how she longed for him to turn his head, or bend down so the moonlight would illuminate his face . . .

"Then where did you go? I looked and looked—" She broke off, chagrined at herself for blurting that out.

"Did you really?" His voice warmed. "How very flattering."

"Don't be ridiculous. I was merely curious to see who would do such a rash thing. I'm only glad it wasn't a waste of time." Mariah heaved what she hoped was a carefree sigh. "I met ever so many more gentlemen whilst looking for you."

"I hope they were more to your liking." Dark amusement lurked in his voice; he was teasing her. Mariah longed to say yes, she had met a dozen immensely fascinating men after he disappeared, but she couldn't. It wasn't true. She hadn't met any man half as intriguing as the mysterious one now sitting on her windowsill.

"None of them felt compelled to leap off a balcony to avoid being seen with me," she settled for saying.

"And none of them climbed thirty feet up a wall to see you again tonight, did they?"

That *was* true. She couldn't stop a glowing burst of feminine satisfaction. "And why did *you*?"

For a long moment he didn't answer. "Because I wanted to see you again."

"Why?" she pressed. "You hardly know me."

"No," he agreed. "It's a risk, I know. You might be as vain and silly and spoiled as any young lady in London. Certainly not worth risking a broken neck, as you were so kind to warn me."

Her mouth dropped open in shock.

"Still," he went on in the same thoughtful tone, "I really had to come, just for my own peace of mind. I couldn't sleep at all last night for thinking of your voice."

Oh, dear. Her stomach fluttered and her toes curled. Mariah licked her lips. "Why didn't you come to call on me today, if you were so curious?"

"Didn't I?" He leaned forward, and a slash of moonlight moved over his head for an instant, too quickly for Mariah to make out any of his features. "Am I not here?"

There was something in his voice, some quiet undercurrent, that made her abruptly, acutely, aware of just how near he was. Here in her dark room, the house slumbering around them in peaceful ignorance, it was just the two of them, alone and unseen and well outside the rules of propriety. Her skin prickled with nervous excitement. "I suppose you are," she murmured, peering into the darkness that cloaked him.

Harry sensed the instant her curiosity became more sensual and less intellectual. He'd caught her off guard with his unorthodox visit, but now she was fully aware that a man was in her bedchamber and that they were completely alone. She had shifted her weight, from sitting cross-legged in front of her bank of pillows to leaning toward him propped on one arm. Her fingers twisted the end of the long dark braid that lay over her shoulder, and her head tilted to one side in a pose of innocent allure.

He stayed where he was. This visit, after all, was not to seduce her, but to see if his impressions last night had been correct. Good God, she was beautiful; when she leaned out her bedroom window, he'd been frozen to his spot in a shadowed hedge, mesmerized by the way she turned her face up to the sky, her eyes closed and a small smile on her lips. He had been compelled then, compelled to climb a vine that ought to have dumped him straight back into the dirt and compelled to ignore every caution and rule imposed on him by asking to come into her room. And she was pleased that he had; with his back to the window, he could see her expression as clear as day without letting her see him. He knew that would only make her more curious about him, but he couldn't afford to give himself away yet.

The thought brought him up short. Not yet? Not ever. Because he was, and always would be, beneath her. Seducing Mariah Dunmore would be ruinous for her and, if he were lucky, merely the most dishonorable thing he had ever done—and thanks to his current employment, that said a great deal. If Mariah knew who and what he was, she'd certainly not welcome him into her room ever again.

"What shall we do now?" came her suggestive whisper, driving home the point.

Harry clenched his jaw and forced down the surge of desire her question caused. This was no scullery maid or tavern wench, ready and willing to be tumbled. "I think we've talked quite enough."

"R-Really?" The catch in her voice, revealing her to

be at once startled and intrigued, acted like fuel on the desire smoldering inside him.

"Yes," he said, keeping his tone careless even as his body roared to life at the thought of what she might allow him to do if he could just set aside his last few scruples. He wasn't quite prepared for that. He had expected she would hold him at arm's length, where he belonged. "Good night."

"What? No, wait," she exclaimed, scrambling toward the side of the bed. Harry instinctively ducked toward the window, and she leaped back. "Stay," she cried softly. "Please." He paused, hands on the sill, and looked back at her over his shoulder. "Why didn't you come see me during the day, as other gentlemen do?"

He shrugged. "I can't."

"Can't or won't?"

He shrugged again as a clock somewhere in the house began to chime. In eight hours he had to be at Lord Crane's house. "I can't."

She was quiet for a minute. "Who are you?" she asked slowly. "Who can't come calling during the day?"

He took another look out the window. The garden appeared deserted, and temptation loomed behind him. He had better leave before he lost his mind entirely. "Good night, Lady Mariah."

"Stop!" He paused, balanced on the windowsill. "You will come again, won't you?" she whispered, hope unmistakable in her voice.

Harry wavered. If he were caught, neither Stafford nor anyone at the Home Office would be able to save him from her father's wrath, even if they tried—and he knew they wouldn't. No one would fault Doncaster in the slightest for shooting a man sneaking into his daughter's room. It was quite likely suicidal to approach her again. The correct answer, the *only* answer, was a firm and final no.

"Perhaps," he said, and slid down the vines before he committed any unpardonable sins.

Mariah leaped out of bed the moment he was gone and ran to the window. Yanking back the drapes, she strained her eyes into the dark night. She didn't hear anything other than the dying chime of the clock, and what was worse, she didn't see anything. She scanned the garden, but there was nothing, not a shadow moving, not even a rustle of the ivy. How the devil had he slipped into their garden and climbed up the ivy to her room without being seen by anyone or leaving any trace of his presence? She leaned out as far as she dared, craning her neck in every direction, and still saw absolutely nothing.

Slowly, reluctantly, Mariah retreated from the window. Gone, like a ghost or a phantom. But he had been there—she put her hand against the windowsill where he'd leaned his weight, the wood still warm—and instead of curing her fascination, he had only increased it. There was something dangerous in him, something mysterious and compelling that she was helpless to resist. Was he a scoundrel? A thief? A spy? She didn't know, but a coy, delighted smile spread across her face. Whoever he was, he found her as intriguing as she found him.

Farewell to her pose of indifference; she cast it off without a second thought. She might not know much more about him, but she did know she wouldn't rest until she'd found him.

Chapter 6

"**J**oan!" Mariah flew up the stairs of the Bennet house, waving a greeting to Lady Bennet, her aunt Marion. Joan's mother was her mother's sister, and she and her cousin had been close all their lives. Now that Mariah was back in London, they had been coming and going like sisters in each other's homes. Lady Bennet waved back, her only reproof a quick shake of the head. Mariah slowed to a walk until she reached the top of the stairs, at which point she hurried on again. Her heart fluttered against her ribs like a bird straining out of its cage, wanting to be free to soar. "Joan! Where are you?"

"Here." Her cousin appeared in the doorway of her room, head cocked. "What's the matter? You know I'll hear from Mother about all the shouting . . . "

"Never mind." Mariah pushed Joan back into the room, closing the door behind her. She leaned against the wall, breathless with excitement and exertion. "Joan, we must find him!"

"Him?" Joan's eyebrows went up. "You don't mean . . . Harry?"

Mariah nodded, hands clasped to her breast as a dreamy smile floated over her face. "Harry." She, too, whispered the name. Which was absurd, because no one could hear them or would have the faintest idea what or whom they were talking about. Her mysterious visitor was a complete and utter secret, only between her and Joan. And a wonderful, romantic secret, too. The idea made her giddy.

"Why?" Joan took her by the shoulders, serious for once. She peered closely at Mariah. "Have you taken a fever? You look flushed."

Mariah seized her hands and laughed. "No doubt! Oh, you'll never guess . . . " She trailed off, thinking again of how he had scaled the wall to her bedroom to see her, like a knight of old braving the sleeping dragon to court the fair princess. The very thought was enough to make her hands tremble and her stomach feel fluttery.

"Well, tell me!" Joan exclaimed. "What happened?"

"He came to see me last night."

Joan frowned. "He did? But then you know who he is."

Mariah shook her head. "I didn't see him. It was very late. And very dark. I was almost asleep when he climbed in the window."

Joan's mouth opened as if she would scream, but no sound came out. Mariah nodded. "He came into your bedroom?" Joan whispered, incredulous.

Mariah nodded again, spinning away from the wall in a lazy waltz step. "Yes, indeed."

"In the middle of the night?" Joan followed, eyes still leaping from her head. "You're ruined, then!"

She stopped. "Of course not! Don't even say such a thing." She softened her stern tone. "He never came near me. A perfect gentleman—well, aside from the fact that he was in my bedroom at midnight—but Joan!

It was so romantic," she said on a sigh. "And I could have talked to him all night."

Joan sat on the chaise with a thump, still stunned. "Like a knight rescuing a fair maiden," she said, echoing Mariah's thought. "Like Romeo risking his life to see Juliet . . . Do you know, I believe I am quite jealous of you for the first time in my life."

Mariah laughed. "You should be! I feel like I could fly! Or at least run through the streets laughing and singing. I think I've never been really alive until now."

"You're in love."

Mariah snorted. "No. I don't think so. Not yet. But I am well and truly infatuated." Both of them laughed.

"That settles it: we *must* find him." Joan crossed the room to her writing desk and pulled out the chair. She took out her journal and opened it with a determined air. "As soon as possible. How intolerable that you still don't know his name!"

Mariah twirled around again, then threw herself onto her cousin's bed. "I quite agree. Where shall we start?"

Joan dipped her pen in the inkwell, ready to write. "What do you know about him?"

Mariah sighed, sadly this time. "Nothing. He might be a Whig for all I know, although I didn't ask—it was bad enough to receive a gentleman at night, let alone a Whig gentleman—"

"Bother all that," Joan interrupted. "What *do* you know about him? How tall is he?"

Mariah frowned up at the ceiling, thinking of his shadow against her window. "Half a foot taller than I am, I think. Perhaps a little more."

Joan wrote it down. "Hair?"

"Yes."

"Mariah," Joan grumbled.

She laughed, then shook her head. "I cannot tell you anything beyond the fact that he has hair. Not too long, but not too short. I'd wager it's dark, but cannot say for certain. Perhaps wavy."

Joan snorted, but made a note. "I suppose nothing about his face."

"He has a very handsome profile," said Mariah dreamily. "And he must be very strong and agile to climb up that old ivy—do you know, it must be thirty feet from the ground—"

"Stop! You're making me want to plant ivy outside my own window, even though I'd be an old woman before it grew high enough for anyone to climb." Joan stared into space for a moment. "So he must be a young man," she said thoughtfully. "But not too young. Strong. Tall. Witty. Charming. And he has hair. Why can I not meet such a man?"

"You will," said Mariah. "And you must help me look for this one."

Joan sighed and shook her head. "But you don't know anything useful. The only thing you would recognize in daylight is his voice."

Mariah rolled over and sat up. "Then that's how we'll find him. We'll simply talk to every man in London."

Joan looked doubtful. "It will take forever."

Mariah thought for a moment. That was unacceptable. She wanted to start searching for him this very instant. "The park. We'll go to the park. Everyone goes there, and it would be quite natural and ordinary to greet gentlemen passing by."

"You could just force him to tell you himself," said Joan. "That would be much faster."

She bit her lip. She didn't want to tell Joan her vague suspicion that Harry was someone not quite . . . proper. She couldn't think of any other reason why he wouldn't tell her his name or come to call on her properly or even let her see his face. She wasn't even entirely sure she wanted him simply to tell her; he was a mystery, rather exciting and undeniably romantic. "I don't know how I could. I don't even know if he'll come back to see me."

"Of course he will!" Joan exclaimed. "How could he not?"

Mariah hoped she was right, but Harry had defied her expectation at every turn so far. "I did ask him to—"

Her cousin gasped in shocked delight.

"—but he only said perhaps. He might decide it's not worth the trouble."

Joan made a face. "If he doesn't come back, that will solve your trouble over him."

But not to her satisfaction. Not only would it be very unflattering if he never came back, it would be disappointing in a way she didn't even want to consider.

Joan apparently realized that, and abandoned the topic. "How long do you think we'll have to walk through the park before you manage to speak to him?"

"I don't care." Mariah bounced off the bed, determination taking root in her breast. "All I need to hear is a few words. If we go every day, surely a week will be sufficient."

"A week!" Joan put down her pen. "Well, I suppose. When do you propose we start?"

"Why not now?"

Joan, who was not fond of exercise, groaned again.

Mariah headed for the door. "Do you really want to remain here and listen to lectures on shouting in the halls? I suppose I could take Sally, to speak to all those gentlemen . . . "

"Oh, wait!" Joan stuffed her journal back into her desk and hurried after her. "I could hardly subject you to that torment without suffering with you," she said primly.

Aunt Marion gave her permission for the stroll, eyebrows raised. Mariah fidgeted impatiently while Joan went to change her shoes, but finally they were off, with Janet, Aunt Marion's imposing abigail, marching behind them. Mariah hoped Janet wouldn't frighten off any and all gentlemen who might speak to them, but knew they wouldn't be allowed to go without the woman.

"So," Joan said, slipping her hand around Mariah's arm, "tell me more."

"I already told you all I know about him."

"No, no," her cousin said with a flip of her free hand. She leaned even closer. "What did he say? How did you know it was he? Tell me everything!"

Mariah couldn't hide a smile. She cast a quick glance back at Janet—still striding along, three respectful paces behind them—and lowered her voice, too. "It was so unexpected. I had already gone to bed, but was not asleep—"

"Were you thinking of him?" Joan wanted to know.

Mariah pursed her lips. "Only because I had quite given up on finding him."

"No, you hadn't, but go on." Joan's eyes sparkled as if she, too, had a secret suitor.

"Then I heard a voice at the window, asking if he might come in. I asked who it was—"

"As if you didn't know!"

"And he said Harry," Mariah finished with a blissful smile. "I said yes, before I thought better of it, and then he climbed through the window!"

"Oh." Joan sighed happily. "What did you talk about? How long did he stay? Are you not worried your parents will find out?"

Mariah shuddered. "I don't want to think what would happen if Papa learned of it. And you are the only soul on earth who knows, so if he discovers it, I shall know whom to blame."

"You can't think I would reveal it! Even if it weren't the most exciting secret imaginable. If my mother were to find out I had anything to do with it, I would never be let out of the house again."

Mariah nodded. "Right. It is our secret, then."

Joan heaved another sigh. "All I have is the secret part, while you have the suitor, too."

"That's just luck," Mariah said. "I would do the same for you."

Joan laughed, somewhat wryly. "I expect no less, if anything remotely like it should ever happen to me."

They had arrived at the park, and Mariah's steps quickened as they left the city streets behind. It was early still, but the day was so fine there were already many people taking the air. The most fashionable ladies wouldn't come until later, but gentlemen were exercising their horses and flirting with the ladies who had ventured out. Even though she knew there was no guarantee of success, even though the chances of meeting one particular man this particular morning in the sprawling park were very small, her heart skipped a beat, and that strange fluttery feeling invaded her stomach again.

They walked for over an hour, cheerfully greeting every gentleman they passed. Mariah smiled and chatted with all of them, listening carefully to every word they said. Some she had met the other night at her parents' ball, and some knew Joan, who couldn't keep from offering her thoughts on each gentleman as soon as he had gone on his way.

"He's a terrible rake, you know," she would whisper. "Douglas says he's gambled himself to ruin!" Douglas was Joan's older brother. Mariah could only laugh and whisper back that Douglas knew a great many scandalous gentlemen. They even met Douglas himself at one point, and he introduced them to some of his friends, all of whom were deliciously wicked in Joan's opinion. But otherwise they had no luck, and Mariah was beginning to grow discouraged when they reached the path around the lake.

There they met Sir George Bellamy, a friend of Mariah's father, who looked as pleased as punch to see them. "Good morning, young ladies, good morning," he cried. The five dogs he was holding all began barking loudly at them. "Hush, there, hush, I say," he said to the dogs. "Just some girls, don't you know. They're always on the lookout for a squirrel, or even better, a skunk," he confided to them. Joan choked and began coughing into her handkerchief, but Mariah, accustomed to Sir George, smiled politely.

"I hope we are neither," she said.

Sir George blinked at her, then cackled with laughter. "No, no, no, not at all! And never say I said so." Something caught the dogs' attention, and as a pack they swerved to the left, barking and baying at the shrubbery nearby. Joan's fingers dug into Mariah's arm as Sir George tried to haul them back out of the bushes.

"Mariah," Joan murmured, her voice rising in excitement. "Look."

Mariah had already seen him. He was standing farther down the path with some other gentlemen, just about the right height, with casually tousled dark hair and a very charming smile. She stared hard, wishing he would turn his head so she could see his profile. Could it possibly be? He was handsome, that was undeniable; not as she had pictured Harry, but she'd already told herself not to put any credence in the way she thought he looked.

He saw them then. She could see the interest spring into his eyes. A pleased smile crossed his face. Her heart jumped. He looked happy to see her; Harry would know her by sight, wouldn't he? He said something to his companions, his gaze drifting back to her. As eager as she had been to find him, Mariah found herself suddenly unprepared. She wet her dry lips and gulped in a deep breath. He was heading their way. Her stomach had stopped fluttering and twisted itself into a hard knot. She realized she had stopped dead in the middle of the path and was squeezing Joan's hand in a vicious grip. Joan didn't seem to notice.

"Good heavens, such a handsome man," her cousin was saying. "And he seems to know you! Mariah, he's coming directly to us! He even ignored Lord Tilburton's greeting. What shall you say to him? How shall we get an introduction? Good heavens, how on earth have I never met *him* in two entire seasons in London?"

"Joan," Mariah said in an unsteady voice. "Be quiet."

"If you want me to walk about with Janet," Joan managed to say as he approached them, "squeeze my hand twice."

And then he was there. She tipped back her head to see him. Up close, he looked even less as she had imagined Harry, but his attention was fixed on her in a very flattering way. For a second they just looked at each other. Perhaps this was the moment, Mariah thought dazedly, that she would tell her children of, years from now: *When I first met your father . . .*

Fortunately, Sir George was still at hand or there would have been a brutally awkward moment. "Ah, another young man wanting an introduction, I'll wager!" he boomed cheerfully as he dragged his pack of dogs over. "Like bees to the lilies, these young men," he teased Mariah. She tried to pretend she hadn't heard him while her heart pounded, her palms grew damp, and her smile felt about a foot wide. "Lady Mariah, Miss Bennet, may I present to you Mr. Tobias Crane, nephew to Viscount Crane," said Sir George. "Mr. Crane, Lady Mariah Dunmore and Miss Joan Bennet."

Tobias? thought Mariah in confusion. Who would call someone named Tobias Harry?

"Miss Bennet. Lady Mariah." The gentleman bowed. Although he spoke to both, his eyes remained on Mariah, filled with admiration. "What a very great pleasure to make your acquaintance."

No. No, it was not Harry. For a moment the disappointment was crushing.

"Thank you, sir," said Joan when Mariah couldn't make a sound. "How kind of you to say so."

He glanced at Joan, still beaming. "It is not a kindness at all, when it is the plain truth." He turned to

Mariah again. "And it is a lovely day for a stroll in the park. When it is nice out, I always try to walk outdoors."

"One can go so much farther than walking indoors," trilled Joan, who seemed to understand Mariah's problem at once. "Tell me, Mr. Crane, do you prefer London or the countryside for your walks? I adore London, but one must simply go round and round in circles in a park to get a good long walk, whereas in the country, one could walk all the way to Wales."

"Er . . . yes." He looked sideways at Joan, then back at Mariah. "I prefer London as well. But outdoors, as much as possible." He paused. "I like parks."

"Then we mustn't detain you from your walk," said Mariah, finally finding her tongue again. "We are bound for home."

"Of course!" He paused again, as if thinking over his words. "Might I have the honor of escorting you there?"

"No!" Joan squeezed her hand in warning at her sharp tone, and Mariah gave herself a mental shake. "Thank you, but we are only a short distance away." She smiled as sweetly as she could manage and bobbed a curtsey. He looked positively dumbstruck, his jaw sagging open. "Good day, sir. Good day, Sir George." She turned on her heel, as Mr. Crane swept a grand bow, and started for home.

Mariah began to recover herself as she walked. That had been a setback, no doubt. It was her own fault; she should have made sure of matters before she started staring at him like a half-wit. What did it matter if she hadn't met the elusive Harry yet? She'd only been looking one day, barely an hour. The battle was not over, and she was not about to surrender. She must be more circumspect in the future, though. She didn't want to let her hopes rise and then be crushed like that again.

"Well," Joan said through her laughter when they were safely away from Mr. Crane. "You've made another conquest! Not Harry, I assume, but still a handsome fellow. No doubt he would have told you so himself if given enough time."

"Nonsense." Mariah kept up a steady, brisk pace. "Besides, he didn't look at all the way I expected Harry to look."

"No, indeed not," said Joan gravely. "You've never seen his face, of course, but when you see him, you'll know him at once."

Mariah stopped. "Don't be ridiculous. I don't expect to know him at sight. I already told you I must speak to him to have any chance of identifying him. But there is something in his voice, something in his manner . . . I do feel I should be able to make a good guess if a stranger might be Harry."

Joan cocked her head. "And of course he'll look like a handsome, charming, intelligent gentleman. Mariah, what if he is not handsome?"

She pushed away that thought. "I'm not so shallow as that. I could like a plain gentleman as well as a handsome one."

"What if he is not even plain, but ugly? What if he is maimed or scarred or otherwise ill-favored? What if that's the reason he doesn't want you to see his face? Would you still patrol the whole park looking for your beastly suitor?"

Mariah opened her mouth, then closed it without a word. She started walking again, not waiting for her cousin. How could Joan think that of her, that she would only be pleased if Harry were handsome? Was that what Joan thought of her? Naturally, her mind had filled in a handsome face to go with his voice. But still . . . What if he were—she swallowed hard—*ugly*? It was a terrible thought, all the worse because she didn't know if Joan mightn't be right, that her interest in Harry would slip if he did turn out to be beastly.

"Mariah!" She stopped at Joan's cry. "Wait!" Her cousin hurried after her, face creased with remorse. "I'm sorry! I should not have said that. I'm sure your Harry is a handsome fellow—how could he not be, when he's so romantic? I should never have teased you about it."

Mariah managed a smile. "It's all right, Joan. You may be right; he may be a fright. I shall have to worry about that if it's true. But . . . " She hesitated, lifting her hands helplessly. "I have to know. Does that make sense? I would rather discover him, and find him hideous, than never know."

"Hideous?"

Mariah bit her lip. "I cannot believe he is, but . . . even so, Joan, I must find him. It's not an idle fancy on my part, it's . . . Well, it's something more than that."

Joan searched her face for a moment, then the crease between her brows faded. She linked her arm through Mariah's. "Then we shall find him, even if we have to summon every man in London, handsome or hideous, for an interview in the drawing room. For I want to know, too."

Mariah smiled gratefully. "Thank you. It's ever so much better to have an accomplice."

Joan flipped one hand modestly, though she was grinning now. "Of course I couldn't let you have all the fun! Even if we have to walk around the entire park a hundred times to find him."

"No," she said slowly. "We needn't do that. I don't think we'll meet him in the park."

"Why not?"

She thought again of a man who leaped—climbed—from a balcony when someone approached, who refused to tell her his name, who said he *couldn't* come calling during the day but instead scaled the wall into her bedroom at midnight. Would a fellow like that be standing around the park, like Douglas's scandalous, no-account friends? She was silly not to have realized that sooner. "I just know we won't."

Joan was staring at her. "Then what?"

Mariah did another survey of the park. She'd been so impatient to find him, but it was too much to think they would succeed so easily. She wouldn't give up, but needed a better plan. "I don't know."

Chapter 7

Harry bounded up the stairs of the Fenton Lane house two at a time, pulling off Towne's jacket. Crane had kept him late annotating drawings of the planned hothouse expansion at Brimstow, and now he had only an hour to dress in Wroth's costume and get across town to the Avery affair, which the Earl of Doncaster was scheduled to attend.

Angelique Martand met him at the top of the stairs. She wore a gown of blue satin that appeared to have been sewn on her body, but just barely. With a garish blond wig on her head and her face heavily painted with cosmetics, she looked nothing like a secret British agent and every bit like a cheap courtesan. "Harry," she said with a smile. "I hoped to meet you tonight."

"Oh?" Harry stuffed his spectacles into his waistcoat pocket and began undoing the buttons.

"I know you are late; I want but a moment." She didn't blink an eye as he continued to strip off Towne's clothing. "Ian says it is wearing on you, being three people."

Harry scowled. Angelique's maid, Lisette, hurried past with a pitcher of water and plucked his discarded clothing from his arms. Harry handed it over without looking away from Angelique. "Ian should mind his own responsibilities and let me mind mine."

She sighed. "I am not scolding. I know what you feel, and I know you are not a normal man if it does not tax you."

Angelique would know how it felt. Not only was she posing as Mrs. Smythe, private nurse to the Marquis of Bethwell, she went out on the town in this costume almost as often as Harry went out as Lord Wroth. Of course, she had done this for years and was more accustomed to the demands, but Harry was not about to admit he wasn't up to it. He gave a careless shrug and said nothing as he untied his neck cloth.

"Do you need a night free?" she went on. "I can pull Alec from his post and send him after Doncaster tonight."

"Why? I'm fine, just a bit tired."

Her gaze turned sharp and probing. "Ian said he nearly had to throw cold water on you to wake you this morning, and now you will be out past midnight again. I do not wish to push you too hard. I shall tell Alec he must find a way to accompany Doncaster's carriage in the future. We must have a plan in case you find yourself mortal once more and require a night free." She said the last with a perfectly straight face, but Harry heard the dry humor in her tone.

So he just rolled his eyes. More protest was useless; Angelique was the leader of their group, and however much she liked him personally, he knew she would do what was necessary to complete their mission— including report him to Stafford if she even suspected what he'd done the previous night.

A call from below saved him. Ian had the carriage ready for her. "You're off to the theater, I presume?"

She gave him a twinkling smile and held out her arms, turning slightly from side to side and setting her skirts swirling around her. "The opera. Bethwell favors the dancers there. How do I look?"

She looked like a Covent Garden whore with airs. Harry grinned, knowing there was likely a knife or two inside her low-cut bodice and a pistol under her skirt. "Well worth a few shillings."

She laughed, swatting at his shoulder as she moved past him to go downstairs. Harry turned into his room, pulling his shirt over his head and kicking off his shoes. Lisette came in again, laying Wroth's coat on the bed and pushing a slice of cold meat pie into his hand. To call her a maid was an extreme understatement. Whenever something needed doing, Lisette was usually already doing it, calmly and efficiently. Harry made an indistinct noise of thanks as he bit into the pie, his first bite to eat in hours. With Lisette's help, he was dressed in record time, and polished off the pie while she rubbed the gray powder into his hair.

"There, so handsome again," she said with satisfaction, fluffing up Wroth's wild mane.

"Mind your hands, impertinent wench," he said in Wroth's creaky voice as he pulled on the padded woolen coat and slumped into it. "Be gentle on my old bones."

Lisette, who was old enough to be his mother, snorted with laughter. "*Alons*, you scoundrel! Off with you. Ian has arranged for a hackney; it should be waiting."

Harry took the walking stick she held out and winked at her over Wroth's half-moon spectacles, then clattered down the stairs. In the hall he slowed, letting her open the door for him like a proper servant before shuffling out into the street to the waiting carriage.

He kept a close eye on Doncaster that night at the Avery soiree, trying to get a better feel for the man and his habits on a night when he had only the one man to watch. He had to learn to predict the earl's actions and judge his moods. He had to pay attention to whom the earl spoke with and the manner of their conversation. And he must be ever mindful of his duty and not watch the earl's daughter as much as he could.

When the earl and his family left, Harry followed. He hailed a hackney and gave a direction near Doncaster House, alighting quickly and doubling back to see the family reach the safety of their home. Doncaster appeared an attentive father and husband, giving an arm to both his wife and daughter to help them up the steps. Mariah lifted her face to him and laughed, the sound drifting across the street to where Harry lurked in the gloomy night, watching in silence until a footman closed the door behind them.

Harry let out his breath quietly. He was done, his duty fulfilled for another night. It was not quite midnight, still early. He could get a full night's sleep for a change, and not fall asleep on his feet tomorrow.

He took one more searching look up and down the quiet street, then turned and walked into the wispy fog.

Mariah bade her parents good-night and went to her room in a pensive mood. Lady Avery's soiree had been entertaining, but not enough to divert her from her thoughts. When Sally had gone, she sat in bed with her knees drawn up under her chin and frowned at her toes. How was she to discover more about Harry?

She had hoped against hope that she might meet him again this evening. She had pinned a bright smile on her face and sallied forth at her mother's side, determined to make the acquaintance of every unfamiliar gentleman in the room. She lingered on the terrace until it began to drizzle, then spent a great deal of time strolling slowly around the ballroom and any halfway private alcove where he might approach her, all to no avail. She danced every dance with a different partner without hearing half of what any said to her. But there was no sign—or sound—of him anywhere.

Perhaps I imagined him, she thought. A man with no name and no face who only appears in the dead of night. Surely if someone else had told her this story, she wouldn't believe him real. She sighed and rested her cheek on her knees, turning her gaze toward the window.

"Good evening," said the figure sitting on the sill.

Mariah started so violently she almost toppled to the floor. "You startled me!"

He dropped to the floor with barely a sound. How could a man his size move so quietly? "I apologize. It seems to be a failing of mine."

Mariah took a deep breath to calm her thundering pulse, and then another. Just his voice could make her heart jump, let alone the shock of his appearance out of nowhere at the very moment she was wondering if he mightn't be a figment of her imagination after all. "You must try to improve yourself in that," she said, trying to be poised and serene, outwardly at least.

He laughed. "Must I? Or perhaps, mustn't we all?"

"What do you mean?" She sat up straighter and discreetly tucked a loose lock of hair behind her ear. She must look a fright with her hair down.

"You startled me."

Her lips parted in surprise. "How on earth—"

"By not screaming," he said.

"Why would I do that? I hoped you might come." So much for poise. She sounded as eager as a child. She bit her lip in consternation. "Even though I am still vexed you won't tell me your proper name."

"Does it matter so much?"

She wanted to know so badly she almost said yes, but couldn't. He might call her bluff and leave. "I think you must not trust me if you won't tell me," she muttered.

"Ah, but what would it change? It's just a name."

"It's improper for me to call you by your Christian name."

"Is it?" Still shrouded by the darkness, he pulled out her dressing table chair and straddled it backward, a very ungentlemanly pose, and folded his arms across the top of the back. "More improper than wishing I would come again?"

"But you address me as Lady Mariah," she said, ignoring his pointed question. "I can hardly call you . . ." She hesitated. "I should not call you Harry when you address me so formally."

"I like you to call me Harry, Mariah." His voice dropped on her name, making it sound even more intimate. Her heart leaped again, her hands grew a trifle unsteady, and she felt a bit breathless.

"Why is that?"

"If we must mind that rule of propriety, then why not others? It will be one rapid descent from cordiality to stiff formality. It will start with correct address, and then soon we shall be sitting uncomfortably upright in the drawing room, drinking tea neither of us wants, discussing the weather with great civility and a complete lack of wit. If that is your desire . . . " He trailed off as she tried to hide her laugh behind a cough.

"Of course not!"

"That is a great relief," he said. "I should be hard-pressed to discuss this weather in civil terms. Absolutely beastly out tonight . . . "

This time she did laugh out loud. "Then I suppose we must be content with this very odd and improper conversation."

"Indeed we must, Mariah."

Again a little shiver rippled over her skin at the way he said her name. "How did you know who I am?" she asked on impulse. "It is unfair that you know more about me than I know about you."

"It is."

Hope rose. "May I light my candle, then?"

"No."

She exhaled in frustration. "Why do you come to see me if you can't actually *see* me?"

"Who said I can't see you?"

"I can't see you!"

He laughed. "Do you need to? Must I leave if you cannot?"

"No," said Mariah with reluctant honesty, "but I want to."

"Ah, I see. Because you want to be certain you're

not wasting your time speaking to a coarse, common fellow with big ears and missing teeth?"

"Because I think I deserve that small courtesy," she said, trying not to laugh again. "No matter how large your ears may be."

"No, no. I'll tell you if I must. Big ears, several missing teeth, thinning hair. A crooked leg. Spots on my face, naturally—"

"Stop." She couldn't resist laughing now. "You're being ridiculous."

"Am I? And does it matter?"

Mariah sobered. She peered into the shadows that cloaked him and considered Joan's question again: would she lose interest if he were beastly? "No," she said at last. No one else she had met in London mocked himself just for her amusement. Whatever he might look like, he made her laugh.

He got to his feet, still in shadow. He seemed to find the darkest parts of the room, preventing her from catching even the most fleeting glimpse of his features. Mariah vowed to sleep with the lamps lit every night from now on. "Close your eyes," he said.

She blinked. "Why? I cannot see you anyway."

"Do you trust me? Can I trust you?"

Mariah hesitated, then closed her eyes. "Yes."

For a long moment all was quiet. What was he doing, she wondered. "Harry?" she whispered uncertainly. Had he left?

"Yes," he said, and the mattress dipped. He was sitting on her bed, within arm's reach. Her breath came faster and her skin prickled all over with awareness. There was a man in her bed, and she was wearing only a fine lawn nightdress. She felt exposed and vulnerable; this was shockingly improper, far more so than inviting him into her room in the first place . . .

"When you cannot see with your eyes, you must trust your other senses." He took her wrist lightly between his fingertips and brought her hand to his face.

Mariah's eyelashes trembled, but she didn't open her eyes. Gingerly, tentatively, she let her fingers drift over his face. His skin was warm, especially given how chilly and rainy it was outside. She touched his cheekbones, the bridge of his nose, his upper lip. There was the beginning of a beard on his jaw, a roughness she had never felt before. Of course, she had not touched a man's face since she was a child, and then it was her father's face—not the face of an enigmatic stranger who slipped into her bedroom only under cover of night to fascinate her until she could hardly bear it.

He sat patiently under her hand, not speaking or moving. She grew a little bolder and explored his forehead, running her fingers along his brows and even delicately touching his short, thick eyelashes. Gradually an image formed in her mind, still somewhat indistinct but more definite than before. He had a smooth, straight scar at his temple, and she wondered how he had gotten it. His nose was straight and his jaw was square. It was . . . She scrunched up her face in thought. It was a strong face. It wasn't the same as seeing him in the light, but it made her feel that she *knew* his features better than if she had simply lit the lamp.

"What made you think of this?" she asked as her fingers brushed over his lips; softer than she had expected, but still firm.

"My sister," he said. "She is blind, and this is how she sees."

"You have a sister, then." She smiled, pleased to have learned even that minor fact about him.

He laughed, very quietly. "Two, in fact. The bane of any man's life, sisters."

"Are you a good brother?" Mariah touched his jaw again, fascinated by the texture of his skin, the shape of his face. She felt his grin lift his cheeks.

"Not the worst, I suppose. They might have a different answer, of course."

Mariah laughed, too. "I daresay you torment them and tease them, as you do me—"

"I can safely promise that I tease them in *entirely* different ways, Mariah." That flicker of awareness licked her skin again, but he went on in the same light tone. "They are the ones who torment me."

"Well, who would not," she said airily, "when faced with such a brother: warts, missing teeth, thinning hair—"

"True, they caused all that."

Mariah choked on a laugh that burst out as a giggle. "And shockingly impertinent, too! I feel no evidence of any of it, sir." She rested her fingers lightly on his lips. "Although I have not checked your teeth . . . "

Harry's breathing changed, and Mariah's heart skipped a beat. "Are you satisfied?" he whispered, his lips barely moving under her fingertips.

"It is not the same—"

"But it must be enough," he interrupted. "Can it be?"

She had been about to say much the same thing.

She had been about to say it was perhaps even better, for it gave warmth and texture to him, proving him a flesh-and-bone man and not some phantom of her romantic imagination. "Yes," she whispered. "For now."

Her fingers drifted sideways, and he caught her wrist. "Careful," he whispered. "Mind the warts."

Mariah's laugh ended in a silent gasp as he brought her hand to his mouth and pressed his lips hungrily into her palm. She trembled as he kissed her palm, her fingers, the throbbing pulse in her wrist.

"You bewitch me," he breathed, holding her hand against his cheek. "Why did you wish I would come to you again?"

"You—You intrigue me," she stammered. It was hard to speak with her heart in her throat.

He sighed against her hand. "I should stay away."

"No . . . "

"I should." He kissed her fingers once more, then took her hand from his face and laid it back on her knee. "But I don't think I can."

"Tell me your name," she pleaded, leaning forward, eyes still closed. "Please."

He laughed under his breath. The mattress shifted again. "Henry Arthur. Harry, to those who know me." With the lightest of touches, his fingers brushed her jaw, then her lower lip, lingering there. Mariah gasped and quivered, thinking—expecting—hoping—he would kiss her next . . .

"Good night, Mariah." She couldn't move, not even to open her eyes, as he rose from her bed and walked away. She felt his absence keenly now, as if a warm cloak had been pulled from her shoulders. He was right; without her sight she was far more aware of her other senses, and they all seemed to be acutely attuned to him.

"Good night, Harry," she whispered, even though she was sure he was no longer in the room. "But you must not stay away."

Chapter 8

Mariah slept late the next morning, kept awake almost until dawn by her own wicked thoughts. After Harry had gone, she realized the ribbon around her neckline was tied too loosely, and that her night-rail must have gaped alarmingly low. It made her blush to think what he might have seen, but not with much shame. She pressed her hands over her breasts to stop them from tingling, but her mind conjured up the question of what Harry's hands would feel like there, and then it took her a very, very long time to fall asleep.

This was all a new world to her. She'd told him true last night—he intrigued her, in a purely intellectual sense—but now her body had come alive to the fascination as well. When he kissed her hand—her palm—with almost palpable desire, something hungry and sinuous stretched to life inside her, awakening a craving she had never known. It felt as though she'd shed her old skin and now moved in a sleeker, more sensitive one, a skin that prickled in anticipation of a man's touch. Of Harry's touch. She thought she might burst if she didn't tell someone, and so she gulped down a few bites of breakfast and hurried off to talk to Joan.

But the sight of the flowers in the drawing room stopped her short, and before she could recover, her mother came up beside her.

"There you are, Mariah. I've been waiting for you to come down."

"Oh." She didn't like the sound of that. "You have?"

Her mother nodded. "Yes, indeed. These are all for you." She smiled at Mariah, looking very pleased and proud. "I knew you would be a success."

Mariah went over to the bouquets on the table. A thought roused her curiosity, and she ripped open the card with each one. Not one of the names could be Harry; some she didn't even recognize. She put the cards down, curious no longer, and turned to go. "I shall be at Joan's, Mama."

"Mariah, really." Her mother came forward with an exasperated sigh. "Who sent them?"

She glanced at the cards with disinterest. "Sir Edward Riley, Mr. Ingleby, Lord Dexter . . . and . . . " She thought hard. "Lord Burke and . . . ah . . . two others."

The countess clucked in disapproval, taking up the cards. "One would think you had no interest in the gentlemen, Mariah. We must decide now whom to receive, when they come to call." She flipped through the cards and promptly discarded four. "These are flattering, but of no consequence. Mr. Ingleby is in search of a fortune, and Mr. Brimmer and Lord Christopher are nobody. Lord Burke . . . No, I think not. He's terribly dissolute." She frowned. "Where did you meet Lord Burke? He was not at our ball, and I cannot think Lady Avery invited him last night."

Mariah lifted one shoulder. "In the park, I suppose.

Joan and I went for a stroll the other day and Douglas introduced us to several people."

Her mother sighed. "Douglas! Marion should not let him run so wild. That explains these." She still held two cards. "Lord Dexter would be a fine match, though; an earl, very eligible, and handsome as well. Many young ladies would be overjoyed to catch his notice. We shall receive him." She studied the last card. "And Sir Edward Riley. Well. A fine family, although I have my doubts about his suitability. We'll receive him as well."

Mariah wasn't terribly interested in receiving either of them. One reason she hadn't remembered any of the gentlemen from the park was that they seemed just like the ones at the ball: dull. Perhaps it wasn't fair to judge them on so little observation, but then, she'd seen for herself that at least one man in London could be fascinating in a few minutes' time. And she still wanted to find him more than she wanted to investigate the suitability of other gentlemen.

However, she would have to explain this to her mother if she refused to receive the other gentlemen— an untenable choice. "Of course, Mama. May I call on Joan now?"

Her mother shot her a keen glance, but before she could say anything, a footman brought in a bouquet that put all the others to shame. Lilies and roses interspersed with ferns and vines overflowed the vase, almost as wide as it was tall. It was magnificent, in an overpowering way. "Just delivered, my lady," said the footman, setting it down. It was too large to fit on the same table as the others.

"Indeed," her mother said, and retrieved the card. Her eyebrows rose again. "Mr. Tobias Crane?"

Mariah tried not to grimace. That was one gentleman she would really prefer *not* to receive, after the way she had embarrassed herself. And he had obviously gotten the exact wrong impression, judging from the size of the bouquet, which would make his call all the more tedious.

Her mother extended the card. "There is a poem, Mariah."

Worse and worse. She took the card, all but cringing at the verse. He wrote a nice hand, she thought; too bad that was the best thing about the card. She managed a weak smile for her mother, who was watching her with an air of expectation. "I met him in the park," she murmured again. "Sir George Bellamy introduced us."

Her mother exhaled slowly, the sound rife with suspicion. "His uncle is a very prominent advisor to Lord Eldon, although his own parents were nobody of consequence. I suppose we cannot avoid receiving him." She paused, a frown pinching her brow. Mariah had a blinding flash of hope that her mother *would* think of a way they could avoid Mr. Crane. If anyone could wiggle her free of this, it would be Mama! "Although," the countess continued thoughtfully, "he is his uncle's heir. A very handsome man"—she smiled knowingly at Mariah—"and an ambitious one, although I have heard he is not as intelligent as his uncle. Not that many are. Still, we should receive him."

Mariah had to smile and nod; what else could she do? "I shall be late meeting Joan," she said, sidling toward the door.   •

Her mother threw up her hands. "You may go, then. But Mariah . . . " A note of reproof entered her voice, and Mariah paused in the doorway, clutching her bonnet. "Be sure you return soon. You must be ready to receive your callers."

Mariah's eyes strayed to the bouquets. "Today, Mama?" she asked plaintively.

The countess laughed and shook her head. "Yes, today." She paused, tilting her head to scrutinize her daughter's face. "Is something wrong, dear?" she asked in bemusement. "You don't seem at all as pleased as I imagined you would be. Don't you wish to have your choice of gentlemen?"

I do, Mariah thought helplessly. But he hasn't sent me flowers, and most likely won't be coming to call today. For a split second she considered telling her mother that someone *had* caught her eye, that she had met a gentleman she liked very much. But she had already tempted fate enough by asking to see the guest list the other day. As tantalizing as it was to imagine her mother's formidable energy focused on the search for Harry, it was even more daunting to imagine the consequences if Mama discovered he had visited her at midnight—twice. "Yes, Mama," she replied. "But I don't want to keep Joan waiting. I shall return after luncheon."

Her mother sighed and waved one hand, and Mariah flew out of the house before she could change her mind. She would have to adapt her plan to be less cordial, it seemed, or she would be doomed to spending her days sitting in the drawing room with the same gentlemen she had already marked off.

Joan, unfortunately, found it funny rather than alarming.

"But what am I to *do*?" Mariah complained as her cousin dabbed a tear from her eye.

Joan stopped laughing, although a huge smile still

sat on her face. "Prepare yourself to drink a great deal of tea."

"*Ugh*. I hardly paid attention to most of them. I shall have nothing to say to anyone."

"That's not necessary. Most gentlemen don't care much for what you have to say. My mother told me they admire a quiet, retiring girl." Joan affected a dramatic swoon into a nearby chair. "Needless to say, I have not been much of a success at that."

Mariah flipped one hand in disgust. "Unless they admire a mute girl most of all, I shall be a crushing disappointment to them."

"Does that bother you?"

"No. But it will be a terrible bother and a wretched waste of time!" She sat down on the chaise with a thump.

"You oughtn't to ask me in any event," said Joan. "I haven't much experience with having too many suitors."

Mariah looked at her. Even though she had spoken in her usual droll way, Joan wouldn't meet her eyes, fiddling instead with her journal. Suddenly Mariah felt awkward. In two full Seasons Joan had not received a single serious marriage proposal. For two years her letters had been full of the gentlemen who did court her, and Mariah had spent many an hour laughing over Joan's descriptions of them. Joan never seemed dismayed that none of them took her fancy or swept her off her feet. But then, Mariah thought, she had never had a suitor like that, either—not until now.

"Then I shall send them all to you, for I don't want any of them." She flopped into the cushions behind her. "They only want to call on me because of Papa, you know. But what shall we do now?"

"You could be very rude to everyone." Joan gave a practical nod. "Then they won't send you flowers or come to call."

Mariah laughed. "A tempting thought. No, I meant about Harry. My mother looked very suspicious when I admitted I met Lord Burke in the park—who is he, anyway? She said he was very dissolute."

"Oh, he is," Joan said with relish. "Douglas has known him since Eton. He gambled away his entire quarter's allowance once with Lord Burke, not two days after Papa paid it to him. Well! You can imagine how Mother scolded Douglas, and Papa declared he wouldn't give Douglas a farthing more before the next quarter, which naturally only made Douglas gamble even more with Lord Burke. I think Lord Burke wagers on everything, but he's wealthy enough to afford it, unlike Douglas, and there are shocking rumors about him and actresses." She paused. "Did he send you flowers, too?"

"Douglas?"

Joan laughed. "No, Lord Burke! Douglas wouldn't recognize a rosebud if it fell on his head. Besides, he prefers tavern girls, who don't require flowers." Mariah's eyes went wide. Joan looked quite smug for a moment. "Really, Mariah, since when has Douglas been able to keep any secrets from me?"

"I did think he might try to keep *that* a secret," she managed to say. Douglas and Joan had always been very close, and Joan heard the most shocking things from him. Mariah, with no brothers or sisters of her own, had envied her cousins her entire childhood for that. "But enough about Douglas. I shall have to be more circumspect. You've been in London for the Season before. What do you think I ought to do?"

Joan pursed her lips. "I suppose if you simply accept a great many invitations, you'll be able to meet all the gentlemen eventually. It will take a while, mind, and you'll be bored out of your head at times, but most of the acceptable gentlemen go out sooner or later."

"Only most?"

"Some are almost never seen; the odd reclusive duke, you know, or the most scandalous rakes who simply aren't received."

"Hmm." Mariah thought for a moment. "I shall have to think about that. Mama won't let me accept every invitation." She paused, then slowly went on, "He came to see me again last night."

Joan bolted upright. "Really? And you wasted all this time telling me about bouquets? What happened?"

Mariah blushed. "He just appeared in the window. I never heard a thing until he said good evening."

"And then?"

She spread her hands and studied her fingers. "I— We argued, a bit. I was trying to discover more about him, and he was refusing so calmly, and then . . . "

"Then . . . what?" Joan looked puzzled at her halting description.

"I said it wasn't right for me to call him Harry when he addressed me as Lady Mariah—for he always had, Joan—and then he began calling me Mariah, and then I said I wanted to know what he looked like, and then I—then he—"

"What did you do?" Joan whispered, aghast.

"Nothing," cried Mariah, feeling a guilty blush steal up her cheeks nonetheless. "He— I touched his face. That's all." Her cousin's horrified expression didn't change. "And he kissed my hand."

"Well, that doesn't sound so bad . . . " Joan said slowly.

"No! It wasn't. But after he had gone, I felt . . . Well, I felt different."

"Like you wished he had touched *you*?" Joan leaned so far forward, she almost fell off her chair.

Mariah's eyes widened. "Yes! That's what I mean. But—" She blushed again. "Have you ever felt that about a man?"

Joan's face turned bright pink and she sat back with a jerk. "Oh! Well, once or twice. I never did anything, of course."

"Of course not," Mariah quickly agreed. They looked at each other for a wary moment, then away.

"How was it?" Joan asked a moment later, very softly. "When he kissed your hand?"

Mariah sighed, remembering the feel of his fingers on her cheek, his thumb on her lips, his grip on her wrist as he kissed her palm. "Heavenly."

Chapter 9

The girl was making quiet squeaks of discomfort as Bethwell grunted and panted against her. Harry slouched lower into his dirty longshoreman's coat, trying to shut out the sounds while not breathing too deeply of his coat's odor of dead fish and sweat. The alley where Bethwell was taking his pleasure smelled even worse, so he was skulking just outside it, near enough to be at the ready but as far away as he could manage.

He hated this part of his job, he truly did. Apparently recovered from the heart palpitations that had kept him chastely at home the last several nights, Bethwell was making up for it tonight on a debauched spree through Whitechapel, drinking and gambling and now rutting, and Harry had drawn the straw to follow him.

No, that wasn't fair. Angelique couldn't possibly do it. Not because she couldn't take care of herself, but the only women out on the streets now were whores and slatterns. Angelique would stand out just for her sobriety, and Bethwell might conceivably recognize her.

Not that he wished this job on anyone. Angelique

had warned him about Bethwell's tastes, but it still turned his stomach. The fight was bad enough, a vicious brawl between two hulking brutes who looked ready to kill each other—and might have. One man was coughing up pints of blood when the marquis left. Bethwell enjoyed it greatly, roaring with approval at every blow and wagering with a very dangerous-looking character who looked quite capable of cutting a man's throat. Harry had watched with his teeth gritted and his hand on his dagger, certain he would be required to intervene sooner rather than later. But to his relief, Bethwell lost with dignity, paid his wager, and the Captain Sharp left him alone.

The whore, though . . . Harry hadn't liked the whore from the start. He shifted his weight, searching for a more comfortable patch of brick wall at his back. He didn't like Whitechapel in general, but particularly not on a dank, cold night when the fog seemed to swallow every sound of warning or alarm and every glimmer of light. He felt blind and deaf tonight, and in Whitechapel those were dangerous things to be.

A loud groan interrupted his thoughts. Bethwell had concluded his business with the young prostitute. Harry didn't move, and a few minutes later the marquis stumbled out of the alley with dirt on his coat elbows, still buttoning his breeches. He passed Harry without a sign he even noticed someone lurking in easy earshot of his sordid encounter. For a moment the marquis stood on the street, fumbling at his clothing, and then he gave a terrific belch. Harry glared at the ground in disgust while Bethwell thumped on his chest as if trying for another.

There was a noise behind him, and Harry instinctively tensed, gripping the handle of the dagger at his waist. But it was just the girl, a small, pale creature who couldn't have been more than fifteen, emerging from the alley. "My shilling, sir," she said to Bethwell in a high, reedy voice.

The marquis didn't even look at her. He picked a clump of dirt off his sleeve and frowned at it before flicking it away. "I never promised. You weren't that satisfying after all." And he started to walk away.

Harry saw the girl's mouth fall open and her eyes narrow in anger. More than one man had been murdered by an irate woman, and even a half-starved young whore could put a knife into someone's ribs with deadly effect. He eased away from the wall, but she made no effort to follow. After a moment her anger faded and she seemed to droop where she stood as if she didn't have the strength even to be outraged any longer. Harry glanced at the departing Bethwell, strolling away with complete indifference. He cursed under his breath, then came forward to drop an arm around the girl's shoulders.

"'Ere, no," she complained, trying to twist away. "You got to pay first, see. That one promised me another shilling after, and din't pay it. Two shillings, in my hand now—"

"Wheest, luv," muttered Harry in guttural cockney as he propelled her down the street while keeping one eye on Bethwell. He could feel the bones of her shoulder like a sharp bird's wing through the thin fabric of her dress. She was fair and small, a girl who might have been pretty if she'd been decently fed and cared for. She had no coat, only a thin shawl clutched around her arms. "No worry, no worry. Oughtn't you get home to yer mum?"

"Not without a few more shillings I can't." She had stopped resisting and started pleading. Her thin fingers groped at his heavy coat in clumsy imitation of a caress. "Come on, just two shillings, and any way you like it."

"Get you home." He pressed a coin into her hand. It was a better use of Sidmouth's money than usual, in his opinion. "It's cold out this eve."

Her eyes flashed toward him in shock, but the silver crown had already disappeared into her ragged dress. "Coo," she breathed. "Thank 'ee . . . "

Harry released her and jerked his head in a curt nod. Without breaking stride, he jammed his hands into his pockets and scowled after the man he followed. Bethwell appeared to be unaware of his surroundings as he strode along with a cocky swagger. Harry was sorely tempted to bash the man over the head, stuff him into a hackney, and send him home. Either that or leave the self-righteous prig on his own in Whitechapel.

Finally the marquis made it to his own doorstep, where his servants would tend to his filthy clothing and putrid odor without comment or reproach. His servants were waiting for him, in fact, holding the door open and lifting a lamp to light his way into the house. No flicker of scorn or disapproval touched their expressionless faces. They weren't paid to judge, after all, just to obey orders without question. Much like Harry himself.

He turned and walked without looking where he was going, furious at Bethwell for carrying on like a sailor on shore leave and frequenting such shabby, dangerous places while holding such a prominent station. The man had a responsibility, damn it, if not to his family to live a decent life then to his country, to live the life he promoted for others. Bethwell was a crusader against the rookeries, the gin houses, the poor laws. The poor ought to live more moral lives, he declared in Parliament, and that would improve their lot—not schools or government programs or higher wages. Harry had read accounts of his speeches in the newspapers and wondered what the marquis really knew of the poor. It couldn't have been much. Certainly not tonight, when Bethwell wagered fifty pounds on a fight where one man might die from his injuries, then paid a half-starved girl a mere shilling for the use of her body.

The marquis had no use for people like that—the fighter with the broken ribs and blinded eye, or the whore with no shoes and bones that protruded through her skin. They existed only for his amusement, Harry thought darkly, just as he himself existed only for Bethwell's safety. The man wouldn't give a damn if someone stepped in front of a knife or a pistol meant for him; he probably wouldn't even notice. Not that Harry was in this job for Bethwell's gratitude, but it made him angry that Bethwell didn't have the slightest care for anyone other than himself. What was the benefit in protecting Bethwell's life if the marquis did nothing admirable with that life?

Harry didn't intend to visit Mariah. He wasn't thinking of her at all. He walked blindly for a long time before looking up to find himself outside Doncaster House. For an even longer while he stood there staring up at the facade, the gas street lamps reflected a hundred glittering times in the many windows. Lord Doncaster, at least, seemed an honorable man, the sort of man worth sacrificing himself for. That made it all the worse, perhaps, that he was lusting after Doncaster's daughter with a ferocity that unnerved him.

While he slipped through the iron gate into the garden, shed his foul coat and cap, and shinned up the ivy to her window, Harry told himself he would deserve nothing less if Doncaster discovered him and put a bullet through his wicked heart. Wicked, for wanting what he couldn't have, as he saw Mariah innocently asleep against her pillows, an open book under her hand and candlelight spilling over her smooth cheek and white nightdress. Wicked, for climbing into her room and crossing to her bedside to gaze on her sleeping face with a desperate longing that had no excuse and no hope of being gratified. And most wicked for knowing all that, and staying anyway.

Mariah awoke just as he pinched out the candle beside her bed. She lurched upright, blinking rapidly, her heart pounding from being startled awake. "What? Who—"

"Only I."

She recognized Harry's quiet voice and searched the darkness, finally locating his shadow as he moved away from her bed. She shook her head, trying to clear her brain. She'd been dreaming of a ball, where dozens of gentlemen holding flowers pursued her while her mother insisted she drink another cup of tea after every dance. A remnant of her day, she thought in disgust, remembering the endless, dull-beyond-words calls from four suitors today alone. Mariah didn't want to think of them as such, but her mother persisted in naming them so, and their actions had been uncomfortably like those of suitors. For three days now she'd been trapped in the drawing room by the parade of gentlemen—including Mr. Crane, twice—and wasn't at all surprised it was giving her nightmares.

But now Harry was here, for the first time in three nights, and if she hadn't fallen asleep, she might have seen him. He had put out her candle before she woke, and she knew he'd done so by design. "Why did you do that?" she snapped in sleepy frustration.

"You were asleep," was his infuriating reply. "You no longer needed a light."

"But now I am awake, and I should like to relight it." She put aside her book, and on impulse started to get out of bed to retrieve the flint.

"Please don't."

Mariah frowned, although she stayed where she was, sitting on the edge of her bed. She had agreed, after all, at his last visit, that touching his face would be enough. And she supposed it would have to be, even though she had deliberately left her candle burning every night since in hopes he might return and she could catch just a glimpse.

"Where have you been? It's been three nights since you came to see me."

He was by her dressing table. She heard the soft clink as he picked something up. "Here and there. Have you missed me?"

She lifted one shoulder, unwilling to admit how much she *had* missed him. "I was merely curious. Of course it's no matter to me what you do, or whom you visit at nights."

"It shouldn't be." He put down whatever he had taken from her dressing table. "It couldn't possibly interest you."

Mariah's brow puckered. This was not like Harry, this thread of bitterness. "Well, I did wonder," she said cautiously. "I thought perhaps you had forgotten me, or decided you didn't care for my company."

His laugh was short and harsh, with no amusement in it. "Did you? I can't imagine how you would reach that conclusion, Mariah."

Her frown deepened, but she didn't say anything, waiting to see where his odd mood would lead next. This was not the darkly charming fellow she had expected.

He was quiet for a moment, and when he spoke again, it was in a more normal tone. "You were lovely last night."

A surprised smile curled her lips. "Thank you." Then realization hit her. "You were at the Spencer ball? Why didn't you speak to me there?"

"You were surrounded by admirers from the moment you arrived until the instant you left. There was no room for one more."

Mariah rolled her eyes in the darkness. She had been hounded all evening by gentlemen gazing at her with calf love—or social ambition—in their eyes. Her quest for male acquaintances, undertaken in pursuit of Harry's identity, had reaped her some tiresome consequences. With the exception of the dances, she had spent the evening as she did most evenings, with Joan and other young ladies. "Nonsense. You have proved you weren't there, for I was most certainly not surrounded at all times."

"Indeed," he murmured dryly. "Sir Christopher is completely besotted. He was very disappointed when you refused to dance with him. Lord Chipping worships you, but from afar; do be kind to him, he's a gentle fellow. Lord Howard fancies himself also in love, but I could see by the way you paid him no attention during the waltz that you don't return the feeling. Viscount Travers spent more time looking at your bosom than your face, until your father came by. That one's after your connections and most likely your fortune. And Mr. Crane would have danced every dance with you if you allowed him. He hardly took his eyes off you all evening. Has he made an offer of marriage yet, or merely hinted at it?"

Her lips had parted with shock before he finished his second sentence. Not only had Harry been at the Spencer ball, he must have watched her the entire evening. She had suspected Lord Travers was looking down her bodice, but never managed to catch him at it. She didn't like him at all, with his small, bright eyes like a weasel and his overloud laugh. Lord Howard was a fool, and Sir Christopher Knightly needed to marry a fortune. But Harry—how could he not have spoken to her and saved her from the lot of them? "You are a coward," she managed to say. "To watch me all night without so much as a word of greeting."

"Perhaps." He spoke without anger, almost absently, and he continued to move restlessly about her room.

Mariah's temper heated another degree. "Actually," she said, "I doubt it. No, I think the reason is far more mundane. I think you must be frightfully ill-favored, to want me never to see you—"

He just chuckled.

"—painfully shy or awkward, since you will not speak to me in company—"

"Of course."

"—and you cannot dance at all. That is unfortunate, for I love dancing."

His tall figure leaned back against the writing desk. "I can dance well enough."

She put up one hand the way her mother did to stop all argument. It made her wild with frustration that he had been near enough to see whom she danced with and what her expression was, yet made no effort to dance with her or speak to her himself . . . even though it also sent a tingle of excitement through her that he had paid enough attention to know. He must have been watching her every move. "Easy enough to say, sir, when you cannot prove it."

Harry fought to subdue his seething sense of discontent. She was trying to provoke him but didn't know how well she was succeeding. Not only had he been tormented all last night by the sight of her, ethereal in a pale blue gown that clung to her every curve as she laughed and danced with every other man there, but after the miserable hours he'd spent tonight trailing Lord Bethwell, his temper, his patience, and his control had frayed a bit too much.

So he replied to her taunt instead of letting it go. "I'm not much given to overstatement, miss."

"Well, perhaps the next time we attend the same ball, you will ask me to dance. Just to prove your prowess, of course."

He kept hearing the young whore's muffled sounds of pain as Bethwell used her. He kept seeing the thin pale face begging him to do the same, for only two shillings in her hand. The contrast between that ruined scrap of a female and the lovely, pampered creature before him made him sick. It made him angry. Bethwell was a hypocrite and an arrogant ass, but he was living the life he was born to. No one would protest his treatment of the whore; he was a gentleman and a marquis, while the girl was nothing. Just as he was nothing, while Mariah was a wealthy young lady of aristocratic blood.

"Come, then." He put out his hand, his desire to blot out the memory of his evening conspiring with his desperation to touch her.

"Come where?" As if sensing his dark mood, she pulled her feet back up onto the side of the mattress.

"Dance with me," Harry said, knowing he should despise himself for this but doing it anyway. "Or perhaps you are the coward."

Her chin came out. She slid off the bed and came toward him. "There is no music."

He didn't move, just remained with his hand outstretched, waiting, dying. He couldn't make himself do anything else; if she wouldn't touch him, how could he blame her? He reeked of the rookeries and sweat and vice, nothing she should know about, nothing she could want.

She came one more step forward, then another—and laid her fingers on his.

Harry inhaled a long, controlled breath. Her hand was so soft, so smooth. She smelled of lavender and clean linen, everything comforting and right, and for a moment the blackness inside him abated. He craved her touch and presence like some men craved gin or opium; a weakness, but not one he could deny tonight. He drew her close, then stepped back and bowed. She dropped a quick curtsey.

"What is the dance, sir?" she asked.

In reply, he softly whistled the opening bars of a popular country dance. Mariah almost laughed at herself, for thinking he would propose something intimate like the waltz. When he had put out his hand and dared her to dance with him, she had wondered, just for a moment . . . But a country dance. It was almost respectable. She fell in step with him and danced the simple steps.

There were no other couples, so they simply repeated the steps others would have performed. Neither spoke, but every time their hands touched—their bare hands—she felt a shock that went straight to her heart. His hands were large but gentle, his long fingers firm around hers. They were not the hands of a gentleman, not soft or plump, but then she knew he was not like other gentlemen.

She could also sense that something was wrong. Their other conversations had all been light and teasing. Tonight the darkness she had always sensed in him was at the fore, even in this dance. His fingers lingered on hers; she could feel his eyes on her as they turned about each other; and more than once their shoulders brushed, at his doing she was sure. He was indeed a fine dancer, but she no longer cared about that.

At the next turn she went the wrong way deliberately, facing him just as he stepped toward her instead of promenading around his back. They both stopped cold, no more than a few inches separating them.

"What happened tonight?" she whispered, straining to see his face. "What has changed you?"

He loomed over her, dark and silent. "A girl," he said at last, his voice flat and yet heavy with emotion at the same time. "She couldn't be more than fifteen years old."

"What happened to her?"

"I gave her a crown and sent her home."

He hadn't answered her question. Carefully, she laid

her hand on his arm. He inhaled sharply but didn't pull away. "What else could you have done?"

"She doesn't need a crown," he said, and Mariah realized what the emotion was: anger. He was boiling with it. "She needs a proper place to live and decent clothes and an honest living that doesn't require her to sell herself to a gentleman gone slumming for the night. He only paid her a shilling and then took her up against a brick wall in an alley reeking of shit." The anger was slipping into his voice, sharpening his words. "I could hear her crying, and then he didn't even pay her the second shilling he had promised, but walked away without a care—"

No one had ever spoken to Mariah of such things before. She supposed she ought to be shocked and offended at his crude speech, but was too horrified by what he described. "Where?" she asked. "Where is she? Perhaps I can help—"

He laughed, a harsh bark of bitterness. "Of course you can't. I probably couldn't find her again if I tried. She might not even survive the night, out on the streets in Whitechapel."

"But I would like to help," Mariah insisted, truthfully. She couldn't even imagine a life like that. Who would not want to help such a poor creature, starving and cold and abused? She could take clothing and food, blankets; even money. Papa gave her enough pin money, she could spare some for a girl in need. "I *can* help, Harry."

"Would you? How?" He stepped back, spreading his arms out wide. "Sell your furnishings? Give her your silk gowns?"

"Well . . . perhaps not, but—"

"Feeding her a meal or giving her a warm cloak won't help. That won't change the facts of her situation. She's poor and young and already ruined. What would a meal do for her when she'll be hungry again tomorrow?" He swept one hand through the air as if flinging something away. "Your offer is kindly meant, but it won't help. No one person can help. It requires all men, and women, of decency to stand up for her. How noble can a man be if he allows people to starve to death a few streets from his own home and never makes the slightest effort to help? Your father cares for you and your health, but does he even know what other young women in London endure?"

"I—I don't understand," she stammered, startled by his fury. "Why were you in Whitechapel? Are—Are you a reformer, Harry?"

He was silent. His shoulders fell. "No," he said at last, as if the anger and animation had all drained away, leaving only hollow weariness. He turned his back to her and hung his head. "I'm not. I'm nothing."

Mariah moved without thinking. She stepped forward and put her hands on his back, then rested her cheek against him, too. He was so big and solid, so warm through the soft linen of his shirt. She closed her eyes and inhaled deeply, even though he smelled of fish. Where had he been tonight, and what had he been doing? Why had he watched a gentleman engage a prostitute in the squalor he described if it disturbed him so? But he cared; he cared for the discomfort of a common street girl he would never see again, and he gave her a crown. There was something in that gesture that touched her heart. "You are not nothing, not to me."

He turned. Mariah stared up into his face, only dimly visible even at this close distance. She realized it didn't matter what he looked like anymore. She would know him anywhere, from the way he moved and the way he breathed and the way he laughed. "I'm sorry," he whispered. "I should not have said that, when you offered to help."

"I would help her, Harry, truly."

"I know." His hands came up. His fingertips whispered over her jaw. Her body reacted on pure instinct, swaying toward him as her eyes drifted closed and she arched her neck, raising her face to him. His lips brushed hers, lingering barely a moment. "You're wrong, though," he whispered against her cheek. "To you, I am worse than nothing."

By the time she opened her eyes, he was gone.

Chapter 10

The next morning Mariah saw her room and her life with new eyes. She had been thinking all night about Harry and that girl. Whitechapel, she knew, was a very dangerous part of town, and Harry never said what he was doing there. For the first time, a serious shadow of doubt clouded her mind: Was she being led on by a liar? He certainly could have done any number of things to her—he'd slipped into her room without waking her, after all—but he hadn't. After some hesitation, she brushed aside that concern. She trusted Harry, at least enough to keep enjoying his company. But other questions couldn't so easily be put to rest.

Once again she needed to talk to Joan. She smiled ruefully to herself, realizing that her cousin was as inexperienced with gentlemen and their intrigues as she was. But the other young ladies in London had their eyes and minds filled with wealthy peers and scandalous rakes; there was no one she trusted to keep her secret other than Joan.

Her mother caught her as she was about to descend the stairs. "Mariah, come here. We would like a word with you."

Mariah paused. "Yes, Mama?"

Her mother beckoned her to follow. "Not until we join your father. Come, dear."

Mystified, she followed her mother. Was she in trouble? But no, Mama looked more pleased than angry, which surely wouldn't be the case if—Mariah suppressed a shudder—she or Papa had any suspicions about Harry. But then, Mama's expression also seemed to rule out a scolding for her disinterest in her callers, which Mariah felt was far more likely to get her in trouble. What had she done?

Perhaps it wasn't about her, she thought as they walked down the long hall to her father's study. Perhaps Papa had some happy news he wished to share with her, or perhaps he and Mama had planned another trip, or a ball, or . . . or . . . The possibilities petered off in her mind. What on earth? When her mother had something to say, she usually just said it. More and more curious, she followed Mama into the study. Her mother closed the door behind them, then crossed the room to stand beside the desk where Papa was waiting.

"Mariah, come in. Be seated."

Obediently she sat, turning a questioning face to her parents.

Her father sat down as well, his handsome face relaxing in a fond smile. "Have you enjoyed your Season thus far?"

She blinked at his question. "Yes, Papa. Of course."

"It has been entertaining to you?" She nodded, still utterly at sea. Surely this wasn't what they wanted to discuss. "And you have met interesting people?" She nodded, as he seemed to be waiting for her reply after each query. "Interesting gentlemen?" Papa added with a significant look.

Ice-cold dread poured through Mariah. Petrified, she stared back, finally managing to jerk her head in a tiny nod. Dear God. They knew. Somehow they had found out about Harry. Joan! But Joan had sworn on her life not to tell a soul, and Mariah trusted her. Who, then? No one knew—*no one*.

Unless . . . Her breath caught in her throat. Had Harry himself approached her father? Had he asked permission to call on her? Were all her questions about her mystery suitor about to be answered? And her parents looked pleased! If Harry had called on Papa and asked to call on her, her father must have said yes. She would be able to see him again!

A wild wave of hope rose up in her breast, which she instantly quelled by reminding herself of the debacle with Mr. Crane in the park. She must go cautiously until she knew for certain. Still, her heart, which had almost stopped beating at Papa's questions, began to pound painfully against her ribs. She clenched her hands in her lap to keep them still. "Yes, Papa," she said in as normal a voice as she could. "Some gentlemen have been . . . interesting."

He smiled. "I am delighted to hear it." He paused, leaning forward, his hands folded on his desk. "And is there any particular gentleman who's caught your eye?"

Color flooded her face despite her best efforts. "Perhaps," she murmured carefully.

His smile broadened. "Then I have happy news for you. Your mother and I have just entertained a gentleman who confesses himself quite dazzled by you. He sang your praises for quite some time, and even I, who knew every word he spoke to be true"—Papa winked, his eyes twinkling—"even I felt it was too much. The man is smitten, my dear, hopelessly, head over heels in love with you."

It was all she could do to smile nervously. Something was telling her it could not be Harry her father spoke of. Sing her praises until even her father tired of hearing it? That did not sound at all like Harry, who was more likely to tease her than compliment her.

"He asked me for your hand in marriage, Mariah." Papa sat back, smiling at her with pride and great satisfaction. "I presume he has informed you of his intentions?"

"Well . . . " She wriggled in her seat and cleared her throat. "No, Papa. No, he hasn't." And that also made her believe it was not Harry they spoke of. Surely he would have said something to her directly, at least a hint. A man bold enough to climb into her bedroom window would surely be bold enough to tell her himself if he loved her.

"You must have guessed," her mother chided gently. "I was not surprised at all."

Well, that settled the matter. It couldn't possibly be Harry if her mother knew and was not surprised. Mariah tried to ignore the hard lump of disappointment sinking in her stomach. She couldn't dwell on that now, not while she had to get through this ordeal with some semblance of grace. She merely looked up at her mother in question.

Mama smiled, coming forward to cup her cheek. "Just think, my dear—you would be a countess. Are you not pleased?"

She forced a grim smile. "Actually, Mama . . . I must confess, I—I haven't the slightest idea of whom we're speaking."

Mama dropped her hand. "Really, Mariah, how could you not know? The Earl of Hartwood."

Oh. *Him.* Mariah felt a wave of relief. Lord Hartwood was a nice enough fellow, but she doubted he was truly in love with her. "Lord Hartwood. Yes, I should have guessed."

"Are you pleased?" asked her mother again. "Do you mean to accept him?"

Mariah blinked at her. "Of course not."

For a moment there was surprised silence. Her parents exchanged a look, and then her mother faced her again. "Why not, dearest?"

"Mostly because I do not love him," she said, finding it was easy to explain now that she'd gotten over the first rush of surprise and dismay. "And I believe he doesn't really love me. We would bore each other silly within a month. He is a kind and amiable gentleman, but he is not for me."

Again her parents looked at each other. "If that is your final word on the matter," Papa began, looking more nonplussed than angry or even disappointed, "I shall refuse him."

She smiled at him in gratitude. "Thank you, Papa. You truly are the best father." She got up and went around his desk to kiss his cheek.

He caught her hand. "Are you certain, though? A man does not usually ask twice, Mariah. Perhaps you would care to consider it for a day before I speak to him."

"He is a very eligible match," said Mama quietly. "A handsome man, kind and goodhearted. You would be well provided for. I hope you're not being hasty, Mariah."

She turned to her mother. "I'm not. I know my heart in this, Mama; Lord Hartwood is not the man for me. I don't need to consider it, even though I know him to be a very eligible and decent gentleman, because I don't love him and don't believe I ever would."

For a moment her mother was motionless, then she smiled and bowed her head in acceptance. "Then he is not the man for you. I would never urge you to ignore your heart."

"I know you would not." She clasped her mother's hand. "Thank you for understanding."

"Of course, darling. We want you to be happy." If her mother were disappointed, she hid it well. Mariah felt a burst of love for both her parents. They obviously thought they were bringing her happy news, and were taking her refusal in amazing good grace.

"I was planning to visit Joan," she said. "May I go to her now?"

"I vow, you and Joan are practically attached to each other of late," exclaimed her mother. "What do you two talk about all day?"

Mariah grinned. "We are making up for not seeing each other for five years."

The countess threw up her hands and laughed. "I see. Well, Marion and I were the same, I suppose, when we were young. Go then, and give my niece my love."

"Yes, Mama." She slipped out of the room, closing the door behind her. Just before it latched, she heard her father say mildly, "Well, Hartwood's a bit of an idiot, anyway," and her mother's laughing response, "Oh, Charles!"

Mariah grinned to herself. All was well if they could laugh about it. Lord Hartwood! What a surprise. He'd only called on her . . . hmm . . . She couldn't precisely recall, but it couldn't have been more than once or twice. And she'd danced with him on a few occasions, but nothing out of the ordinary. Which was only fitting for Lord Hartwood, who was nothing if not ordinary, although still, as her mother had pointed out, a decent and eligible gentleman.

As for her hope that it might have been Harry . . . Mariah heaved a bittersweet sigh. As much as it would have made things considerably easier if he had indeed called on her father and asked his permission, she also acknowledged there was an excitement in Harry's midnight visits that she would miss if he began calling on her in the ordinary fashion. Harry, in her mind at least, was the very antithesis of ordinary.

And it worried her, just a little. She tried to be as honest with herself, about herself, as she possibly could. She admitted she was thrilled by her secret suitor and his mysterious habits. She admitted his unpredictability piqued her interest and fanned her curiosity to almost unbearable levels. She admitted his attentions were all the more delicious for being paid in the dark of night, in her bedroom, on the razor's edge of scandal and utter ruin. And so, she worried, what did that say about her character?

She had been raised as a very proper young lady. She knew the rules of the society in which she lived, and gentlemen climbing into ladies' bedrooms were decidedly outside those boundaries. And yet, she loved it. Perhaps she wasn't such a proper lady after all. Perhaps she had one of those rebellious natures that would land her in scandal after scandal throughout her life. She hoped she would be sensible enough not to humiliate her family that way, but if she were so thrilled by something this forbidden, maybe she wasn't.

After all, what if all her delight with Harry were due to his unorthodox courtship? Would she still find him interesting if he did come to call at the proper time? Would she still be intrigued if she knew his name, his family, his station, and his prospects? Or would she find him as boring and ordinary as all her other suitors if he were to behave in a more . . . boring and ordinary way?

"Joan," she hesitantly asked her cousin later, as they walked through the park, "do you think it wrong of me to be so . . . " She paused, searching for the right word. " . . . so acquiescent to Harry's attentions?"

Joan squinted at her from under her bonnet brim. "What do you mean?"

"Well . . . " Mariah lowered her voice. "It's so exciting that he climbs the wall to see me. It's even exciting that I don't know what he looks like or what his full name is."

"It certainly is," her cousin said at once.

"But it's wrong of him."

"Oh, yes."

Mariah frowned. Joan was being very agreeable. "But is it wrong of me to feel that excitement? Ought I not to be horrified, or scandalized?"

Joan snorted with laughter. "But you're not!"

"I know, but do you think I should be?"

Joan stopped laughing and gave her a sideways look. "What do you mean? How could you help it?"

"I can't." Mariah sighed. "I just wondered if it's truly wrong of me, if it makes me wicked or immoral."

Her cousin rolled her eyes. "It makes you *normal*. Who would not be interested in such a man? I cannot think of anything a man could do that would be more intriguing. If I were so fortunate as to have an exciting suitor, I would revel in every lovely, scandalous moment of it, you may depend on it."

Slowly, Mariah nodded. "Yes, I suppose." She certainly couldn't change the way she felt, and surely things like this only happened to a person once in her life. If nothing this exciting were to happen to her ever again, at least she would have this one delicious adventure. "Yes. You are right, Joan."

"You needn't sound so surprised. I am right from time to time." Joan tilted her head. "But now that we're agreed I'm a marvel of wisdom, will you tell me why, after all this time, you're pondering questions of propriety? I thought we agreed it was highly improper and therefore utterly exciting."

She had to smile at that. "No, *you* thought it was highly improper and therefore highly exciting. I think it's intriguing and exciting and wonderful, but . . . can it be right to like something so improper?"

Joan stopped short. "You aren't getting nervous, are you?" she whispered, her face blank with surprise.

"Nervous?" Her laugh did sound high and thin—nervous. "No," she whispered back. "Not if by 'nervous' you mean ready to give up looking for him or not wanting him to come again. I only wondered what it said about me that I find him mysterious and fascinating instead of shocking and scandalous."

Her cousin let out a breath. "I think he's all of those things. And I've never even met the man!" Her face brightened. "Now there's a thought! I could stay over at your house one night and sneak into your room after everyone has gone to bed. Then when he comes to see you, I could be hiding behind the curtains and leap out and catch him!"

Mariah stared at her in dumbstruck amazement before she burst out laughing. A moment later Joan followed, a mite sheepishly.

"Oh, Joan," Mariah gasped, clutching her cousin's arm. "Have you gone utterly mad? How did you plan to catch him?" She lowered her voice abruptly at the end, looking around anxiously, but no one was paying them any mind.

"I . . . I . . . I don't know!" Joan said on a hiccuping giggle. "Borrow Papa's walking stick and rap him around the ankles, or some such thing."

Mariah wiped a tear from the corner of her eye. "Well, that would make it harder for him to climb down, I suppose." The last of her amusement faded. "No, I think not."

"I liked the idea," Joan said with a sigh. "I'm quite perishing of curiosity, you know. If only he would come out in public where I might meet him, too."

Mariah just smiled uneasily. She hadn't told Joan that Harry had seen her out in public, even though he never approached her. It would be hard enough to keep herself in check, wondering if he might be at every gathering she attended, just out of her sight. It would be impossible if Joan were whispering in her ear about it every night.

And yet . . . something had to change. It was thrilling and intriguing and vastly flattering, but she simply had to find out more about the mysterious Harry—and it seemed the only way would be to ask him.

Chapter 11

"**T**ell me about your family, if you will not tell me about yourself." Mariah clasped her hands in her lap, determined to learn something from Harry that night. He was sitting at the end of her bed, just far enough away that she could only make out the pale shape of his face above his white shirt. She didn't ask why he wasn't wearing a coat, even though it was another cool, foggy night. It seemed an artifice now, when she was wearing only her nightdress and dressing gown. And perhaps she had gone past the point of questioning anything he did.

"My family." Harry leaned back against the bedpost and folded his arms. The muscles in his shoulders tightened in protest. Crane had kept him busy all day shelving and reshelving thick reference books on shelves high above his head, according to an ordering system that seemed to change by the hour. Harry's daytime employment had grown so tedious, his late night visits to Mariah had taken on an importance beyond even his craving for her. At least with Mariah he was himself, just Harry, even if he must conceal so much from her.

But she wanted to know about his family. "What would you like to know?"

"Your sister," she said. "You mentioned her the other night."

When her fingers had traced every line of his face. When he had been close enough to see the pulse in her throat and smell the faint lavender scent of her skin. "Yes. Ophelia." He hadn't thought about his family in weeks. It was easier if he didn't; he suspected his father would not approve of what he had chosen to do, and his mother would screech herself hoarse if she knew how many weapons he carried on his person at any time. "She is my younger sister," he went on. "By five years. She is the wit of our family, and none of us are ever spared. When Ophelia is in a temper, we all run in fear, for she will tease us mercilessly."

"And she is—is—"

"She was stricken by a fever when she was not quite three," he said, guessing at the reason for her hesitation. "She was sick for nearly a week, burning with fever, unable to eat, taken in fits . . . " His voice trailed off, remembering that week. He had been a boy of eight and terrified out of his mind. "My father nursed her."

"Your father?" she exclaimed.

"My mother was too overset." He paused. "The doctor told her it was a very dangerous fever, and Ophelia would likely not survive. He recommended they leave and hire someone to care for her. My mother objected." He paused again; his mother had thrown a pitcher at the doctor. He could still recall the sharp explosive sound it made as it hit the stone wall behind the astonished physician. "But my father took Ophelia in his arms—she was so small—and he carried her upstairs and bolted himself into the room with her. He wouldn't open the door except to allow my mother to hand him fresh water and linens, and food."

"That's very unusual for a father," said Mariah slowly.

"My father does not shy away from anything. He knew my mother was too upset." Harry stopped. He remembered his mother pounding on the door, screaming for his father to let her in. He had hidden at the turn of the stairs and watched, cowed by the doctor's somber warning and his mother's hysteria. "He came out when she begged him to open the door and let her see her baby before she died," he said quietly. "He held her until she calmed down and told her he would not let Ophelia die; and he would not let her in because of the danger she would catch the fever herself or give it to me or my sister, Fanny."

"Fanny?"

Harry nodded. "She is two years younger than I."

"Oh. And then—at the end of the week . . . ?"

"Father came out of the room with Ophelia in his arms. The fever had broken at last, but she seemed to have shrunk, from a week not eating, and when she opened her eyes she saw nothing. It was a terrible blow." Harry remembered thinking she might as well have died, the uncomprehending reaction of a child. He would never forget the sight of Ophelia standing in the middle of the kitchen, crying with frustration and fright because she could not locate her mother. Her blindness had been terrifying to him then. "My father removed everything from the room where she had been sick," he went on. "He burned it all, even the clothes he wore while he tended her. And after that we had our heads and necks scrubbed every day whether we needed it or not, as a guard against fever."

"He sounds a remarkable man," Mariah murmured.

Harry smiled wryly. "Indeed."

"And now, Ophelia . . . ?"

"Is quite well. She has the keenest ears and most sensitive touch. We none of us can sneak up on her, and my brother George has tried mightily."

Mariah perked up again. "George?"

Harry laughed. "Yes, the youngest of us all."

"I always wondered what it would be like to have a brother or sister."

"It is a great trial," he replied, and told her all about his brother and two sisters, how they played pranks on each other endlessly, and stood together when an outsider tormented one of them. That was safe enough to share. Mariah would never picture a man who defied his father to join a troupe of traveling players instead of becoming a proper tailor; a woman who was disowned by her wealthy, respectable family for running off with a penniless actor; or four children who were raised in numerous towns across England, sometimes comfortably and sometimes not, sometimes on stage and sometimes working behind the curtain, before their father settled in Birmingham to manage a theater. At least he came by his gift for lies and impersonation honestly, Harry thought; he had been raised to it.

He looked around the shadowy chamber again, a room almost as large as some of the lodgings his entire family had shared at times. The carpets alone cost more than his father made in a year. It was like two different worlds, Mariah's life and his, two separate planes of existence that never intersected. "Now tell me about your family," he said, not wanting to think of the gulf that separated them.

"All right." Mariah could feel his eyes on her, and she straightened self-consciously. It was easier to sit and listen to him talk, letting the quiet tenor of his voice swirl around her. He had a way of putting things that never ceased to make her smile. Once again she thought she could listen to him talk all night long. "My father is a confidant of the Prime Minister. These last few years he has been on government business abroad in foreign capitals. My mother also takes a keen interest in affairs of state, and she wished to go with him. They took me along because I threw a temper fit when they told me they were leaving." She smiled awkwardly. "I was much younger then, of course."

"Such a spoiled child."

She blushed. "Well—perhaps a little. But I am the only child, and am fortunate enough to have very kind and devoted parents." She hesitated again, remembering how well her parents had taken her refusal of Lord Hartwood's offer. "But I suppose they do . . . *indulge* me more than is usual."

"What is the usual indulgence, pray?"

He was teasing her again. She fiddled with the lace on her dressing gown, not in the mood for teasing. "I received an offer of marriage today," she blurted out. "From a very eligible man."

That silenced him. Mariah glanced up, even though it was too dark to see his expression.

"Should I offer my congratulations or condolences?" he said at last, all amusement—all inflection, in fact—gone from his voice. It was a flat, impersonal tone she had never heard from him.

She frowned. "Neither! I did not wish to marry him, nor even to have an offer from him. But it would have been a very eligible match, and my parents were both quite sanguine about my refusal. My father even laughed about it, afterward. That is how they indulge me. Not every parent would be so easy about it."

"Perhaps they had some objection to the man and were relieved."

She shook her head. "I don't think so, although my father did admit he was a bit of an idiot."

"If they knew that, they must have known he was not right for you."

"Many parents do not care," she told him. "A title, a fortune, an illustrious connection . . . That is what they want in a daughter's marriage, particularly when a daughter is as old as I am."

"Perhaps they feel you are old enough to know your own mind."

She smiled ruefully. "I have known my own mind since I was a child. 'Willful,' my governess once called me."

"And why shouldn't you know your own mind? Should you believe yourself incapable of it merely because you have a father to look out for you?"

"No," she said slowly. "Of course not."

"Did you not tell me yourself a woman is not a prize to be won? Wives should not be gotten by bargaining with the father, offering so much in settlements and requiring this much in dowry, when all that is wanted is her family alliance, her bloodline, and the heirs she can bear. A woman has hopes and dreams and affections just as any man does." Mariah's eyes widened in surprise. His white-sleeved shoulders rose again in another shrug. "Why should her desires not be as important as her family's, or her suitor's?"

"I—I am sure my parents *do* want me to be happy,"

she stammered. "They would have been pleased, had
I accepted him . . . "

"Why did you refuse?"

She stared at him. How could he not know? "Because I don't love him."

"How do you know?"

"Because—" *Because I never longed to see him the way
I long to see you.* "Because I just know."

"Ah." He was quiet for a moment. "I'm sure I'm very
sorry for the fellow, but if he had not won your heart, it
was a mercy that you refused him."

Mariah thought about telling him it was *his* fault she
had refused Lord Hartwood, that it was *his* fault she
couldn't begin to think of another man. But that would
be a confession of feelings she wasn't ready to admit.
She found Harry intriguing and exciting and amusing,
and she wanted him to keep visiting her—but beyond
that she would not let herself think. She had no proof
of his affection for her, and was just reserved enough
to keep her uncertain affection to herself. In fact, she
didn't even know what she felt for Harry. How could
it be love, when she didn't know his name or anything
about him? And yet, she did know it was more than
mere interest or liking. If only she had some thought
of his true intentions toward her.

"Don't you think you're a bit—a bit wicked?" she
asked. The question had been burning inside her all
day. If Harry thought his visits wicked, then she would
have to be wicked for taking such pleasure in them.
But if he could offer her any explanation that didn't
admit wickedness, perhaps her own conscience would
be more at ease. And perhaps, just perhaps, it might
prod him to reveal something more about his motives
in coming to see her.

"Wicked? On what grounds?"

"Yes, wicked. To come see me like this." She leaned forward and raised her chin in challenge.

"Ah." He shifted his seat on the mattress with a faint creak of the bed ropes. "I think 'wicked' is a word flung about with distressing ease. Our amiable conversation cannot compare to all the true wickedness in the world."

"Then what do you think this is?" Mariah waved one hand to encompass her darkened room, their nearness, the intimacy of the situation. She felt driven to compel some declaration from him, of anything. Amiable conversation? What did that mean?

"I find it quite pleasant."

"You enjoy climbing the ivy?" she said with a disbelieving huff.

"Especially climbing the ivy," he declared. "I searched all London for an ivy-covered wall with a beautiful woman at the top . . . "

"Then what would be really wicked?"

"Why, wearing a waistcoat that doesn't suit one's complexion, I imagine."

"Oh." She sighed. "Something else you cannot tell me."

He was quiet for a long time, then spoke again, more seriously. "What is wicked, you ask? A great deal, I answer. To say a man may not vote if he isn't wealthy enough, and yet still expect him to support the government that gives him no voice. To pass laws keeping the price of wheat high for the benefit of landowners, when people in the cities are starving for want of bread. To declare swaths of society immoral and indecent because they are poor, and then do nothing to help them out of poverty. All those things are much more wicked, to my mind, than anything you've done."

That was not what she had expected to hear. "You said you are not a reformer."

He shrugged, a quick, slight action. "I dislike unfairness."

"What would you change, then, if you could?"

"Many things." His voice vibrated with an undercurrent of passion. Mariah leaned forward, wishing she could see him better. At the same moment, he moved forward, raising one hand, and she froze at his gossamer-light touch on her skin.

"Why were you in Whitechapel the other night?" she whispered. "When you saw that poor girl. Because you dislike unfairness?"

Harry's fingers stilled on her cheek. "I was watching after someone."

"Her?"

His hand fell away. "No. Not her. I expect no one watches after her."

"Then after someone else. Someone special?"

Another long pause. "In a way."

She wet her lips. "And what would you have done, if something had befallen that person?"

"Anything I had to do." His voice had fallen into a murmur. "Do you have any more questions?"

"Yes." She could feel his breath on her lips. Her heart beat so hard he must be able to hear it every time she opened her mouth. "When you watched me the other night . . . at the Spencer ball . . . what did you hope to see?"

Now his hand returned to caress her cheek, more boldly this time but no less gently. "I wanted to see you, so beautiful and elegant, like a faerie goddess come to earth for the night. I wanted to see the candlelight on your hair, and dream of seeing it down. I wanted to see your smile, and imagine it was meant for me." His voice dropped even lower. "I wanted to see you dance, and pretend it was my hand you took. To hear you laugh and hope that someday you might laugh with me that way . . . "

"You're such a scoundrel, to say such things to me," she whispered as his lips brushed hers.

"You have no idea," he murmured, and then he kissed her.

She almost forgot to breathe. His lips brushed once over hers, and then his hand slid around the back of her neck and he pulled her closer, so close she threw out her hands to keep herself from falling into him. Her palms hit his shoulders. He made a smothered sound deep in his throat, and her fingers curled into the soft fabric of his shirt as his mouth pulled at hers.

His head lifted; his lips moved to her forehead, her temple, the corner of her eyelid. He cupped her face in both hands and dragged his thumb across her lips. Mariah sighed, her head swimming, and he kissed her again, nudging her to open her mouth with a soft flick of his tongue. She gasped, surprised, but then moaned as he tasted her mouth, at first delicately and then more hungrily as she kissed him back.

When the kiss ended, a lifetime later, she sat shaken and breathless, still clutching Harry's shirt by the shoulders. Her heart galloped along in her chest and her lungs burned, but her mind seemed to be ringing with a chorus of joy. Yes, *that* was what the hidden creature inside her craved. She had never felt more vitally alive than when Harry touched her.

He tipped up her chin and kissed her once more,

lightly, on the mouth. "To answer your question," he whispered, "I most definitely am."

"Am what?" She smiled dreamily into his shadowy face.

"Wicked." One more kiss. Mariah sighed, feeling a little drunk from the pleasure of it.

"In the very best way . . . "

His laugh was more a sigh. He ran his thumb once more over her lower lip. "Unfortunately, my darling, also in the worst."

Chapter 12

Mariah hesitated at first to tell Joan about the kiss—her first true kiss—but in the end the joy of it was too great to keep to herself. Two days later, as soon as they reached the Plympton home for Lady Plympton's annual garden breakfast, she rushed her cousin to a quiet corner and related the tale.

"Oh," swooned Joan, laying one hand over her heart and fanning her face with the other. "Good heavens!"

"Stop," said Mariah, blushing. "Everyone will wonder what we're saying."

"The gentlemen will know. Would that one of them would kiss me so." Joan grinned and dropped her hand. "Perhaps he is here today."

Mariah looked around. Lady Plympton was an old friend of her grandmother's, and Mama had come because of that connection. The guests were mainly older, with hardly any young gentlemen present, but there were some. "Perhaps," she said, "but it seems unlikely."

"Well! That bodes well for discovering him. It always seems people turn up in the most unexpected locations."

Mariah laughed and had to agree, even though she

privately doubted it. Joan's mother was beckoning to her, so Joan squeezed her hand and promised to look about for any men who might be Harry before hurrying off.

Mariah slowly wound her way through the gathering. Just thinking about Harry's kiss had made her stomach fluttery and her breath short. Could he be here? She and Joan were probably the youngest guests in attendance among their grandmother's set, but there were a few gentlemen, standing about the sideboard talking. Most of the guests had gone outside. Aimless without her cousin, Mariah drifted through the open doors to join them.

It was a glorious day, especially bright and fresh after the recent rain. Beautifully decorated tables had been set up at various points, each of them surrounded by a profusion of greenery and color. In the middle of the garden a tall fountain gurgled away, the spray sparkling like diamonds in the sunlight. A large white tent was erected near the house, over a buffet laden with enough delicacies to feed half of London. Mariah's eyes caught on the trays of sweet buns and platters of roasted fish. Would Harry think this wicked, she wondered, this sumptuous spread of food for people who had never gone hungry in their lives? Were there truly people starving in London? Funny how he had made her think about such things for the first time.

Not really hungry, she was walking past the buffet when a man spoke behind her. She didn't even hear what he said, just caught the tenor of his voice, but it was enough; she jerked to a halt in disbelief. That voice. She knew that voice—it was *his* voice. She'd been searching all London for it, and here it was, right in

Lady Plympton's garden. She whirled around, her eyes flying about in search of the speaker.

He had his back to her, a broad expanse of dark cloth, and was bent over the buffet table. He spoke again, the familiar rumble that sent her heart straight into her throat and completely emptied her mind. Good heavens, what was she to say to him? In all the time she had been looking for him, she still hadn't worked that out. A triumphant *I found you!* seemed out of order at a garden party. She didn't want to seem rude or impolite or, worse, silly. She touched her hair nervously, wishing there were a glass nearby. Oh, where was Joan? With a friend at her side for support, she would be much more confident and composed.

He turned, a laden tray in his hands. Mariah stepped back, yet stayed on the path he was taking. She gripped her trembling fingers together. Almost here—five steps—now three—now one—

"Good day, sir," she said airily. "What a surprise to meet you here."

He paused, glancing at her from behind plain round spectacles with calm hazel eyes. He was tall, with brown hair neatly combed flat. He could not have been more than thirty, a modestly handsome but unexceptional man. "Ma'am." He bowed politely, as well as he could with his tray. "May I assist you?"

"Wh-Why," she stammered, thrown completely off stride by his lack of recognition, "do you not know me?" She lowered her voice to a whisper and added, "Harry!"

He blinked as if surprised. "Pardon?"

She shifted her weight uncertainly. It was his voice, she would swear it—but he was not responding as he ought to. "It is I, Mariah. Surely you've not forgotten me."

"Indeed, I should not say that . . . " He trailed off. There was something terrible in his face—a shade of deferential pity that made Mariah shrink with horror. And yet, the one sentence he spoke crystallized her conviction that it *was* Harry. She wet her lips and plunged ahead, ignoring the doubts and misgivings multiplying in her mind. There couldn't possibly be two gentlemen in London with the same voice . . . could there be?

"Then you must recall—you can hardly have forgotten our conversations! Nor the place where we met." She watched closely, desperately, for any flicker of recognition, even as she began to wish she had not spoken to him yet; how humiliating to have to quiz him on this! Better to have maneuvered into a formal introduction, or a walk in the garden where she might speak to him in private. But there was no such sign of comprehension in his face. The horrible silence dragged on. "But I know you," she said helplessly.

"Towne!" Mr. Crane appeared at her side. "My uncle is waiting for his tea." He turned to Mariah. "How lovely to see you today, Lady Mariah." He bowed, beaming at her. Her stunned gaze veered back to Harry, still standing mute and passive.

"Yes, sir. I beg your pardon, my lady." He bowed politely and moved past her.

Mariah could say nothing, struck dumb with shock and heartsick confusion as she watched him walk away without a backward glance. It was Harry, it really was, and he was either pretending not to know her or . . . or he didn't want to know her.

"I hope the fellow didn't bother you," Mr. Crane was saying. "My uncle's secretary—Uncle depends on him, particularly of late." He paused, but she couldn't have spoken to him if she wanted to. A secretary. A common secretary. And she had invited him into her bedroom and let him kiss her. "You look rather pale, Lady Mariah," said Mr. Crane. "May I fetch you a glass of wine?"

She nodded faintly, anything to get him to leave. *Just a secretary . . .*

"Or perhaps lemonade?" Mr. Crane pressed on in oblivion. "I could send for a cup of tea, if you wish, I'm sure it wouldn't take but a moment. Or water?"

"Yes, tea," she said desperately. Go go *go*, she willed him.

He beamed at her. "Tea at once. I shall return in a moment, Lady Mariah."

The instant he was gone, she pushed her way through the guests to an open space, where she could see him. Harry was well away, crossing the grass toward old Lord Crane. Her chest felt tight and her stomach heaved. A *servant* . . . No wonder he wouldn't tell her his name . . .

"Mariah! There you are." Joan scurried over, her skirts in her hands. "Come, there's a group of gentlemen beyond the fountain. Some of them I've never met, and two are fearfully handsome!" Then she noticed Mariah's expression. "What is it? What's wrong?"

"That's Harry." Mariah's lips barely moved as she stared after the secretary, now almost back to Lord Crane, sitting in a sunny spot by the camellias, the pride and joy of Lady Plympton's garden.

Joan followed her gaze. "Mariah, that's Lord Crane. He must be nearly a hundred years old."

"No, not him. The young man with him." The words choked her. "His secretary."

Joan gasped out loud. "No! His secretary is Harry? No!" She swung around to squint at his figure, then back. "Mariah, you must be mistaken. Your mother would never invite a secretary to her ball. It must be a relation, or someone who sounds like him . . . "

Mariah shook her head. "I heard him speak, Joan. He spoke to me. I heard him as clearly as I ever heard Harry and it was the same voice." Her knees trembled and she caught Joan's hand. "He lied to me—he led me to believe he was a gentleman—"

Joan threw her arm around Mariah's shoulders. "Come sit down."

She let her cousin guide her to a bench a short distance away and collapsed onto it, all her dreams and fantasies mocking her. How could he have deceived her so? How could he have presumed to sneak into her room when he was nothing but a servant? How could he have let her think he meant to court her?

"Well, now you know why he was too cowardly to give his name," Joan said. "What a snake! As if he had any chance of being acceptable. I for one think you should consider yourself lucky you found him out this way. Now he has nothing to hide behind, and is exposed for the liar and trespasser he is. You should tell your parents at once; they should know a common servant is sneaking into their affairs masquerading as a gentleman."

"No," said Mariah, her voice faint but calm. "He—He did deceive me, but he never actually said he was a gentleman. I assumed . . . " *I assumed he was what I wanted him to be.* "I assumed he was one," she finished aloud. "But I won't tell my parents. It—It would cause more trouble, for them to know."

"But then what will you do?" exclaimed Joan. "How shall you make the wretch suffer? He deserves that, you know. Why, I myself was half in love with him, just from the way you talked about him." She leaned closer, squeezing Mariah's hand. "Do you know, perhaps that was his goal all along! If he could have kept up his masquerade, he might have fooled some poor girl into falling in love with him and even persuaded her to run off with him. Think how she would feel when she found out she was married to a common nobody."

Mariah heard what her cousin was saying; *Mariah* should count herself lucky, for unlike Joan, she had been more than half in love with Harry, and could indeed have considered marrying him, if only . . . if only . . .

But that had never been possible. Her hands balled into fists as the shock of discovery gave way to disillusionment. Harry had to know the Earl of Doncaster would never allow his daughter, his only child, to marry a man so far beneath her station. Once Harry knew who she was, he must have known her father would disapprove of them speaking, let alone marrying. Every single moment of his attentions had been a cruel trick, letting her grow attached to a man she would never have.

Of course, he hadn't been *so* dishonorable, she argued with herself. He had hardly done anything she hadn't invited or permitted, and overall their meetings had been fairly innocent. Not that it excused him sneaking into her bedroom—no matter that he had asked permission—but he hadn't taken advantage of her, not really. Every time he touched her, she had wanted him to, allowed it and welcomed it. And perhaps he had known he was unacceptable and yet just couldn't help himself because of his feelings for her . . .

Mariah leaped to her feet, appalled with herself for defending him, for still wanting him to be someone he wasn't. She hoped he *was* madly in love with her, so her rejection would hurt him just as much as his deception had hurt her. She hoped he suffered a decline and wasted away and died of a broken heart. Then she would be happy again.

Tears stung the back of her eyelids. "I want to go home," she said to Joan. "Now."

"Of course." Joan wrapped a comforting arm around her waist and they went into the house. Mariah refused to look back, not wanting to see the lying rogue again as he served old Crane his tea.

Not that she would have noticed him watching. Harry couldn't allow himself to look directly at her, but he did steal several glances back. Her shocked expression was branded on his mind, the hurt and betrayal in her eyes piercing him like a white-hot lance—of guilt, most likely. He felt it eat away at him—the knowledge that he had hurt her by indulging his personal desires, desires he knew damned well were forbidden and ultimately doomed. And at the same time, a part of his wicked soul exulted that she cared enough to be hurt. He ought to be flogged, he told himself in a fury of self-loathing as he arranged the tea and cakes on the table at Lord Crane's elbow.

"You brought kippers," grumbled Crane. "I detest kippers."

"Of course, sir." Harry moved that plate back onto the tray, sneaking another look in Mariah's direction. She was huddled on a bench with another young lady. It hadn't taken too much effort to discover that the tall brunette was her cousin, Miss Bennet. Mariah's face was pale, except for two spots of red in her cheeks, and from the expression on her face, he guessed she was agreeing that he should be flogged.

"And I don't want tea. There must be port somewhere in the house."

"The physician says you should not have port," Harry reminded Crane for the hundredth time.

"Ballocks," snapped Crane. "I think I know what's better for me than the leech knows. Fetch some port, Towne."

"Now, sir, I cannot in conscience contribute to a decline in your health."

Crane snarled some more. "I don't pay for your bloody conscience."

"No, sir, I believe my conscience remains in my own employ." Harry barely noticed Crane's peevishness today. If only Tobias hadn't persuaded his uncle to come to this garden party, where he had been required to go along and attend to Crane. He'd known that Crane would dislike it and take it out on him. But of course he hadn't known Mariah would be here, intent on seeking him out and confronting him.

"I want to move over there, into the shade," Crane said, just as Harry had the table arranged. "The sun is too hot here. And where's my nephew? That useless fribble; he cozened me into this party, and now he's nowhere to be seen. No respect for his elders, no appreciation." Crane got to his feet, clutching his cane.

"I'm going inside," he announced, and started in that direction.

"Will you want your tea there, sir?" Harry asked dutifully.

Crane swore. "Damn it, Towne, I want no tea! I'll find some port if I have to search every cupboard in the house! Drink the tea yourself."

"Yes, sir." He ought to follow him. Crane was exposed, surrounded by dozens of people in strange surroundings. His duty today was to stick closely to the old man, no matter how prickly Crane was and no matter how pointless or unwanted his presence might seem.

Instead, Harry remained where he was, silently replacing the dishes on the tray, barely registering the sharp clink of china on china. Mariah and her companion had disappeared. Even if they hadn't, he couldn't have done anything; there was no explanation he could give, no excuse, that would pardon his actions, even had there been any way he could have spoken to her.

With a great effort, he picked up the tray and straightened his shoulders. He still had a job to do. A job that did not, and never would, involve Lady Mariah Dunmore. And he had never been more heartily sick of it.

Chapter 13

That night, Mariah went to bed late. Not wanting to spend any time awake in her room, she waited until she was dropping with exhaustion. She hated her room now, where she'd lost her silly, naive heart to a liar, bared her soul to a common scoundrel who never had any intention, or hope, of marrying her. No wonder he had sneaked around! Papa would have set the dogs on him for approaching her. She should have known better than to trust any man who would slip into her room . . . after climbing a thirty-foot wall . . . at midnight!

She dismissed her yawning maid; she didn't need anyone tonight, not Sally and certainly not Harry. The cad. The bloody blighter. She called him every bad name she could think of, even as her heart twisted in her chest.

With a snort that drifted into a sigh, she flopped into bed, deliberately turning her back on the windows. If it weren't so hot, she would close them. She wished it were winter. She wished her room faced the street. She wished the gardeners had never planted ivy. Why couldn't they have planted climbing rosebushes, with plenty of thorns? That would keep any lying, sneaking imposter from disturbing her peace.

And yet . . . She sniffled a little, then scrubbed one hand across her face. It wasn't entirely Harry's fault. She did tell him to come in, that first night he appeared at her window. She did ask him to come back when he left. If he had been guilty of an overreaching presumption, she had been equally guilty of accepting and even encouraging his advances. If she had behaved with the circumspection proper in a young lady, this might not have happened at all.

But the worst part was, she wasn't even sure *that* would make her happy. Would she be better off if she had never known him? Perhaps she would have met someone else, someone more suitable and just as interesting and charming . . . and perhaps not. After all, she had spoken to nearly every other gentleman in London while looking for Harry, and many of them had called on her. Not one had captured even half as much of her interest as he had. She heaved another sigh, rolling over and trying to find a comfortable position. Deep down, she suspected, part of her would always treasure the memory of her mysterious, romantic suitor. If only—

She sat up and pounded her pillow, wildly annoyed that it should be so lumpy tonight of all nights. Then she lay back down and closed her eyes, determined not to open them again until morning. A small drop leaked from one eye and slid down her cheek. She refused to move, even to wipe it away, willing herself to sleep. Finally, after several more tears had followed that one, she drifted off.

* * *

Harry melted into the deep shadows of a hedge that surrounded the Doncaster House gardens. He really ought not to be here. He could only make things worse, after all, either for her or for himself or, most likely, for both—and yet, here he was, unable to listen to his own good sense and stay away.

As usual, the gardens were deserted. He had never encountered a gardener or other servant, and the gate was a child's game to open. For a man supposedly in danger of his life, Doncaster seemed strikingly unaware of how easy it would be for someone to walk into his gardens, climb a wall of his house, and . . . and fall hopelessly in love with his daughter. Harry scowled. He was the fool, not Doncaster.

All right, he decided grimly. In for a penny, in for a pound. He wouldn't be able to stop thinking about her until he saw her one last time, saw how she turned up her nose at a lowly secretary and heard her scathing dismissal of a man with neither title nor fortune to his name. Once he felt the lash of her scorn in person, he might recover from the madness that had gripped him since the moment he first saw her. At least he wouldn't be able to deceive himself any longer.

Taking a deep breath, he strode across the lawn, ducking into the shadows of the towering ivy. With one last glance around to make sure he was as unnoticed as always, he took hold of a vine and scaled the wall.

He slipped through the window, bracing himself for a scream, a curse, an order to leave. The room was silent. She obviously wasn't waiting up for him as she once had. That was probably for the best, he thought with a silent sigh. As his eyes adjusted, he took a step farther into the room. "Mariah?" he whispered.

There was no response, and then he saw she was asleep. She had kicked off the bedclothes, her legs bared to the knee. She lay on her side, facing him, one hand tucked under her cheek. Something wrenched at his heart. She looked exhausted, and for a moment he thought he should just leave her in peace.

But that would only prolong the agony. Mariah deserved a chance to tell him just how dreadful he was. He deserved to hear it, too, for he had known all along they had no future. He had known, but selfishly came back again and again, letting her believe a lie because . . . He cursed under his breath. He had let her believe it because he wanted to believe it, too.

Not that it excused his actions in any way.

Quietly, he crossed the room. The moon was full tonight, and the sky cloudless; silvery light filled the room, revealing the luxurious furnishings more clearly than ever before. Inside, he laughed mockingly at himself. Had he truly believed, for one moment, he could have a girl who lived in such splendor? He could never provide her with half this much elegance, and was a fool even for wishing he could. Ladies like Mariah didn't marry scoundrels like him.

At her bedside he stopped, greedily watching her sleep. God above, but she was the most beautiful woman he'd ever seen. He reached out and lifted a stray curl from the pillow, letting the silky lock slip through his fingers. The pillow looked damp beneath her cheek, another sign of the harm he had done her. Oh, yes, he was every kind of fool for ever speaking to her. Brandon had been right from the beginning: she was not for him.

"Mariah." He went down on one knee next to the bed, hoping she didn't wake with a scream and scratch out his eyes. "Mariah."

She didn't move.

He touched her shoulder. "Mariah." Her eyelashes fluttered but didn't rise. "Wake up, Mariah." Her nose twitched, and a thin line appeared between her brows, as if she were annoyed that her rest was being disturbed. Harry smiled in spite of himself. "I'm so sorry, love," he whispered. He touched her cheek, his fingertips barely skimming her soft skin, and felt the full force of his folly.

Slowly her eyes opened. She blinked twice, not moving. "Harry?" she murmured thickly.

He snatched his hand away. "Yes."

"Oh, Harry," she gasped, lurching upright to throw her arms around him and pull him close. Caught completely off guard, he fell against the side of the bed, instinctively throwing his arm around her. "I'm so glad you came!"

Harry froze. Was she truly awake? That was not the greeting he had expected. "Why?"

"Because I missed you!" she said against his shoulder.

Even though he knew it was wrong, his heart took a great leap. He rested his cheek against her silky hair and inhaled warm, rumpled woman, wishing yet again that there were any way . . .

But there wasn't. He lifted her arms from his neck and sat back to look at her. "You ought not to. I only came so you could give me a proper dressing down."

She blinked again. "But why? Of course I was terribly surprised at the Plymptons' party—I'd been looking for you simply everywhere, and then I didn't know what to say when you were there right in front of me. So I jumped at you and insisted you act as if we were old acquaintances, which would have been dreadfully improper—"

Harry's eyes narrowed. That sounded suspiciously like an apology, which wasn't right. He was here to apologize to her.

"—and then Mr. Crane came up and I couldn't think. I only wanted him to go away, and Joan wasn't there to distract him, and then I was so flustered I just went home. But I've thought about it all night, and only just now, while I was sleeping, I think, did it come to me—"

"Mariah, what are you talking about?" he interrupted.

"Why you are employed with Lord Crane," she said. He could only stare at her. She smiled, her face glowing. "But it's fine! You're not the first, you know; my mother's youngest brother was also a secretary for some time, I had completely forgotten—then he went into Parliament—"

He must have made a noise or done something to betray his dawning realization. She thought he was a younger son, still a gentleman. Still someone of her class.

"What?" she whispered anxiously.

Slowly, woodenly, Harry shook his head.

She opened her mouth, then closed it. "But . . . but you must be," she said in a voice that began to tremble. "Many younger sons take employment as secretaries, particularly with men like Lord Crane. It would be such a good opportunity . . . "

Harry sat back on his heels, a vague sense of contempt filling him. But for whom? He could hardly blame her for wanting—expecting—him to be a gentleman. Her life was filled with gentlemen. He, on the other hand, knew he was no such thing and had known it from the beginning, despite all the times he'd let her continue assuming he was one. He had known, even if he hadn't admitted it to himself, that he wanted her to want him, and he knew she would never speak to him if he weren't good enough. *This* was his just reward, he told himself bitterly.

Suddenly he was angry. Angry at her, for trying so hard to make him acceptable by her standards. Angry at himself, for wanting her so desperately that he had deceived her. She was a wealthy elegant lady, born for someone in the peerage. He was nothing more than a common actor, playing at being a spy with the hope of becoming more, but still no one worthy of her.

He surged to his feet and paced away, trying to suppress his resentment and anger and knowing they both sprang from his frustration with his circumstances. It wasn't Mariah's fault. She had been born to her lofty station just as innocently as he had been born to his lowly one. At least she had not pretended to be what she was not.

She interpreted his actions correctly. "No!" she gasped after a moment. "I cannot believe it. You—You must be a gentleman. You're the younger son of an earl, or a viscount—even a barrister—"

He put up a hand to stop her. "No," he said shortly. "No, I am not."

There was a moment of dreadful silence. Harry scowled, wishing he could have said yes. But his father was an actor; his grandfather had been a tailor. He was not a gentleman.

"It's so bloody unfair!" Mariah exploded abruptly, pounding her pillow. He turned and rocked back on his heels.

"What isn't fair?" *Besides the fact that I'm falling in love with you and can't have you . . .*

"It's not fair that you should have to sneak around to see me while dull, boring people like Mr. Crane may call on me and waste the entire day. And why, I ask you? Because his *uncle* is a viscount!" Harry, about to speak, paused. She rushed on. "Just because he's going to have a title someday, he may speak to any female he chooses. But I must sit and *wait* until a proper, acceptable man finds *me*. What an unfair thing it is, to be a female!"

That disarmed his anger like nothing else could have. He laughed ruefully. "Perhaps, but you're far too beautiful for a boy."

Her mouth twisted, and she punched the pillow again, without force. Her dark hair was coming loose from her braid and fell forward, hiding her face. He drew in a deep breath and let it out, all at once tired and resigned. "I came to apologize—"

"How did you get into our ball?" she demanded. Harry tensed. "Secretaries don't go to balls. They aren't invited. Lord Crane would never bring you, not to my mother's ball. How did you get in?"

"Perhaps I snuck in," he said, dodging a direct answer.

"But you would stand out. No one would know you, and at my mother's ball, everyone knew everyone, or at least *of* them. And if you snuck in, why? What did you intend to gain?"

A plausible story was on the tip of his tongue; every step he took, he had a story prepared. Things could go wrong, people could make mistakes. He might be caught out or suspected at any moment. But he had already lied to Mariah enough. Even though it went against everything he had been told to do, Harry thought it might be better to tell her something like the truth, if only to keep her from trying to discover it herself.

"You must believe me," he began, "when I swear I had an honorable purpose. Beyond that you must trust me, if you can. It was not for personal gain—I did nothing to harm or embarrass any of your guests or your family—but I can't tell you precisely why."

She had listened with eyes growing rounder at each word. For a moment she didn't reply. "Is it dangerous?" she whispered.

Harry said nothing.

She gave a muffled squeak. "I—I shan't tell! I don't want to cause you any harm . . . "

"I can't come back to see you," he said. "I dare not. And you mustn't speak to me again if we should meet." She wet her lips. Harry returned to her bedside in one stride and reached out to take her hand without thinking. "Promise me."

"I promise," she said, her voice barely audible. "But when will you be . . . free?" Harry stiffened. "When can you come to see me again?" she clarified. "Don't tell me you won't. Not at night, but during the day, as yourself." He started to shake his head, and she put her hands on the sides of his face, stopping him in place. "You must," she implored. "Please! I will only give my word if you give me yours that you will."

Her face was so near, her eyes so bright in the silvery moonlight, and her words so tempting, Harry heard himself say "I will try" before he was aware of even thinking it. She let out her breath and her face softened with relief.

Refusing to think about what he was doing, he tugged her forward. She came easily, moving into his arms without hesitation. Her arms went around him and her head nestled against his shoulder, her body fitting perfectly to his. For a moment he just held her. She was soft and warm, her hair smelled like spring flowers, and her cheek felt like the finest silk against his. Harry closed his eyes and thought he might sell his soul to stay like this with her.

But not even that bargain would suffice, not in her father's eyes, not in society's eyes, and doubtless not even in her eyes if she knew what he really was. So he gently set her back. "Good-bye."

"When, Harry?" she whispered. "When will you come again? I can't bear it, not knowing . . . "

He pushed to his feet. "I don't know."

This answer displeased her, he could tell, but she let it go. Perhaps she sensed that he was unwilling to tell her the truth—that he didn't expect her parents would ever receive him no matter what he promised her. "Why . . . " Her voice faltered. "Why did you approach me?"

Harry frowned. "What do you mean?"

"That evening at my parents' ball, when you were on the balcony and I came out for some air. And why—why did you come to see me later?"

Still frowning, he thought rapidly; how on earth was he supposed to answer?

"Was it, by any chance," she went on, her voice a little higher-pitched, "because of my family?"

The suggestion was so completely absurd, he

almost laughed. If anything, he had come in spite of her family; her father could have him sacked and thrown in prison for what he had done. But then he thought back to what she'd said that evening on the balcony, and understood. He didn't like it that she thought he might also be a greedy, status-crazed suitor, but she must have met several of them. He could hardly blame her for wondering, after he refused to tell her what he *was* doing or anything about himself. "No."

"Not at all?" There was an almost accusatory bent to the question. It reminded him again of just how far above his touch she was.

"No," he repeated sharply.

"Because it wouldn't be unusual, you know," Mariah went on, unable to stop herself. "My father is a very important man. Marrying me would be an enormous advantage to someone like you."

The instant the words left her lips, she wished them back. Her feelings had been so unsettled and so confused today, it seemed she wasn't in control of them anymore. All her bitterness at the thought of Harry being just like all the other men who wanted to marry her for her money and her family had risen up inside her again, with the echo of Joan's words running underneath—*as if he had any chance of being accepted . . . you were lucky to find him out this way* . . . When it crashed into the sudden joy when she thought she had figured it out, followed abruptly by his denial, she wasn't able to moderate her emotions or her tongue.

But she hadn't meant to blurt that out so baldly. "I didn't mean it that way," she said swiftly, but he turned away.

"No, you're correct." His voice was low but controlled. "The advantage in such a match would be entirely mine. But I assure you, never once did I think of your family when I spoke to you." He started toward the window without a backward glance.

Mariah leaped from her bed and ran after him. "I'm sorry, Harry, truly I am! I said that very badly. I never thought you were like all the other useless idiots and fops who called on me, but—" She stopped, wringing her hands as he paused with his hands braced on the sides of the window and glanced over his shoulder. "I just want to know," she said desperately, "why you would sneak into my room if you didn't even hope to court me."

For a moment he said nothing, regarding her grimly. In the moonlight he was silver and black, halfway between reality and fantasy, everything she wanted and nothing she understood. If only, if only he would *explain* . . . She thought she would be able to bear almost anything so long as he told her for certain . . .

Slowly, as if making a deliberate decision, he turned, his hands falling to his sides. "Because you are the most beautiful creature I've ever seen," he said in a dark whisper. His eyes seemed to burn into her. "Because the sound of your voice echoes in my dreams every night until I think I might go mad from it. Because I would rather see you like this, for these few stolen moments, knowing I have no hope of anything more, than not see you at all. Why? Because I can't seem to stop myself, Mariah, even though I know I should."

She felt tears gather at the back of her throat. Why oh *why* couldn't he have been somebody, anybody, proper enough for her parents to accept? Harry might not die of a broken heart, but she very well might. "How dare you," she said, her voice shaking. "How dare you come and make love to me—"

He gave a caustic huff of laughter. "You haven't the slightest idea what that means."

"I do," she burst out, unaware that her voice was rising. "I do know, and you—"

In two long steps he reached her. "Do you?" he whispered harshly, seizing her by the arms and giving her a small shake. "Do you know what I long to do to you?"

"What?" she demanded. "Torment me more? How could you *possibly* do that?"

For answer he spun her around, wrapping his arms around her to hold her against him. "I long to hold you like this every night," he said, his breath hot against her ear.

Mariah couldn't move, shocked. She could hardly believe he had grabbed her so roughly, and yet . . . that sinuous thing inside her seemed to loosen and uncoil with satisfaction as her body molded against Harry's almost unconsciously.

"I long to touch you," he told her. His fingers brushed her cheek, lightly, then trailed over her jaw and down her throat. She shivered. "I long to kiss you," he murmured. "Every inch of you." And he pressed his lips to the side of her neck, ending any chance that she might have protested.

She had never guessed a man could be so overwhelming. He seemed to envelop her completely, much taller and bigger than she had thought before. His mouth moved up her neck, setting her skin tingling and sending sparks through her entire being, and his hands moved down her body, stroking the length of her arms, the curve of her waist, and the plane of her belly. She gasped for breath. Her knees threatened to give way, and she clutched at him to keep her balance.

As if Harry knew, he pressed her against him until she could feel every solid muscled inch of him—his chest against her back, his arms around her, his thighs behind hers. She wore only her nightrail, and the fine lawn might as well not have been there for all the barrier it provided. He was hot, so hot; surely that must be why she felt as if a sudden fever had overtaken her as his hands continued to move over her in leisurely purpose, stroking that stretching, writhing creature inside her into life.

"You drive me mad," he whispered, dropping kisses all along her shoulder. With one tug of his fingers he pulled the ribbon at her neckline loose, and her nightrail drooped, sliding off her shoulder. Mariah looked down, shocked anew, and watched his fingers steal inside. If she could breathe, she would say stop, surely . . . But then she didn't breathe or speak as his hand cupped her breast, his thumb stroking over her nipple. She tried to say his name, and only managed a small, strangled gasp.

Harry laughed under his breath, a dark and wicked sound. "Do you see? Do you see now why I came back?" His hand flexed and tugged, holding her against him as he tilted his hips forward, and a disquieting burst of heat seemed to dissolve between her legs. He moved again, his breathing strained, and released his grip on her belly to draw up her nightrail.

The air felt cool on her heated skin. In some dim recess of her mind she knew she should protest, but Harry kissed her shoulder again, and so instead she whimpered, leaning more of her weight against him and not making the slightest effort to stop anything he did. This was why young ladies were warned never to be alone with a gentleman, she realized; if the young ladies knew what could happen, there would be a dozen new scandals every week.

And then—oh heavens—his fingers brushed her thigh, his palm smoothing over her skin. She arched her back, gripping the arm that circled her waist and digging her toes into the carpet to push against his touch as his fingers dipped tantalizingly between her thighs. The blood rushed to her skin, and the feverish heat ran down her belly. The lustful creature within her purred and surged against the inside of her skin. Her head fell back against his shoulder in abject surrender, her knees fell apart, and he stroked one long finger through the soft folds between her legs.

He pressed his lips just below her ear. "I want you to burn for me," he murmured as he stroked her again and again.

"I do," she moaned, shamelessly abandoning all pretense of modesty or outrage. No one else had ever touched her there—and she herself had only done so a few, furtive times—but already he had brought forth that hot dampness between her legs, the dark illicit hunger that was almost frightening. Her blood hammered through her veins, burning with longing. She didn't know quite what to make of that yawning ache inside her, nor what to do about it, but she was desperate for Harry to show her.

"No," he said. "Not yet." His hand shifted, turned, and then—she made a choked sound of shock—he pushed his fingers inside her body, without stopping the maddening, marvelous stroking on that one exquisitely sensitive spot. And it felt even more excruciatingly good.

"What—What else?" Her voice was a breathless quaver.

He only laughed quietly in reply, nuzzling aside her braid to lick the back of her neck. His mouth moved along the back of her neck, over her shoulders, nipping at her skin. His fingers began a hard, pulsing slide in and out of her. His other hand still played with her breast, rolling her nipple between his thumb and forefinger. Mariah felt light-headed as her hips jerked and her spine undulated in time with his wicked fingers. Her heart beat as though it would leap out of her chest. She tried to pull away from him, wanting to catch her breath and clear her head of the sensation of drowning, but he refused to let her go, yanking her back against him and pressing his cheek to hers.

"Do you feel it yet?" he whispered as his fingers seemed to delve deeper and deeper within her. "That burning craving inside you that threatens to drive you mad? Tempts you to throw aside every propriety, every modicum of sense and restraint because you can't *not* risk it? Because you would give everything you have for the chance to find what comes next?"

"Yes—no," she whimpered. A blistering tautness was spreading through her belly, agonizing in its intensity. Tears sprang to her eyes. "I can't bear it, Harry . . . "

"You can." His breath was ragged. "Let yourself . . . "

"No—yes—oh!" Abruptly, she stiffened. The taut-ness strained and then broke, and her entire body con-vulsed about his fingers. A moment of shimmering, sparkling darkness engulfed her and she cried out against the hand Harry clapped over her mouth at the last second.

Mariah sagged in his arms. If he hadn't held her, she would have slid to the floor in a helpless puddle. She would swear her heart had almost stopped for a moment. Never in her life had she felt anything like that. This is but a dream, she told herself numbly; it cannot be real . . . She clutched at Harry's arms, still tight around her, his strength all that held her up. "Oh," she moaned, rubbing her cheek against his shoulder. She couldn't think coherently enough to ask anything beyond one all-important question. "When will you come again to me?"

Harry pressed his lips to the bared side of her throat and tasted the sweet saltiness of her skin, flushed and damp with the aftermath of her climax. He gathered her closer in his trembling arms, one hand falling nat-urally around her breast and the other still cupping the soft, wet curls between her legs. Her passionate whimpers echoed in his ears and made him painfully hard. The way she had come to life in his arms would torment him for the rest of his life. Slowly, he rocked his hips, pushing his straining erection against the curve of her bottom, just once, just to punish himself a little more. He breathed deeply of her soft lavender scent and felt his heart twist with agony and longing, a pain even deeper than his physical torment. He was a fool twice damned now, and so he told her the truth: "I can't."

Chapter 14

Still reeling from what he had done to her body, Mariah wasn't capable of arguing when he scooped her into his arms and carried her to her bed, tucked her gently under the coverlet, and left with only a light kiss on her temple. Alone in bed, she curled her arms around herself and closed her eyes, letting every moment of his visit unfold again in her mind.

He wasn't a gentleman. She supposed she had known that all along but hadn't wanted to think it. All the times he'd asked her if his name mattered, if his appearance mattered, she had said no. Had she lied? To whom? Certainly to him, although she suspected Harry hadn't been fooled. But she . . . Ah, that was a different matter. She had never quite faced the fact so plainly: Harry was not what he appeared to be, no matter which appearance he gave. She was as much in the dark about his true self as she ever had been.

But he wanted her as a man wanted a woman. Mariah inhaled deeply, stroking one hand over her breast, down to her belly, as the echoes of Harry's touch shimmered across her skin. He had made her burn, made her ache, and then thrown her into a pleasure she never suspected existed. She knew he had not found a comparable pleasure from that lovemaking. Joan once stole a book of naughty poetry from her brother, and Mariah had giggled with her over the rhymes that said a man found his greatest pleasure when his—she blushed just thinking the word—his cock was inside a woman. She blushed again; Harry had only put his fingers inside her, and wicked creature that she was becoming, she wanted him to do it again. Perhaps even—she slid deeper under the covers—perhaps even his cock. If he could affect her so much with just his fingers, what would it be like with more? And now that he had pleasured her so thoroughly she couldn't stand upright, she felt the most wicked desire to do the same to him, to leave him shattered and breathless and utterly enthralled.

The only question left was . . . what mattered to her? His lack of status? His secrecy and vagueness? Or the way he kissed her and held her and made her laugh? Mariah squeezed her eyes closed and tried to summon his face to mind. She had seen him, after all, as clear as day at the Plymptons' and the moon had been full tonight . . . and yet, no matter how hard she tried to recall his image, what she remembered was the face she touched in the darkness.

A lone tear leaked from the corner of her eye. She had been deceived, but very willingly so. If only it could have continued.

The sparkle went out of the Season for her from that night onward. She hoped, at first, that Harry hadn't meant it when he said he wouldn't come back, but he was true to his word and didn't appear in her bedroom window again. Joan, blessedly, didn't mention his name again, either, and if she could have just blotted that last night from her mind, she might have been able to cling to her sense of betrayal and disappointment and dismiss him as a presumptive liar who fooled her for a time. Instead she left her lamp burning every night and slept with her window open even when it rained and the night air swept through her room, cold and pitiless.

She tried to carry on. Two other gentlemen approached her father about courting her, and she refused them both. She went with her parents to all the usual balls and parties, and out of habit danced with the gentlemen who asked her. Nothing worked. Day after day she found herself distracted and out of sorts, unable to pay attention to anyone or anything. And every time she saw Lord Crane, she had to restrain herself from bursting out and asking after his secretary.

That part puzzled her more than anything. Harry hadn't answered her when she asked why he attended her parents' ball; he just said he had a good reason. What could it be? And might it possibly recur? He had once seen her at the Spencers' ball, so he was out among the ton at nights. Might he be here tonight at Lady Arnold's soiree? He said it was an honorable reason that took him into society, and she wanted to believe him. She just couldn't think what it could be.

It meant she had to trust him, even as she knew he was keeping things from her. But in return he was trusting her. If she were to tell her parents about him, her father would set out to find Harry and expose all his secrets, if not do worse. She and Harry were bound together in their private little world, each relying on the other to be honorable—and discreet.

Something caught at Mariah's attention. She lifted her head, glancing around and realizing she'd been sunk in her own thoughts for some time. Her last partner had left her side and she hadn't even noticed. She was standing by herself on the edge of the room, staring blindly at the couples dancing. But something had routed her out of her reverie. What was it? She couldn't even say, and now her thread of thought was gone. She bit her lip and turned to look for her mother, wondering if she could persuade her parents to allow her to return home early yet again.

" . . . careful . . . more than . . . "

Her eyes widened as it sank in. Harry's voice, quiet and low. *Here.* Just behind her, somewhere in the crowd. She whirled around, scanning the faces, looking for the speaker. Where was he?

" . . . watch . . . not again . . . "

Without thinking she began crowding through the guests, not even bothering to murmur excuses. He was here—somewhere—if only everyone else would be quiet for just one moment—

A hundred voices seemed to rise and swell around her, laughing, talking, almost shouting. Still she strained her ears, listening for any hint of that maddeningly familiar voice. She batted her way past the drooping plumes in a lady's headdress, squeezed past a rotund little man roaring with laughter—she hated him for being so loud—and went up on her tiptoes, trying to see, straining for just a glimpse of his dark head, his wide shoulders. She didn't know why she was looking but she couldn't help it.

She stopped, overwhelmed. The dozens of conversations around her beat at her ears, each drowning out all the others. She listened as hard as she could, and heard nothing. Helplessly, she turned in a circle, still on her toes, searching in vain. Where was the blasted man? Was he even truly here? Or was she simply going mad and imagining his voice everywhere?

"Lady Mariah."

She turned to see Tobias Crane looking immensely pleased to see her. He bowed, forcing her to curtsey, albeit reluctantly. "What a pleasure to see you again," he said.

"Thank you, sir," she murmured, trying to glance around under her eyelashes. Harry was probably on the other side of the room by now, while she was stuck with the prosy Mr. Crane.

"Might I beg the honor of a dance this evening?"

"Er—yes. I should be delighted." She handed him her dance card without another word. There was nothing else she could do, and she didn't care whom she danced with anyway.

He marked her card and gave it back, then stood there beaming at her. Mariah kept back a sigh as he asked, "May I offer you my arm? You seem unsettled."

"No, no. I am fine. I—I was looking for my mother." It wasn't the most inspired reply, but it would have to do. "Do you see her, sir?"

His face fell with disappointment, but he obligingly lifted his head and searched the room. "Ah, yes, I do. She is near the doors."

When he offered his arm, she gave in and took it. He escorted her through the room, a very stately progress, and more than once he stopped to greet someone, making a point to present her. Mariah was left with the unmistakable feeling that she was on display, which only made her more desperate to be away from him. Mr. Crane was polite enough, but he was behaving as though he had accomplished something merely by offering her his arm, as if this promenade across a crowded ballroom indicated an attachment. She thought again of Harry diving off a balcony so he wouldn't be seen with her. Why couldn't it be Mr. Crane who fled from her, and Harry who would storm across the room to reach her, instead of the other way around?

Something occurred to her then. Perhaps there was something to be gained after all. "Mr. Crane," she said. "How is your uncle?"

He glanced at her in pleased surprise. "Very well, Lady Mariah, thank you. Shall I give him your regards?"

"Yes, of course," she murmured. "I was thinking of his secretary, whom I encountered at the Plymptons' garden breakfast the other day. Do you remember, sir?"

"Every moment." He smiled meaningfully. "Although I was very sorry to find you had left early. I had hoped we might take a turn in Lady Plympton's tulip garden. It is reputed to be the finest in Mayfair, and—"

"Yes. But your uncle's secretary," she persisted. "He reminded me very strongly of someone I know. Perhaps it is a relation of his. What was his name?"

Mr. Crane did not appear terribly pleased anymore. "Henry Towne is his name," he said stiffly. "I know nothing about him, Lady Mariah, except that he is a competent fellow. Keeps my uncle bumping along well enough, as any good servant ought."

Henry Towne. She wondered if that were his real name. "Has he been employed long with your uncle?"

"No, perhaps a month or two. Uncle has always insisted on being self-reliant, and only this Season when I came to town could I prevail upon him to hire someone . . . "

Mariah didn't hear the rest of his reply. Only a month. Then Mr. Crane would know nothing of real import. Fortunately they had reached her mother. "Thank you, Mr. Crane." She curtsied.

"It was my pleasure, Lady Mariah." He bowed again, leaning close with a private smile. "Until our dance."

Mariah clenched her teeth and smiled. "Of course."

Mr. Crane beamed and bowed some more, to her mother and then to Lady Arnold, who was standing nearby. Finally he had no reason to linger and excused himself.

Mama raised her fan and inclined her head toward Mariah. "A change of heart regarding Mr. Crane?"

"Not at all," she whispered back, her eyes flitting about the room without thinking. She had been so sure it was Harry's voice she heard earlier. No doubt it would be merely another disappointment, but she still wished she could have known for certain. "He came upon me as I was looking for you."

Her mother turned away from Lady Arnold and drew Mariah closer. "Dearest, what is wrong? You can hardly hold still tonight. I can see you aren't attending to the gentlemen you dance with, and you always seem to be glancing over your shoulder. Is something troubling you?"

The concern in her mother's voice made Mariah's face grow hot. She should have known Mama would notice. "I—I don't know," she confessed. "I feel as though I am missing something, something important."

"Mariah, it is all here in front of you. You must look around and see it, and let yourself enjoy it."

Mariah sighed. "I know." And she did. It was just easier said than done.

Enough, she told herself. She would banish Harry from her mind, at least for tonight. She would stop trying to discover him in every man who walked past, and she would stop listening for his voice. If only she hadn't thought she overheard him earlier, she might have been able to enjoy this evening. She was ruining her entire Season by brooding on him so much. For tonight, at least, she would pretend she had never crossed paths with her mystery man. Even if she had to go sit in a quiet corner somewhere.

The Arnold soiree was a difficult test of Harry's fortitude.

As expected, Mariah was there, stunningly beautiful in a green gown with silver lace that framed her bosom like a setting for a rare jewel. As expected, she danced with a number of gentlemen, each of whom carried her hand to his lips and smiled at her and held her close enough to know the smell of her skin. Harry hated them all, for having what he could not, and he hated that he had to be here to witness it.

He tried to focus on his duties. Ian slipped around to one of the windows and warned him of some grim-looking guests just arriving, who turned out to be an austere Whig politician and his sons. That threat ruled out, Harry forced himself through the motions of monitoring Lord Crane and the Earl of Doncaster. But he couldn't be social, not tonight when his heart swelled with bitter longing every time he saw Mariah, so he found a chair with a good view and stayed slumped in it for most of the evening, ruminating on his well-deserved sufferings.

To his shock, Mariah herself came walking toward him after the second waltz. Harry tensed, bracing himself, but she wasn't looking at him. She took a seat near him with only a distracted nod in his direction. Hard on the heels of his relief that she hadn't recognized him came a fierce satisfaction. He was near her again, almost near enough to touch her. Of course, to her he looked tipsy, slightly unkempt, and old enough to be her grandfather. Only a fool, or someone driven mad by desperation, would be glad to see her now.

Harry, though, was a little of both. It had been almost a week since he made his vow to stay away from her, and although he wasn't about to break that vow, he hadn't enjoyed a minute of it. He had gone through his duties with a grim efficiency, and then gone to his bed every night and dreamed of what he was missing. But this was beyond his control. He was sitting here minding his duty, and she simply appeared next to him. Perhaps it was a gift from heaven, or a temptation from the devil, but he didn't care.

"Tired of the dancing, are ye, miss?"

She glanced at him, startled. "No, sir, not at all."

He persisted, leaning toward her on his cane. "Aye, well, their loss."

She exhaled slowly and turned a polite smile on him. "How kind of you to say so."

"It was my pleasure to say so," he retorted with a

leering wink. "Never say Henry Wroth can't tell the prettiest gel in the room."

"You are too generous, sir," she said. Her eyes drifted back to the dancers.

Lord Wroth chuckled; deep inside, Harry laughed recklessly. The longer he played at being an elderly rogue, the more it felt as though the old man became a sort of second skin. "I'm feeling generous, not that my compliments are ever accused of being so. But since I am so fortunate to find myself sitting next to you, I'll not keep my own counsel tonight."

The glance she gave him was half amused, half perplexed, as if she didn't know what to say and would rather not have to converse with him at all. "What a rogue you are, sir."

You don't know the half of it, he thought, and cackled again. "There's not much else left in life for me to be! Better a rogue than dead. But I can see you've a preference for younger company." He got to his feet, making a show of his supposed infirmities. This might be the last time he ever spoke to her, and he couldn't say a word of farewell. "I'll leave you to these young gents—although mind you choose wisely, for there's many a young rogue dancing there now!"

Mariah stared at the strange old man in fascination. He was an uncommon character, no question, but there was also something about him that seemed somehow familiar. He bowed, leaning heavily on his cane. "Good-bye, my lady. It has been my pleasure."

She bobbed her head, murmuring something polite in reply. He shuffled off, skirting the crowd, and she watched him for a moment, puzzled. What was familiar about him? And why had he said good-bye instead of merely good night?

Then she mentally shrugged it off. It must be her imagination. It had certainly played enough tricks on her tonight. She turned back to watching the dancers, catching one more glimpse of old Lord Wroth several minutes later. He was standing in profile to her, speaking to someone she couldn't see. Again her eyes lingered on the curious fellow. He was an odd one, to be sure.

Then he lifted his head and laughed.

Mariah looked, and looked again. It was impossible, and yet . . . She gasped out loud. She could swear she'd seen that profile before.

In moonlight.

Chapter 15

The notion that Harry might be related to Lord Wroth bothered her well into the next day. It was surely impossible, and yet there was just something, a nebulous, indefinable something, that refused to let the thought die. It was absurd, of course. She already knew Harry was Lord Crane's secretary. She was imagining things. Lord Wroth was just an old roué who delighted in shocking young ladies, just as Harry always managed to catch her off guard, and that similarity was putting ideas into her head.

Perhaps he was a distant relation. That thought was rather pleasing, to tell the truth. Lord Wroth wasn't the most acceptable gentleman in town, but he was a . . . Mariah wasn't certain. A baron, most likely. Perhaps a viscount. He might be Scottish, or Irish even, which didn't help much but at least he was a titled Scot. Or Irishman. She would have to look up Lord Wroth in the peerage. Any sort of title in the family would help, even if Harry weren't to inherit it himself.

She made her way to the library the next morning to check. Excitement made her steps quicken, not only at the idea that she might finally learn something about him, but at the hope that he might have any connection of consequence. She turned the corner, trying to think where she would find a copy of the peerage, and almost bumped into her father.

"Good morning, Papa."

"Good morning, Mariah." He laid his hands on her shoulders and kissed her forehead. Then he stepped back and studied her face. "You're up and about early today."

She was dying of curiosity and hadn't been able to sleep another minute. "It's such a lovely day, who could stay abed?"

He laughed. "Who? Why, you, miss, many days! I've had luncheon before I've seen you the day after a ball."

"Papa," she said severely. "Mama will not like you teasing me about that."

"No doubt." His eyes gleaming with mischief, Papa lowered his voice. "Would you care to accompany me, since you are awake so early, Lady Mariah?"

Having her father's undivided attention was a rare treat, so great it diverted her from her quest. "Where are you going?"

"I've a petition to deliver to Hastings, and thought to walk. It's barely a mile."

Mariah debated less than a moment. The peerage would still be in the library when she returned, and it had been a while since she walked with her father. He was so busy, especially since their return to London. "Of course I shall walk with you."

They set off a short time later. Papa laid his hand over hers, nestled in the crook of his arm. "Are you still enjoying London?"

She thought of Harry, with his visits that made

her blood run hot and fast, and his infuriating lack of openness and possible unsuitability, which made her mind burn with intrigue. She sighed half in dismay, half in pleasure. "Yes, although I shall also be glad for the quiet of Doncaster again. It seems an eternity since we've been home."

Her father nodded, seemingly gratified by her words. "I miss it, too. I knew it would be a great imposition on you and on your mother to go along on my travels—"

"No," Mariah protested.

"Nonsense," he said firmly. "Of course it was. If you both hadn't been such hardy creatures, it might have been disastrous. I would never have forgiven myself if either of you had come to harm on our journeys."

"Neither of us would have willingly stayed behind."

"No, but I am glad to have you safely home all the same." He patted her hand. "Although it seems I have only postponed the inevitable. I foresee that I shall lose you very soon."

Mariah smiled nervously. "Oh, perhaps not . . . "

Papa snorted. "How many men have I refused, Mariah? You have had your choice of the finest men in England, and just because one has not suited you yet does not mean one won't, all too soon."

She wasn't sure what to say to that. They walked in silence for a moment. "Papa," she began, choosing each word with care, "whom do you think I should marry?"

His eyebrows went up. "Ah. You have never asked my opinion before."

"Now I am." And it wasn't something she did lightly. She knew he would be livid if he discovered her scandalous behavior with Harry, and she was quite certain he wouldn't approve of Harry's actions in the least. Papa was likely to name some other man, perhaps even one of the ones she had rejected, and then she didn't know what she would do. Her father was a very perceptive man, and he knew the gentlemen of London much better than she possibly could. Her father was, after all, a man; and who better to judge other men than the man who had loved her best all her life? If he named a man she had already met and dismissed, she would have to consider the chance that she'd made a mistake.

"I think you should marry a man who deserves you," he replied after a moment. "You are not like many other young ladies. Your mother and I have always taken great pride in your poise and insight, your charm and your intelligence. You . . . I fear you would be wasted on a country squire, Mariah, or even a placid duke. You, I think, need a man who will rely on you, who will respect you and appreciate your talents, who will interest you and excite your respect in return."

"Do you think any of the men who have approached you fit those requirements, Papa?"

He thought for several minutes as they crossed the park. Riders cantered along the path across the rolling grass. It was quiet in the park at this hour, almost like being in the country.

"No," he said at last, and he sounded regretful and relieved at the same time. "I cannot say I do."

Mariah breathed a sigh of relief.

"Perhaps I am too indulgent," her father said with a wry smile. "I cannot think of anyone I would like to give you to. He will have to be a rare man, my dear."

She thought of Harry and forced a smile. He was a rare man, but perhaps not in the way her father intended. She wondered just what would happen when the two came face-to-face. She couldn't see Harry being intimidated by her father, and yet, everyone else was.

They reached Viscount Hastings's home and were offered tea. Hastings was a jovial gentleman, a bit single-minded but in a charming way. Mariah poured the tea and listened with half an ear as her father and Lord Hastings argued good-naturedly over the petition Papa had brought. She was used to this. She had been privy to more political discussions than she could remember, so many that she'd always assumed she would marry a man in politics, just because she couldn't imagine life without debates over the Corn Laws or Catholic emancipation. She didn't find it tiring, although not all of it was engrossing. What would she discuss, she wondered, with the man she eventually married?

She was still thinking about it, trying to form a picture of her future, when they left. Papa was quiet, no doubt pondering the petition or perhaps Lord Hastings's arguments. Mariah walked beside him and felt for the first time a bit of melancholy for her waning girlhood. She could feel it fading away, and while she looked forward to what life would bring, it was moments like this when she liked being a girl still, able to walk with her father.

"Mariah, I see Silton approaching," Papa said then. "I believe he wants a word. Do you mind waiting, or should I put him off?"

"No, I don't mind. I shall walk down to the lake and back." She smiled and strolled off as Lord Silton strode up, doffing his hat to her.

She wandered slowly down the path toward the water, her thoughts returning to the question of Harry and Lord Wroth. Harry had already told her he was not the younger son of an earl or other nobleman, but he might still have connections to a good family. He must have some level of respectability to obtain his post as Crane's secretary. Wroth was a kind old man, she told herself, and seemed fond of her the other night. Perhaps if she could discover a link between him and Harry, she could implore him to recognize Harry as his cousin or nephew, and he would. It would help so much if she knew Harry's last name, she thought in frustration.

Just as she was growing impatient to return home and look up Lord Wroth, who but the man himself should come limping around a clump of shrubbery. Mariah stopped and gasped out loud.

Lord Wroth looked up and started, then clapped a hand to his chest. "Eh, goodness there, young miss. I might have run you down."

The thought that an old man with a cane might run her down made Mariah bite her lip to keep from smiling. She ducked her head and curtsied as all her questions and hopes flooded back. "Good morning, Lord Wroth. We met last night."

He frowned, peering closer at her. "Oh, yes, so we did, much to my pleasure. Good morning, Lady Mariah. How do you fare this fine day?"

"Very well, sir." Mariah studied his face as intently as she dared. "I am walking with my father."

"What, what?" He tilted his head as if he couldn't hear her.

"My father," she repeated. And then the question burst out before she could stop herself. "Sir, I cannot help but think I know a relation of yours. He reminds me of you so strongly—"

"I am sorry to say, you are likely mistaken," he said sadly. "All my family are dead. My wife and sons fell to the consumption, years ago . . . 'Tis a sad thing to find oneself alone at the end of life, my dear."

"Of course," she said quickly, wishing she hadn't said anything. He did look somewhat like Harry, but it might be coincidence, or even just her imagination. It was hard to say now, while Lord Wroth's face sagged into lines of sorrow and his gray hair fell around his temples.

Lord Wroth coughed and groped in his pocket, drawing out a large handkerchief to blot his face. "How kind you are. I miss them still . . . "

"Mariah, are you ready to return home?" Papa had come up behind her.

Lord Wroth's eyes moved past her to her father. "Good day, sir. And to you, my lady." He glanced at her again, a sad, polite smile on his mouth, and bowed, his head cocked slightly to one side.

Mariah's eyes widened as some faint memory caught and held, of Harry bidding her good-night before slipping out the window, only visible in silhouette, his head dipping just a little to one side. Her mind whirled. Harry wasn't a relation of Lord Wroth's. No, indeed—Harry *was* Lord Wroth. It was all a disguise.

Before Lord Wroth could move more than a step away, she leaped forward and latched onto his arm. He started, but kept them both upright even though she had all but jumped on him.

"A moment more, Papa," she said, frantically searching Lord Wroth's face, now very close to her own. It was spectacularly unlined for a man of his age. And his eyes—his *hazel* eyes—so sharp yet so opaque behind his spectacles. Her fingers tightened convulsively on his arm—not the bony, frail arm of an elderly gentleman, but the firm, well-muscled arm of a young man who could scale ivy-clad walls at midnight. "Lord Wroth has asked permission to call on me," she blurted out. That strong arm tensed under her grip. "And I have consented."

For a moment there was a shocked silence. Mariah dared a glance over her shoulder to see her father staring at her with his mouth all but hanging open. Lord Wroth—Harry—was as still as stone. Then he gave a wheezing laugh.

"Good gracious, gel, such a start you gave my old heart. What a thought! An old scoundrel like me paying court to a young lady like yourself!" He patted her hand rather condescendingly, then turned to her father. "No insult intended, good sir. It was a momentary breath of youth again, speaking to such a lovely child, but of course I'm much too old for her."

"None taken, sir," her father said in a strangled tone. "Mariah, do come here."

Mariah refused to let go of Wroth's arm. "But you did say you enjoyed speaking with me, sir, and I would very much like you to call! Please say you will come."

He chuckled again, his eyes flickering toward her father. "That is very kind of you, Lady Mariah, but I would not wish to impose. Every young man in London will wish my *other* foot in the grave if I should take up your time."

In desperation, Mariah turned to her father, beyond caring what he thought of her sanity. She was holding onto Harry's arm—she was sure she was—and she would not let go until he agreed to call on her. "It wouldn't be improper, would it, Papa?"

Of course he couldn't possibly say no. With a very strange expression the earl inclined his head. "We would be delighted, Wroth."

For a moment Lord Wroth didn't move. Then he coughed. "It would be my honor." He eased his arm out of Mariah's grasp. "Good day to you, sir, Lady Mariah. Until another day." He bowed again, gingerly, creakily, like an old man, and hobbled off, leaning on his cane. Mariah watched him closely, looking for any trace of youth in his departing figure. She could see none. A shadow of doubt clouded her mind. She was still sure she was right—probably—although if not, she had just made a spectacular fool of herself.

"Mariah?" Her father took her chin in his hand and tilted her face up to his. "Are you well, child? I've never seen you so . . . " He frowned in worry. "So overset."

She managed a smile. "Perhaps I am a little light-headed. The sun is very bright."

"Let us return home then." He tucked her hand securely around his arm and led her slowly back in the direction of Doncaster House. "You startled Lord Wroth by your declaration."

I'll wager I did, she thought in silent satisfaction. If she were right, she had just seen through a disguise that had all of London fooled. But why? Why would a young man masquerade as an old one? Was he a spy after all? For whom? And why on earth was he posing as an old man and working as a secretary?

But that was how he had attended their ball, as Lord Wroth. She remembered an old-fashioned gentleman's shoe, the sort of shoe an old man would wear, the sort of shoe that would pinch a young man's foot. That was how he had avoided her notice that evening, and every evening since; she had been looking for a young man, and like everyone else, completely overlooked the elderly man. He had thoroughly taken in everyone in society.

Not that she would give him away. She would be as silent as the grave, to show that he could trust her. But she would still do everything possible to see him. Perhaps a secretary couldn't call on her, but Lord Wroth certainly could—provided her parents didn't prohibit it. "He really is quite amusing, Papa, when he wants to be. I suspect he believes people are entertained by the crusty old tartar he usually projects—"

"Projects?" Her father frowned again. "Mariah, you must not believe you know the man better than anyone else, when you have only spoken to him a few times. Why, Lord Wroth is old enough to be your grandfather! Who knows what he is really like?"

"Do you know him, Papa?"

His mouth closed into a thin line. "No."

"But he was invited to our ball last month," she said innocently. "I remember seeing him."

His eyes remained straight ahead. "An invitation does not imply a close acquaintance."

"Oh. Perhaps we will become better acquainted when he calls."

Her father stopped and turned to face her. "I am not pleased that you accused Lord Wroth of wanting to pay his addresses to you. It was not well done of him to suggest such a thing, and it was even more ill-mannered of you to respond to it."

"But he's far more interesting than any of the men who call on me every day to sit and stare, not just at me but at the furnishings and the art and the china," she burst out. "Papa, everyone sees me as just an object, something rich and worthy of trying to get, but not because they care about me. Why may I not have at least one caller who listens to what I say and even gives credence to it?"

"I did not say you may not receive him," countered her father, looking more and more annoyed. "But he is not a harmless old man, Mariah. Young ladies your age have married old men before, and if that is in his mind, you must know I will *never* allow it."

Momentarily forgetting that he had no reason to suspect Lord Wroth was other than he appeared, she gasped. "Not even if I wish it?"

"No," he said with grim finality. "Not even then." Mariah could only gape at him. Her father took a firm grip on her arm and led her home without another word.

Harry let himself into the Fenton Lane house, gasping for air. His lungs burned as if he'd run from the park instead of walking doggedly along in Wroth's shuffling gait. Damn it! Why did he have to see her there? And what on earth was she thinking, to force him to call on her? He threw down his walking stick and stripped off the suffocating coat. With an oath, he pulled the cravat from his neck and kicked off the terrible shoes. He hated Wroth now, hated the old man he must don like a second skin. He faced the terrible likelihood that Mariah had seen right through him. And he'd thought he was safe from her, after extracting her promise!

And now what was he to do? He'd just given his word to the Earl of Doncaster that he would call on them. Stafford would throw him in Newgate. How was he to get out of this mess?

He let his head fall back against the door with a sharp crack, welcoming the spike of pain. The pain was good. It might prod his brain to produce a solution to the problem, a problem he knew all too well was entirely his creation. He never should have spoken to her in the first place. He certainly shouldn't have dared to slip into her bedroom and talk to her not once, but night after night. And he ought to be drawn and quartered for almost making love to her.

The hard wall at his back was beginning to feel too comfortable. His head might as well have been stuffed with wool. He had crept too far out on the limb, and now felt it begin to give way beneath his feet. Unfortunately, if he came crashing down, everyone else would come with him.

He gathered up his discarded clothing and trudged up the stairs to his room. He only had a short time to change back into Mr. Towne after shadowing Lord Crane to a botanical lecture in Wroth's clothing. If Ian hadn't been occupied driving Angelique, he would have gone in the carriage and not even had the choice of walking home through the park. And he'd walked because it was a fine day, and knew he would spend the rest of it closed up in Crane's study. Cursed sunshine, he thought as he jerked his shirt off and hung his head.

Harry pressed his fists to his forehead. "Bloody hell," he whispered. It seemed his sins were catching up to him at last.

Chapter 16

Three days later Harry had his half day free from Lord Crane's employ. After a minor quarrel with himself, he put on Wroth's clothing and powder, muttered something to Lisette about reconnaissance around town, and headed out. All too soon he found himself on the doorstep of Doncaster House, his heart thumping and his palms damp. He felt exposed and out of place on the steps, and glanced nervously about; if he were seen by anyone in Stafford's employ, he'd be sacked before supper. But if he didn't call on Mariah, who knew what she would do when next they met? Pushing his spectacles back on his nose one last time, he rang the bell and stepped back to wait, hoping she would be out and praying she would be home.

His prayers, and not his hopes, were answered when the butler returned very quickly after bearing away his card, to usher him into the drawing room. As he followed the man, he rehearsed what he would say to her. In the space of a scant half hour, he had to be boring, unfashionable, and dull-witted, everything that would dissuade her from seeking him out again, and cast every possible doubt on her suspicion that

Lord Wroth and Henry Towne were even remotely related. Then he would excuse himself and totter off before he made another critical lapse in judgment, something he seemed very prone to doing in Mariah's presence.

The butler opened the door before him. Harry gripped his cane. "Lord Wroth," the butler intoned, stepping aside, leaving him no choice but to enter the room. He shuffled forward, keeping his eyes firmly on the countess, a tall handsome woman whose serene smile hid any surprise or displeasure she might feel at his appearance. Harry murmured a reply to her greeting, hunkering into a shaky bow. He took advantage of the respite to draw a deep breath, gathering himself, bracing himself—

"Lord Wroth." She curtsied. "How splendid to see you again." And his heart all but stopped in his chest at how beautiful she was in sunlight, her hair gleaming like polished ebony and her gray eyes as fresh and clear as dawn. For a moment all he could do was stare, blissfully, helplessly, idiotically besotted.

"The pleasure is mine," he heard himself say.

Mariah beamed. "Do come in." She extended a hand toward the seat nearest her own. Harry hesitated a split second, then shuffled over to it. "I am so glad you've called," Mariah went on as soon as they were seated.

"Well, it was very kind of you to receive me." Harry gave a wheezy chuckle. "Very flattering, it is, to be welcomed by such lovely ladies."

"How good of you to say so, sir." The countess smiled. "Mariah has told me of your kindness to her in the park."

"Oh, it was a trifling matter—" he began, but Mariah interrupted.

"To me it was not trifling at all! I must thank you, sir."

Harry smiled uneasily. He had already lost control of the situation. "Eh, well, all the better! Not every day I can please a lady without so much as a spot of trouble to myself." That came out less politely than he had intended, but it couldn't be helped.

"Would you care for some tea?" asked the countess.

He nodded, resting his hands on the cane, propped beside his knee. Tea would be wonderful; he could hold the cup and stir the tea and have something to look at besides Mariah.

No sooner had the countess handed him his cup than two other callers were announced, and they all rose. Harry nodded his greetings, noting the covertly assessing looks the two newcomers gave him, as if wondering just what his business was here. He told himself he was glad to see them, for they would draw attention from him until he could manage to leave. He told himself that as he sipped his tea and watched both Lord Carteret and Lord Whitting maneuver for Mariah's attention and her mother's approval. Neither was having great success, he thought, if only because Mariah kept trying to draw him into conversation and her mother kept trying to divert her from him. Finally the countess seemed to have had enough and spoke to him directly.

"You hail from Scotland, I believe, Lord Wroth? The Lowlands?" She looked at him with determined eyes.

Harry sensed more than saw Mariah perk up her

ears, as if he might accidentally reveal something. Of course, everything he was about to say was a lie, fabricated by Stafford to mesh with the true, long-dead, Wroth family. "Yes, yes, fine and lovely Scotland," he answered. "I miss it more each day."

"Indeed," she replied. "I often miss our home near York."

"Ah, that is understandable, madam. True comfort cannot be achieved anywhere but at one's own hearth and home."

"Every time I have had the pleasure of visiting the Lowlands, I have remarked on the excellent gardens."

Harry barely kept from laughing. She'd done him a favor, in some sense; a neutral topic he could discuss at great length, if not with great enthusiasm, thanks to Lord Crane. "'Tis the most beautiful place on earth," he said, ruthlessly launching into a long-winded discussion of horticulture and botany designed to bore everyone within earshot. Thus far he had managed to avoid any attempts by Mariah to draw him apart, and with two other gentlemen insulating him now, he felt confident in his ability to prose on and on until he could conclude his call.

The countess smiled, pleased to be bored so long as she held his entire attention. Mariah now had no choice but to turn to the other gentlemen or risk being appallingly rude.

The next quarter hour seemed to last half the day. By the time Harry's mental clock chimed that he had stayed long enough and could make his escape, he half expected to see the sun setting out the tall windows. "Eh, I must take my leave, Lady Doncaster, Lady Mariah," he said, reaching for his cane. "It has been a rare pleasure, indeed."

Mariah almost leaped from her chair. She'd been waiting all this time, and now he was about to leave before she had spoken more than ten words to him. She couldn't let him go before she discovered if she'd been right—or wrong—about his real identity. "Oh, no! But you've only just arrived, sir!" There was a silence as everyone except Lord Wroth looked at her. He seemed absorbed in finding the perfect spot on the floor to place his cane. "Perhaps you would care to see some of my father's collection," Mariah said, trying to sound calm when her heart was beating furiously. Every moment of his visit had been agony for her as she waited for an opening to suggest a stroll in the garden, a viewing of the gallery, anything to get a moment alone with him. She was barely even aware of Lord Whitting's and Lord Carteret's presence anymore.

Slowly, Lord Wroth turned to her, his hazel eyes keen over those dreadful spectacles. "What's that? What's he collect?"

"Why—Why, many things," she blurted, suddenly forgetting what was in the gallery. It was amazing, how he made her wits go wandering so easily.

"My husband has a fine collection of antique arms," provided her mother, with a veiled stern glance. Mariah knew she was running on like a blathering idiot, and would have to account for it later, but that was *later*. He was sitting here now, and Mama had wasted nearly his entire visit asking about plants!

Lord Wroth nodded his shaggy gray head. "Now that's—"

"Perhaps you would like to see the garden, then," Mariah said. "The laurels, and the ivy"—she cringed; not the ivy!—"and the roses."

He shifted in his chair. "A very kind offer, indeed. However . . . "

He was trying to leave. "But you must at least see the Reynolds portrait of my grandmother. I recall you mentioned a fondness for his art," she lied in desperation.

This time Lord Wroth seemed caught. He hesitated, his gaze shifting back to her mother.

"By all means, sir. It is a fine portrait," her mother said with a gracious smile that didn't fool Mariah at all. Mama would never correct her in front of others, but Mariah knew she would have her ears blistered later. *Later.*

Slowly, Lord Wroth turned back to her, his expression almost grim. "Thank you, Lady Mariah," he said. "That would be very kind."

The walk to the gallery had never seemed so long. Mariah was acutely aware of every scrape of his cane on the floor, every labored breath he exhaled. He was such a good actor, she could see why all of London believed wholeheartedly in his masquerade. But why? The unknown reason hammered away at her; she had to know. After an eternity of walking, they passed through the wide double doors of the gallery where portraits of her ancestors hung. Mariah managed to give the door a little push behind her so it swung slowly closed but did not latch. For the first time in hours, it seemed, she let out her breath, alone with him at last.

"Where is this Reynolds?" He peered around the room, his humped back seeming more pronounced. "Mustn't hang too near the window. Fades the paint, don't you know."

Suddenly tongue-tied, Mariah indicated the portrait.

His cane tapping loudly, he hobbled over to peer at it closely, studying it for just a few moments before nodding. "Excellent work. Fine eye for light, Reynolds."

"There are some miniatures in the case there, also by Reynolds, I believe." She wasn't sure of any such thing, but he was already turning toward the door. At her words he stopped as if curbing his eagerness to leave, and went to the case.

Mariah gathered her courage in both hands. This was it. If she didn't speak now, there might never be another chance.

"Harry." She said it very softly, still somewhat fearful that she might turn out to be wrong. "Do you not know me any longer?"

Lord Wroth remained bent over the glass display case. "I think it's you who don't know me," he returned in his scratchy voice.

Mariah's courage almost gave out. She wet her lips and made one last effort. "I think I do know you. I think you are posing as an old man to move about town without drawing much notice. I think you must be a—a spy, of sorts. Not that I think you are an *enemy* spy," she hurried to add as he darted her a shocked glance. "I trust you, truly I do. And I will never, ever say a word to anyone, not even to my parents—"

He turned and started walking away from her, his cane making a loud tap on the floor that echoed through the gallery—*not not not*, it seemed to say.

Mariah hurried after him, on the verge of tears. Tears that he was refusing to admit who he was, or tears that she had been wrong and was thus still in the dark about her mysterious suitor, she didn't know. "Please don't run from me," she begged. "I'm sorry for the things I said. I've missed you so, please don't go just yet . . . "

He stopped outside a small alcove. Mariah stopped, too, wringing her hands and waiting in agony. He gestured toward the alcove. "What's this?"

"It's—It's some things which belonged to the first Earl of Doncaster, five hundred years ago," she said. "But will you—"

"Show me," he interrupted. "I do love something older than myself."

And that was when she admitted defeat. Either she was wrong, or he was simply determined not to tell her. Either way, Harry was lost to her forever, keeping to his promise never to return. The thrilling lover scaling her ivy tower was gone, and she didn't even know why. She wanted to turn and storm away, leaving him to play at being Lord Wroth without letting him break her heart. But she had brought this on herself and would not show how much it hurt.

She straightened her slumping shoulders. Head held high, she swept past him into the alcove. "This sword belonged to William More," she said coolly. "He was known as the 'dun More' because of his dark colored armor—"

Abruptly she was yanked back, against the wall and almost behind the drape that partially shielded the alcove, keeping the light off the most fragile portraits. Lord Wroth crowded close to her, one hand over her mouth and one arm around her waist, holding her in place.

"As God is my witness, you'll be the very death of me," he whispered. Mariah made a muffled squeak—it *was* Harry!—and then his mouth replaced his hand on her lips, and everything else vanished.

"It *is* you," she sighed when she had caught her breath. Her arms tightened around his neck. "I thought I would never see you again!"

He sighed. "You shouldn't have." He still held her close, and she could feel his heart thumping rapidly.

"But why? Why must you pretend—"

"*Shh.*" He silenced her with another hard kiss. "Don't even ask. I cannot tell you, and prefer not to lie."

She swallowed her next ten questions. "Will you do this forever?"

He was quite still for a moment, his eyes roving over her face. "No."

She let out a pent-up breath of relief. "Then when you said you couldn't come to see me again—"

He sighed, releasing her and pushing up his spectacles to pinch the bridge of his nose. "I meant it. But you . . . " He shook his head. "Mariah, I'll be in terrible trouble if anyone discovers what I've done, visiting you as I did. And not just from your father, who would be well justified in shooting me."

"Oh." That silenced some of her curiosity even as it made her heart flutter. When she had asked before if he were doing something dangerous, he hadn't answered. She never suspected he risked his life by coming to see her, though.

"I ought never to have even spoken to you," he went on. "I've broken so many rules, it hardly bears contemplating . . . "

"Then why did you?"

His eyes flashed toward her, hot with raw desire, and with a shock Mariah recalled the feel of his hands, pulling aside her nightdress to free her breast. She felt the hungry pull of his lips against her inner wrist, and the sensual creature within her stirred. "Why did you accost me in the park?" he asked quietly.

Her cheeks were burning, but she didn't look away. "You know why," she whispered.

He turned aside first, pushing the spectacles back into place. "We must neither of us do it again."

"I don't agree to that. I promise to be patient," she added quickly as he gave her a dark look. "But only if you promise me—"

"I cannot promise you anything."

She didn't like that line of conversation. He wanted to promise her something, she could sense it in his tense posture and clipped tone, but he wouldn't. She changed the subject. "Will you be punished?"

His face softened and a slightly cocky smile quirked his mouth. "Not if no one ever knows."

"I won't tell a soul," she vowed. "No one."

"Not even Miss Bennet?"

Mariah blushed. She'd completely forgotten about Joan. "How did you know I'd told her?"

He just raised his eyebrows and looked at her over the top of his spectacles. Then he shrugged. "You cannot change it, so it doesn't matter. But you mustn't reveal anything else, and not just for my sake."

Her eyes rounded. "Why?"

Harry could see he'd frightened her, and even though he'd meant to, he felt badly about it. He gathered her close again, knowing he had only a few more moments with her. "Don't ask me any more," he whispered. "Not now."

She clutched at him, then pulled back. "Will you at least show me what you really look like?"

He met her eyes for a moment. He shouldn't. He never shed any part of his costume except in the safety of Fenton Lane. But she was looking up at him with those luminous eyes, her body pressed against him as if she couldn't bear to let go. He had refused her so much, what was this one small thing, after he'd already unmasked himself? Slowly he straightened, his hunched shoulders falling back, the cotton padding shifting against his back. He rarely stood upright in Wroth's clothing, and it felt strange. He removed the spectacles and peeled off the misshapen coat.

"Do you always wear spectacles?"

"Only to read," he said. She brushed her fingers over the lean slope of his cheek, the joint of his jaw. His eyes closed and he inhaled a deep breath at her touch. "Your hair is . . . ?"

"Brown." He opened his eyes and ran one hand lightly over his head. "It's powder. A stage trick."

She nodded solemnly, scrutinizing his face as if trying to commit everything about it to memory. Perhaps she was. Who knew when they might have another moment like this? Harry stripped off his gloves and took her face in his hands.

Her hands crept up his chest. Slowly, almost tentatively, her fingers slipped under the edges of his waistcoat. "I thought—I began to suspect you weren't real," she whispered.

A wry smile curled his mouth. Many parts of him weren't real. "And now?" he murmured, his lips brushing hers.

A tremor passed through her, and she tugged on his clothing. "Kiss me again, so I might know for certain."

Harry kissed her, deeply and desperately. Then he caught himself and gentled the kiss, in case this were the last one. She tasted like tea and cherries, sweet and crisp and delicious. Until the day he died, he would remember the taste of her mouth today, when she clung to him with both hands and whispered to him to kiss her again. The fact that she knew he was beneath her, and yet was here in his arms anyway . . . He held her tighter, knowing he was far beyond merely besotted.

"Call on me again," she whispered, her breathing growing uneven as his mouth moved over her cheek, her jaw, her neck. "Come as yourself . . . "

Harry groaned. "I can't."

"Please," she begged. "Tell me your name, I swear I will receive you."

"No."

"Then come to me as you usually have . . . "

He hesitated. "Perhaps."

"Perhaps?" she cried softly. "No, tonight . . . "

He placed his hands on the wall on either side of her head and leaned in to kiss her once again without rumpling her dress even more. "No."

"Mariah? Lord Wroth? Mariah, are you here?"

Mariah's horrified gaze flew to Harry's. In a flash he had shrugged into his padded coat, his chest slumping back into Wroth's usual posture, and slid the spectacles on his face. "Fix your dress," he breathed, yanking his gloves back on. She slapped at her skirt with one hand, patting the bodice with the other to make certain she was all in order. "Now tell me about something," Harry ordered.

Mariah obligingly turned, her eyes flying about the small alcove. "Yes, of course," she whispered back. "This painting is of the first Earl of Doncaster," she began in an overly loud, bright tone. "He was elevated to the earldom by Edward the Third, who was in fact a cousin of his." They could hear footsteps now, coming closer. Mariah took a deep, ragged breath, and forged on, blurting out everything she could remember about her ancient ancestor. It rather surprised her she could pull anything from her brain now, with her blood still pulsing hot and fast from Harry's kiss. "There you see his coat of arms, chosen in honor of Edward, with the lion for England and the lily for purity. Lilies have ever since been the badge of the Dunmores—"

"There you are." The countess stood in the doorway.

"Yes, Mama." Mariah turned and smiled at her mother. "I was just showing Lord Wroth the first earl's things."

Her mother smiled back politely. "Of course. Do you have an interest in landscapes, sir? There are a fine pair of Wilson landscapes in the dining room."

"Eh? Ah, right." He pulled out a handkerchief and coughed into it. "Landscapes," he said, and coughed again. Mariah waited, too relieved at the close escape and too excited about their stolen moment to say much of anything. Her mother shot her a questioning glance as Lord Wroth kept coughing into his handkerchief. "Pray, excuse me, madam," he croaked. "I think I must go."

Mama bowed her head graciously. "Of course. It was so good of you to call, sir."

"The most delightful call I've made this Season. Your daughter has been so kindly attentive to an old man. You must be very proud of her."

Mama's smile seemed painted on her face. "We are indeed."

Slowly they walked through the house. He did not look at Mariah again until they reached the front door, where he bowed over her hand and said a polite farewell. She didn't let herself watch him leave, but turned away at once.

"I believe I would like to take some air. May I walk with Joan in the park, Mama?"

Her mother gave her a severe look. "Come with me a moment, Mariah."

She knew a terrible scolding awaited her, and she couldn't have cared less. Obediently, she followed her mother back into the drawing room, where a maid was clearing away the tea tray. Once the servant left, Mama closed the door and turned on her.

"Mariah, what on earth has come over you?"

"Oh—nothing, Mama." She shrugged. "I find Lord Wroth amusing, more so than Lord Whitting and Lord Carteret."

"I could see that, from the way you all but insisted he tour the gallery. Mariah, he is old enough to be your grandfather!" Her mother's face was taut with concern. "You have had offers from some of the most eligible men in England, and rejected them all. What makes you prefer Lord Wroth?"

Mariah frowned to keep from giving anything away. How astonished Mama would be if she knew the truth! "He doesn't look at me as a wealthy society wife. He just looks at me as a person. He is interesting, and I am well aware that he is far too old for me. But you have always advised me to heed my heart—"

"Not if it looks toward him," her mother said sharply.

She bit her lip and looked down. "I have no intention of becoming Lady Wroth," she said quietly. And it was true; she could never be Lady Wroth because Lord Wroth didn't exist. She only then realized that her hope of finding a respectable connection of Harry's had come to naught. His true name was as unknown to her as ever, and even more so: he was an admitted spy and an imposter. There was no denying it now.

Her mother seemed to wilt with relief. "I am so pleased to hear that." She crossed the room and placed her hands on Mariah's cheeks. For a moment her worried eyes searched Mariah's face. "I've been concerned about you, dearest. Your father and I do so want you to be happy, and yet it seems you are not content. Is there something you desire? Are you not pleased with London?"

And Mariah felt a flood of guilt, at least equal to the relief her mother must be feeling. She had never kept something like this from her parents. They had always been firm but kind, and she had never been a deceitful child. But this was different, and she saw no way out of the predicament—not one that pleased her. "I—I am content," she said at last. "Or becoming content. It seems as though I had forgotten, or perhaps never really knew, what it is like to be a

Londoner. Everything feels so different than the last time we were here, Mama. I was only sixteen then, and I was different." She shook her head. "I think I was a girl then, and now I am not, or at least am less of one. It has not been easy for me to see how gentlemen add up my worth as a bride in the pounds of my dowry and the advantage of Papa's connections. I know you and Papa have been puzzled by my refusal of so many eligible offers, but I want someone who will want me for who I am. I want someone who will love *me*, Mama."

For a long moment her mother was quiet. "I see."

"You have been so good to me, and I am sorry to disappoint you, but I want a marriage like yours and Papa's, with a man I can respect and trust and who will respect and trust me, even if he is not the most eligible man in town." She lifted her hands and let them fall. "I won't marry Lord Wroth, but at least with him I don't feel as though I am on parade."

Her mother's eyes grew damp. "Oh, Mariah." She opened her arms, and Mariah stepped into them. Everything she had told her was entirely true . . . except that she'd already found the man who fit her requirements. Harry was a spy, an imposter, and a commoner—and she would rather have him than the richest duke in Christendom. Somehow she doubted her mother would be well pleased to hear that, though.

"Would you like to come with me, Mama?" she said on impulse. "It is a very fine day out, and it's only a few streets to Aunt Marion's home." She wouldn't be able to talk to Joan, but Mariah realized that what had happened today was not something she could tell Joan. In fact, perhaps she could never speak to

Joan again about Harry at all. Before, it had been like a game between them, trying to discover the elusive Harry. Now, she saw that there was nothing of a game about it; Harry's safety—his life—might depend on her discretion.

Mama smiled again. "Yes, I think I shall."

Chapter 17

When Harry returned to Fenton Lane that night, he had a visitor.

Alec Brandon stood in the back of the hall. He still wore his footman's livery, although with a plain black greatcoat instead of the sage green Doncaster coat, and he wasn't wearing his powdered wig. He might have come just to report in with Angelique, but something about the set of his chin put Harry on guard at once.

"Can I have a moment, Sinclair?"

Harry paused a moment, then nodded, divesting himself of the longshoreman's coat. It had been a long day. After his call at Doncaster House, he'd spent the evening following Bethwell on another Whitechapel ramble and had to pull two drunken sailors away from the marquis, getting a bit of a thumping in the process. He had been looking forward to his bed with an almost passionate eagerness. "Of course."

Brandon jerked his head and went into the small parlor. Harry laid aside his coat and unstrapped the knife from his waist. The hilt had been digging into his ribs all night. Pressing one hand against the bruise already forming, he followed Brandon. "What is it? Something about Don—"

Brandon's punch to his gut caught him mid-word. Harry doubled over, his hand instinctively flying to where the dagger would have been. His fingers closed on nothingness, and he slowly straightened, still holding his stomach, and met Brandon's eyes warily.

"Stay away from her." Brandon kept his fists up and at the ready. "I warned you once before she was not for you. You'll ruin everything, being led around by your prick!"

Harry didn't move, not even to blink.

"I heard all about it in the servants' quarters," Brandon went on in a growl. "Lord Wroth calling on Lady Mariah! What a surprise! I wonder what that old fool could want with our beautiful, wealthy, young ladyship!"

"Nothing," said Harry quietly, then more loudly, "Nothing! Damn it, Brandon, I didn't want to go!"

"Then why were you there?"

Slowly, Harry raised his hands in surrender, his gaze steady on Brandon's face. He lowered his voice calmingly. "I met her with her father in the park the other day. The earl invited me to call. What was I to do?"

Brandon lowered his fists a little. His eyebrow dipped in suspicion. "Then you have no interest in her? Your word of honor, Sinclair, that you've kept away from her and will continue to do so?"

Harry's expression must have betrayed him, or else Brandon merely wanted to reinforce his warning. He threw another punch that just clipped Harry's shoulder as he ducked. Harry put up an arm to defend himself and tried to shove the other man away, but his shoulder connected with Brandon's midsection. Then Brandon slammed him into the wall so hard his teeth rattled, and all cooperation between them was forgotten until a sharp voice cut through the room.

"What on earth are you doing?"

Brandon gave Harry one last shove before he turned to face Angelique. His chest heaved and his face was red. "Nothing."

She turned to look at Harry, slumped against the wall and holding his side. He gritted his teeth and nodded. "Nothing."

Angelique rolled her eyes. "I am not so simple to believe nonsense. Stop beating each other and explain."

"We were just reviewing our instructions," muttered Brandon.

"I see." Her gaze swung between the two of them. "And which of you has forgotten?"

Brandon shot a bitter look at Harry, who hadn't moved. "Neither, I hope."

Angelique's expression didn't change. "I see," she said again. "May we speak in the hall, Alec?" He hesitated, then nodded once and followed her, shaking and flexing his hand as he went. He closed the door behind him.

Harry slid all the way to the floor and hung his head, gingerly. Brandon had a punishing jab. He deserved that, though. Again he felt the weight of his presumption, his arrogance that he thought he could do what he wanted and no one would be hurt or even know. Today's visit to Doncaster House had a reasonable explanation only when he admitted to the rest of the story, that he had incited Mariah's curiosity by sneaking into her room in the middle of the night until she was searching for him in every man she met. There was no chance she would have pressed him to call on her today or even spoken to Wroth at all if he had done as he ought, and stayed far away from her from the beginning.

He was still sitting there when Angelique came back into the room. She regarded him a moment, then crouched down beside him. "Look at me." Reluctantly, he raised his eyes. Angelique was not pleased. "Are you risking this entire enterprise for the sake of your cock?"

He scowled. "No."

"That is what Alec tells me. He says you are drawn to this young lady, that she distracts you from your work."

"I have never compromised my duties."

Her eyebrows went up a little. "I see." For a moment there was silence in the room. "Is she very beautiful, this Mariah?"

Harry let his head fall back against the wall and sighed. "She's utterly out of my reach."

Angelique tilted her head to one side, studying him. "That does not always matter to the heart, does it? Out of reach does not mean out of mind."

Harry glanced at her, then looked away from her perceptive eyes. "I haven't let it interfere with our work."

"I see." She smirked. "You are too ambitious, *non*? Not only the Home Office's gratitude, but an earl's daughter."

"It's not ambition," he muttered.

Angelique's smile grew. "Perhaps not."

"And it hasn't interfered in any way with my work," he went on, repeating it to convince himself. "Never."

"Good. See that it does not, or I will hand you over to Stafford." She reached out and lifted the hair that had fallen over his forehead. "At least Alec did not hit you in the face. That would be difficult for Lord Wroth to explain."

Harry winced, pressing a hand to his ribs again. Brandon had hit him plenty of other places. "It was a bloody hard blow nevertheless."

"Then you will not forget it soon. Alec has as much to gain, and to lose, as you do, Harry."

He grimaced and got to his feet, putting out a hand to help her up as well. "I have never forgotten it, Angelique."

Nor would he.

For several days Harry applied himself to his duties with renewed focus and concentration. Staying away from Mariah and getting a full night's sleep was a great deal of help in that regard.

Crane was more querulous than ever, dictating a dozen letters a day and then sending him off on a variety of errands, once even all the way up the river to the botanic garden at Chelsea. It took him an entire day, and yet Stafford said not a word about the lengthy absence from his post.

In fact, the more he thought about it, Stafford never said much of anything about their performance. Every night he and Ian, and sometimes Angelique, sat around the kitchen table and put together their reports, in excruciatingly tedious detail. Bethwell attended the opera with his wife and spoke to Lord

Canning while eyeing the girls onstage. Doncaster spent the night at his club in company with several other members of the House of Lords. It was hard to see the threat, even though Harry dutifully lurked in the rain waiting to see them safely home. Bethwell in particular, with his pompous demeanor, should have offended someone badly enough to cause a scene, but it never happened.

And still Stafford pushed them. Instead of his fears being allayed, the lack of incident only seemed to agitate him. He pressed for more information, more detail; he wanted to know the times they arrived and left parties, whom they spoke to, what they spoke of. He wanted lists of their correspondents and accounts of the gossip in their household. He wanted to know who called on them and when, and if they underwent any sudden changes in overall demeanor, as if overtaken by fear.

"If a scullery maid wants to sneak through the house at midnight and bash one over the head with a soup ladle, there's not much we can do," Ian grumbled one night, reading through the papers as he copied them into Phipps's peculiar code.

Angelique laughed. She lounged in her chair across the table from him in a very unladylike manner, occasionally correcting Ian's code. "No! We are expected to know and anticipate these things. You must be waiting in the closet to spring out and arrest her."

Ian gave her a sour look. "Stafford doesn't pay me enough to hide in Bethwell's closet. I might see him tupping his wife and go blind from the sight."

"No, you'd never see that," replied Angelique. "He might chance to bend a maid over a chair, though. He likes the girl young, and the encounter quick."

"Bloody prig." Ian put down his pen and shuffled through the papers. "This is all of them?"

"I'll take them tonight." Harry put out his hand. Usually Ian traipsed across town to deliver the reports, but since depriving himself of the illicit pleasure of visiting Mariah, Harry had become restive at nights. A walk would do him good, even if not to Doncaster House.

Ian tossed them across the table without protest. "More fool you. It's a long walk."

Harry shrugged, pulling on his coat. "I need the exercise." He folded the sheaf into his pocket and grabbed a battered old cap from the assortment by the kitchen door. As he left, Ian was leaning back against the wall, arms folded behind his head, and saying to Angelique, "Now, if it were *your* closet I were to hide in, that would be a different story . . . " and Angelique was smiling at him in that catlike way she had. Harry tugged on the cap and slammed the door behind him. And Brandon gave *him* a hard time for thinking with his cock.

The delivery point was a draper's shop in Cheapside, with a narrow alley just wider than a man running between it and the neighboring chemist. All the shops were closed up for the night, the street quiet; no one was about to see what he did. Harry turned down the alley, pried away the loose shutter around the back of the draper's, and deposited the reports through the slot hidden underneath, hearing them slide down a chute with a tinny hiss. He didn't know who owned the shop, which looked neat and respectable enough, but Phipps would get the reports, probably within a few hours. He slid the shutter back into place and walked away, his duty done but his mind uneasy.

It was a long walk back to Fenton Lane, but Harry didn't even proceed in that direction. Instead he just walked, deep in thought. What did it matter what time Doncaster went to his club, so long as he returned home safely? Stafford's new demands were complicating the once simple business, turning him and his companions into hapless clerks. If a madman were to attack, Harry thought darkly, he would have to stop and note the time before intervening to save his man's life. It didn't make sense, and one thing he had always believed in was Stafford's ruthless sense.

So what was the truth? He could well believe Stafford would add to their responsibilities without telling them why; but if the danger to Bethwell, Crane, and Doncaster had grown so markedly, why not take steps to put them on guard? Bethwell still went whoring and gambling in Whitechapel, where he might be gutted by an angry whore or her bull. Doncaster went about as publicly as ever, and even Crane rode out in his barouche on fine days to take the air. Shouldn't they know the government had evidence of threats against them? Shouldn't they be warned to take more care? And just what was the Home Office's interest in hour-by-hour diaries of their actions?

Harry stopped and took a deep breath, realizing his mind was wandering down dangerous paths. There was a pub up ahead; he could use a pint, to calm his head. He pushed open the door and slid onto a bench in the shadows, lifting one hand to beckon a serving girl. Within a few minutes he had a foaming mug of ale in front of him, and he hunched over it, letting his thoughts stew in his mind.

Stafford had to be lying to them about something. Harry wasn't much surprised at this, as Stafford's stock in trade was lies. And, Harry was compelled to admit, he had his own secrets from Stafford, despite the pledge of absolute loyalty Stafford had required. They were made for each other, he thought with a spark of black humor, two liars lying to each other.

Still, it was his life on the line, not John Stafford's, and that made all the difference. It made a man more cynical and more suspicious, knowing that his employer would sacrifice him without hesitation to achieve his goals, and then discovering that the employer was lying to him about even the fundamentals. So he drank his ale and thought of all the things about his job and his instructions that didn't make sense.

A shout roused him from his thoughts. One of the serving wenches had been sitting in a customer's lap, laughing and smiling with him. Now she was on her feet, her hands on her hips and her nose in the air. She turned her back and walked away from the man, the imprint of her hand still clear on his face. Behind her the man—a sailor, by his dress—and his companions shouted at her back, some laughing, but her former suitor was red-faced with drink and too unsteady to follow her. The woman made a rude gesture to them before swinging around another table.

Harry's gaze lingered on her absently. Had he been to this tavern before? He didn't think so; it was far from Fenton Lane, close to the docks and more frequented by sailors and dockworkers from

Wapping. He rarely came out this way, and tonight only because he needed more exercise before going home. But something about that wench was familiar in a strange way, as if he'd not only seen her before but seen her often.

She was leaning over another table, taking an order. He watched her profile as she nodded. Not a friendly one, he thought as she snapped at the customer when he leaned forward and leered at her bosom. Not that tavern wenches were known for their genteel manners in any event, but this one—

She turned her head then and Harry's idle ruminations stopped cold. Oh, he knew this one, indeed.

The woman grabbed two empty mugs from a nearby table and forged through the clutter of tables and men. He watched her shove chairs and arms to the side as she passed, saw her kick more than one foot out of her path. He didn't move a muscle but his eyes never left her. She collected some more empty mugs and gave a table a halfhearted swipe with the tail of her apron, all with a hard frown on her face. She might be voluptuous, but her expression could cow any man—except Harry, who had no interest in her figure.

She turned sideways to edge between two tables jammed together. A man at one of them called out drunkenly to her and she turned, to tell him off, no doubt. But then Harry seized her wrist and yanked, pulling her backward and off-balance into his lap despite the splash of ale that flew out of the mugs as she dropped them, wetting both her skirt and his trousers. Before she could react, he bent her arm behind her back and wrapped his free arm around her waist, holding her tight.

Her eyes shot daggers at him as she twisted. "Let me go, mate. I'm not looking for a tumble tonight," she warned in a plain, coarse accent.

"Aw, that's fine wi' me," he replied in kind, holding her in place despite her struggles. "All's I want's some conversation, sweeting."

The patrons around him shouted with laughter as Harry cast an exaggerated look down her bodice. The serving maid hissed in fury. Harry ignored it all, leaning closer to press his cheek right against hers. She smelled of ale and sweat, not French perfume, but he knew exactly where he'd seen her before.

"Such a pretty thing. Come on, just a kiss, love." More raucous appreciation around them. Harry lowered his voice to a bare murmur as he pressed his mouth against her ear. "Come down in the world a bit, haven't you, Madame? Last I saw of you, you were tempting Gerry Wollaston into a bit of treason."

Her reaction was slight, but definite. Had Harry not been holding her pinned against him, he might not have felt it. But for a split second she froze, her muscles tensing and her mouth twitching ever so slightly before she recovered and hurled a vile epithet at him. He grinned as the crowd roared again, but he kept all his attention focused on her.

"Who's 'at? I don't know what you mean." She twisted in his grip to peer at his face.

"I think you do," he muttered back. "Just a quick tickle, mum," he said out loud. "I promise, you won't mind a bit . . . "

Her gaze sparkled with pure malice. "Let me go, or you'll not have much to tickle the maids with anymore."

Harry dragged her back, grinning lewdly when she shoved against his chest and bucked to escape. "I'll take my chances." Then more quietly: "I want answers."

"Answers," she sneered just as softly. "Yours is not to ask, just to do."

Phipps's words exactly. Harry blinked, startled, and she took advantage of his surprise to get one hand loose and slap him hard across the face. "Take that for your damned answer," she cried. "And that—" Harry caught her wrist as she swung again.

"Tell me," he demanded through his teeth. "What was your role?"

"You saw it," she hissed back. "Poor Polly must miss you dreadfully."

Harry squeezed her wrist tighter. "Why? What were you after?"

Sal the serving wench, formerly known as Madame de la Tource, raised her eyebrows. "The same thing you were. Didn't you know?" Her mouth curled with mockery as her voice dropped. "Didn't think you were the only one he had on Wollaston, did you?"

"No," he said evenly. "But I didn't know about you. What brings you to a place like this, I wonder?"

Some of her animosity relented. She must know as well as he did what would happen if he stood up and named her a government spy. Just in the time he'd been nursing his ale this evening, Harry had heard enough rebellious talk and inflammatory boasts to land half the patrons in Newgate with Sir Gerald. They wouldn't be kind to any spy. She calmed a bit, draping one arm around his neck. "All right, let's see the coin," she said for the benefit of the audience. Then, under the racket of catcalls and laughter, she whispered, "Speed the job up, that's all. They knew there was a traitor, so I set the trap and he fell into it. You turned the key. And if you call me out here and now, you'll not be in line for such plum jobs again, aye? Fancy serving ale, or maybe your fine arse, to this lot?"

This time Harry let her go when she made a show of elbowing him in the ribs and jerked free. Everyone around him shouted as she stormed off toward the back room, some with glee and some with disappointment. Harry ducked his head and waved one hand, nodding as a few fellows called out to him not to give up, that a half hour between Sal's thighs was worth a few clouts to the head. Little did they suspect a night between Sal's thighs might lead to a life in prison. He shoved his ale away and tossed down a few coins to pay for it, then made his way out into the street, where his thoughts calcified into bitter realization.

Madame de la Tource, Gerald Wollaston's seductive paramour, had been one of Stafford's spies. Harry had known there was another spy in her household, a footman who'd been his contact and conspirator in the plot to get him into the house. That man hadn't been able to locate any proof of Wollaston's guilt, which was why Harry had been sent to work next door, or so Phipps had told him. It had taken Harry barely a fortnight to have all Madame's maids swooning over him, giving him ample opportunity to slip into the house and have a look around. And lo, what did he discover but Wollaston passing stolen secrets to his mistress. An easy job, Harry recalled with scorn as he paced along the street, even though he had wondered at the time why Wollaston bore the brunt of the blame for stealing the secrets and his French mistress none for taking them.

But now it was all clear. The supposed Frenchwoman had been working for the same man as Harry,
to the same end. And Harry had heard her, with
his own ears, exhorting Wollaston to give her more
information, more secrets—to commit more treason.
Whether Wollaston had begun giving her information
on his own or at her prompting, he couldn't say, but it
was indisputable that she'd pressed him to continue
doing so, even when Wollaston had reservations. That
wasn't spying, as Harry saw it; that was entrapment.

He walked faster, his boots slapping on the wet
cobblestones and his hands in fists in his pockets.
Stafford had framed Wollaston. Harry's whole mission
there had been a lie, stealing stolen government secrets
from a fellow spy who had seduced her victim into
treason. Wollaston's fate had been sealed by Harry's
own testimony, given in Stafford's office to the Home
Secretary himself, that he had indeed heard Wollaston
pass the information to his mistress, and that he had
retrieved it from her bedroom moments later. Lord
Sidmouth had been so grave, acknowledging his service to the Crown with magnificent condescension.
Did Sidmouth know, Harry wondered in growing
fury, or was it just Stafford trying to please his
superior?

He stopped on the street corner, glaring into the
dark London night. Everything he had believed in
had been set off-balance. If Stafford could lie to him
about that, about *treason*, what wouldn't he lie about?
All Harry's doubts about his job came flooding back,
more threatening and more ominous. Why had
he been given this job, this soft, easy job following
wealthy nobs around like some sort of guardian
shadow? Why was he supposed to be invisible and

silent, even if danger were to confront them? And why hadn't he seen so much as a disgruntled street sweeper scowling at any of them?

It had begun to rain, a light drizzle that steamed off the cobbles like ghosts released from their graves. All the smells of a London street rose up around him in a mist, a putrefied miasma of rotted food and vomited ale and horse dung and human waste that turned his stomach almost as much as the realization that he had been used.

He turned on his heel and headed for Bow Street.

Chapter 18

Phipps was still at Bow Street, as he always seemed to be. He had told Harry and the others they were to come directly to him there if they ever had urgent need. Perhaps he lived in his cramped, nondescript office in the rear of Bow Street; Harry didn't know or care. He pushed open the door without knocking and strode in.

At his entrance, Phipps surged to his feet, a curious eagerness filling his face. "Yes?" he barked. "What is it?"

"Madame de la Tource was working for you." It wasn't a question.

The eagerness faded. "Ah." Phipps came around his desk and closed the door. "That's not your concern, Sinclair."

Harry swore. "You coerced a man into treason!"

Phipps raised a finger in warning. "Mind your tongue. We don't much like that word around here."

With difficulty, Harry mastered his anger. He glared at Phipps, so infuriatingly calm. Phipps had the cold eyes and pale skin of a fish. Harry had no trouble believing he would entice victims into his snares, then kill them slowly and painfully. "I don't much like being told I'm doing one thing—a grand and noble thing—only to find I'm risking my neck trying to tempt a half-witted clerk into a bit of betrayal."

Phipps lifted his chin. "You know nothing about that—"

"Nothing." Harry jerked his head impatiently. "And who kept it that way?"

"It wasn't necessary for you to know." Phipps's lip curled. "Really, Sinclair, you did your job. Perfectly competent. And it worked out well for you, didn't it?"

"And now?" Harry folded his arms. "I'm creeping around spying on a viscount—on an earl. What mightn't I need to know whilst I'm impersonating a peer?"

Phipps smiled, his eyes veiled and watchful. "Traitors come in all stripes and sizes. Don't forget that. They're here, there, everywhere, right under our noses."

Harry flipped one hand in disgust. "You overstate the matter—"

Phipps snorted. "Do I? Do I, indeed? You wouldn't have much of a job then, would you? Now, I suggest you go back to it, or I shall find someone who will." And he pulled open the door and stood, waiting with magnificent unconcern for Harry to leave.

It slowly sank into his brain, as he stalked away from Phipps, what the real point of his assignment was. Sidmouth and his men were a suspicious lot, fearful of being caught unawares by rebellion. They sent the mounted yeomanry into a demonstration in Manchester and rode down women and children. They passed the Six Acts to contain and control dissent wherever it existed, or seemed to exist. They hired

people like Madame de la Tource—and himself—
to be something they weren't and to report back on
what they saw and heard. And when someone like Sir
Gerald Wollaston fell into their hands, they whisked
him off to prison with nary a word or reason made
public.

And now there were government agents living
anonymously in the shadows of three English noble-
men, even in their homes. Three highly influential men
but not members of the government itself, men who
wouldn't discover what Stafford and Sidmouth were
about. All widely respected for one reason or another,
all consulted by Cabinet ministers and secretaries and
the King. All with far-reaching, intimate knowledge
of political affairs and plans. If the radicals Sidmouth
so feared were to persuade one of them to sympathize
with their cause . . .

He thought of the reams of reports he, Angelique,
and Brandon had filed on each of their marks. Every
waking moment of their lives was scrupulously docu-
mented by Harry and his fellow agents for Sidmouth's
files. They were to know everything about Crane, Doncaster, and Bethwell—*everything*. But most importantly
of all, no one was to know they were watching, not
even the men supposedly in danger of being attacked
at any moment. And now he knew why.

They weren't guarding Doncaster, Crane, and
Bethwell.

They were watching them.

Three hours later Harry pulled up a chair near the
bed and watched a man sleep.

John Stafford was a nondescript fellow, the sort one
could see every day and yet never quite say what he

looked like. He slept on his back, mouth slightly open, a red nightcap on his head. He might have been a clerk or a duke or a pig farmer instead of a spymaster. Harry gazed dispassionately down at his superior, so calm and secure in slumber, and considered one last time before he crossed the Rubicon, so to speak, and put his entire future at risk. He had done well at his job. He might never again have an opportunity like the one he had been offered upon completion of this assignment, and it would hurt—badly—to lose it.

But every man had to have his limit. He struck the flint.

Stafford awoke with the faintest of flinches. His eyes opened a mere slit, and for a moment he and Harry regarded each other in silence by the light of the single candle.

"How dare you," Stafford finally whispered.

Harry gave a careless shrug. "Is it really so shocking?"

"This is my bloody home! My bedchamber!" Slowly, Stafford pushed himself up against his pillows, his expression fierce. "Explain yourself, Sinclair, if you wish to see tomorrow."

"Now that you mention it, that's why I've come," Harry said conversationally. "My seeing tomorrow, that is. Obviously I've already handed over much of my life to your direction, but some parts I like to keep a close eye on. Particularly the longevity."

"Talk sense," Stafford snapped.

Harry leaned forward and rested his elbows on his knees, his clasped hands hanging loosely between them. "You've been lying to me." His employer's eyebrow arched cynically, and he added, "To all of us. I want to know why."

"I am not in the habit of explaining myself," the other man began in a sharp voice.

Harry smiled without humor. "Well, we all have some unsavory habits, don't we."

Stafford pursed his lips and said nothing more. It was at his instigation that Harry's habits included breaking into houses in the middle of the night, unseen and unheard and almost always well-armed.

"Now," Harry went on, "I met a woman this evening. Fascinating creatures, women. There's no more potent force on earth for muddling a man's mind and making him do the damnedest things. Wouldn't you agree?"

"Get to the point, if you please."

"Ah—yes." Harry leaned back in his chair, draping one arm over the back. "As I said, I met a woman this evening. At first glance I thought she was a mere tavern wench, but it turns out she was once much more. Almost . . . nobility, if my memory serves. French. Expensive. Spoiled and arrogant and capable of twisting a weak-willed Treasury deputy around her little finger." Stafford's face didn't change but Harry knew he had touched a nerve. "And what should I discover but that she was also taking orders from you. How many agents did you have trying to catch Gerald Wollaston with his fingers in the Treasury till?"

Stafford's stare could have chipped stone. "This is not your concern."

"That's what Phipps said." Harry stroked one finger down his throat and tilted his head back to look at Stafford from under lowered eyelids. "I have to disagree."

The other man's mouth flattened. "Are you offering your resignation?"

Harry thought about it a moment. "Not . . . necessarily." Stafford snorted, and Harry leaned forward. "Tell me why," he demanded in a soft voice. "Tell me why we're spying on Doncaster and the others. This isn't a guardian assignment. Tell me the truth."

For a long moment it seemed Stafford wouldn't reply. His jaw tensed and relaxed several times, as if he were swallowing his words, before he finally exhaled in disdain. "These are dangerous times, Sinclair. I expected you would know that. After all, one presumes you wished to do your patriotic duty when you came into my employ. One wouldn't want to question the motive of a man who agrees to housebreaking, impersonation, lying, stealing, and any number of other activities some might judge criminal."

"No, nor would one want to question the motive of the man who charges others with those same tasks and then rewards their success in them," Harry shot back.

Stafford dismissed this with a slight twist of his mouth. "Indeed." He studied Harry with piercing eyes. "I hired you in part for your intelligence, so I suppose I ought not to be surprised at this."

Harry just looked at him, waiting.

Stafford's lips pinched. "From time to time," he said, speaking each word as if he wished he needn't, "it is necessary to engage in anticipatory behavior. Naturally one would prefer not, particularly in situations where some delicacy is required, but when the dangers outweigh the reservations, one must act. It would be dereliction of my duty not to do so. I placed you and my other agents with the utmost care, trusting in your ability to act with discretion and wisdom in the pursuance of your tasks. I trust you will continue to do so."

Then he said no more. For a moment he and Harry just gazed at each other, before Harry leaned forward even more.

"So, which one do *you* suspect is the traitor?"

Stafford simply looked at him, coldly and silently.

Harry took that silence for confirmation. "All right," he said quietly. "I understand."

"I expect you to continue following your orders—" Stafford began.

Harry lifted one hand. "I will. But from this moment on, I follow my own instinct as well."

Stafford shot him a cutting glance. "Whatever is required."

Harry inclined his head, partly to hide his surprise. Stafford didn't care what he did, just as long as he caught the traitor. He hadn't quite expected that. "Then we comprehend each other. At last." He got to his feet and crossed the room.

"How did you get into my house?" Stafford asked behind him.

Harry glanced back from the doorway. "All too easily."

Stafford glared at him, clutching the blankets to his chest. "Do not do it again."

Harry just flashed a tight-lipped smirk and slipped through the door.

Back out in the street, he took a deep breath. That could have gone rather badly for him, but it hadn't. Stafford hadn't sacked him or promised retribution; instead he implicitly confirmed the charges he made and gave him carte blanche to catch the traitor. That meant Stafford was quite desperate to find the man, for he had already seen how repressive his employer was regarding his missions.

And if the reward for safeguarding a few wealthy gents were as he'd been told, how much more would it be for discovering a traitor in the upper reaches of society, almost within the Cabinet itself? The government—even the new King himself—should be very grateful indeed.

Harry strode along through the dark streets, his blood beginning to surge at the thought. It was an awful risk as well. If he made a mistake and accused the wrong man, Stafford would gut him and spit him without hesitation. Harry would take the entire blame, not an inconsiderable drawback, as the penalty for falsely accusing a nobleman was death. And if he were correct, no one would ever hear his name associated with the matter, even though he would not be shy in claiming his reward.

But one of the possible traitors was Lord Doncaster, Mariah's father. Harry didn't want to consider the possibility that he could be the guilty party—for tonight. He didn't want to confront that thought, or the choices it would demand, unless he was absolutely forced to do so. It seemed unlikely Mariah's regard for him would withstand the sight of him rising to testify against her father, ruining her family and disgracing her forever. He couldn't think about that now.

By the time he arrived back at Fenton Lane, he had decided on at least a beginning. It was easiest to spy on Crane, so he would begin there. Crane's diary and correspondence went through his hands every day, and he had been watching the old man for weeks now. The actions that must have caught Stafford's eyes had to have happened some time ago, so he would have to go through as many of the viscount's papers as he could. As long as he didn't get sent off on too many pointless errands or dragged out of the house by any more of Tobias's larks, it should take only a few days, weeks at the most.

Tobias. Harry stripped off his clothing and scrubbed his face and neck, thinking of Crane's nephew. Perhaps that was the source of the treason. He didn't think Tobias was clever enough to plot to overthrow a cricket pitch, let alone a government, but Tobias was a young man with lofty ambitions and no fortune of his own. It would be fairly easy for him to sell information gleaned in his uncle's house to a radical group, possibly even without realizing what he was selling. The more Harry thought about him, the more plausible Tobias became. And searching Tobias's belongings for any telltale signs of treachery would be easy enough to do, since Tobias had resided with his uncle since he came to town.

Harry fell into bed, exhaustion finally overwhelming him. Bethwell would prove difficult, since he had no entrée into the marquis's house and only followed him sporadically. He would have to think on that. But as he drifted off to sleep, it was the earl he thought of.

Please God, don't let it be Doncaster.

Chapter 19

Several days went by without any sign or word from Harry. Mariah felt at once weighed down and buoyed by his secret. A man did not masquerade, very convincingly, as an elderly man and a secretary without help, nor without a very strong reason. She had plenty of time to think about that and what his reason might be. He might have lied to her, and he might be as scheming and detestable as Joan had said. But she had seen no sign of that, and in the end she realized she must choose to trust him, or not, without having any of her questions answered. Despite all his secrets, she couldn't distrust him. She missed his company and the way they talked so easily to each other. She missed his laugh and the tenderness in his touch. And when she finally heard the soft scrape and swish at her window again, she threw back her blankets and bounced upright in bed. "Harry!" she whispered in delight.

He rose to his full height and ran his hands through his hair. Cold rain was beating against the window behind him, and it had been the sound of him pushing up the sash that caught her attention. She hadn't thought he would come to her in a storm, but was overjoyed that he had. "Come in," she said, scrambling off her bed and grabbing a shawl from the chaise. "You must be soaked!"

He peeled off his dripping wet coat—Mariah could hear the drops hitting the floor—and folded it over the windowsill before taking the shawl she offered. His fingers were like ice when they brushed hers. She gasped. "You'll catch your death of cold! Why are you out tonight?"

He swung the shawl around himself and slumped against the window frame. "To see you." Even his voice sounded cold and tired.

"Come by the fire." She took his hand and pulled, but he resisted.

"No. I cannot stay for long."

Mariah bit her lip but didn't argue. Her teeth were chattering, thanks to the cold breeze through the window, so she rummaged inside the wardrobe for another shawl and waited for him to explain.

"I've missed you," he said instead.

Warmth filled her heart. "I've missed you as well."

He shook his head and smiled. The fire gave off just enough light for her to make out his expression. "You undermine all my intentions to stay away. You should be out dancing with proper gentlemen, not wishing a scoundrel would come see you."

"But the scoundrel is more interesting than all the gentlemen put together," she said as she pulled her dressing table chair closer to him. He was still leaning heavily against the windowsill, and Mariah could sense that his good cheer was somewhat forced. "Why are you out in this weather?"

He wiped his face with one corner of the shawl. "No very good reason, it seems."

"Why not?"

Instead of making light of her question or refusing to answer, Harry simply gazed at her for a long time. As Mariah's eyes adjusted, she could see him a little better. His hair was slicked back from his face, his cheekbones thrown into high relief by the flickering firelight. Water trickled from his wet hair down his throat, running across his skin and melting into the collar of his soaked shirt. She tried not to stare at that little stream of water. "It's difficult to explain," he finally said. "I hope your evening was more enjoyable."

"We went to the theater," she told him, changing the subject to something other than the cares that seemed to have worn him down tonight. "It was a fine performance, although my cousin, Joan—Miss Bennet— thought it was silly and whispered the most awful things in my ear the whole evening. Joan is dreadful, capable of making sport of nearly anything. And the worst of it is, she does so with such humor, I cannot help but laugh at what she says." She paused. "Do you enjoy the theater?"

This seemed to amuse him. A wry smile curled his mouth. "Moderately well."

"I think it's wonderful. I could go to the theater every week, but Papa says we might not return for a while."

"Why is that? Does he not share your enthusiasm?"

"No—yes—that is, he likes it well enough, I suppose. But near the end of the performance, some people in the gallery stood and began shouting. They tossed handbills into the air, and Papa was very displeased."

Harry lifted his head. "Why?"

Mariah flushed. "They were handbills in support of the Queen. Some in the audience cheered as they were thrown about. Joan caught one when Papa had his back turned, or else I'm sure we would never have known what they were."

His expression changed, becoming strangely guarded yet alert. "Does your father sympathize with the Queen?"

"Papa?" Mariah asked in surprise. "No, of course not. He *is* a Tory, you know. I think he was angry at the way the Queen's supporters behaved, ruining the play. Papa feels the people should respect the dignity of the King, even if they do not *like* him."

"Then he believes they have good reason to dislike the King."

"I . . . Well, I suppose he knows they do dislike the King, whether the reasons are good or not. Papa has always been more of a diplomat, used to dealing with the way people are instead of the way people should be." She gave him a puzzled look. "Why?"

Harry just shook his head. "Does he support the King's divorce?"

Mariah rolled her eyes. "No one supports the King's divorce except the King. Even I know that."

"Ah." Harry pulled the shawl from his shoulders and folded it into a neat square. "What do you think of it?"

She tore her eyes from his wet shirt, plastered to his arms and chest. "I—I think . . . well, I think the King should not be able to divorce Queen Caroline when everyone in London knows he's had a dozen mistresses. However badly she has behaved, he has done much the same. That doesn't seem fair."

Harry heaved a sigh. "No. It doesn't seem fair." He hung his head for a moment, looking so tired Mariah's heart melted. She leaned out and took his hand. His fingers wrapped firmly around hers, as if he drew strength from her touch. She still longed to know what he had been doing and why, but held her tongue. He would tell her, when he could—if he could. Wordlessly, she raised her free hand to hold his hand between her two, offering him what comfort she could.

Harry's throat tightened as he gazed down at their clasped hands. He'd needed to see her tonight, even though he had no strength to be charming. It was freezing cold and raining hard, and he'd been out in it for several hours shadowing Lord Bethwell. Now that he knew it wasn't to protect but to watch, he didn't see the point in waiting outside the Cavendish mansion while Bethwell dined there, but if he didn't go, Angelique would want to know why. He had kept his conversations with Phipps and Stafford to himself so far. He didn't know what his fellow agents would do. He didn't know what Stafford would do if the entire team mutinied. He had discovered the truth about their work, but it didn't make anything about it easier.

Mariah believed her father loyal—and why wouldn't she? Doncaster was a Tory, part of the government party. What motive would he have to turn against it and aid its opponents? But Sidmouth and Stafford thought he might have done just that. And Mariah would be devastated if it were true.

"You are very fond of your father."

She looked up at him, no hint of distrust in her gaze. "Yes, of course. I could not ask for a better one."

Harry nodded. It made no sense. Doncaster was publicly allied with the King. What had brought suspicion on him? "I'm glad," he murmured. "Everyone should have an affectionate father."

"Harry . . . " She stopped, then got to her feet. "I

wish I could help you," she said helplessly. "I hate feeling as though you might be in danger or troubled and I can do nothing."

In spite of everything, he smiled, and raised her fingers to his lips. "This helps," he told her, brushing her knuckles against his cheek. "Just talking to you helps."

Her smile was tender and a little bit sad, as if she knew it was only a moment of comfort. She stepped closer and put her arm around his neck, until he rested his head on her bosom. He snaked one arm around her waist. "I'll get you wet," he mumbled even as he drew her closer.

"I don't care." Her fingers stroked his hair. She rested her cheek atop his head. "I'm glad you came to see me," she whispered again.

So he kept his arm around her waist and his head on her breast, and shoved away the thought of what he had to do next.

Tobias had moved into his uncle's house early that spring, coming from his own home in Dorset. From what Harry had seen, Crane took him in rather ungraciously while Tobias was determined to enjoy the Season in town if not his uncle's company. Tobias Crane had given every appearance of being what he seemed to be—a genial fellow of very modest intelligence and even less wit. But there were enough flashes of ambition to make one wonder—or if one were in search of a traitor and not inclined to miss a suspect, to make one break into Tobias's rooms and search them.

His weeks of service in Crane's house had taught Harry much. He knew the little window next to the scullery door wouldn't close all the way, and he knew how to mount the back stairs without making a sound. He knew the lone lamp burning in the front hall was all Crane would allow to light Tobias's way upstairs when he came home, and it told Harry that Tobias was still away from home even before he glided into the deep, silent shadows around the house and pressed gently at the scullery window. All told, it took him less than five minutes to gain entrance to the house and find his way to Tobias's sitting room and bedchamber.

For a moment he stood just inside the door, letting his eyes adjust. Tobias's rooms were at the front of the house, overlooking the street and admitting no quick exit. They were plain, simple rooms, with little place to hide anything. It was a stroke of fortune that Tobias could afford no valet of his own. Harry knew Tobias had tried to persuade Jasper, Lord Crane's man, to assist him, but Jasper had been too long under Crane's misanthropic influence and stiffly refused. Thus, the rooms were completely empty, and would remain so until Tobias himself returned. Harry drew off his thin leather gloves and set to work, not knowing how much time he would have.

He began in the bedroom, carefully turning over every item of clothing in the clothespress and probing every pocket. He inspected the few books, all the obvious places someone might hide stolen documents, and then every other nook and cranny he could see. Taking up his tiny shielded lantern, he moved silently into the sitting room. A few coals glowed weakly in the grate, making it a little easier to see. He searched the room with the same swift thoroughness; he didn't want to miss anything, but also knew he wouldn't have the entire night.

He left the writing desk for last. Surely even Tobias would be more devious than to hide anything incriminating on top of his desk, but one never knew. Harry sat down and slid open a drawer, feeling a tinge of frustration. For the first time, he felt the pressure of time, that his quarry might act before he could catch him out. Of course, if Stafford had been honest with them from the start, he and Brandon and Angelique could have been searching all these many weeks for the villain instead of powdering their hair and lurking in the shadows doing nothing.

The desk contained bills, several overdue and some clearly replies to letters Tobias had sent asking for more time. Harry totted up the value of Tobias's new lifestyle as he skimmed through them, and thought again how much the man could use a source of income. There were a pair of letters from his mother, exhorting Tobias to be a good nephew and not to fall in with those who thought too highly of themselves. Harry smiled a little at that, and went on with his search.

He'd almost reached the end without finding anything. Carefully, he replaced everything as it had been, then began picking through the letters and papers all jumbled on the desktop. To his enormous amusement, many of the pages appeared to be drafts of love letters and poems addressed to several young ladies, chief among them Lady Mariah Dunmore. His eyebrows went up as he read one heavily edited missive with her name on it. A few lines of verse were written in the margin, comparing her hair to freshly mined coal and her eyes to a rainy sky. Tobias must not have been pleased with it, for the bit about rainy sky had been scratched out and amended to "the dewy dawn." That had ruined his rhyme, though, for *dawn* didn't rhyme with *freshly baked pie*—which was apparently how appealing she smelled—and the poem wasn't finished. Harry grinned and shook his head, putting it aside with the other pages.

There was nothing. He finally got up from the desk, his amusement over Tobias's painful poetry vanishing under the realization that Tobias's apparent innocence meant his search was far from over. He sighed, looking around the room for some hiding place he might have missed. It wasn't that he wanted Tobias to be a traitor; but given that there *was* a traitor, it would have been nicer to find the man out at once with minimal danger and inconvenience to himself. It would be considerably more difficult to get into Lord Bethwell's home, and he didn't even want to contemplate searching Doncaster House. If only Stafford would tell him what, precisely, had alerted the Home Office to those three men as the most likely parties.

He put out his little lantern and turned toward the door. By his internal clock, he guessed he'd been in the house a little more than an hour, making it late enough that he should be on his way. After all, he—or rather, Henry Towne—had to be back in just a few hours, ready for another day copying diagrams of leaves and vines and other flora. Already thinking about his next step, he was reaching for the doorknob before he heard the sound of footsteps in the hall. Hand outstretched, he froze, listening and waiting. A thin line of light appeared under the door, and the steps paused, then quickened, as though the walker had stumbled before slowing in front of the door.

In a flash Harry turned and vaulted over the small sofa in the corner, folding his body in half and pulling his knees up into his chin. He held himself utterly still as the doorknob turned and someone staggered into the room.

The man was drunk. His steps wandered around the room for several moments, and a swish of cloth hit the floor, probably a coat. He hummed a bawdy tavern song under his breath, off pitch and far too slowly, and finally sat somewhere with a great thump that rattled the uneven feet of the sofa Harry hid behind.

For a while it was quiet. The room hadn't grown any lighter since the door opened, as if Tobias had just brought up the lamp left burning by the door and not bothered to light any others. Carefully, a fraction of an inch at a time, Harry raised his head from behind the sofa until he could just see over it.

Tobias Crane sat sprawled in the armchair across the room, legs outstretched toward the fender and arms hanging out to the sides. One hand clutched a bottle, which Tobias raised to his mouth for a long drink. The lone lamp sat on the table, casting barely enough light for Harry to see him, certainly not enough for Tobias to spy him peering stealthily over the shabby little sofa.

"Shall I compare thee to a summer's day," Tobias mumbled, then shook his head. "I like that. 'S good rhyme. But not summer, already been done." He frowned. "Winter day. Shall I compare thee to a winter day." He said it a few more times, as if tasting the words, and drank from his bottle again. Brandy, Harry guessed from the way Tobias grew rapidly drunker. He slowly eased his muscles, just enough to settle silently into a more comfortable position. It might take a while for Tobias to drift off to sleep, and Harry couldn't go anywhere until he did.

"Compare thee . . . winter's day." Tobias was still talking to himself. "Yes, winter's very good. Sparkle

like snow. But cold." He frowned, drinking some more.
Drops dribbled down his chin. "Lady M'riah's not cold.
Warm, lovely girl. Like fire in winter."

Harry felt an odd urge to laugh even as he scowled.
Tobias's poetry was terrible, not at all the sort of thing
to appeal to Mariah—and yet, who was he to say Tobias
had no right to compose odes comparing her to a fire
in winter? The heir of a viscount could call on her and
flirt with her and dance with her in full view of society, and could ask the Earl of Doncaster for permission
to court her without fear of being thrown out on his
face. It would be a better match for him than for her,
but Tobias would be Lord Crane someday, and most
likely not a distant someday. Crane was over eighty
and in uncertain health, and Tobias was his only heir.
The considerable Crane fortune would fall to Tobias
along with the viscountcy. The fellow would be an eligible match someday.

Harry closed his eyes, no longer feeling the urge to
laugh. Tobias was still muttering to himself, but less
distinctly. He was falling asleep, though not quickly
enough for Harry. The floor was hard and cold and he
didn't dare move. Even drunk as a lord, Tobias would
notice a man suddenly rising from behind his sofa.
All Harry could do was sit and ruminate on the utter
impossibility of his own hopes and dreams while a
possible traitor composed bad poetry to the woman he
loved.

Finally, at long last, the rasp of faint snoring
drifted across the room. Harry dared another peek
from behind the sofa. Tobias had slid sideways in his
chair, the bottle cradled in the crook of his arm. He
was sound asleep, and the lamp had burned very low.
Harry stayed where he was until the snores turned

deep and regular, then slowly crept from his hiding place and from the room.

The next several days proved an excruciating test of Harry's patience and subterfuge. On pretext of cataloging and organizing Crane's papers, he skimmed through months' worth of letters and documents. Crane's letters of course were missing, but Harry could see with whom he corresponded and what they discussed. There were letters from the Lord Chancellor, arguing details of the Six Acts and other laws. Polite notes from members of Parliament. Letters from friends and acquaintances abroad and at home, even a letter from his sister-in-law, Tobias's mother, timidly asking for funds in her son's absence. And of course the voluminous correspondence from the gardener at Brimstow, John Rusk.

To Harry's amusement, Rusk was impatient with Crane's horticultural vision; there seemed to be a quarrel between Crane and Rusk over the importance of *Quercus robur*—a large oak tree near the gates of Brimstow, as Harry well knew—versus fields of lilies and tulips that were to be planted or uprooted, it was difficult to tell. The passions of gardeners were quite beyond him, Harry thought, moving on to examine the tradesman's bills for anything out of the ordinary.

He didn't truly expect to find incriminating papers in Crane's own desk; Crane was too intelligent for that, if he were a traitor at all. But it must be done, and he would search until he was satisfied there were no treasonous papers in with the rest.

Tobias broke up the monotony one day, knocking on the door and coming in before Crane could tell him not to. "Uncle," he announced, "I have come to seek your blessing."

Harry immediately turned his face to his work. Even aside from the way Tobias provoked his uncle's temper, Harry didn't care to see the man and remember him comparing Mariah to a winter's day.

Crane shot his nephew a sour glance. "To visit your mother? Yes, yes, go."

Tobias, still grinning, shook his head. "No, indeed, sir. I am going to take a wife."

Crane grunted. "More fool you. Who is the lady? Some impertinent chit, I suppose."

His nephew flushed. "Not at all! She is a lady of the highest standing, the most impeccable character—"

"Well, just tell me," snapped Crane, "since you seem determined to make it known to me. And why do you require my blessing in any event? I am not your father."

"But you are the head of my family, and I value your blessing very highly, since my father is dead." Tobias said it with a straight face. Harry kept his head down to hide his own expression. Tobias would be sunk without his uncle's financial support, not to mention the inheritance Crane could leave to the Horticultural Society if he chose.

Crane seemed to have the same thought. "I suppose you have weighed this blessing in pounds," he said irritably. "Who is your object, then?"

"Lady Mariah Dunmore." Tobias puffed up his chest with pride.

Fortunately for Harry, Crane's reaction was derisive enough for both of them. "Damned fool," he said at once, cackling with laughter. "She won't have you."

His nephew blinked and raised his chin, stung. "I believe she might."

Crane seized on the telling word. "Might! And the moon might crash into the sun. Might! Doncaster won't have you, even if she would. Unless you've managed to find your way beneath her skirts and leave your babe in her belly, you've not a prayer."

"Uncle!" Tobias was shocked. "Of course I would never abuse her that way!"

His uncle shrugged. "I never said you should. But your only hope is that she's lost her head over you, silly girl, in which case she might have allowed you certain liberties that would force her father's hand."

Harry's fingers clenched on his pen. He could no longer force it to keep moving across the page. For a second he could feel the velvet skin at the back of Mariah's neck, the soft brush of her lips against his, the breathy gasp she made when he slid his hand under her nightdress, around her breast. Just like that, his body reacted merely from the memory of holding her. He swallowed and tried to tamp down the flush of anger and desire rolling through him.

"You insult me," Tobias was saying, sounding mortally offended. "I intend to make an honorable offer for the lady's hand, and I believe she might be inclined to accept."

"Why?" Crane's voice was like a silken whip, soft but stinging.

"Well—because . . . " Tobias flushed. "She has rejected every other suitor. She is kindness itself every time I speak to her. She clung to my arm very sweetly at the Arnold soiree a fortnight past. I think she favors me, Uncle, and I intend to propose marriage."

Crane squinted at him for a moment as though he couldn't quite believe Tobias was serious. "Eh, go to it, then." He waved one hand in dismissal. "You're a fool, whether you get her or no."

Tobias chose to declare victory and retreat. Beaming, he bowed. "Thank you, Uncle. Good day."

The viscount sighed as the door closed. "The damned fool doesn't know what he's doing. The Doncasters may be what he wants, but I warrant he's not all they want. He'll end like our noble King, stuck with an unsuitable wife he can't be rid of . . . Well, well, Towne! What are you doing there?"

Harry rose at the peevish query. "Finishing the diagram of the new knot garden at Brimstow, sir." His employer snatched it from his outstretched hand and scowled at it, but Harry knew it was perfectly done.

"I wish to add something here," Crane said, stabbing one palsied finger at an open space. "Something clean and bright, but delicate . . . " He muttered to himself, then tossed aside the drawing. "Oh, off you go."

A short time later, an exhaustive list in his pocket, Harry walked down the steps of Crane's house and headed for the Horticultural Society to discover which little plant would be added to Crane's collection. It was a bright sunny day, after a week of rain, and he strode along briskly, stretching his legs and inhaling the crisp fresh air. He turned toward St. James, intending to make the most of his reprieve from drawing and spying on his way to Piccadilly.

Before he had reached the end of the street, a small but smart phaeton flashed past. It made him think of Tobias, preparing to propose to Mariah. His steps slowed. He didn't think Mariah would accept Tobias, not because of her feelings for *him*, which he didn't know for certain in any event—but because Crane was right: Tobias was a fool, and Mariah had never spoken fondly of fools. She would never be happy with a buffoon, no matter how charming and handsome he was, and she could hardly appreciate Tobias's extreme interest in her family status and connection.

Still, it struck black murder in a man's heart to see another man pursue his most passionate desire. Harry resumed walking, telling himself he was a bigger fool than Tobias, but it did no good. Fool he might be, but he was a fool desperately in love.

The wide boulevard through St. James's park was filled with Londoners out savoring the sunshine. Every man seemed to have a woman on his arm. Harry imagined strolling though a park with Mariah at his side, her smiling face turned up to him, the sunlight warming them both. She had been glorious the day he met her in the park as Lord Wroth, and even more beautiful the day he sat in her mother's drawing room hunched over his tea and tried not to stare at her with his heart in his eyes. It was bad enough he couldn't call on her today, but to know Tobias Crane was on his way to propose marriage to her on this perfect spring day . . .

Harry cursed under his breath, abruptly turned at the end of the park, and went up into the main road, where dozens of busy shops lined the street. It took him out of his way, but he didn't care. Crane could wait a little longer to discover a new plant. In fact, he felt less and less obliged to hew strictly to the viscount's directives now that he knew the true requirements of his actual job, and today he felt rebellious enough to drop all pretense of being Crane's man for a while.

It took some time to locate the right shop, and then more time to choose his purchase, but when he left, he walked along with a spring in his step and a smile on his face. A week ago he would have never dared, for fear of discovery or Stafford's wrath or any of a dozen other reasons. But today . . . today he thought it was a grand thing to do.

"Mr. Tobias Crane to see you, Lady Mariah."

Mariah's first instinct at the butler's announcement was to flee. She was cozily nestled in a sunny spot in the garden, an open book on her lap, enjoying the warmth of the sun and daydreaming about when Harry might come to see her next. It seemed an age since he had climbed through her window. She'd kept to her promise not to know him if they met in public but she never promised not to *look* for him in public—and all her promises had been in vain anyway. She hadn't caught sight of Lord Wroth or Mr. Towne the secretary anywhere, and was past being ashamed to say she had looked for both. Harry had disappeared entirely from her life, and although she felt more at peace with that, his absence left a sad hole in her world.

And now Mr. Crane had come to cast a shadow over the rest of it. For a moment she debated telling the butler to send him away, but decided against it, reluctantly. Her mother was already watching her with concern, and Mariah knew turning away visitors would alarm her even more, no matter who the visitor or what the reason.

She set aside her book and got to her feet. "I'll see him in the drawing room, Hawking."

"Very good, my lady." The butler bowed and glided away.

Mariah followed more slowly. She had a dreadful apprehension she knew what Mr. Crane had come about; no one could have missed his devoted regard and constant presence near her. Joan would tease her to no end about this one, even though her cousin found her other marriage proposals less and less amusing as the number of them mounted.

He was waiting in the drawing room and swept a deep bow as she entered. Mariah curtsied, and left the drawing room doors wide open. With any luck, her mother would come by and save her.

"Good day, Mr. Crane."

He always wore the same broad, slightly foolish smile when he looked at her. "It is a very fine day, indeed, Lady Mariah."

"Won't you be seated?" she murmured, gesturing to the furniture behind him. Purposely, she took a single chair. He sat on the edge of the nearest sofa, never taking his eyes from her face.

For a moment neither spoke. It made Mariah uncomfortable, the way he looked at her with such focused admiration. "How is your uncle?" she asked, thinking more of Lord Crane's secretary. "I trust he is in good health."

"Indeed he is." Mr. Crane wet his lips and inched forward in his seat. Before she could react, he reached out and took her hand. "Shall I compare thee to a winter's day?"

Mariah blinked. "A winter's day? Am I cold, sir?"

Horror flashed across his face. "No, no, no! Never, dear lady! I—I should have begun with another poem—"

"Oh, please do not," Mariah said hastily. "That is— please just speak your mind, sir. I am not a devotee of poetry."

"You aren't?" It seemed to confound him; his brow wrinkled in confusion and his grip on her hand slackened, just enough for her to pull free and quickly clasp her hands together in her lap. "But—then—oh, dash it all!" He lurched to his feet, looking almost like a boy about to plead for a treat. "I adore you," he blurted out.

Mariah blinked again. "Sir—"

"Truly I do. Since the moment I saw you. I'd have told you then, except that it seemed bad form, and perhaps a trifle out of place, what with your cousin standing right there and a crowd of people close at hand—"

She blushed in mortification at the memory of their first meeting. "Mr. Crane, *please*."

"I would be a faithful servant to you," he barreled on. "A most loyal, devoted, tender and kind husband. You would rule me with one soft glance from your beautiful eyes."

She bit her lip. She didn't want a husband who was her servant, nor did she want a husband cowed by a glance. "Mr. Crane . . . "

"And I shall inherit my uncle's title, so it would not be too far a fall in the world for you. Of course, you would still have your connections through your family, and eventually I might rise enough to join the circles you now inhabit."

He was making her head hurt. Mariah closed her eyes and waited for him to finish.

"In short, I would do anything to win your hand, my dear. You have but to name it, and I will grant it. It shall ever be so, between us, if only you will consent to be my wife." Thus concluding his speech, Mr. Crane fell to his knees and tried once more to capture her hand.

Mariah resisted. "Sir, please! Stop!"

"Yes, my heart's most precious darling?" His expression was almost tragic in its hopefulness, his eyes shining, a fine sheen of perspiration on his upper lip. Mariah felt as though she were about to break a man's heart, even though part of her felt he was ridiculous to fancy himself in love with her when he hardly knew her. He knew nothing of her temper, her humor, her wit, nothing at all of her moods and passions. It was calf love, but it was sincere calf love, and she felt a moment's remorse.

But just a moment's remorse. It was kinder to refuse him now than to give false hope. "I am greatly honored by your declaration," she said gently. "But I must refuse."

His eager expression didn't change. "Why? You needn't refuse. What is my fault? Tell me and I shall remedy it."

"Er—no, no." She squirmed backward in her chair, wishing he would stand up and move away. "It is just that—while I hold you in very high esteem—my affections are not engaged as they should be for marriage."

"Oh." The surprise was obvious in his voice. He sat back on his heels. "I see."

"I am very honored by your offer and thank you most humbly," she said by rote. "But I am certain we would each find greater happiness with other people."

He nodded once, as if dazed, then got to his feet and barely managed a bow before turning and walking from the room, his steps quick and jerky. Mariah held her breath until the main door opened and closed, then exhaled in relief. It was becoming uncomfortable to refuse so many offers of marriage. It was so much easier when the gentlemen went first to Papa and he could refuse for her.

A tap on the door roused her from her thoughts. "Beg pardon, my lady," said the footman who entered. "Just delivered." He handed her a florist's box, plain and rather small.

It contained a single lily, stark and lovely in its simplicity, with a few ferns to surround it. The card, though, was the true gift. There was no signature, just a delicately drawn strand of ivy with a suggestion of stonework behind it. Mariah stared at it a moment, then a delighted smile spread across her face and she laughed aloud in joy as she clasped the card to her breast.

Harry had not forgotten her any more than she had forgotten him.

Chapter 20

The next night, they were to attend a musical evening in Chelsea. Lady Fromby had engaged a Scottish soprano, Mrs. Campbell, and was holding a benefit for the Royal Hospital, which lay nearby and where Lord Fromby served as a director. Mama was keen to hear the singer, and Papa would no doubt end up in a heated discussion in Lord Fromby's study. Mariah had no interest in going. She was quite sure Harry wouldn't be at a benefit in Chelsea, where only wealthy guests of the highly connected and proud Frombys would be invited.

But she was wrong.

It was indeed a very elegant affair, and Mama was soon deep in conversation with several other ladies. Mariah stood quietly, until a stooped figure across the room caught her eye. She even took a step back to be certain her eyes didn't deceive her. No, she was quite right, and an involuntary smile bloomed on her face. Quickly, she looked away, raising her fan to hide her expression. She followed her mother into the large, ornate drawing room without a word, but temptation was already whispering in her ear. Could she manage it? And did she dare? It was a risk, after both her parents had expressed their disapproval . . .

Mariah wet her lips and debated. Hang the risk, she finally decided in a burst of recklessness. Just as the singer came out to the applause of the guests, she leaned toward her mother. "I have to visit the powder room," she whispered, and jumped out of her chair to hurry quietly out of the room before her startled mother could say a word. As she walked past the last row, where Lord Wroth sat in solitary dignity, she thought she saw a hint of a smile on his face.

She hurried to the powder room, patted her hair and fluffed her skirt, then hurried back to the drawing room. She almost shrieked aloud as Lord Wroth shuffled out the door at the same moment she almost rushed in, then fell back with her fist at her lips.

"Eh, there, are you going to be ill?"

He stepped closer and grasped her elbow. She stared into Harry's warm, laughing eyes and shook her head mutely.

"Good thing. A mighty blow to this old man's pride, it would be, if young ladies fainted at the sight of me." He winked at her over his spectacles, and Mariah smiled, her heart settling back into place after its leap into her throat.

"You aren't leaving, are you?" she murmured. A servant stood at the end of the hall, but otherwise they were alone.

He shook his head, his eyes steady on hers.

"Oh, good. I am so glad." Mariah hesitated, but it was too risky. If she didn't return to the concert, her mother would come look for her. And she had promised Harry not to do anything to give him away. "Then should we return?"

He put out his arm. Her fingers trembling, Mariah took it, and they slipped wordlessly back into the drawing room. It was dark at the back of the room, all the candles having been lit at the front to show off the singer. Instead of returning to her seat, she followed Harry—moving soundlessly in spite of his cane—into the darkest shadows. As they turned to face the musicians and Mrs. Campbell, Mariah let her hand hang at her side, behind the folds of her skirt. Harry's fingers closed around hers, strong and sure, where no one else could see. She felt a peaceful warmth steal over her, and when she darted a sideways glance at Harry, he was watching her the same way. There they stood, shoulder-to-shoulder and hand in hand until the song ended.

The audience applauded. She had only a few minutes before her parents saw her. "I have to go," she whispered. "I wish I did not. I wish we could slip away somewhere and be alone for an hour . . . "

He pressed her hand, then let go. "It has been a pleasure listening with you. I shall take a turn in the garden, I believe. The fresh air will be good for my chest." Every word he said had been in Lord Wroth's scratchy, quavering voice. "Good evening to you, my lady." He gave a brief bow and shuffled off. Mariah closed her eyes and laid her hand on her bosom; the garden. She could find him in the garden.

"Where did you go, dearest?" asked her mother in concern when she made her way back through the guests. "Are you feeling well?"

"Ah—yes. Well enough. I felt a little overcome—the heat . . . " She fanned herself vigorously in illustration.

Mama looked a bit perplexed, but smiled. "Shall we step outside? It is warm tonight."

"Oh yes." Mariah obediently followed, wondering how she would manage to get away. Harry had disappeared, although she'd expected that.

On the terrace outside they met her father. He was talking to Lord Dexter, one of Mariah's early suitors. Mama drew her toward them, greeting Lord Dexter warmly; she had always thought him most eligible. Mariah curtsied, casting a longing glance at the sunken garden. Could she profess a sudden interest in tulips?

"Are you enjoying the concert, Lady Doncaster?" Lord Dexter asked politely. He must have gone out with Papa and the other gentlemen to discuss politics while the ladies listened inside. Many gentlemen were caught up in politics these days, mostly the question of whether Queen Caroline would return to England and fight for her crown. Mariah had no interest in it, not now.

"Very much, sir," Mama replied, fanning herself. "If only it weren't so warm."

Papa smiled. "I cannot complain, if the heat has driven you out here to us."

"Indeed no," Lord Dexter agreed.

The conversation ran on in that manner for a bit, although Mariah paid no attention. Was Harry waiting for her? Could he know she had been caught and delayed? How she wished he would come to her again; it was easier for him to sneak into her room than it was for her to get away for even a quarter hour, apparently. Not for the first time, she bristled against the unfair advantages gentlemen had over ladies.

Then Lord Dexter turned to her, startling her out of her thoughts. "Lady Mariah, might I persuade you to take a turn about the garden with me?"

Mariah's lips parted in dismay. She turned to her mother in appeal. Her mother mistook her hesitation, and smiled graciously at Lord Dexter. "How kind, sir. You may go, Mariah, if you wish."

She bobbed a curtsey to hide her frustration. "Thank you, sir." With no choice, she put her hand on his arm and let him lead her across the grass and down the steps into Lady Fromby's Dutch garden.

It was cooler and much darker in the garden. A few lanterns cast flickering shadows across the path, but otherwise it was quiet and still. Not many guests had come all the way out here.

"What a lucky man I am, to have the most beautiful young lady on my arm tonight."

Mariah smiled uneasily at the way he pulled her even closer to his side. "You flatter me too much, sir."

"I should like to flatter you more." He reached out to touch her face, but she turned away at the last moment.

"And I am sure you also wish to be quite proper and gentlemanly." She tugged at her hand but he wouldn't let her go.

"I have been, my dearest Lady Mariah. Part of my desire to speak to your father hinged on it. I have asked his permission to call on you."

"Indeed?" Mariah glanced over her shoulder. Had no one else come into the garden? "What answer did he make?"

"He indicated your choice was yours alone, and that I had his blessing to try to persuade you."

The faintly patronizing amusement in his voice stung her temper. "I must warn you I am not easily persuaded against my inclination," she said coolly, hoping he would get the hint.

"That sounds like a challenge." Only as he bent his head toward her did she smell the wine on his breath. He wasn't drunk, but had probably had enough to make him bold. She twisted in his grip as he put one arm around her waist and pulled her against him.

"Stop," she protested, shoving at his shoulder. "I believe I have made up my mind against you already!"

"Can't have," he muttered, trying to kiss her. "Come now, you're an intrepid female, smiling at every man in town . . . " Mariah pulled one arm free and swung, smacking him on the side of his head with her forearm. He ducked under her flailing and pressed his mouth to her cheek. She squeaked and protested again when his hand, trying to grasp her shoulder, slid down to her breast.

"You're drunk!" she cried. "Let me go!"

And he did. With a strange choking sound, he released her and bowed his head.

Mariah stumbled backward, breathing hard, and rounded on him in anger. "How dare you, sir," she began, only to stop as she realized that Lord Dexter was not standing in penitent silence before her; he was slumping, unconscious, into the arms of another man whose hand was still wrapped around Lord Dexter's throat.

Her stunned gaze jumped from Harry's face—so foreign still, under the wild mop of Lord Wroth's hair, but taut with controlled fury—to the man in his arms, then back again.

"Are you hurt?" He spoke in a harsh whisper that hummed with intensity.

Wordlessly she shook her head.

His eyes locked with hers for a moment. Then he turned and lowered Lord Dexter onto the grass, prop-

ping him up against a tree. Dexter's head lolled back
on his shoulder, his mouth gaping, and Mariah's heart
took another sickening leap—but then a distinct snore
drifted out of that mouth, and she stumbled away,
weak with relief.

"You should return to the house." Harry rose from
settling Lord Dexter and turned to her. She gasped
as the deadly gleam of a knife disappeared under his
coat. He held out his hand. "Come. I'll see you out of
the garden." His voice had become that of Lord Wroth
again, crackling and thin. She looked at him in amazement. He appeared every inch an elderly gentleman—
except that now she knew there was a dagger under
his coat, and he had just taken down Lord Dexter with
one hand. Lord Dexter was a large man, tall and broad
in the shoulders. He was strong, too; Mariah had
always thought she was a fairly sturdy woman, but
Dexter easily held her with one arm while he groped
her with the other. She glanced down at him again as if
to remind herself this had all truly happened.

"Is he . . . ?" She swallowed, unconsciously touching
her throat.

"He's had too much to drink," said Harry. It was
eerie to hear Lord Wroth's voice from his lips. It didn't
sound a thing like his normal voice. Mariah swallowed another gulp of hysteria at his unnatural abili-
ties. "He'll have a splitting headache on the morrow,
and doubtless not a single memory of this evening."

"What did you do to him?" she whispered.

He hesitated, then stepped closer. "Here . . . " His fingers trailed down her cheek, then curved around her
jaw as if to raise her face for a kiss. His thumb rested
lightly on the side of her throat. "Here runs a vessel of
blood. Press firmly for just a moment, and the stron-

gest man will fall senseless. The wine did the rest."
His hand slid down her throat, his touch still feathery
light, then stopped at her collarbone.

Mariah stared back at him in the faint light of a
nearby lantern. Stooped over as he was, his eyes were
level with her own.

"You should return," he murmured again, even
though he didn't move.

She had to clear her throat before she could speak.
"Yes."

"I'm sorry I frightened you."

She shook her head. "No—no, I just—I was frightened before you appeared. He seemed like a perfectly
decent gentleman. . . . " She put her hand on his arm,
clinging to him. He had just proved himself not the romantic gallant of her dreams but a dangerous man—
and she had never felt safer. Lord Dexter snored behind
her in drunken oblivion, and she stepped closer to
Harry, wanting to fling herself into his arms and hide
within the safety he offered.

Harry clenched his jaw as she crowded against him.
His body reacted to the feel of hers, his cock growing hard and heavy as her soft breasts pressed into
his arm and chest. The fury that had roared through
him when he saw Dexter holding her as she struggled
hadn't abated, only mutated into a blazing desire that
strained his conscience and his soul. Part of him remembered that he was still Wroth tonight, that he
would be caught out and exposed as a liar and imposter if anyone had seen what he had done. The other
part of him, the greater part, wanted to pull Mariah
farther into the shadows, push her up against a tree
and make love to her hard and fast, marking her as
his in the most primal way. Because she was; whatever

chasm of propriety and situation lay between them, he knew without a shadow of doubt that he would die for her.

She raised her face to him. Her lips trembled and her eyes glistened. "Harry . . . "

Harry swore. He could feel her pulse beneath his thumb, throbbing rapidly. His conscience made one last token objection, and then he was pulling her deeper into the darkness to a sheltered arbor, trapping her against the trunk of an oak, and taking her face in his hands to kiss her with a hunger that threatened to consume him.

"Don't stop," Mariah moaned as his mouth left hers and moved to her neck. His hands were sliding down her back, pressing her against him even as she clung to him with all her strength. She could feel every inch of his body, lean and strong and capable of sliding through the darkness like a shadow. He made her feel wicked and alive, and she would have granted him any liberty he demanded at that moment.

"*Shh.*" He put his finger on her lips. She captured his gloved fingertip between her teeth and lightly bit down, trying to wriggle closer to him. "Minx," he whispered in her ear. "You'll pay for that."

She sucked in her breath as his other hand cupped her breast. Her nipples grew tight and hard, and so sensitive she almost cried out when he rolled his thumb over the taut peak. Sensation rippled through her, and a fierce heat bloomed in her belly. Her body softened, opened, and she slid one foot along the side of his boot, trying to hold him to her with all her limbs.

And then he kissed her once more on the mouth,

a hard, demanding kiss. Her head spun. Her knees started to buckle, but he raised his head. "You have to go back."

Mariah shook her head, refusing to open her eyes or to release him. Fire seemed to be licking at her bones. "I don't want to."

"You must." His lips brushed the corner of her mouth. "If anyone else should come into the garden . . ."

"I would not betray you for the world."

His chuckle was muted. "I would betray myself, if you were to keep looking at me that way." He brushed a stray wisp of hair from her temple, and she felt his fingers shake. "But we can't give in to madness, not here. You must return."

With an effort, Harry released her and stepped away. He closed his eyes, forcing himself to breathe in and out. He couldn't make love to her, even though he burned to, even though he knew she wanted him to. He shouldn't have kissed her, nor even touched her. He had to take her back to the house while he still remembered that. "You should return to the house," he repeated once more, to himself as much as to her. "Your parents will be missing you."

She bowed her head and nodded. When he put out his hand, his desire once more in check if not diminished, she gave him hers.

He led her around the wisteria path, pausing to pick up the walking stick he had dropped. With his blood racing and his heart still pounding, it was hard to fall back into the slow, shuffling gait of Wroth, even had the source of his arousal not been hanging on his arm. He stabbed the stick into the ground with more force than necessary. God, he was tired of this facade.

"Why are you here?"

He almost missed Mariah's whisper, he was so caught up in his thoughts. As it was, he barely remembered to speak in Wroth's voice. "Eh? What's that? Why, 'tis a rare privilege to hear a soprano of Mrs. Campbell's quality," he replied, leaning on his cane and bending a kindly glance on her. At least, he hoped it was kindly instead of burning with thwarted desire. "And she's a fetching Scottish lass, as well."

"Oh." The sound was soft with disappointment. "I see."

Harry hesitated, then lowered his voice and dropped Wroth's accent. "Just watching out for someone—and keeping my eyes open, should any ladies need rescuing."

Her eyes shone. "Have you rescued many other ladies tonight?"

"No." He could get lost in those eyes. "But I was only watching one."

Her next breath was shaky. Her body swayed toward his. Their progress had slowed to a halt, and Harry forced himself to start off before he forgot himself again.

"There, you're not overset from your tumble into the shrubbery, are you, Lady Mariah?" He watched until realization flashed in her face. She had been in the garden a long time, and someone would ask her why. She would have to explain the dirt on her gown, as well as any scrapes or marks Dexter might have left on her, and Harry offered her a reason that didn't require a rescuer. For both their sakes, his part in the evening must remain unknown.

"No, no," she murmured. "But it was so very, *very* fortunate you happened along at that moment, sir. I was never so happy in all my life to see anyone as I was you."

Harry nodded as lust swelled and surged within him. Keep going, he told himself. They had reached the steps of the garden. Light from the mansion spilled out onto the grass, and anyone could see them. He stumped doggedly forward, right to the edge of the small terrace, and stopped. He turned to her and bowed. "I am relieved to hear it. No doubt you will want your mother. I hope you are able to enjoy the rest of the evening."

"Yes, thank you." She released his arm and stepped away.

Harry lowered his head, and she bobbed a quick curtsey. Over her shoulder he could see her father approaching.

"Come to me tonight," she breathed.

Her words went straight to his groin, and Harry forced a grim smile, groping in his pocket for a handkerchief and hoping no one noticed his state. "I am always pleased to be of service. Ah, good evening, sir." He looked up into the earl's set face.

"Wroth." Doncaster barely acknowledged him as he took his daughter's hand. "Mariah, where have you been?"

"I stumbled over a tree root, Papa, and fell into the shrubbery. Lord Wroth was kind enough to walk me back to the house."

Doncaster glanced his way again, a measuring look. "My thanks, Wroth."

Harry inclined his head. "I could never overlook a young lady in distress. I was delighted to be of some slight assistance."

The earl nodded once. "Indeed. We shan't detain you any longer, sir. I shall see to my daughter now."

Harry bowed to Mariah. Then he excused himself and shuffled away, saying a prayer of thanksgiving that Doncaster obviously still saw him as an old man and nothing more.

"Mariah, are you hurt?" her father asked in concern.

Mariah shook her head, unable to keep from watching Harry walk away. Harry, who had emerged from the darkness like a silent, deadly angel with a knife in his hand to protect her from Lord Dexter. Harry, who had pressed her up against a tree and kissed her as if it would kill him not to. Just the memory of it made her skin feel hot.

Papa took her chin in his hand and inspected her face. She dragged her eyes away from Harry's retreating back. "Wroth was not impertinent, was he?"

She blushed. She had seen the raw desire in Harry's eyes when he touched her throat, and she knew he'd seen the response in hers. He could have been impertinent in a dozen wicked ways and she wouldn't have stopped him or protested at all. Her body still throbbed in frustration that he hadn't. But she mustn't betray any hint of that to her father, who cast another suspicious glance after Harry. "Not at all!" she said. "But Papa, Lord Dexter was not a gentleman. I don't wish to see him again."

"What did he do?" her father demanded, successfully diverted.

"He—He tried to kiss me when I didn't want him to." The wobble in her voice was unaffected. It gave her serious pause to think about what might have happened, out there alone in the dark with Lord Dexter.

"And I think he was foxed. He also tripped in the dark, and never got up. I heard him snoring when Lord Wroth came upon me." There—no one could possibly suspect what Lord Wroth had actually done. She said a quick prayer that Harry was right and Lord Dexter would have no memory of the evening.

"I see." Papa looked grim. "Let us find your mother. Perhaps we should return home early."

"Oh, *yes*," blurted Mariah. Harry had to come see her tonight after what had happened. Surely he would. "Let's go this instant."

Her father nodded. "Very good," he replied, and led her back into the house.

Harry watched her leave, clinging to her father's arm. That ought to be the end of his work tonight. He'd watched Doncaster carefully, noting whom he spoke to and even lingering close enough to know what he spoke of. He hadn't seen anything exceptional in the earl's words or actions—but that was proof of nothing. He would still have to get inside the house and look, unfortunately, or persuade Brandon to do it. So far he had not dared speak to his fellow agents about Stafford's true purpose, but he was forced to admit he was making no progress on his own. And somehow following Mariah into the garden made him feel as though he'd broken his vow, even though he had not intended to speak to her or touch her or kiss her.

He took up his walking stick and left without taking proper leave of his host. Stafford continued to procure invitations to events that Doncaster, Crane, and Bethwell attended, but Harry felt free of his obligation to shadow them as he had before, or even to maintain his disguise as rigidly. He found a hackney and gave the Fenton Lane direction. Phipps could pay for the long drive back across the river. Besides, tonight he was sure it would be fatal to go near Doncaster House, where Mariah would be waiting for him, and where his own mind and body longed to go.

Harry balled up his fist and rapped himself on the forehead. No matter how desperately he wished it, he had no right to go to her, no right to hold her close and soothe her fears, no right to promise her that he would never let anyone else hurt her ever again. He had no right to kiss her when she raised her lips to his, no right to touch her with the possessiveness he had almost killed Dexter for attempting . . .

No right at all.

Chapter 21

"**U**ncle! I have some shocking news!" Tobias burst into the room the next morning, flushed and breathless with scandal. Crane glanced up from his leaves.

"Oh? Have we no watercress for luncheon?"

His nephew shook his head, oblivious to the sarcasm. "No, it is far more serious than that. An attempt was made on Lord Liverpool's life."

Harry's pen stopped mid-word. Crane put down his magnifying lens with a soft clink. His eyes never left Tobias. "Indeed . . . ?"

Tobias drew a deep breath. "Someone attempted to poison him. He was to dine at a dinner party given by the Marquis of Bethwell, and then the soup was found to be tainted." Harry abandoned his pretense of working and put down the pen before ink ran all over his page. Was this the plot he had been hired to thwart? Had it unfolded in Bethwell's kitchen right under their noses?

"Attempted," Lord Crane repeated. "He is alive, then? And well?"

"Completely unharmed," Tobias confirmed. "But it was a very near thing, I believe. The villain was a cook—imagine! But he was caught attempting to put a fatal herb into the turtle soup. Not only the Prime Minister and Lord Bethwell, but all their dining companions would have been poisoned."

"The cook," Crane exclaimed, his color fading. "It simply cannot be."

Tobias nodded. "I am afraid it is, Uncle. Naturally, Lord Liverpool wishes to keep the news to a small circle. It wouldn't do for the populace to know how close to danger the government was."

Crane just looked at his nephew as if he spoke a different language. Tobias seemed to puff up with importance at having rendered his uncle speechless. He glanced at Harry. "Of course, I must ask you to keep this news in strictest confidence, Towne."

"Of course, sir," Harry murmured, watching Crane. The old man looked thunderstruck, even though Harry suspected he didn't hold the Prime Minister in as high regard as Tobias did.

"The villain was carted away to Newgate at once," Tobias went on. "No doubt he'll be tried and hanged for treason within the month. Imagine! A cook in the man's own kitchen! His housekeeper must be quaking in fear for her position."

Crane pressed one hand to his forehead. He was deathly pale. "Who told you this?"

"Lord Liverpool sent a man over to inform you, Uncle." Tobias pasted on a smile probably meant to look comforting, and instead appeared self-satisfied. "I insisted I should break the news to you myself, delicately, for the sake of your health."

Crane only nodded, sinking back into his chair. He looked frail and unwell all of a sudden, in stark contrast to his demeanor only a few minutes ago. Harry moved forward discreetly. "Perhaps you would like to rest now, sir," he said quietly.

"Oh, yes, Uncle," Tobias rushed to say. "Do rest. You must have a care for your health in the wake of such a shock. How appalling that assassins penetrated Lord Bethwell's very own kitchen! I intend to go into our own kitchen and question all the staff myself. If there are any poisoners in our midst, never fear, Uncle, I shall catch them out." Without waiting for his uncle's reply, Tobias bowed and left.

In the quiet in his wake, Harry collected the leaf specimens and put them away. Crane still sat slumped in his chair, fortunately silent. Harry's mind raced. If this were the plot, and the villains had been caught, Stafford would soon notify them all, and they would begin disengaging themselves from their posts. He would be his own man again, free to pursue his own interests . . .

He didn't dare let himself think further. He could hardly present himself in the drawing room of Doncaster House, a penniless commoner without a handful of dirt to call his own, and ask for the hand of the earl's daughter. But at least his part in spying on the earl need never come out; he could rest easy that he'd only acted in a protective fashion toward Doncaster, which only doubled his relief that Doncaster had not been the treasonous party Stafford and Sidmouth sought. That fact alone, more than anything else, lifted a monstrous burden of care from his shoulders.

"Put it all away, Towne." Crane's voice startled him out of his thoughts.

"Sir?"

"All away," Crane repeated quietly. "I shan't wish to do any more today." Surprised, Harry put away the journals and instruments. Crane rarely put away his botanical work before late afternoon. Perhaps Lord Liverpool's brush with death was more unsettling than expected. Crane might have thought him cold and vain, but the man was the leader of the government.

"May I bring you anything, my lord?" Harry asked.

Crane didn't move. "No. Nothing."

Harry hesitated. "Is there anything else I can do for you, sir?"

"No, nothing," Crane said again. "It all seems rather pointless now." He looked up. "You might go protect the kitchen staff from my nephew. He seems quite determined to expose another poisoner in our midst, and I should hate to lose my chef. I assume if he had wished to poison me, it would have been done long ago."

"Mr. Crane means well, sir."

"He may mean well, but Liverpool might as well have sent a notice to the *Times*. Tobias cannot keep a secret for long. How gleefully he rushed up here to tell me!" Crane sighed. "He means to do well for himself. And I suppose my own death would be a great aid to him in that ambition."

Harry could hardly argue with that. "I am sure Mr. Crane meant nothing like that, sir," he murmured diplomatically. "No doubt Mr. Crane is merely somewhat carried away in his relief that the Prime Minister and his companions were fortunately unharmed."

"Fortunate?" Crane looked up from under his brows. "Yes, fortunate for the minister, indeed."

That was spiteful, even for Crane, but for some reason Harry couldn't leave it alone. Just a few months past, a band of radicals had plotted to assassinate the entire Cabinet over dinner, and then to overthrow the government. They had planned to behead all the ministers and set Sidmouth's and Castlereagh's heads on pikes. Stafford had a hand in foiling that plan. Harry couldn't imagine it hadn't been of significant interest to Lord Crane, as it had rippled through the town like a clap of thunder, far off and muted but threatening nonetheless. "It would have thrown the country into a crisis," he said to Crane now. "Any attack on the government in these times must cause alarm."

"There would not have been a crisis England could not withstand," Crane retorted, some of his color returning.

Harry straightened the journals on the shelf; something about Crane's reply was not right. He knew the viscount did not much like Lord Liverpool, but it was a different level of dislike entirely to say England would be just as well without him.

"But then, it does not matter," said Crane, subsiding again. "The minister is alive and well—completely unharmed, Tobias assures me. England can sleep well tonight."

Harry wondered again, but Crane said no more. His chores complete, he had no choice but to leave.

Tobias had been to the kitchen, but the butler had been able to soothe the chef's ruffled feelings. Harry thanked him on behalf of Lord Crane, who did not suspect his staff of poisoning, indeed not. Mr. Crane had been unduly alarmed by rumors of poisonings, which would doubtless prove false. Lord Crane was very satisfied no one in his household would be so disloyal, and no one was so accused.

Then, unneeded by Crane and having done his part to restore calm to the household, Harry put on his hat and left.

Papa came in while Mariah was having tea with her mother. "There has been an assassination attempt on Lord Liverpool," he said, white-faced and somber.

Mama put down her cup. "Charles, no!"

He nodded, sinking into the chair beside her. "A cook in Lord Bethwell's house attempted to add a large dose of toxic herbs to the soup. By a singular stroke of fortune, a maid observed him doing it, recognized it was not savory as it should have been, and raised the alarm in the kitchen in time to have the soup recalled. If not for her, Bethwell and all his guests, including Liverpool, might have been poisoned and killed."

"Good heavens." Mama reached out her hand and Papa grasped it. "The Bethwells shall be outcasts; no one will ever dine with them again, even if they sack their entire staff. Who is responsible? Surely no mere servant would have done such a thing on his own."

Papa glanced at her with admiration gleaming in his eyes. "You have put your finger on it as usual, Cassandra. It is not entirely certain yet, but it appears the man may have been related to one of the murderers who attempted to assassinate the Cabinet this spring. Under interrogation, he claimed he was fulfilling the mission of the Cato Street conspirators and avenging their deaths at the hands of Liverpool's government."

Mariah sat very still in her chair. Mostly she didn't want to call attention to herself and risk being sent away while her parents discussed this shocking event, but partly she was thinking of a man who spied and watched after people and lurked in the shadows with a knife under his coat. Could this be the reason for all of Harry's secrets? Had he been involved? She had heard the Cato plot was discovered by a spy . . . like Harry? Might he have been hurt? Her heart seized at the thought.

"What a relief it all came to naught." Seeming to recall her presence, Mama threw a significant look in Mariah's direction. "You may go, dearest."

Her father glanced at her. "No, let her know, Cassandra. Mariah will be discreet, and there is no reason she should not hear. It will be whispered about everywhere, I have no doubt."

"Thank you, Papa," she murmured, thankful as ever for an indulgent father. "What will happen now?"

He sighed, taking the glass of port a servant had brought at her mother's signal. "I don't know. The Cabinet has been under enormous strain lately, thanks to this business with the Queen, and this will not make things easier. It will be common knowledge about London by the end of the week, I daresay, and no doubt only embolden those who mutter against the government. Liverpool already has his hands full, and now he must walk about in fear of his very life, even in the homes of trusted friends. I would not have his place for all the world at this moment."

"Nor would I have you in it," murmured Mama.

"No, I was not in it," Papa said grimly. "But that may yet change."

Shortly afterward gentlemen with grave expressions began calling on Papa. Mariah watched them come and go; she heard raised voices in her father's study, where they all met and talked and argued, late into the evening. Papa did not come to dinner, and his guests were still there when she went to bed.

She lay awake until late, burning to know what, if any, role Harry might have played. She was certain he was involved, in some way, although she could not for the life of her say how. And she might not ever know, for she had no way to contact him, not even a name to inquire after. Just Harry, she thought, watching the shadows of the tree branches flit across her window. She placed her hand atop the little card with the delicate scroll of ivy, lying on the table beside her bed, the only proof she had of Harry's existence, and a lone tear ran down her cheek.

The next day Papa revealed more about the plot. It had been kept out of the newspapers so far, and Liverpool was of the opinion they should keep it that way. "Some of the lower classes are already hinting assassination may be an acceptable method of protesting the Cabinet's policies," Papa said, looking worn and weary over breakfast. "Two attempts in three months might inspire others to try again."

"But the villain will be dealt with," said Mama. "Quickly and decisively, no doubt."

"Yes, but did he work alone? So far he has confessed nothing more than a desire to kill Lord Liverpool. Sidmouth would hang the man this day, but if he is part of a larger plot, his death could lead to worse. The worst we could do is to make the man a martyr." Papa sighed and shook his head. "But that is not my main concern.

It is time for cooler heads to intercede, and apparently I have been selected as the first to try."

"Ah," said his wife with a knowing look. "How do you intend to do that?"

"I shall call on His Highness. This business with the Queen has unnecessarily agitated people, giving them a rallying figure for all who feel abused by His Majesty's government. The King's persistence in seeking a divorce has transformed her from a spoiled, indulgent woman into a victim of royal petulance. He must be persuaded to cease promoting, for a time, his desire to eradicate her from the monarchy. And since I think it wisest to begin softly . . . " He turned and glanced over his shoulder. " . . . I should like Mariah to come with me."

Mariah, who had been eating quietly, hoping to discover more about any possible connection to Harry, started in surprise. "Me, Papa?"

"Yes, you." Mariah put down her fork and faced her father. "You know the king wishes to divorce his wife."

She nodded. That was common knowledge, although most people didn't approve of the idea. Even in her deepest fascination with Harry, she had heard the talk about the King and Queen.

Papa sighed again. "And that he is determined to keep her from his coronation? That he has had her name removed from the prayers of clergymen across England?"

"What does this have to do with Lord Liverpool?" she dared to ask.

"Liverpool opposes the divorce, but he is the King's man. There is great unrest in England now, Mariah. Newspapers exhort the masses to revolt. Some of the radicals have chosen to rally around the Queen as a symbol of their discontent. Rumors have been flying thick and fast that she is about to embark any day from France for England, to claim her right as Queen. The King is just as determined that she shall not be recognized in any way. Do you see the storm brewing?"

"Yes, Papa. But what is to be your role?"

His expression turned rueful. "I am to persuade His Majesty, delicately and gently, that talk of the Queen, at least, must die down. Divorce is out of the question; procuring it would be very costly politically, if not impossible, and England has more important worries now. If the populace is not distracted by a pointless uproar over her return, it may calm the unrest and give the government a chance to bring down the most virulent of the mob. Some people are stirring a dangerous pot, and we must not let it boil over."

"And why am I to come with you?" Mariah darted a glance at her mother, who sat in watchful silence.

"Because it is meant to be a persuasive call, diplomatic and friendly instead of confrontational. His Majesty must take just such a tack in dealing with the Queen, and allow his ministers to persuade her not to return to England by whatever means they can, even if it injures the royal pride. The people's goodwill is a powerful thing, and His Majesty must remember that." Her father smiled. "And His Majesty has always been fond of a pretty female face. It will put him in good spirits if I bring one with me."

Mariah smiled and ducked her head. It would be quite a thrill to meet His Majesty. She had missed a chance to be presented to the old Queen, being too young before going abroad with her parents. The King might be older and less dashing than he had once been, but he was still the King. She glanced once more at her mother, who gave her a small nod of agreement. "Of course, Papa."

He pressed her hand. "Good girl. I shall request an audience as soon as His Majesty will see us."

The rumors were true. A cook in the Bethwell household was found to be a cousin to John Brunt, who had recently been hanged in Newgate for the failed conspiracy to assassinate the Cabinet in February. The cook, also a radical Spencean, had vowed to avenge his cousin's death and so had been putting a large quantity of toxic foxglove into the turtle soup. A maid became suspicious of him and so had been watching. By good fortune she recognized the herbs he added and was able to call others' attention to it. The cook was currently in Newgate, apparently spilling his secrets in an attempt to save his own life, but so far he had only named other petty rabble.

"Is Stafford satisfied?" Harry pressed. They were sitting in the kitchen having breakfast. Angelique had been to see Stafford late last night and was relating what he told her.

Angelique shrugged. "For now. He is beside himself with relief, even joy, to have caught someone. It proves he was right, and that always pleases a man."

"Of course. And the maid who intercepted the soup? She was one of his as well?"

Angelique smiled coyly. "She was not, until I befriended her. It is always good to have another pair of observant eyes about, and her eyes miss nothing. One hint that Lord Bethwell was anxious about his digestion, and she reported everything in the kitchens to me. And now she will have a rich reward, so it has gone well for all of us."

"I should say so," exclaimed Ian, pushing back his plate and slapping his hands down on his thighs. "And us? Are we to have our reward now?"

She nodded. "*Oui*. Stafford considers our business to be at an end. I will give my notice today. Harry, you are also free to leave Crane's service."

"And I?" Ian winked at her. With his broad Scots accent and imposing physique, Ian hadn't been assigned to anyone's household on the belief that he would never blend in. He'd always said he was happier with horses than with people anyway, and Harry had to admit they needed a coachman who knew what he was about. Angelique raised one eyebrow and crossed her arms.

"You wish to leave my service?"

The cheeky Scot grinned. "Not that I mind driving you about town—especially not when you wear that blue gown that looks like you can barely breathe in it—but sleeping above the stable leaves something to be desired. Or am I to improve my sleeping quarters as part of my reward?" Angelique regarded him with a thoughtful smile, running one fingertip along her lips. Ian seemed to recognize it as encouragement, for he leaned toward her. "I stand ever ready at *your* service, ma'am."

Harry got to his feet, annoyed at their flirting. He had heard Ian talk like that to every female on the street. "I'm off, then." They bade him farewell distractedly, still making eyes at each other. Harry took up his hat and coat and left, his mind much occupied.

Was this matter truly over? Stafford was not a fool, and if he believed they had caught their quarry, odds were they had. Harry didn't flatter himself that he knew more than, or even as much as, Stafford did about this whole affair. He supposed it was possible a cook could have been passing the treasonous information that had so alarmed Lord Sidmouth. Heaven knew it had been easy enough for him to get into houses and rooms he had no right being in and search for information. There was no reason a determined revolutionary, willing to sacrifice himself to his cause, couldn't have done the same thing.

But something didn't seem right, although he couldn't quite figure out what it was. Perhaps it just seemed too anticlimactic—a cook, of all people—or perhaps he had expected to be the person who unmasked the villain and gained whatever glory was to be had. Perhaps he'd somehow wished the guilty party would be Tobias Crane because of the man's interest in Mariah. Harry felt rather disgusted with himself for that possibility, and arrived at Crane's house cross and late.

His tardiness was unnoticed, however. When he slipped into the room, braced for a reproof, Crane was sitting in his Bath chair wrapped in a shawl and looking ill and old. Crane barely acknowledged his entrance and then was silent for a long while, sitting and staring out the window. Harry quietly went to his desk and set to work tidying up the journals that were always present. Any relief from Crane's temper ought to be a blessing, but somehow it only unsettled Harry's mood even more. It was just one more thing that was not normal, and therefore did not seem *right*.

"Towne," said Crane after a while.

"Yes, sir?"

The viscount sighed. His color was not good, as if a shadow had fallen across his face and stayed there.

On impulse, Harry asked, "Are you well, my lord? Should I ring for Jasper?"

"What?" Crane frowned at him, then raised a blue-veined hand to his forehead. His hand shook noticeably. "No, I am well enough for an old man. Jasper cannot do anything to remedy that." He sighed and sat a little straighter in his chair. "Take a letter."

"Yes, sir." Harry knew this routine; he took out a sheet of paper and uncapped his ink. Pen poised over the page, he looked up, and Crane nodded.

"To John Rusk. *Syringa reticulata*," Crane began, his voice regaining something of its usual vitality. "Prune delicately along the branches where the blossoms have faded. I shall be bringing several cuttings when I return to Brimstow, and may remove some existing *Syringa* to make way for them. Note any which may be unhealthy or losing vigor, and burn any that are blighted."

And so it went, for another three pages. Harry wrote dutifully, keeping in mind that he would not be doing this much longer. Although he would be happy never to write another botanical letter again, he was reluctant to walk away from his post immediately. Crane would be leaving soon for his country estate, and he could stay until then; he could claim he had no wish to leave London. After working so hard at maintaining his disguise, it seemed wrong to give notice abruptly and just vanish, even though it didn't matter what Crane thought of him now.

"And lastly," Crane said, causing Harry to straighten in relief. "*Lilium candidum.*" He paused, pursing his lips. "Yes, *Lilium candidum.* Harvest all the foliage from the bed in the southern garden; crop it close and low to the ground. Take care not to miss any, for it must all be cut. This must be done today, with great care. You must oversee the work yourself." Crane fell silent and the only sound was the faint scratching of Harry's pen.

When he finished copying the letter, Harry looked up. Crane's face was set in a brooding frown. The old man looked small and almost woebegone, huddled in his shawl, his fingers plucking at the fringe while he stared out the window. "No, it must be cut from my garden," he muttered to himself. Harry brought the letter across the room and waited. Crane shook himself, turning back. "Yes, yes," he said. "Give it here."

Harry handed over the letter and Crane glanced over it before reaching for the pen.

"This must go off at once," he said, handing back the signed letter.

"Yes, sir." Harry folded the letter and sealed it. He went to give it back to Crane to frank, but his employer seemed not to notice him. Harry laid the letter quietly in front of him.

Crane looked at it and sighed. "One of the oldest, finest plantings in my garden," he said wistfully. "So lovely."

"Why cut it, then?" Harry ventured. Better than anyone, he knew how attached Crane was to his plants; this was the first time he'd ever given instructions to remove any.

Crane's mouth quivered. "It will not grow with the *Syringa reticulata* I intend to plant there. And nothing must impede the *Syringa*." He picked up the letter. "No, no, you needn't send it," he said when Harry reached for it, seeming to shrink as he spoke. "Ring for Jasper; he will take it. I am unwell, and have no more need of your services today. You may go."

Surprised, Harry bowed, and left.

Chapter 22

He found Angelique at the Fenton Lane house already, looking herself for once. He stopped in the upstairs hall, leaning against the jamb of her open door. "Anxious to be done?"

"*Mon Dieu*, you cannot imagine." She was packing, folding severe gray dresses with white lace around the collar into a trunk. "Are you not?"

"I am." Harry peeled off his coat and took off his spectacles, tossing them aside, then rubbed the pinched bridge of his nose. "I plan to give notice next week." His thoughts drifted toward Mariah; perhaps in a week or so he would have cobbled together a plan to see her again, perhaps even openly and honestly. In the meantime, he thought he might go mad with nothing else to do. Working for Crane at least occupied the hours of the day.

She looked horrified. "Why then? I could not wait. *Fah!* Even giving notice took too long."

"What—do you mean you were sacked?"

She smiled, her dimples showing. "One tantrum about the danger here in London, the threat of poison in every mouthful, and he could not wait for me to be gone. For a man so fretful of his own health, he cares nothing at all for the welfare of his servants." Harry started laughing. "I did not receive a reference, of course," she added with a dramatic sigh. "What a pity."

"You'll never be a nurse again."

Angelique pulled a face. "I shall only pray it is so. It is a most disgusting employment, tending another's body."

Still chuckling, Harry surveyed the room. The house had become disorderly, with people moving through it at all hours of the day, changing clothes in a rush, occasionally catching some sleep or a bite to eat. None of them spent much time straightening up, not even Lisette. Angelique's bedchamber looked as if a theater wardrobe had exploded, with wigs lined up on the dressing table beside the cosmetics and somber nurse's attire piled up alongside revealing courtesan's clothing on every chair. "Bit of a mess we're leaving here."

She shrugged it off. "I am not paid to clean."

"No, of course not." He shifted his weight. "So Brandon will leave his post, too?"

"I suppose. He has not enjoyed being sent out on the carriage." She held up a particularly plain dress and scowled at it. "I should burn this one," she muttered, then tossed it into the trunk anyway. "But you—apparently you have taken a liking to your job. Shall you ask Stafford if he has need of any more clerks?"

He grinned halfheartedly at her teasing. "Not at all. Crane is leaving in a fortnight for his country estate. It seems less noteworthy if I quit his service then."

Angelique shrugged again. "As you like. Crane keeps you busy, yes?"

"Usually. Oddly, today he was ill and sent me home. And I am *not* sorry," he said, seeing her mouth curve. "I have never been so bored in all my life as when copying Crane's letters."

She laughed. "Bored is sometimes the best one can hope for. You could be fondled and touched by drunken gentlemen on a nightly basis." She held up one of her more garish wigs in illustration.

"Sometimes I would prefer it to fruit trees and bulb propagation and rose bed care. I have learned far more than I ever cared to know about gardening in these last weeks. Horticulturalists are lunatics, I tell you. Even today, so ill he could not even upbraid me for being a quarter hour late, Crane dictated pages and pages of instruction for his head gardener. Prune the *Syringa reticulata* and crop the *Lilium candidum* . . . It never ends." Harry shook his head.

"Crop the lilies?" Angelique said scornfully as she wrapped a bonnet before packing it in a hatbox. "The English, they think they are such gardeners. Crop the lilies now, before they enter their prime, before they bloom? What a waste. If they are cut too close, they will not grow back."

Harry lifted his head. "He said to crop it close and low."

"He must not wish lilies in his garden. It will surely kill them."

Harry stared at her, his mind racing. Cutting the lilies . . . before they enter their prime . . . it will surely kill them . . . *Lilies are the badge of the Dunmores*, echoed Mariah's voice in his head. *The lily for purity . . . the lion for England . . . Edward the Third was a distant cousin* . . . A comment here, a fact there. In an eerie procession, unrelated bits of information marched into order and spelled out the answer he'd been searching for all along. Stafford had been right—and very, very wrong. "Bloody Christ," he said numbly.

Angelique looked up from her packing. "What?"

"Go . . ." He crossed the room. "Go to Stafford, now. Tell him it's Crane . . . Crane's the one directing the radicals—and Doncaster is their target."

She looked at him with alert, unblinking eyes. Harry seized her arm and shoved her ahead of him toward the door. "Hail a carriage—or send Ian—tell him to bring a dozen men, Coldstream Guards, to Doncaster House—"

Angelique stopped, looking at him as if he'd gone mad. "Harry—what are you saying? It cannot be! They have caught the villain—the cook—"

"It is. I don't know if the cook is part of it or not, but this—this is the danger now."

"How do you know?" she demanded, stubbornly blocking the doorway.

Harry swore, running both hands through his hair. "The lilies are Doncaster—they're on his arms. Doncaster would be the radicals' worst nightmare: he's a shrewd politician who is friendly with both Whigs and Tories, he's descended from royalty himself, and he's dedicated to supporting the King while still sympathizing with the populace. The radicals want the government—the whole bloody monarchy!—to fall, and if Doncaster forms a new government, it won't."

"So? Why would Crane care? He is also from an old family . . . "

"He's eighty years old," said Harry bluntly. "His time is past. He thinks Liverpool is an ass and Castlereagh is a jumped-up country lawyer. When I said the death of Liverpool would throw the country into turmoil, he said it wouldn't be anything England couldn't survive. I think he *wants* to see a revolution, to prune away the deadwood so something new can grow."

"You must tell Stafford," she said, her voice low and her eyes glittering. "He set us to protect this man you accuse."

Harry clenched his fists in frustration. "Stafford hasn't been guarding these men, he's been watching them—*we've* been watching them!" He gripped her arms. "He's had a web of agents spying on them. We were never to interfere, were we? Never to give away our 'protective' presence, not even if we should have to save them from the jaws of death. Did you never wonder why Stafford insisted on that?"

"He never explains anything. Harry, you are imagining things—"

"He admitted it!" Harry snapped. "As did Phipps. They suspected someone was feeding information to the radicals, someone who would know the inner workings of the government. Somehow—I don't know how—they fastened on Bethwell, Doncaster, and Crane as the most likely. Think of all those reports we made on their every action. Stafford just couldn't figure out which one had turned traitor, so he set us to gather the information for him while he and Phipps sit in Bow Street like two spiders surveying their web."

"Why did you not tell me this sooner?" Angelique said furiously. "He admitted it?"

Harry cursed again. "I should have told you. Another agent gave me ideas. My last assignment was not all I thought it was, either. I confronted Stafford and he didn't deny a thing. And if you don't believe me now, Crane could still pull it off. The letter I wrote for him this morning said it must be done *today*, cropping all the lilies. And he wouldn't let me send it as usual, but said Jasper would. He might well intend to harm the earl today!"

Angelique let out her breath in an angry hiss but still she didn't move. "But how do you *know*?"

Harry took a controlled breath and forced himself to let go of her. "I don't."

For a long moment she stood there, her eyes boring into his. "If you are wrong . . . " she said slowly, at last.

Harry dismissed it with an impatient jerk of his head. "Then I'll have made myself a great fool. What if I am right?"

She pursed her lips and said nothing for a moment. "Very well. I shall go tell Stafford of your suspicions—for that is all you have presented. But why do not you come with me and explain for yourself?"

"I'm going to Doncaster House to put Brandon on alert." Angelique had moved from the doorway enough for him to squeeze past her. "I'll come to Bow Street directly after."

"Harry," she said in warning.

"Angelique, I must." He took one step down the stairs.

She followed him. "You wish to go there because of *her*. Harry, think—you must be right in this—wait until Ian returns, he has taken the horses to the farrier—"

Harry was already down the stairs, his hand on the door, straining toward it. He didn't bother to deny anything. "If I go because of Mariah, do you think I could bear to wait until Ian returns?"

Angelique cursed at him in French. "What will you do?"

"Whatever I have to do. Now go—*please*." He grabbed his coat hanging beside the door, shoved a pistol in his pocket, and was gone before she could say another word.

He struck out across town, pulling on the coat as he went. He walked as quickly as he could, and still felt like he was moving through sand. He was sure he was right—it explained everything, except *why*—but none of that would matter if he failed to keep Mariah and her family safe. The irony of it was cutting: All that time he had written out Crane's letters, those endless horticultural missives, unwittingly sending off the directions to the radicals in his own hand at Stafford's instigation. It wouldn't surprise him at all if there were a precisely detailed code in the plants and gardening instructions he copied out. And he supposed he could still be wrong—he admitted cutting lilies was slim basis to accuse someone of attempted murder and insurrection—but would rather bear the consequences of this mistake than the other.

He traveled the familiar path to Doncaster House in short order, but this time went to the servants' door. He had to put Brandon on guard first, and then go to Stafford. Once he knew Mariah and her family were safe, that Brandon was alerted to the possible danger, he could breathe easily enough to go to Stafford and persuade him to look at Crane. He knocked on the door and asked to speak to John Jameson, as Brandon was known at Doncaster House.

The maid who answered raised her eyebrows. " 'Ere now, like 'e's a fancy gentleman? And who're you?"

Harry didn't let his simmering impatience show. He pulled off the cap and bobbed his head politely at her. "I'm from Mr. Cooke's office—Mr. Cooke being a solicitor, miss—and there's an important message I must give to Mr. John Jameson."

"Important, huh." She cocked her head with a little smile that said quite plainly she thought he was making it up. Which he was.

He tried a different tack. He edged closer, glancing from side to side. "Thing is, miss," he said in a low friendly voice, "he's come into some funds, Mr. Jameson has. Great-uncle, it was, what passed on. So now, Mr. Cooke's sent me to find Mr. Jameson, let him know his good fortune, see?"

"Funds, is it?" she whispered, stepping out of the doorway toward him. " 'Ow much funds?"

Harry leaned against the doorjamb, giving her a coaxing little smile, the same smile that had melted the reserve of chambermaids and millinery assistants in the past. "Can't say, miss; Mr. Cooke didn't say. He and I had a falling out, so to speak. To tell the truth, I'm about to get the sack, if I make another mistake. So could you help me, fetch Mr. Jameson?"

She pursed her lips, her eyes flicking up and down over him. "Well, I would if I could. After all, ain't every day a man comes into funds, is it? And o' course you oughtn't get the sack just 'cause you can't find the man. Still, if he ain't here, he ain't here, right?"

"When do you think he might be free?" She looked over her shoulder as someone called behind her, and Harry added, in a burst of desperation, "I think it's a great deal of money, miss."

"He's gone on the carriage," she said in a rush. She stepped back into the house, her hand on the door. "To Carlton House, with his lordship. Can't say when he'll be back, they've only just gone."

Harry froze. Carlton House?

"Why—to see the King? The King himself?" he asked, thinking fast.

The maid shrugged. "I expect so; who else lives there? His lordship's a great one, even the King listens to him. He's gone to call there with Lady Mariah." Someone called from behind her again and she turned to answer, leaving Harry reeling on the doorstep. Mariah and her father had gone to call on the King— they would be out on the public street—easy targets for a man concealed with a pistol. Or perhaps more traitors lurked in the King's own household, waiting to serve them all a fatal cup of tea.

Without waiting for the maid, he strode back around the corner of the house. Brandon hadn't notified them of this visit; it must have been a last minute arrangement. People like Doncaster, Harry reflected, could probably call on royalty without too much ado. But why did Mariah have to go as well? He didn't like this, not the visit itself, not the timing, and certainly not Mariah going along. He thought of Crane's words again—cut the lilies close and low—and fought down a surge of fear. What would it gain Crane to kill Mariah? She was just a girl. She couldn't even inherit her father's title. There was no reason he could think of for her to be in danger . . . except that she had gone with her father to visit the King.

Several hours had passed since he wrote out Crane's last letter. Even if Jasper handed it straight out the window to an assassin, it was unlikely the event would take place today, no matter what Crane wrote. Who could know where Doncaster was, or intended to be? Surely if they intended to kill Doncaster, they would try in a more discreet way, not when he walked up the steps of Carlton House.

Harry rounded the corner and looked up and down the street with sharply critical eyes. Plenty of places to lie in wait and watch, just as he had done on several occasions. And it was easy enough to follow a carriage across town.

He turned toward Whitehall and broke into a run.

Chapter 23

It took a long time to get ready for a visit to the King. Her mother was in her room early, surveying her wardrobe with a critical eye and sending Sally running back and forth to her own rooms for various hair combs and jewelry. Trying to calm her own nerves—she was taking tea today with the King of England!—Mariah gave herself into the hands of her mother's maid without hesitation.

By the time a servant knocked on her door to say her father was ready to go, she was amazed at what had become of her. She looked very much as she always did, but brighter and prettier in every way. She wore her mother's pearl ear drops, and her pale green silk gown with new lilac ribbons. Her hair was curled and pinned up even more elaborately than it had been for her ball, and a light dusting of powder covered the freckles she'd acquired during her rambles with Joan. As the footman stood waiting in the doorway, she glanced at her mother, smiling in relief when she saw Mama's beaming pride.

"My darling," her mother said, squeezing her hand. "You look lovely. You shall do the Doncaster name proud."

"Thank you, Mama." She swallowed a nervous giggle, then walked carefully down the stairs to meet her father.

"I shall be invited to visit His Majesty more often," said Papa, his eyes lighting, "for bringing such a companion."

Mariah laughed with her mother, afraid to move much more than her face. "I am not sure I could stand to do it more often, Papa!"

He smiled and held out his arm. "Let us go, then. The King awaits."

It was a slow journey. Carlton House was only a few miles distant, but the streets were clogged with people and carriages. Mariah, whose life in London had mainly consisted of parties in other mansions and expeditions to various fashionable locations, looked around with interest as they drove into the heart of the city, where the government was seated and Carlton House stood.

Somewhere in the great crush of Piccadilly the crowds grew denser and louder. Mariah, sitting carefully still on the seat to avoid wrinkling her gown, couldn't see everything, but she could hear the volume rising. Risking a crumpled skirt, she leaned forward to peer out the window better.

The horses stopped. The carriage rocked a little, then lurched forward, only to stop again. She could see men in the crowd pressing forward, angry faces turned toward them. Toward her. The shock made her sit back abruptly. "Papa?"

He patted her hand, but his expression was grave. "Sit back," he said quietly. "Do not lean forward." They started again, and proceeded slowly but steadily for some time before stopping again. The crowd was yelling now, jeering at them. Papa's mouth compressed in irritation and he patted her hand once more. Then he pushed open the door and stood in the opening, one arm hooked inside the carriage to keep his balance.

"What is the problem?" He spoke calmly and politely, his voice carrying over the rumble of the crowd. Someone shouted back at him, Mariah couldn't hear what, and a crude laugh rippled around it.

"I have already inquired," Papa replied with dignity. "Surely you can reply in kind."

Another chorus of voices rose up, some challenging, some protesting, some imploring. Someone called out her father's name, and a few huzzahs mingled with the catcalls. Mariah listened in growing alarm as they grew louder and more strident.

"I ask only the right to drive down this street unmolested, no more than every Englishman would wish." Papa chose to address the loudest voice, who had asked what business they were on, the people's or the King's.

"If only every Englishman had your fortune!" someone yelled, which was followed by a dull roar of agreement.

Papa raised his hand. He continued speaking to the crowd in the same reasonable tone, but Mariah didn't hear him. She slid to the center of her seat and tried to make herself small and invisible, not at all tempted to peer out the windows anymore. The crowd's discontent was palpable and frightening. There was a danger, an anger, in the hard faces surrounding them that she had never expected to see in the faces of her fellow countrymen. She had seen enmity abroad and been snubbed on occasion, but never seen such naked resentment.

And still Papa spoke, exhorting them to remember their own families, to reflect on the decency of their actions. From her seat, she could see a sliver of the crowd, a handful of faces. Papa's words seemed to have effect; gradually the anger faded, leaving somber expressions.

Mariah realized many of the faces were thin and worn, people accustomed to a hard life. Edging closer to the window, her eyes were caught by one particular woman at the back of the crowd, lingering to listen to her father. Her dress was a muddy brown, and very coarse fabric from the look of it. A strip of cloth was knotted around her shoulders, the frayed edges waving gently in the puffs of breeze, and Mariah could see how thin her figure was. There were hollows in her cheeks, and when the woman raised one reddened hand from the large basket she carried to push her straggly hair from her face, Mariah could see the outline of every bone in her arm. And her eyes . . . there were decades of misery in those bleak eyes, far more than she could possibly have lived. It shocked Mariah to realize that woman was probably very near her own age.

She turned her gaze to her lap. The silk of her dress was fresh and light under the fine kid of her gloves. The velvet of the squabs was lush and soft behind her. Suddenly, she wondered how it would look to her, if she were in the street wearing coarse, ragged clothing and carrying a heavy basket to market, to see a carriage drive past gleaming with such luxury. She curled her hands into fists, feeling again the worn texture of old linen beneath her palms and against her cheek, and closed her eyes. Harry, she thought; that woman in the crowd was the sort of girl he had helped one night with a crown. *No one looks after her,* he had said so bitterly. No wonder he had thought she could never understand his world.

The crowd had grown quieter and when she peeped out again, it seemed only half as many people were clustered about their carriage. The woman with the basket was gone. Papa paused in his speech to stoop inside and ask if she were well. She nodded, grateful for his concern and presence; if this had happened when she was out with Mama, it would have been much more frightening.

The coach swayed to one side. Papa nearly lost his grip and tumbled to the ground. Mariah gave a little shriek, reaching for him, but he recovered, waved to the crowd, then swung back into his seat as the carriage started forward again at last, but very slowly. "Papa, what is wrong? What do they want?"

He glanced at her. She could see the worry in his eyes, but his tone was unruffled. "There are too many men out of work. Wheat and corn are dear, and they have drunk too much of the Spenceans' rot."

"Why did they turn on us? We did nothing to them."

He covered her hand with his. The crowd was moving along with them, it seemed. "They resent the wealthy, my dear. Do you see now what I meant by the people's goodwill?" He shook his head, looking out the window. "The King was once well-liked. If he can regain that regard, things will improve immensely."

Mariah nodded, but was not sure. Papa must know, she thought, but to her eyes, the unrest in the crowd was more than envy, or disgust for the King's activities. It was desperation. And suddenly she was less certain that her father's visit would make a great difference in those people's opinion of the King.

Harry plowed around the wide corner into the crush of Piccadilly and finally caught sight of the Doncaster carriage. The street was busy, and traffic moved slowly. He stopped, flooded with relief that all seemed well, and braced his hands on his knees to catch his breath. Thank God he hadn't been wearing Wroth's shoes. He raised his head and tracked the carriage through the street as it rolled toward Carlton House. With a spy's eye, he scanned the crowd and picked out potential troublemakers at once, men who wore the clothing of various tradesmen but were oddly out just walking in the street instead of making candles or butchering. But still, everything seemed normal.

When the carriage stopped, he tensed and began moving more purposefully through the crowd. Hands reached out to shove at the carriage, and the driver flicked his whip at them, sparking more hands to push. On the back of the carriage, a footman—Brandon?—was waving people away, trying to clear a space around the vehicle. Harry broke into a trot, shouldering aside everyone in his way. A coal wagon had drawn up next to the carriage and also stopped, seemingly blocked by the crowd. Harry dodged a dray going in the other direction and waited for two horses to pass. The men in the coal wagon were standing, yelling at the crowd.

Except one. One slim fellow slid off the back of the wagon and disappeared between the wagon and the Doncaster carriage. Harry couldn't quite see him, but then the footmen leaped from their positions and he realized Mariah and her father were alighting. He craned his neck and caught sight of her, as beautiful as spring in a pale green dress and straw bonnet. Doncaster was speaking to the people, hands raised in placation, while Mariah stood close behind him. Carlton House stood only a little ways down the street. Some of the King's Life Guard were already approaching, in fact, hustling down the street and barking at the crowd to stand aside. Doncaster was clearly expected.

His muscles were burning. He paused to let another wagon go by as he sucked in a deep breath. He was beginning to think he had worried over nothing, that everything was fine, when the wagon drove by and the crowd parted, just for a moment affording him a clear view of the short man from the coal cart. He was crouching almost under the Doncaster carriage, setting light to what looked like a small powder keg between the rear wheels.

Harry bolted. The street was full of people, innocently going about their business. "Fire," he shouted as he ran, waving one arm. "Fire!"

People cried out and jumped out of his path. He hoped they would flee the street entirely as he caught another glimpse of the Doncaster coach. The earl was still standing beside it with his daughter, the royal guard too far away. And above the carriage, drifting on the lazy breeze, a thin, faint puff of smoke.

"Brandon!" he roared. "The carriage! Under the carriage! It's a bomb!"

One of the footmen, just about to jump down from the back of the coach, whipped around in his direction. For a moment Brandon seemed frozen, then he sprang into action, disappearing around the side of the carriage.

His lungs burning, Harry ran harder, sprinting along the street, in front of horsemen and pedestrians without regard for the curses called after him. The men on the wagon had seen him, and most of them leaped off and disappeared, scattering in all directions. The little fellow who had placed the powder key remained, grimly guarding his deadly work and standing between Harry and his target. A thin knife shone in one hand, the barrel of a pistol in the other.

Harry charged right at him, ducking the swipe of the knife. He grabbed the man's arm in one hand, forcing it high as the pistol discharged, and kicked hard at his knee at the same time, bashing him across the face with the hilt of the dagger he didn't even remember drawing. And then he ran on, leaving the man to crumple in a bloody, screaming mess on the street, or to die, or walk away; Harry didn't even care.

At the sound of the gunshot, pandemonium broke out, everyone suddenly running and screaming, some toward safety, some unwittingly toward danger. The thin trail of smoke was just barely visible beneath the rear wheel. Harry knew it could explode at any moment—there was no time to move the keg, and no safe place to move it to. Mariah was glancing around in alarm, unaware of what was really happening, turning instinctively toward the supposed safety of the coach. He refused to look toward the bomb as he rushed forward—just ten feet more—the muscles in his legs aching and about to give out as he shoved people aside and down—

The blast was deafening. Harry felt his ears go numb just as he slammed into Mariah, bowling her flat to the ground and throwing himself on top of her. Debris rained down on his back, and he closed his arms around her, tucking his own head down. Something heavy hit him in the shoulder, but then rolled away. A mangled coach door landed with a thud mere inches away from his head. Grit and splinters and dust showered down on them for what seemed an eternity, then finally stopped. All was eerily quiet.

As his hearing started to return, he heard dim screams and shouts, felt the pounding of running feet. Nothing else had struck them. Cautiously, he lifted his head a few inches.

"Are you hurt?" he asked, giving Mariah a gentle shake. She hadn't moved since they hit the ground. Her eyes were wide and unfocused with shock, her lips parted. He must have knocked the breath out of her. Blood oozed from a small cut on her forehead, but otherwise he could see no injury. At his anxious question, she slowly turned to look at him.

"What . . . ? Oh, my *dress*," she muttered, struggling to raise her head. He cupped her cheek and restrained her.

"There, love. You may be hurt. Lie still a moment."

"Oh," she said weakly, then abruptly her gaze fixed on him, sharpening and clearing. "Harry?" she whispered incredulously.

He grinned, incapable of doing anything else. His heart seemed to have just resumed beating. "Yes. Are you hurt?"

"No, I don't think so. But what . . . ?"

People were tugging at his arms, trying to pull him

off her. "I'm glad," was all he managed to say before servants in royal livery yanked him to his feet and swarmed to Mariah's side. One asked if he were hurt, in a cursory sort of way. Harry shook his head even as he was pushed farther back by the swelling crowd and the Life Guards attempting to control them. He lost sight of her, then caught another glimpse; she was sitting up, one hand on her head, and scanning the crowd. Their eyes met, and he smiled just a little, then took a step back as the earl shoved his way through all the people around her, calling his daughter's name in a panic-stricken voice.

Harry allowed himself to be pushed back. Now that it was over, he felt weak, his knees shaking, his back aching, and his lungs straining painfully inside his chest. But she was safe, Doncaster was safe, everyone—

Abruptly, he jerked around. There was a smaller cluster of people a few feet away, bent over another figure. A pair of legs extended from their midst, clad in footman's stockings and shoes, and utterly still. Harry felt his blood turn cold. He edged closer, trying to see—

Someone moved aside, and he caught a glimpse of Alec Brandon, lying on his side, his face covered with blood. His footman's wig had fallen off, and his entire head was scarlet with the blood that pooled under his cheek.

Good God.

Harry was still standing there, stunned, when someone took his arm. "Come," Stafford muttered in his ear, pulling him away.

"Brandon," he said, resisting.

"I'll see to him." Stafford pushed him toward a

nearby carriage. "There's nothing you can do. Are you hurt?"

"No. Is he dead?" Harry demanded.

Stafford hesitated, glancing back before pushing Harry again, through the open carriage door. "I think not; they are calling for a doctor. Go back to Fenton Lane. Angelique will meet you there."

Harry leaned out the window, trying to see Brandon again.

"Sinclair." Stafford's firm tone recalled his attention. "Well done," said his employer with a ghost of a smile. "I'll inform you as soon as possible. Now go," he called to the driver as he slammed the door closed.

As the carriage lurched forward, away from the mayhem and confusion and cries still filling the street, Harry scrambled to the other window and caught one last glimpse of the earl, embracing Mariah. She was pale, but seemed otherwise unhurt, on her feet and moving about. Thank God for that much.

But Brandon . . . The crowd around him had only grown, and the expressions were grave. Harry's elation was poisoned by fear. What had happened to Brandon?

The belated shock of it bore down on him. He kept seeing that lone puff of smoke above the coach, the unsuspecting look on Mariah's face as she turned to climb back into the doomed coach, the blood running down Brandon's face. He heard the terror in Doncaster's voice as he called Mariah's name. Too late. He had almost been too late.

He bent over until his forehead touched his knees, his hands shaking uncontrollably, and didn't look up until the carriage reached Fenton Lane.

Chapter 24

I will never allow it.

Her father's stern words echoed in Mariah's mind as she made her way to the servants' rooms. Of course Papa didn't know the truth about Lord Wroth, but she didn't think that would matter. Would he be more likely to approve if he knew Lord Wroth was really Harry, a nameless young man, probably a commoner? Not if she knew her father at all. If Lord Wroth were what he seemed, Papa might at least expect her to be left a widowed Lady Wroth in fairly short order. But she could be married to a poor young fellow for a long time, and she didn't think Papa would find that any more acceptable, even if the young fellow had saved her life.

That meant it was up to her to do something. Harry was the man she wanted, and she had been raised to get what she wanted. Since she wouldn't get him if he came to call and asked her father in the usual, proper, way, she decided it was time to resort to other methods. Sneaky and even underhanded methods, but infinitely more likely to succeed.

The uproar of the previous day had died down only a little. Footmen were now standing at every door of the house that wasn't barred and chained shut, and members of the Coldstream Guards were on the grounds, at her father's request and the government's agreement. Her parents were badly shaken; Mama had insisted that Mariah sleep in her dressing room that night, with the door open and Sally on the floor, even though she had not been hurt beyond a cut on her temple and a bruise or two. The servants flitted around with frightened expressions and hushed voices, as if more bombs might be tossed through a window at any time. Papa was closed up in his study again with government men, and this time their air was angry as well as alarmed. He had not been hurt when the carriage exploded beside him, much to Mariah's and her mother's relief. A footman—a man named Jameson—had leaped from his perch and dragged Papa to safety, shielding him with his own body. Just as Harry had done when he threw himself on top of her.

Mariah rapped at a narrow door at the end of the long bare hall. "How is he?" she asked when a maid opened the door.

The maid shook her head. "Resting, my lady. The doctor was here not half an hour past."

Mariah stepped into the darkened room, which had the still, apprehensive feel of a sickroom. She looked at the figure lying propped up in the bed, gazing vacantly into space. Jameson had been hit on the head by a splintered piece of the carriage axle, and the doctor told her father it was a miracle he survived at all. "You may go," she told the maid. The girl nodded and slipped out, drawing the door partly closed. Mariah pulled a stool close to his bed and sat down, watching him intently.

"Jameson?" He turned his head, fixing startlingly blue eyes on her. "I hope you are feeling better," she began awkwardly. A bitter smile bent his mouth.

"Of course," he said without a trace of the deference she was accustomed to hearing from her servants. Mariah flushed, feeling as though she had somehow insulted him.

"I can never thank you enough," she said softly. "For what you did. It was . . . heroic. It was more than heroic." She wet her lips. "You and Harry both."

He said nothing, just looked at her with unnerving directness. She resisted the urge to squirm. "I must find him," she went on. "Harry. Can you tell me how? What is his true name? Where does he live? If you could help me at all, I . . . I would be forever in your debt."

He made no response.

Mariah bit her lip and forged on, aware that she was pleading, and that she would sink to begging if necessary, just before she got to bribery and blackmail. "I know you are not just a footman. I know he is not just a secretary." Jameson showed no response to anything. "I love him," she blurted out, unable to keep the desperate longing from her voice. "Please help me."

The small window under the eaves admitted only a little sunlight. It fell across his bandaged head, the dark hair cut short to allow his footman's wig to fit. She wondered who he really was, what he really was. What had made him pose as a footman, then throw himself in front of a bomb to save her father? That was not the act of any mere footman, no matter how loyal. Whatever his true purpose, Harry's must have been the same, for Lord Crane. That must be why he'd worked for the viscount. And if not for Harry, she would be dead now.

"You're a fool," Jameson said bluntly.

Her blush was painfully hot. "Perhaps. Please help me."

He looked away, turning his face to the ceiling again. "Fenton Lane," he said in a low voice.

"Fenton?" Mariah seized on it. "His name is Fenton?"

A sharp shake of his head. "Fenton Lane. Number twelve."

"He lives there?"

A long moment of silence. "You can reach him there. Send a message on plain paper."

"Plain paper," she repeated. "Should I address it to Harry?"

"To H.S." A frown came and quickly went. "An answer may not come immediately. If he answers at all."

"H.S." At last—an initial! Impulsively, she clasped Jameson's hand. "Thank you," she said fervently. "Thank you."

His fingers twitched in hers before he pulled free without another word, his expression closed and remote, and turned away from her. Feeling dismissed, Mariah slipped quietly from the room, forgetting any pique in her excitement.

"Fenton Lane, number twelve," she repeated over and over to herself as she hurried through the house to her room. At last she knew how to contact him, a way to find him. *If* he answered, Jameson had said! Of course he would answer her; she simply couldn't conceive of him not answering. He loved her, she loved him, and now that he was a bona fide hero, there was nothing at all to separate them—save, perhaps, her father, which was why she was taking drastic action.

Back in her room, she rummaged through her desk until she found a sheet of perfectly plain paper. Why plain paper? she wondered. Would any special marking cause the letter to go astray? For a moment she tapped the end of her pen on her chin. Now, what to say . . .

It mustn't give too much away. Jameson had only said she could send a message to him. That could mean someone else might be opening and reading letters first. She was not about to pour out her heart for a stranger to read, particularly a stranger who might not be all that sympathetic. Harry had said he was breaking the rules to see her, and the last thing she wanted was to cause him trouble. But it must be specific enough that he would know who sent it and what she meant by it. After a few false starts, she thought it was good enough.

> Dear H—I have something of the greatest importance to tell you, if you would be so kind as to return to our usual meeting place at the usual time. M

Now she only had to have it delivered without anyone finding out about it. She giggled nervously as she folded and securely sealed the note, writing the direction on the front. Her parents would know for certain if she had one of the servants take it. How did one deliver secret messages?

She decided to ask Joan's opinion. Even if Joan were no help, visiting her cousin would at least let Mariah work off some of the nervous energy building inside her. She slipped her note into her reticule and headed for the Bennet home, this time with a muscular footman at her side.

"Mariah! We were so worried when we heard the dreadful news!" Aunt Marion swept her into her arms the moment she arrived. "Your father? Your mother?"

"Both are well. Papa was unharmed almost entirely. Mama will recover from the fright, in time."

"Not quickly, I should think." Aunt Marion studied her, taking in the cut on her temple. "And you, dear?"

"My dress was quite ruined and I lost one of Mama's pearl earrings, but I am quite unhurt, as you see." She made herself smile. Behind her aunt, Joan grinned back with a relieved expression.

"That is very good news. Your mother sent me word of the incident and that you had both returned home, but nothing more." Aunt Marion shook her head, embraced her once more, and then released her to Joan.

Joan, of course, wanted to know every detail, and Mariah obliged, leaving out only the identity of the man who had burst from the crowd and shielded her from the exploding wreckage of her father's town coach. She had promised not to tell anyone about him, not even Joan, and if she mentioned him in any way, her cousin might guess what she planned to do. Joan likely did anyway, from the odd pursing of her mouth as she revealed that she'd discovered where to contact Harry and wanted to send him a message.

"Are you certain?" Joan asked, completely serious for once. "About him, even after . . . ?"

Mariah took a deep breath. Yes, she was. She had thought long and hard on everything about Harry and what he'd done. He had never hurt her; he had never coerced her. She still didn't know all the answers, but she knew she could trust him with her life. "I am." She hadn't spoken a word to Joan about him since that disastrous day in the Plymptons' garden, and Joan hadn't asked. For a moment it seemed her cousin would protest; her forehead wrinkled and she appeared to be biting her lip very hard.

"But he was—"

"Yes."

"And you said—"

"I know."

Joan's frown deepened. "If you are wrong," she said slowly, "there would be terrible consequences . . . "

"I believe in him," Mariah whispered. "I will understand if you can't help me."

Joan stared at her for a long moment, but then she reached out and squeezed her hand. "All right. If you trust him, I shall, too. Go on."

Surprisingly, her cousin came up with the answer immediately. "Douglas," she said when Mariah explained about needing a messenger. "Douglas can take it. No one will care if he goes out by himself."

"Do you think he would?" Mariah asked anxiously.

Joan waved one hand. "Of course he will. We can always tell Mother and Papa about the barmaids."

Mariah gave an uneasy smile. It was easy for Joan to tease her brother, but this was too important to risk Douglas getting irked at them and refusing to do it, or even worse, telling his parents that they were up to something. "Joan, you must ask him nicely," she said.

Joan rolled her eyes. "Then he'll know for certain we're up to no good—I meant, that's what he'll think," she amended hastily. "Douglas would think I've taken a fever if I ask too nicely." She opened the door. "Trust me, if handled properly, Douglas will do it."

They found him in the hall, dressed for riding and on the verge of stepping out the door. "Douglas, wait!" Joan cried, running down the stairs.

He turned and looked up at them. "Why? What did you do now?"

"Nothing." Joan scowled at him. "We need to ask you something."

"A favor," said Mariah, hiding her note in the folds of her skirt. If he wouldn't do it, she didn't want him to know what it was.

Douglas shrugged. "What sort of favor?"

"Come in here." Joan dragged him into the nearby drawing room, and Mariah closed the doors behind them. "We need something delivered."

"To whom?"

"To someone in London, not far from here."

"Where?"

Mariah hesitated, but Joan blurted out, "Fenton Lane. Do you know where that is?"

Slowly, her brother nodded, a faint line between his brows. He wasn't going to do it, Mariah realized; he was too suspicious. But everything hinged on this letter being delivered without anyone knowing, and she didn't have an alternative to Douglas. "It's just a note," she said, drawing out her message. "Only . . . " She glanced at Joan and felt a blush rising in her cheeks. "Only . . . "

Douglas's face cleared and he put out his hand for the letter. "Oh, *that* sort of note. Who's it for?" He weighed it in his hand as he eyed it.

"Oh, what does it matter?" said Joan. "We're sending a report to the young lady who's hired us to spy on you."

"Hmm." A terrible gleam came into his eyes. "What does she look like?"

"She's bald, wears spectacles, and weighs twelve stone," said Joan impatiently. "It's not about you, you dunce!"

"It would be a very great favor to—to both of us," Mariah interjected with a sharp glance at Joan. They had agreed it would be best if Douglas didn't know it was solely on her behalf, just in case.

His gaze slid to her face. Cocking his head to one side, Douglas considered a moment longer, then lifted one shoulder. "All right. It can't hurt to have both of you in my debt."

"Thank you, Douglas," Mariah said before Joan could say anything smart and make him change his mind.

He looked at her a little too curiously, but didn't say anything. He promised to deliver it while out on his ride, and left.

Mariah's knees felt suddenly shaky, and she sank onto a nearby chair. It was done. The die was cast. Now she only had to wait—and for who knew how long? She would have no way of knowing when or even if Harry had gotten the message. She would have to be prepared for the next step immediately, and just as prepared to wait awhile.

"Well, what next?" Joan sat down beside her.

She clasped her hands together and avoided her cousin's gaze. It probably was not a good idea to tell Joan just what she had in mind, for several reasons. "Wait, and see if he answers."

Joan was duly disappointed. Having promised to follow Mariah's lead and trust him, her earlier enthusiasm for Mariah's secret suitor had returned. "Wait? How long?"

Mariah lifted one hand helplessly. "As long as it takes him to answer, if he even answers at all."

"If! Of course he'll answer—how could he not?"

Mariah laughed with her, even though inside she wasn't so sure. When she had written the note, when she had badgered the direction out of poor Jameson, when she had rushed over to Joan's house, she hadn't doubted that Harry would respond at once, exactly the way she envisioned. Now that she had committed herself to a course of action, though, it suddenly seemed possible something would go wrong. He might not be there and someone else might get the note. He might be unable to come for weeks, and she would go mad in the meantime. He might not wish to come to her any longer . . .

She pushed the thought out of her mind. She was not going to torment herself like that. She was going ahead with her plan, and would worry about those problems only if they actually occurred.

Harry lay on the sofa, staring at the ceiling while Lisette changed the dressing on his arm. When he'd tackled Mariah to the ground, he had skidded along the street with all his weight and hers on his forearm. His coat sleeve had been shredded away, along with a good portion of his skin. The ugly burn stung, but not as badly as his pride. For almost two months he had sat beside the man plotting to overthrow the government and never once suspected. Was it no surprise he felt like a prize idiot? Angelique told him to forget his blindness. He had seen it in time, and the result was what mattered, she told him firmly. She had done this far more than he had, but he couldn't help thinking he should have noticed things earlier.

Stafford sent word that Brandon was injured but expected to recover. He didn't come to Fenton Lane himself until the next day. Angelique thought he was dealing with more immediate concerns, like informing the Cabinet and questioning Crane. But Stafford finally arrived as Lisette finished cleaning the wound, and Harry stayed on the sofa and waited.

Stafford stopped inside the door. He and Harry eyed each other in silence as Lisette bundled up her medicinal supplies and left without a word. Then the older man turned and moved toward a chair.

"What happened?"

Stafford inspected the chair, then took out his handkerchief and dusted it off before sitting. He made no reaction to Harry's terse query. "Congratulations are in order, Sinclair, and, I suppose, thanks." He flashed his rare, dry smile.

Harry just glared at him. Stafford sighed.

"Much of it you must have already guessed. Lord Crane had grown to sympathize with some of the radicals plaguing England. He had taken to writing to one of them, Arthur Thistlewood, before Thistlewood was hanged earlier this year for his role in the attempted assassination of the Cabinet."

"Why?"

"Why?" Stafford repeated in disdain. "The man's gone mad, Sinclair, quite obviously."

"He hid it rather well from everyone. I attended some of the finest parties in the city, trailing after him."

Stafford's lips pinched. "Indeed." He cast a sour glance at Harry. "He hid it even from you."

Harry shrugged. "How was I to know? The letters to Rusk were as dull as ditch water, plant this and prune that and rake everything into oblivion. Perhaps if I had been told sooner it was a traitor we hunted, instead of some rubbish about being a guardian shadow—"

"You have made your point," Stafford snapped, but an instant later regained control of his temper. "Yes, the horticultural instructions were the code, with the lily representing Lord Doncaster, as you suggested. Cabinet ministers were referred to as various other plants, according to what we have deduced so far. I gather Lord Crane came to see England as a vast personal garden, where he might plant and uproot men as he pleased." Stafford's tone indicated what he thought of that presumption.

"Is anyone else in danger?"

"We are examining the letters for that very question."

"What will happen to Lord Crane?"

Stafford's mouth flattened. He crossed his legs. "He shall be suitably dealt with. We do not prosecute men of Lord Crane's stature publicly."

Harry nodded. There would be no trial, no public acknowledgment that an esteemed member of the nobility, whose advice had been sought by the Lord Chancellor just last week, had turned traitor. Crane would live out his days in lonely but secure house arrest somewhere, and the men he had incited would hang. Tobias, of course, might find his social standing somewhat reduced. Harry's arm ached, and he felt a headache coming on. He slumped on the sofa, pushing out his legs and letting his head rest on the cushion behind him.

"You were right, Sinclair," Stafford said then. "To

act when and as you did. We managed to apprehend a pair of the men involved in the plot. They did receive Lord Crane's letter from Jasper and were waiting near Doncaster House for his lordship to emerge. They followed his carriage into Westminster and stirred up the crowd deliberately, to mask their true purpose in setting a bomb beneath the carriage. If you had delayed, I am quite afraid they might well have injured or killed his lordship."

"And his daughter," Harry said, staring at the ceiling.

"Yes. And his daughter."

"Or any number in the crowd," he added, irked by Stafford's single-minded focus on Doncaster. There had been women on the way to market, children out running errands to earn a penny, ordinary, decent, hardworking Englishmen who never dreamed of revolution or murder in that street. Harry felt the weight of their souls, if Stafford did not.

"Er—yes."

"How is Brandon?"

"He is injured, but not mortally," Stafford said, resuming his normal distant tone. "Lord Doncaster credits him with saving his life. Brandon shall be well-rewarded, and he is better off receiving care at Doncaster House."

"And what of us?"

"You have done all I asked of you, and more. I wish you well in recovering from your injuries."

"And then?"

Stafford gave one of his humorless smiles. "We shall speak later. I have not forgotten your ambitions, Sinclair." He got to his feet and bowed very briefly. "Good day."

And that was that.

Harry spent a long time wondering what exactly had made Crane do it. In the course of his employment as Crane's secretary, he had come to respect the old man, even if he hadn't admired him overmuch. He racked his brain for any signs of madness he might have overlooked while in Crane's employ, but even in hindsight could come up with nothing. It took two chance remarks from Mariah and Angelique to give him any sort of clue to the true meaning in Crane's communications, and he thought only a trained botanist could have known if Crane's letters were sensible otherwise. In fact, now that he thought back on it, it had been quite a leap of logic on his part, and if not for the weight of Crane's directive—*it must be done today*—he might well have had time to talk himself out of it. It was unnerving to think that even a few minutes' hesitation could have meant Mariah's death.

And Brandon's, who'd been in his post at the back of the coach before he yelled. He could not forget that glimpse he'd caught of Brandon, lying limp on the ground, unmoving and covered with blood. And the horrible thought gnawed at him that it was his fault. Brandon had shielded the earl because he had gone for Mariah instead. The instant he saw her standing next to the carriage, he'd not thought of anything but protecting her. He knew, deep down, that he wouldn't be able to do it differently even if he had the chance, but it didn't keep him from feeling that Brandon had suffered because Brandon had done exactly what his job required while he had not, and yet he was the one who escaped serious injury.

He didn't know what he should do next. He couldn't bear to sit around and wait for Stafford to offer him another assignment, not when this one was still unsettled. But there was nothing he could do to help Brandon, and there was just as little he could do regarding Mariah.

Did he have any chance of winning her father's consent? He had taken Stafford's offer with the hope of gaining some useful friends, even patrons. His political ambitions were just dreams without connections. While he didn't expect to get public credit for his part in stopping Crane's schemes, he had hoped Stafford would recommend him quietly to a few important people who might give him a leg up. But he didn't think any letter from John Stafford of Bow Street, or even from Lord Sidmouth himself, would persuade the Earl of Doncaster to grant Harry his daughter's hand in marriage.

And what was left to him then? To watch her make a brilliant marriage to someone else. Even if all his plans worked out as he had hoped, he would still be nothing but a backbench member of the House of Commons. It didn't sound nearly as appealing as it once had, especially when he considered the probability that being in London for Parliament would bring him face-to-face with her, married to someone else and forever lost to him.

But perhaps . . . His heart lifted despite the long odds of this possibility. Perhaps she loved him as madly as he loved her. Even after she knew he was posing as Wroth, she had told him to come to her. Could she give up her life of ease and elegance for him? His own mother had done that, following her heart to marry the man she loved even though it meant being disowned. She left a comfortable life to become the wife of a traveling actor. Could Mariah do the same?

If she ran off with him, her father's wrath would surely ruin any chance he had at Parliament—he had already decided that spying was no longer for him, never knowing if Stafford were telling him the whole story or even any truth at all. To marry him, Mariah would have to give up the most glittering society in England—and what could he offer her in return? A small cottage, perhaps only rented rooms, while he took what employment he could find to support them. Harry wasn't sure he could wreak such havoc in the life of the woman he loved.

So he lay on the sofa, veering between guilt and despair and reproach. Lisette returned to finish bandaging his arm and then left him alone in his gloom. He heaved himself upright with a sigh and rolled his sleeve down over the bandage. Perhaps he should go for a walk and try to clear his thoughts. It had been a while since he'd been able to come and go as he pleased, without looking for murderers and revolutionaries behind every shrub and lamppost.

There was a tap at the door, and Angelique came in. "How do you feel?" she asked, remaining by the door with her hands behind her back.

Harry shrugged, pulling on his waistcoat. "Well enough."

"Hmm." She strolled into the room. "Not guilty?" Harry said nothing. "It was not your fault," she said gently. "It could have been you, just as easily as Alec. Had you protected the earl, Alec would surely have thrown himself in front of the young lady. Stafford would not have either of you allow her to be harmed." Harry ignored her and reached for his coat. "The fact that you are in love with her would not have made any difference."

He flinched.

"Are you still?" Angelique prodded. "I have waited and waited for you to speak of her, and what you intend to do, but you say nothing."

"What can I say?" He flung out his hands. "Do you think her father will give me permission to see her, let alone court her and marry her? Would any man want a spy for his son-in-law, even if the spy hadn't been spying on *him*? It's a different world she lives in, Angelique. I don't *know* what to do."

Angelique exhaled slowly, a faint smile creeping over her lips. "But you love her."

He gave a short, sad laugh, propping his elbows on his knees and dropping his face into his hands. "Beyond reason. I'm considering impersonating Lord Wroth's young nephew, just to be able to call on her once or twice." To say good-bye, he thought in despair.

"So you would do anything for her, yes?"

He looked up, something about her tone catching his attention. "Why?"

She held out a note. "Even if you have no idea what to do, she has."

Harry snatched it. "Did you read it? How do you know it's from her?" His eyes raced over the writing on the outside, only his initials and the direction. Mariah didn't know any of that . . . did she?

Angelique made an indignant noise. "Did I read it? As if one cannot tell without reading. It is a woman's hand. It smells very faintly of perfume, although I imagine she did not want it to. It is addressed to this house, even though few people would know to reach you here, one of whom resides in her home. And it was delivered by a well-to-do young man."

"Young man?" He looked up as he broke the seal.

Angelique's smile widened in triumph. *"Oui.* The sort of young man who would know an earl's daughter." She turned and walked out of the room, closing the door behind her.

Harry had read the brief message almost before the latch clicked. The usual place and time? Did he interpret that correctly? Something of greatest importance . . . What could it possibly be?

He yanked his watch from his pocket; barely half past four. He had never climbed into her room before midnight, which meant he had over eight hours until he found out. He put the note into his pocket and strode out of the house to take a long walk after all.

Chapter 25

If one could suffer a collapse from nervous anticipation, Mariah thought she might be on the brink
of it. It was impossible to sit still. She paced the suddenly small confines of her room, wringing her hands.
Would he come? Had he gotten her message? Had
someone else intercepted it and dragged Harry away
for an interrogation? How would she know? Would she
wait forever, wondering? She certainly couldn't sleep.

With a thump, she sat on her dressing table chair,
her fingers digging into the cushion. She'd be half mad
by morning at this rate. Anxiously, she checked the
clock again; it was most definitely past midnight, by
a good two minutes or so. What if he didn't want to
come? What if all his attentions had been part of his
masquerade? What if he didn't realize she had sent the
note? What if—

The soft sound of cloth against wood almost escaped
her notice. For a moment she sat frozen in uncertainty,
then whirled around to see the familiar figure unfolding in front of the window. Her lips parted—after
longing so desperately for him to come, she seemed
struck dumb now that he was here—and he stepped
away from the window. "Mariah?"

She jumped at the sound of her name. "Oh! Oh, Harry, you came." She surged out of her seat and half-way across the room toward him, then stopped, wring-ing her hands. "I didn't know if you would."

"Did you not?" She had left a single candle lit, and it picked out the highlights of his features. He wore plain dark clothes that rendered him almost part of the shadows, although the collar of a white shirt showed around his neck. His eyes, bright and sharp, were fixed unwaveringly on her.

"Well—Well . . . " She cleared her throat. "I hoped you would."

"Ah." He finally glanced away from her, then back. "Why did you ask me to come?"

"Because . . . " All her courage and fortitude seemed to have fled. She could barely speak more than a word at a time. She wet her lips and raised her chin. "Be-cause I must speak to you. And—And because I have missed you so!" The last burst forth before she could restrain herself, and it seemed to release the tension in the room. Harry's face relaxed, and then Mariah was running the rest of the distance to him to be caught up in his arms and held against his heart.

"Having been unable to stay away thus far, why should I begin now?" His arms tightened around her. "Are you all right?"

She pushed back to see him. For a moment she just looked, feasting on the sight of him. In clothing that fit, no longer stooped and powdered, he might have been a completely new man—except for the familiar gleam in his hazel eyes. He seemed taller this close, more powerful; nothing at all like the hump-backed old man he had appeared to be, nor the quiet, almost invisible secretary.

"Are you all right?" he repeated with a small smile.

"Oh yes," she said fervently. "Very much so, now that you are here."

His smile deepened and he pulled her to him again. She closed her eyes as he held her. "God, how I've missed you." Then his arms loosened. "But this can't be why you sent for me."

Feeling steadier now, Mariah shook her head. Her nerves had made her uncertain before, but the feel of Harry's arms reassured her. This was no fancy or whim she would regret in the morning. This was what she wanted more than anything. "You can't keep sneaking in to see me at nights." Looking grim, he shook his head. "And you won't be Lord Wroth anymore, will you, so you can't even come to call in that way." Again he shook his head. "Then there is only one thing we can do. We must run away together."

He stared at her, then released her and stepped away. "Do you know what you're suggesting?"

She followed and put a finger on his lips. "Listen to me. My father will never give his permission for you to call on me, but if we run away together, he'll have no choice—"

"Oh, he'll have a choice." Harry sighed. He took her hand and pressed her knuckles almost absently against his cheek. Mariah's heart fluttered at the gentle affection in the gesture. "You think he'll relent and forgive all if we run away and force his hand. Perhaps he will—but perhaps he won't. He could disown you, cut you off and never see you again."

She had considered that, but didn't think it was possible. Her father adored her, and if he even considered disowning her, he'd have her mother to deal with. "No, he won't."

Harry dropped her hand and paced away from her. "He might. Believe me, he might." He ran his hands over his face, looking weary. "My mother . . . My mother was from a good family, very well-born and proud. My father was no one. She ran off with him thirty years ago and hasn't seen or heard from her family since. Believe me, Mariah, it could happen to you, no matter how much your father loves you. Men like him don't like to be crossed."

She thought about that for a moment. Would she regret it, if her parents refused to speak to her again? She would be sad, no question . . . but she would still have Harry. "Did your mother regret it?"

His mouth tightened. "You are not the same person as my mother."

"I should hope not!" He smiled reluctantly, and Mariah beamed back. She took a step after him. "Did your mother regret it?" she asked again, softly. "Is she happy with your father still, with you and your brother and sisters?"

"She had to learn to cook, you know, and mend and clean. It was not easy for her."

"So she's miserable, and wishes she'd never met your father?"

He sighed, but his eyes crinkled. "No, she's still very happy. But you should consider the risk."

"Hmm." She clasped her hands behind her back and took a nonchalant step after him. "So to warn me off, you tell me about a woman who ran off with a remarkable man who adores her, and she's blissfully happy. That is a terrible consequence indeed. Unless . . . " She sidled another step closer. "Unless you are trying to let me know, delicately, that you don't really care for me."

"You know I am not."

She lifted one shoulder, still inching toward him. "But you've never said anything on the subject one way or another. Perhaps it is all my imagination—perhaps you would rather I had never come onto the balcony that night of my parents' ball. Perhaps you came creeping into my room all those nights after because you felt sorry for me—"

Finally, ruefully, he laughed. "Sorry? The last thing I have ever felt for you was pity, darling."

"Good," she said, "because I have been in love with you since you kissed me in the garden at Chelsea."

Harry looked at her for the longest time. If she hadn't felt the rapid beat of his heart beneath her cheek when he'd held her, she might have doubted; she might have begun to worry. Instead she waited, sensing he was arguing with himself. He thought he was beneath her. He would try to tell her he was nothing to her, or a danger to her, or some other nonsensical idea Mariah didn't even want to hear unless it was to reject it so firmly and clearly, he would have to believe her. She had seen more worth and admirable qualities in Harry than in most other men of London, even before he threw himself in front of an exploding powder keg to protect her.

Abruptly, Harry walked away from the window. He picked up the lone candle she had left burning on the dressing table and began lighting the other lamps. As light filled the room, Mariah watched him greedily, his face and form materializing in living, vibrant flesh as the shadows were banished.

When the room was filled with light, Harry put down the candle and turned to face her. His hands fell to his sides and for a long moment he just stood, letting her look her fill at him without disguise or subterfuge.

"My name is Henry Sinclair," he said quietly. "My father is Thomas Sinclair, manager of the New Towne Theater in Birmingham . . . " He paused, as if waiting for her response. Mariah managed a tiny shake of her head, at a loss. "He is a commoner—an actor. Nobody of consequence, no family, no fortune, no connection to speak of. And I . . . " He paused again. "And I am a spy."

She had guessed as much. "For whom?"

"The Home Office." He was picking at the cuff of his heavy woolen coat. To her shock, he slid a long slender blade from the cuff, rapier thin and glittering sharp. He placed it on the dressing table. From his pocket he produced a pair of small thin tools, and from somewhere inside his coat a small pistol. He shrugged out of the coat to reveal a leather sheath strapped under his arm, the dagger she had seen the night he pulled Lord Dexter off her. All this he placed on the dressing table. Then he faced her, in his shirtsleeves, and raised his hands wide. "You have always had questions, and I have never answered you, never as completely as you deserved. Ask me anything, and I will tell you, even the ugly, unpleasant parts. You cannot declare your heart"—his voice caught for a second—"without knowing."

Mariah looked at the weaponry, so foreign and so dangerous amid her feminine toiletries and hair combs. *Deadly weapons for a dangerous man,* whispered a little voice in her head, but the shiver that went down her spine wasn't fear. "Have you ever killed anyone?"

He lifted one shoulder. "Perhaps. I have certainly wounded a few men badly enough they could have died."

"Whom do you spy on?"

"Everyone."

"Why?"

A bitter smile cracked his somber expression. "My patriotic duty."

She stared at him. "My father?" she asked incredulously, a number of curious coincidences falling into order. "Of course . . . You were at my mother's ball. You saw me at the Spencers' ball. And the Avery soiree, and the musicale—"

"Other men as well." He folded his arms and looked at the floor. "I didn't realize that's what I was doing until recently. We were told it was to protect and not to watch."

"The Home Office is spying on my father?" she repeated. "Why? He's done nothing wrong—"

"No," said Harry curtly. "He hasn't. And now they know it."

She opened her mouth, ready to vent her rising outrage, then closed it as realization sunk in. "You proved it." He jerked his head down, just a fraction of an inch, his expression still closed and dark. Mariah steadied herself with a hand on the wall. He had saved her more than once because he was lurking about. Spying? Watching? Protecting? If not for him, she and her father might well have died the other day near Carlton House. "And you saved our lives."

Harry let out his breath as if he'd been waiting for her to get to that. "By a lucky chance."

"Very lucky, I should say," she muttered.

"Yes. But you should know— Before you rashly declare your affection, you should know what sort of scoundrel you've gotten involved with. Don't promise what you'll regret in the morning."

Again her eyes strayed to the pile of weapons. "Do you love me?" she whispered. "Please tell me if I have been so mistaken . . ."

Harry was shaking his head before she finished. "The first sight of you bewitched me. You held my heart in your hand the moment you asked me to come see you, even after I climbed into your room at midnight and wouldn't tell you my name. If Dexter had hurt you, I'd have slit his throat without a moment's regret, and if I hadn't caught up to your coach in Piccadilly in time, I might have slit my own throat in grief. Do I love you? More than that small, simple phrase can convey. I love you enough that I cannot bear to ruin your life by taking you away from this life"—he swept one hand around the room—"and condemning you to mine."

"I see." She raised her chin and put her hands on her hips. "Instead you will condemn me to an unhappy marriage to someone I could never love half as much as I love you. You shall be off 'watching after' people in Whitechapel and throwing yourself in front of bombs while I will have to suffer through some other man's insipid lovemaking, always wishing it were *you* kissing me, and *you* making me laugh, and *you* holding me at night in bed—"

Harry cursed, crossing the room in two long strides. Mariah gave a small, involuntary squeak as he caught her to him and kissed her, a deep, demanding kiss that made her stomach leap and her bones wilt.

"You're a plague," he murmured, his nimble fingers unfastening her plain traveling dress. "You've infected my brain with a fever that drives out all sense and restraint."

She laughed, giddy in triumph. "A fine couple we shall be, I in my madness for you, and you with your fever for me . . . "

Harry laughed. "Fine, indeed." He pushed the fabric off her shoulders.

"Shall I tell you my plan?" she asked, helpfully pulling her arms free of the sleeves as he slid the dress down past her hips until it crumpled to the floor along with her petticoat.

"Later." He swung her into his arms and carried her to her bed. Mariah watched with awe as he pulled his shirt over his head. She had seen statues, but nothing as fascinating as Harry. Her breath felt short as her eyes moved over the flex and bunch of muscles under his skin. There was such latent power in his body, she reached out to trace the swell of his bicep to reassure herself he was real. London had thought him a withered old man, she thought in amazement as her fingers skimmed over warm, solid muscle that quivered at her touch. His other arm was wrapped tightly in a bandage, and she felt a fierce tenderness well up inside her, that he had been injured protecting her.

"Make love to me, Harry," she whispered. His muscle clenched under her hand. "Please."

His eyes gleamed with amusement. "Forward wench."

She blushed, from excitement and anticipation. With some inborn female instinct, she knew he hadn't been waiting for her formal invitation, that he'd been intent on making love to her since climbing in the window. And it was intoxicating, to know she had such power over *him*, this dangerous man who deposited an arsenal of weapons on her dressing table but kissed her so gently and sweetly. She ran her fingertips down his arm once more, shifting around until she was sitting on her knees close enough to see the pulse at the base of his throat. "I have thought about what you did once before. When you made me burn for you . . . "

He kissed her, a light, lingering contact. "Have you?" Her corset loosened, the string coming undone in Harry's hands.

"Yes." She shrugged her shoulders as he stripped the corset off, leaving her in only her thin chemise. "Every night you did not come to see me, I thought of it."

He made a soft growl low in his throat. "Did you? And what did you think of it?"

Her heartbeat was so strong she could feel the blood throbbing through her veins, pulsing between her legs. "I wondered how long it would be until you did it again," she whispered. "Until you touched me again . . . here." She cupped one breast. His eyes dropped there and seemed to ignite. "And here . . . " Her voice was barely a thread of sound as she slid one hand between her legs. She was already warm and wet there, and she stroked her fingers back and forth, leaving a damp spot on her chemise. Harry's face darkened with pure, feral desire as he watched, and she felt a heady rush of exhilaration. He was right to call her a forward wench; she certainly wasn't a lady when he looked at her that way.

"Far be it from me . . . " His hand closed over hers,

large and callused but gentle, his fingers moving between hers to touch where she had touched. " . . . to
disappoint a lady." He kissed her mouth, bearing her
back into her pillows, and Mariah pulled her hands
free to wind her arms around his neck. Then there was
no more conversation as her chemise came off, and
Harry demonstrated how thoroughly he would not
disappoint her, finding every sensitive spot and tender
area on her body until she was shaking.

"Tell me once more," he whispered between kisses.
"One last time, tell me you want this—*me*. Because
you're going to be very thoroughly ruined in a few
minutes . . . "

"I already am," she said on a sigh, running her
hands over the lean, firm lines of his back. "For
every other man but you." His eyes half closed as
she scraped lightly with her fingernails, and Mariah
stretched beneath him. The sensual creature no
longer slumbered inside her; it had become her,
writhing with need.

"You bring me to my knees when you say things
like that." He slid down, trailing kisses over her collarbone. His breath warmed her nipple, and Mariah
trembled even before he kissed her there, too. His
hands had been running all over her, and yet when he
touched between her legs, her whole body tensed in
giddy anticipation.

"I don't want to hurt you," he murmured. She
thrashed her head from side to side, already feeling
the storm gathering inside her belly. "God, you're so
beautiful, so wet . . . " His fingers were inside her now,
just as before. She pressed her heels into the bed and
pushed her hips against the delicious pressure he was
exerting, making her body hum.

When he pulled back, she could hardly see straight and her limbs shook. She murmured some inarticulate protest, grasping for him. Harry laughed, the sound strained and dark, and then he moved over her, rising to his knees and unfastening his trousers. Sprawled on the bed, Mariah watched breathlessly as he peeled off the last of his clothing. She simply had to see . . .

"Worried?" Harry asked.

She dragged her eyes away from his cock, blushing that she had been caught staring and then blushing harder because she hadn't been worrying, she had been thinking too much about touching him, that mysterious, virile part of him, and what it would feel like when he was inside her. Drat Joan and the naughty poems; perhaps she was too bold. "No," she murmured. "I—I was thinking I would like to touch you."

Harry closed his eyes. His cock bobbed. "Later," he said in a strained voice. "Well—perhaps just once . . . " His words choked off as she reached out and stroked him. "Blessed Christ," he croaked, letting her explore him for a minute before grasping her knee and pushing it toward her chest. He bent down and pressed his mouth between her legs, licking her on that sensitive, pulsing spot. Mariah gasped, her body surging up against him. Then, before she could recover from the shock of it, he had pressed the head of his erection against her and nudged his way inside.

She gulped in small, rapid breaths, feeling her body stretch. It didn't hurt, but it felt tight and full and unbearably intimate. Slowly, he sank all the way into her, his hips settling between her thighs until she just wrapped her legs around his waist. The movement made her more aware of him, thick and hard, inside her, and she shivered, raising her eyes to Harry's.

His head had fallen forward, as if he were studying the place where his body joined hers. The tendons in his neck stood out, and his fingers shook as he slowly stroked one hand down the inside of her thigh until he touched her, there, where it made her gasp and arch her back because it felt like lightning crackling beneath her skin. He moved, sliding out of her, and then moved forward again, rocking his hips against her as he continued to touch her so exquisitely softly until the pleasure was almost suffocating.

Just as she felt it begin to shatter, Harry fell to his elbows, sliding his arms beneath her to hold her tightly while he drove into her again and again as he kissed her everywhere. He slipped one hand beneath her bottom and lifted, tilting and holding her so his every movement set off that lightning, sharper and brighter every time. Mariah gripped his arms and pushed against his every thrust until he sucked in his breath and froze, holding himself deep within her while she clung to him and cried a little as her body shuddered in time with his.

Neither moved for a while as they lay tangled together in exhausted satisfaction. So this was ruin. Mariah smiled sleepily, thinking that she enjoyed it very much, from the feel of Harry's arms around her to the weight of his body atop hers.

"Tell me your plan now," he murmured, pressing his lips to the sweat-dampened hair at her temple.

Mariah turned her head, giving him better access to her neck, where his kisses sent tingles through her. He obliged, nipping lightly at her skin until she shivered. "We can't be married in London. It would take too long to have the banns read."

He mumbled something agreeable, still kissing her neck.

"But a license would also be too difficult to procure, not to mention expensive."

Harry laughed, nuzzling her ear. "I'm not destitute, darling."

She smiled. "Good. Although I have saved my pin money and borrowed Joan's besides, so I am not destitute, either. But I thought the best way would be for us to go to your parents." Harry didn't say anything. "Unless you think they wouldn't approve," she added hesitantly.

He kissed her once more, then rolled onto his back. "They'll approve mightily of you."

"Then why do you hesitate?"

He sighed, gathering her closer in his arms and resting his cheek against her hair. "They might not approve of my actions." There was an understatement, he thought. He could just imagine what his parents would say if they knew how he had pursued Mariah, with no real hope of an honorable conclusion to the business. He didn't want to think what they would say if they knew he'd just made love to her, in her family's home, knowing full well her father would never approve of the match. Of all the questionable things he had done in his life, he suddenly felt the weight of this sin more than any other. So much for saying he didn't want to condemn Mariah to his poor life; now she had little choice, since he'd compromised her in the eyes of her own society.

"To Birmingham we go, then," he said to banish the thought. "What if your father follows us?"

She wiggled her shoulders, her fingers skating in swirls and loops across his chest. "Does it matter now?"

Harry closed his eyes. Christ. No, he had seen to that.

"It didn't matter before, either," Mariah added in the same unconcerned tone.

Perhaps not, but before, there had been no permanent harm. Before, she had still been a virgin and could have walked away from her entanglement with him and no one would have been the wiser. Abruptly, he sat up. "Do you have your things packed?" Looking startled, she nodded. "We'd best be off, then," he said quietly, his spy's instincts returning. "The sooner we're out of London, the better."

"All right."

She followed him off the bed, and in silence they retrieved discarded clothing and dressed. Mariah was not used to dressing herself; Harry had to fasten the corset, then the dress. She flashed him a brilliant smile as she wound her glossy dark hair into a knot at her neck, and Harry helplessly smiled back. This was utter madness, he thought, contrary to every logical, sensible course of action, and yet his blood hummed and his heart leaped every time she looked at him that way. She pulled a small valise from under her bed as he replaced his weapons and pulled on his coat.

"Ready?"

She nodded once at his whisper, catching up a long dark cloak from the chaise. Harry watched with a measuring look. Mariah couldn't climb down the ivy, not in her long skirts and without a single experience to aid her. They would have to go out through the house, no matter how little he liked the idea. "Which way is the servants' stair?"

"To the left, at the end of the corridor."

Harry leaned down to press a soft, silent kiss on her mouth. Putting one finger to his lips to indicate quiet, he took the valise and quietly opened the door.

And looked right into the barrel of a pistol.

Chapter 26

Harry stopped dead, throwing wide his arms, reflexively shielding Mariah behind him. The pistol in the earl's hand trembled just enough to threaten a random shot. Harry had every confidence he could avoid that shot. If he wished, he could have the pistol in his own hand and at Doncaster's throat before the earl could stop him. He had done it before, disarmed a wild-eyed Luddite out smashing weavers' frames and drunken sailors bent on mischief in Wapping. When he started in Stafford's employ, he had learned how to defend himself and turn the tables on an attacker, and an unprepared older gentleman like the earl would pose no problem.

But instead he slowly raised his hands, holding the valise to one side. He never took his eyes off the pistol, just in case.

Behind him, Mariah grew impatient. Harry was blocking the door, not moving, and she couldn't see around him. She couldn't see anything, having put out all the lamps he'd lit. "What is it?" she whispered, clutching his arm and trying to peek over his shoulder.

To her horror, her father stepped around Harry. He

was holding a pistol, pointed right at the two of them. "I thought I heard a rat," he said in a deadly furious voice. "I see I was right."

She gasped. "Papa, no!" She tried to push past Harry, but he wouldn't move; indeed, it seemed he deliberately blocked her way and held her back. "Let me by!"

"No," Papa said sharply. "Stay in your room, Mariah. Close and bar the door. I will speak with you directly." He motioned at Harry with the gun. "You. Walk this way, with your hands where they are."

Without a word of protest Harry turned and slowly moved down the hall in the direction he had indicated, the valise still in his hand. As soon as he moved, Mariah burst out of her room and threw herself on her father's arm. "Papa, put the gun away! Let me explain."

He shook her off, glaring at Harry, who had an eerie calmness about him. Out of nowhere Mariah recalled how he had overpowered Lord Dexter with his bare hands, and remembered as well the weapons hidden on his person. She had a strong suspicion Harry was obeying because he wanted to, not because he felt compelled. She tried again with her father. "Papa, please—"

"What is going on, Charles?" Behind them in the hall, her mother gasped. "Charles!"

"Return to our chamber, Cassandra," he said grimly. "Take Mariah with you."

White-faced, her mother reached for her. Mariah dodged her and scurried toward Harry. So much for a quiet elopement and presenting her parents with a fait accompli. "No! I am going with him!"

Her mother gave a little shriek. Her father's lips turned white. "Mariah, come here at once—"

"Put away your pistol, Papa!" She stepped up beside Harry and curled her hands around his upheld arm.

"Silly chit," her lover murmured. "What the devil are you doing?"

She looked him straight in the face. "I am saving you from my father so you can marry me like a proper gentleman and not have to break your neck on the ivy to see me. Or get shot."

"Ah. Carry on, then," he said, making her want to laugh. She beamed at him, then turned back to her father.

"Please don't let Papa shoot me, Mama." The countess lunged forward then with a cry, clutching the earl's arm. With a curse, her father uncocked his pistol and lowered his arm.

"What is going on?" her mother cried, bewildered and terrified.

"Mama, I am running away to be married." Mariah smiled brightly even though her words made her mother turn pale and sway on her feet. "May I present Mr. Henry Sinclair."

"Not another word, Mariah," her father snapped. "You are not going anywhere, certainly not with this scoundrel."

"But I love him, Papa, and if I must be scandalous and disowned to be with him, I shall be." Her mother moaned, covering her face with both hands. Mariah, calculating at once which parent was more vulnerable, added solemnly, "I shall miss you terribly, Mama, if you mean to disown me, but I shall not change my mind."

It worked. The countess dropped her hands, then drew herself up and tightened the sash of her dressing gown. "In that case," she said with regal tragedy, "good-bye, Charles."

"Eh? What?" Startled, Papa turned to her. "What do you mean?"

"I shall not be deprived of my only child. I am going with them." She gestured to the maid hovering in horrified silence at the back of the hall. "Fetch my cloak, Frances."

"Cassandra," said Papa, flummoxed.

"She is just like you, Charles, just as stubborn and determined. I have long since learned I can never deter either of you, once you set your mind on something." She turned to Harry. "You there, young man—what is your name? Where is your carriage?"

Mariah glanced up. Harry was staring at her mother with a strange mixture of admiration and astonishment. She could hardly blame him. She certainly hadn't expected her mother to say *that*. Still, it had spiked her father's guns and bought her some time to persuade both her parents.

"Where is your carriage?" Mama repeated as the maid came flying down the hall with a long cloak over her arm. "My daughter cannot elope in a hired hack."

Harry finally managed to tear his eyes off her and glance at Mariah. Eloping with the Countess of Doncaster had not figured at all in his plans, even such plans as they were.

Mariah simply smiled as if she had anticipated this all along. "I told you they wouldn't disown me."

"It's not quite a blessing, either," he muttered back. "I beg pardon, my lady, I haven't got a carriage."

The countess sighed. "Frances, run down to the stable and wake John Coachman. He must prepare the traveling coach at once."

"Cassandra, stop this foolishness." The earl ran his hands through his hair as if he would rip it out. Harry half feared the man would shoot him now just because he couldn't shoot his wife or daughter.

The countess faced her husband. "Then you stop your foolishness, Charles. Waving a pistol is not helping."

Doncaster swore some more. He glared at Harry. He shoved the pistol into his dressing gown pocket. "I will see you in my study."

Harry thought it was without doubt the oddest procession he had ever imagined as he followed the earl, with Mariah hanging on his arm. The countess followed, cloak over one arm. The maid, he assumed, took off like a rabbit for the servants' quarters to spread the tale. He wondered if Brandon would still want to cut him down for this, and if he'd be waiting once the earl finished with him.

The earl's study was the picture of quiet English elegance, the sort of room Harry had always fancied, paneled in dark oak and lined with bookshelves, with a large map of Europe on one wall. Deep leather chairs were arranged near the tall windows, now covered in dark green draperies. A thoroughly comfortable, masculine room, evidence of the wealth and stature of the owner. He felt at a distinct disadvantage.

The earl set down the lamp he had caught up from a table along the hall and turned to Harry. "Now, sir," he said coldly. "Who are you, and what the bloody hell were you doing in my daughter's bedroom?"

Harry had been thinking very hard about how he would answer those very questions. His business with Stafford wasn't part of his reason for being in Mariah's bedroom—nor in Doncaster House at all tonight—and he didn't think it would help him anyway. He could still end the night in Newgate, and he knew no one who would or could get him out. He was on his own here. "My name is Henry Sinclair—" he began.

"Papa, I am in love with him!" Mariah burst out.

Doncaster put up one hand and shot her a stern glance. "And who is this man, Mariah? Not one of the eligible gentlemen who called on you"—his lip curled as he glared once more at Harry—"properly."

"No," Harry agreed, tired of lies. "No, I called on her most improperly."

Mariah's mother gasped. Mariah herself blushed and forced an uneasy smile. Doncaster's eyes flashed; he took three steps across the room, drew back his fist, and punched Harry in the face. Harry made no effort to defend himself, but absorbed the blow in silence.

Mariah gasped. "Papa, stop!"

"How dare you," said the earl in a venomous tone.

Harry held up one hand to stay Mariah, gingerly touching his jaw. He deserved that. A sad commentary on his life lately, that he felt people were entitled to assault him. "I should not have done it. But . . . " He glanced at Mariah, standing with her hands clapped over her mouth, her eyes as wide as saucers. "But I found myself utterly unable to obey my own sense and stay away. I have fallen completely in love with Lady Mariah."

"I see." There was pure contempt in the earl's expression. "You are one of those vile fortune hunters, luring a respectable young woman away from her family and friends, seducing her out of her innocence."

"Papa!"

"And who *are* you, sir?" Doncaster went on. His eyes raked over Harry, in his worn linen shirt and plain woolen coat. "Who are you to raise your eyes to her? You have the look of an adventurer about you, a rogue. Plotting to elope with my daughter! To steal her away from her family! I should have you arrested."

"Papa!" Mariah slapped her hands on her hips. "He saved your life, and mine!"

"Mariah, be quiet. One of our own footmen shielded me from the blast—"

"And who protected me? Who alerted our footman there was a bomb?" A tense silence fell over the room. All eyes turned on Harry, who tightened his jaw but said nothing.

"But how did you meet him, dearest?" The countess joined the conversation at last, tactfully turning the talk away from any virtue Harry might have had.

"I—I met him at our ball, Mama."

Her mother looked puzzled, then her face went blank. "The elusive Harry, I presume?"

Mariah's cheeks were pink. "Er . . . yes."

Lady Doncaster turned to inspect Harry with cool eyes. "You were not on our list."

This time he met her gaze directly. "No, madam."

"He was," said Mariah at the same time. "But under a different name."

Her comments were not helping, Harry realized. The countess had looked merely bewildered before; now her expression began to close up, a veil of hauteur coming down over her emotions. The best way to do this would have been to explain, delicately and carefully, from the beginning—and even then he thought the chances of success weren't very good. Mariah's frustration, born no doubt out of her belief that her parents would accept her decision with grace and calm, was making her hasty. She was blurting out facts he would have preferred to ease into the conversation as part of his entire story. Feeling defeat bite at his heels, he focused on her. "Mariah."

She turned to him, impatience stamped on her face. He raised one brow and waited until her frown faded and her pinched mouth relaxed. Then he nodded once at her, for reassurance, before turning back to her father. "I should begin at the beginning, sir."

The earl's expression did not look inviting, to say the least, but before Harry could begin picking his way through the elaborate web of secret motives and hidden agendas, there was a knock on the door. Almost mid-knock it opened and a footman slipped into the room, a bareheaded footman wearing mismatched shoes, with his nightshirt stuffed into his breeches. A footman Harry recognized at once.

"Viscount Camden, sir," Alec Brandon announced somewhat breathlessly.

Mariah heard her father's growl of displeasure, saw the flicker of fury that passed over his face as he turned to dismiss the impertinent servant—perhaps even to sack the man—but Lord Camden was already standing in the doorway. It was past one in the morning; why on earth would Lord Camden be here now? Mariah took a closer look at the footman—Jameson, she realized, the one who had told her where to find Harry. And when she swung around to see Harry's response, his still posture and expressionless face spoke volumes. He was the reason Camden was here.

"Sir." Papa nodded curtly. Mariah could see his temper was on a very short leash.

Lord Camden entered the room slowly, his every movement deliberate. He was tall and gaunt, dressed all in black like a specter from a children's tale, and had not the slightest expression on his hard-hewn face. He nodded back to her father, but his cold dark eyes flashed about the room until they landed, and rested, on Harry. There was nothing in his gaze, though, and after a moment he turned to her father.

"Doncaster, Lady Doncaster." Camden drew off his gloves and bowed slightly to Mariah's mother. "I hope I have not come at an inopportune moment." Behind his back, Mariah noticed another, nondescript man slip silently into the room. The footman, Jameson, closed the door and stood with his back to it. No one remarked on the utter lunacy of receiving callers at this hour.

"Not at all, Camden." Papa's eyes flicked over Camden's shoulder, taking in the other man. "To what do I owe the honor of this visit?"

Mariah took advantage of his distraction to dart to Harry's side. He hadn't made a sound or a move since Jameson opened the door. "Don't worry," she whispered. He didn't look at her. She slipped her hand into his, and his fingers closed around hers. "It will all come out well," she added softly, "I know it will." Although she didn't.

The viscount must have heard her whispering, for he turned in her direction, slowly, ominously. That cold, flat glare landed on her for a moment, and she stood a little straighter and put up her chin. If it fell to her to defend Harry against both her father and Lord Camden, she would.

"My daughter, Mariah," Papa said in a wintry tone. She curtsied. "Mariah, would you please excuse us," he added with a significant look.

Lord Camden gave her a faint nod. "Lady Mariah." Again he turned back to Harry, as if he were a curiosity the viscount couldn't take his eyes off of. For a moment there was silence as Camden stared at Harry and Harry stared back. "Let her stay," said Camden thoughtfully. "I suspect she will be relevant."

Relevant! As if she ordinarily weren't! Mariah blinked, then looked at her father, whose eyes narrowed. He drew breath to speak, but Camden went on before he could. "You have the look of your mother about you," he said to Harry. "Is she well?"

Harry's grip on her hand tightened for a second, then eased and slid away. "Yes."

The viscount made a noise in the back of his throat. "Does she know where you are?"

Harry hesitated, then shook his head once.

"Good." Camden turned back to Papa. "What is your complaint against him?"

Papa drew himself up. "It is a private matter, sir, one I shall deal with myself."

Camden harrumphed. "He tangled with your daughter, didn't he? Looked far above his station and dared to approach a young lady whose handkerchief he wasn't fit to hold." Beside her, Harry stiffened but said nothing. "I am not surprised," Camden went on, slewing a sour glance at him. "I should have expected as much, perhaps."

"That is not true!" Mariah burst out. "I begged him to come to see me! I sought him out every chance I could! How dare you say he's not fit to hold my handkerchief, you—"

"Is the harm irreparable?" Camden asked her father, whose face was mottled red with temper again. Now both of them looked ready to send Harry to the hangman.

She hated being talked about as if she weren't there. "Yes, it is!" she said before her father could respond, unconsciously stepping in front of Harry as if to shield him. "I am irreparably in love with him! I will never marry anyone else—I shall never receive another gentleman, and if you force me to marry someone else, I shall leave him! I shall live the most scandalous life London has ever seen—" She cast about wildly for anything else she could use to frighten her father with. "—and I will never see or speak to you or Mama ever again!"

"Mariah," her father said, his face now white—with fury or with hurt, she didn't know. "You will retire to your room. You are overwrought."

"No! Not until you swear to me you won't do anything to him." She folded her arms and silently defied them. A touch on her shoulder startled her.

"I think I can speak for myself," Harry said with a faint, wry smile. "Not quite so eloquently, perhaps, but you'd better let me have a go."

"Oh." Flustered, she retreated to his side. Her allegiance was unchanged. If her father wanted her to leave the room now, he would have to drag her out himself.

Harry looked over Mariah's shoulder. John Stafford gazed at him with opaque eyes, not making the slightest effort to control the situation for better or worse. That was different, but no less than he deserved. He took a deep breath and turned back to Doncaster, ignoring the other man in the room. "I have never done a moment's harm to Lady Mariah."

"She thinks otherwise," said Camden, who looked almost fiendishly pleased Harry was speaking for himself.

She rounded on him. "I never said that! He never did anything to hurt me—"

"Not all harm is violence, young lady," Camden snapped. His eyes ran over Harry again. "But let him speak: what *has* he done?"

Finally, Harry turned his full attention to Camden. "I have done my job."

"She was never part of that."

"No?" Harry raised his eyebrows. "And yet she was in the coach when the radicals lit a powder keg beneath it."

Camden pressed his lips together in a furious scowl.

"What the devil," said Doncaster, angry once more. "Why have you been sneaking around my house like a thief, trifling with my daughter? Answer me, sir!"

"Now, that only he can answer," said Camden. "But he does have an honorable reason to be about London, particularly when not himself. And in your position, Doncaster, I should be very grateful to him."

"I should like to hear why," Doncaster bit out.

Camden waved one hand at Harry. "Go on, then."

Harry hesitated a moment, waiting, but still Stafford didn't speak, so he turned back to Lord and Lady Doncaster. "The attempt on your life, sir, was not unexpected."

It took a while to outline the facts. Harry didn't hide anything about his mission, although he was conscious of Stafford at his back the entire time, and so skirted a few parts rather delicately. Doncaster listened with a mixture of outrage and anger in his face, and when Harry finished, it was to Camden he turned.

"I was suspected? Of treason?" Fury laced his words. Harry grimaced; he had tried to treat that as lightly as possible, but Doncaster was no fool and had seen between his words.

"You yourself were not suspected," said Stafford smoothly, falsely, finally stepping forward. "We suspected someone in your household could have been selling information, or perhaps stealing it."

Doncaster didn't look as if he believed one word of this. He turned at once on his footman and snapped his fingers. "You." Brandon stepped forward. "You work with these men, don't you?"

Brandon nodded.

A shadow seemed to pass over the earl's face, and he braced his hands on his desk. His voice shook. "All my life has been given in service to the Crown. I have dragged my wife and child across Europe for the sole purpose of doing His Majesty's bidding and preserving England's dignity and sovereignty. To know that my own have turned on me, suspected me and spied on me—"

"But I presume, since you are revealing this, you have caught the traitor," said Lady Doncaster when he broke off. She placed her hand discreetly on her husband's back.

Stafford bowed his head. "Yes, my lady. Mr. Sinclair realized the true threat. His actions alone prevented the attempt on his lordship's life from succeeding. We are greatly indebted to him."

That was a rather ringing commendation, Harry thought, and not something he had expected.

Lady Doncaster turned to him, her lips parted in surprise, and he shifted his weight uncomfortably. "And what does this have to do with Mariah?" she asked.

He looked at Mariah. "I saw her at your ball and was struck," he said. "Every moment I have known her since then has only deepened my feeling, until I have fallen utterly in love with her." Doncaster winced and Camden's mouth twitched.

"And I with him," Mariah said, beaming back at him.

"Mariah," said her father. "Please—"

"It is true I cannot offer her a life to equal her current one," Harry went on. "It is true my family is nothing to hers, and I am no one of consequence—"

"I don't care," she exclaimed. "To me you are everyone."

"Stop," said Doncaster wearily. His shoulders slumped and he looked old all of a sudden. "No more of this, Mariah . . . "

"You might as well let him have her," said Camden. "His mother thumbed her nose at me just the same way, and ignored every word I said." He shook his finger at Harry. "You're just like your father."

Harry bowed his head. "Thank you, sir."

Camden snorted and turned to the earl. "Well, Doncaster? Are you going to let your daughter marry my grandson or not?"

Chapter 27

"Your grandson!" Mariah's mouth fell open. Doncaster raised his head. Everyone turned to Harry.

"I don't claim the relation," he said.

Mariah closed her mouth and poked him in the arm. The grandson of a viscount was at least a plausible match for the daughter of an earl, and despite all her bluster, Mariah didn't want to leave her parents forever. She would have missed them both dreadfully. If there were any way she could have both Harry and her parents, she was all in favor of it. "Why didn't you tell me that?" she whispered.

Camden gave a harsh bark of laughter. "Oh, you'll claim it, all right, young man. You'll claim it to marry the girl you want and win the seat in Parliament you've got your eye on. Either Doncaster or I will see to that, I expect."

Harry said nothing, his face gone hard and taut. Camden laughed again.

"Thought I didn't know? Why? Just because your name's Sinclair instead of Farrington?" He came closer, until he and Harry were almost eye-to-eye. Fascinated, Mariah searched for any resemblance, and found more than she expected. "Why do you think you're in London?" Camden asked very softly. "Who do you think put your name in Stafford's ear?"

Harry could barely hide his astonishment. Camden? The heartless old man who had sworn never to see his mother again as long as she lived with his father? Camden had tapped him for his post? It was more than shocking; he would have wagered that Camden hadn't even known of his existence.

"I've no idea what you mean," he said. Good God. For thirty years his mother had believed herself excluded from her family forever. She was happy with his father—Harry didn't doubt that—but she had regretted losing her brother and sisters, her mother and father. Was Camden relenting? Or did Camden have some other purpose in promoting him?

The viscount snorted again. "You know exactly what I mean." He crooked his fingers and Stafford stepped forward. "Has he served you well?"

There was a trace of dark amusement in Stafford's eyes as he glanced at Harry. "Indeed, sir, very well. One of my finest and ablest men, although somewhat more independent than anticipated."

"Very good, then." Camden glanced at Doncaster. "She is your daughter. I cannot tell you what to do. But I shall claim him, even if he will not have me. I bid you good night, sir. Madam." Without another word, he turned and walked out of the room, Stafford in his wake. Brandon met Harry's eyes for a moment, then left the room as well and closed the door.

"You might have mentioned your connection to Camden earlier," said the countess in the suddenly quiet room.

Harry flinched, dragging his eyes away from the door Camden had just departed through, looking back to his companions. "I do not want any connection."

She shook her head. "Do not be a fool," she said gently. "A man in politics must use every connection he has."

"I'm not—" Harry began without thinking, then stopped when Mariah stepped on his foot.

In the intervening silence, everyone turned to look at Doncaster. The pulse in the earl's temple throbbed rapidly, and his eyes flashed fire. "The man who marries my daughter," he began ominously, "cannot be nobody."

"Papa, you could—" Mariah started to say, before her father held up one hand.

"Yes, I could," he said through his teeth. He turned fierce eyes back on Harry. "You cannot marry my daughter, then, unless I make you *somebody*. I have a pocket borough in Yorkshire—the Aldhampton seat. If you want it, you shall have it."

Harry's stomach took a plunge as his heart took a great leap. Doncaster would never have said that if he didn't mean to give his consent. Not only the wife he wanted above all else, but the political start he dreamed of. Somehow he managed to keep his composure and nod.

Mariah did no such thing; with a happy exclamation, she jumped up and flung her arms around Harry's neck. "I told you Papa would help! And now you shall be able to do something, to help people like that poor girl in Whitechapel!" She beamed at her father. "How wonderful you are, Papa!"

Doncaster didn't look wonderful. "If you are a damned Whig," he growled, a muscle twitching in his jaw, "I beg you, do not tell me now. I cannot take it tonight."

Harry swallowed a grin, sliding a quick sideways look at Mariah. "No, sir," he agreed. "I shan't."

Doncaster closed his eyes for a moment, then sighed. He looked at Mariah, glowing with happiness and still clutching Harry's hand. "This is what you want, darling?" he asked, as if to assure himself one last time. "It is not a flight of fancy?"

She shook her head. "Not a fancy, Papa. I am quite certain. I love him."

The earl looked at Harry.

"With all my being, sir," Harry said, answering the unasked question.

Doncaster sighed once more, then waved his hand. "I suppose I must give my permission, then."

A while later, after Mariah had given her mother a rambling explanation of her acquaintance with Harry, and the earl had quizzed Harry closely on several points of his recent employment, Harry excused himself and stepped into the hall. Brandon was leaning against the wall, nodding off. He raised his head at Harry's appearance.

"Congratulations are in order, I suppose."

"And an apology," said Harry. "I lied to you."

Brandon shrugged. "I knew it. For such a good actor and practiced liar, your affections were pathetically obvious."

He had to laugh at that. "I don't think I'm meant to be a spy, then." Brandon gave a crooked grin and shrugged again. "What made you fetch Stafford?"

"When she asked about you this afternoon, I suspected," Brandon said. "I was sitting up when the earl rang, thinking he'd heard a rat. I gather he listened at the door for a bit . . . But I sent Frances up to see to her ladyship and went after Stafford, on the odd chance you'd finally misplaced your luck.

"The other fellow—Camden—was there with him. Don't know why, but they didn't seem surprised to see me, and when he set his horses to, we crossed London in a matter of minutes."

"Lovely timing."

Brandon coughed. "For you. Camden's your family?"

"My mother's father," Harry muttered. "Not that I've ever seen or spoken to him before in my life."

"It appears that breach has been mended."

Harry doubted it; but it was true that if he went into politics, Camden's connection would help. And it would make his mother happy if he could indeed mend the breach. "Perhaps." A long moment of silence. "I'm a damned fool, I know."

"Without question." Brandon paused. "I was standing right next to the carriage and never noticed the keg. If you hadn't shouted—"

"And if you hadn't fetched Stafford tonight . . . " Harry shrugged. "I should say we're even."

Brandon smiled, just a faint quirk of his mouth. "All even."

"I'm out," said Harry abruptly. "I've had enough of this."

"I expected as much. A married man cannot have so many secrets, nor fling himself in front of so many powder kegs." He put out his hand. "Good fortune to you, Sinclair. And to Lady Mariah. Especially to Lady Mariah."

Harry shook his hand. "And to you, Brandon."

"Give my notice to Doncaster, will you? I expect he won't want me back, and . . . well . . . " He gave Harry a wry look. "I think you're a better messenger than I now." Harry nodded once, and Brandon turned on his heel.

As he walked away, Mariah slipped into the corridor. "Who is he, really?" she asked.

Slowly, Harry shook his head, still watching his fellow agent leave, his posture as straight as a pike. "A good man, of high morals and honesty. Military, I'd say, but beyond that I do not know." He looked down at her. "We all have our secrets."

Mariah put her arms around him, twining her fingers through his and resting her cheek on his shoulder. She looked up at him with soft, luminous eyes. "Do you? What secrets do you have, Harry?"

"From you? Too many. But none I shall keep any longer."

"And you will tell me everything? Why you were Lord Wroth and a secretary and spied on my father and climbed in my window?"

Harry thought of Stafford's words—that he had been one of his best men. Stafford knew he was out. He put his arm around her shoulders and laughed. "Yes, I shall tell you everything. Not tonight, perhaps; we must have something to talk about all the days to come, and it is perhaps best not to exhaust every topic at once."

"I don't think I shall ever grow tired of talking to you."

"Well, should I run on and begin to bore you, you know just how to silence me." He kissed her lightly, then more deeply as she wrapped her arms around his neck and held him in place.

"A useful skill. I shall have to stay in good practice on that one."

"I shall insist upon it." Harry drew her fully into his arms, holding her close despite the chance of being discovered by her parents or the servants. "For the rest of my days."

Epilogue

Two months later

It was a lovely wedding breakfast, albeit a smaller event than one might expect at the home of the Earl of Doncaster. The bridegroom's parents were in attendance, looking very proper and respectable for a pair of actors. The bridegroom's grandparents were there as well, vastly more austere but polite enough when spoken to. The bride's family connections weren't sure what to make of the match, but everyone knew the Earl of Doncaster would never have permitted the marriage if he were not perfectly satisfied, and the earl's judgment was widely respected.

But the bride and bridegroom seemed to have vanished. "Have you seen Mariah?" Lady Doncaster asked her sister quietly as she circulated among the guests in the garden.

"I thought I saw her heading toward the house," Lady Bennet replied.

"Oh, no, Mother. I saw her just a few moments ago walking along the path around the terrace." Joan Bennet craned her neck to one side. "There, I think I can still see her skirt around that tree."

"Ah. Thank you, Joan," said the countess, turning in that direction.

Joan smiled and sipped her champagne until her mother's suspicious gaze grew too heavy. "Yes, Mother?"

"Mariah's not gone toward the terrace, has she?" Lady Bennet had eyes like a hawk.

Joan smiled her brightest smile. "I'm sure I saw her there, Mother."

"Hmm." Her mother was trying not to smirk, Joan thought. "And if you instead saw her heading toward the house, especially if she were with her husband, you wouldn't tell your aunt a lie, would you?"

"Mother," said Joan indignantly, "I cannot possibly answer that question."

Lady Bennet sighed, and then she laughed. Joan grinned, linked her arm through her mother's and led her off, away from the house, with only a tiny conspiratorial glance behind her.

They reached the upstairs without meeting anyone. It was very fortunate the weather was so lovely, for it meant everyone was out in the garden, including most of the servants. No one saw them slip into her bedroom, or heard him turn the key in the lock.

Mariah laughed and pulled the wreath of flowers from her hair. "You don't need anyone's permission to be alone with me now."

Harry grinned, tossing the key in the direction of the dressing table. "I don't need anyone interrupting, either. Come here, wife."

She flung her arms around his neck, burying her face in his crisp white cravat. "How I love the sound of that word. It seemed like this day would never come."

"Two months never passed so slowly." He lifted her chin and kissed her mouth. "Right up until the bishop concluded the ceremony, I feared your father would stand and put a stop to things, and take me aside for one last interrogation."

Mariah laughed, letting her head fall back as his lips moved down her neck. "He wouldn't have . . . "

"There was hardly anything left for him to ask. It's been two long months of examination, my dear, as he tried to make sure I was worthy of you." He was dragging up her heavy, embroidered skirt. Mariah pressed against him, her breath coming faster. It *had* been two long months. Her father had given Harry permission to court her, but then he and her mother had watched over them like a hawk: no more midnight visits, and barely a handful of stolen kisses. She was as desperate as Harry for this moment, which was why she had told Joan to distract her mother so they could steal away even before the wedding breakfast was over.

"And are you worthy?" She tugged the end of his cravat free and wound it around her finger.

Her new husband grinned, that slow, wicked grin that made her heart trip over itself. "Must I prove it to you, too?"

She just raised her eyebrows coyly.

With a growl, he swung her around in his arms, then pushed her back against the wall. He kissed her again, hard, as he twisted up the elegant fabric of her skirts and petticoats between them, and then his hands were under her skirt, inside her pantalets, touching her—so perfectly—*there* . . . Mariah moaned, opening her legs, gasping with want as he slid one hand under her knee and pulled it up to his waist.

"How shall I prove myself worthy?" His whisper warmed her ear. Mariah slid down a little, her supporting leg wobbling as his fingers slid along the already wet folds of flesh there, oh *there* . . . "How shall I please my lady wife?" He slid one, then two fingers inside her, stretching and stroking. She choked for air, overcome by the desire raging through her. It had been two *very* long months, she thought dazedly.

And then it was Harry's turn to suck in his breath, as she pulled loose the buttons on his trousers and reached inside to cup him in her hands, one hand around his ballocks and one gliding the length of his erection. "If you want to please me," she whispered, "stop talking."

"As you wish," he managed to say, and then he was inside her. Mariah raised up onto her toes and tilted her hips, meeting his every hungry thrust. Harry—her darling Harry—cupped her bottom in one hand and stroked her into climax with the other, and when he jerked and shouted in his own release, she truly felt they were one. She had never been so happy in all her life, and the warm light in his eyes indicated he felt much the same.

"I think—I think that will serve," she said breathlessly. "For now."

Harry exhaled, resting his forehead against hers. "I'm not certain I shall ever feel worthy of you, love."

"Why not?" She stretched and smiled, running her hands over his back.

"For the way you trusted me when I told you nothing about myself. For the courage you showed in inviting me to run off with you."

"That was a good plan," she told him. "I had everything worked out."

He laughed. "Yes, but this . . . I do believe this is better."

Mariah held him closer and laid her head on his shoulder. Yes, this was much better. Now her parents approved—rather grudgingly, but without any misconceptions about the man she loved. Her father had taken Harry as his protégé, in a way, although Harry's progressive ideas were already making Papa glower at him. Even Mama was beginning to succumb to Harry's charm.

"This is everything I dreamed of," she murmured, "that first night we spoke on the balcony." Harry lifted his head and gave her a surprised look. Mariah nodded. "I did not know a thing about you, except that you were interesting. And that night, I wished—hoped—that perhaps you would be the man for me, the man I longed to meet and fall in love with."

"That was my plan as well," he said, making her laugh.

"I didn't quite envision how it would proceed, of course."

He brushed the hair from her face and studied her. "You are a rare woman, Mariah. I doubt any other lady in London would have suffered my scandalous visits, or my secrecy, or my impertinence . . . "

Mariah pulled him close again. "But I loved it all. And that is why we deserve each other. Forever and ever."

At Avon Books, we know your passion for romance—once you finish one of our novels, you find yourself wanting more.

May we tempt you with . . .

- **Excerpts** from our upcoming releases.

- Entertaining **extras**, including authors' personal photo albums and book lists.

- Behind-the-scenes **scoop** on your favorite characters and series.

- **Sweepstakes** for the chance to win free books, romantic getaways, and other fun prizes.

- Writing **tips** from our authors and editors.

- **Blog** with our authors and find out why they love to write romance.

- **Exclusive content** that's not contained within the pages of our novels.

Join us at
www.avonbooks.com

AVON *An Imprint of* HarperCollins*Publishers*
www.avonromance.com

Available wherever books are sold or please call 1-800-331-3761 to order.

FTH 0708